I0593516

To the best vet in town, Dr Belinda Wright.

&

The best vet nurse out Danni.

Thank you, Dr. B, and the whole team at Dr B'S vet clinic for all you do for-

Austin, Phoenix, Ghost, Hulk, Jacko and Dude.

And big thank you for our new baby, Pablo, he is such a huge part of our family already.

Xxx

BRUTAL TRUTH

SAMANTHA BARRETT

BRUTAL
TRUTH

CHAPTER ONE

Jessica

"Creed, wait!"

After Davina dropped her bombshell Creed took off, he's walking so fast I have to run to even catch up. I reach out when I'm close and grip his hand, but he yanks free of my hold. "I'm not gonna keep chasing you." I call after him in frustration.

"I never asked you to in the first place." *Ouch,* that hurt. I stand there and watch as he storms away from me heading back the way we came. I feel for him, I really do but his mother is *alive.* I would give anything to have my mom back with me, for her to meet my son. I release a frustrated sigh and cram my hands in my pockets, I could follow Creed or go back and see if I can figure out what Davina's role in all of this is. I decide it's better to let Creed just cool off, if I go after him now, I know he will lash out and I don't need that crap right now. With my mind made up I turn around and head back to the others.

On my way back I notice things I didn't on the way in. There are children here and they don't seem like vampires, mind you I have never met a vampire before until like ten minutes ago but still. People here don't look unhappy or trapped, they almost seem at home. I don't know what I expected when we came ashore but this sure as hell wasn't it. I make my way around the container style home and head toward the back, I hear raised voices and stop. I know I shouldn't eavesdrop but come on, people tend to be more honest when they don't know someone is listening.

"You don't get to tell me what to do with *my* kids, Davina, you lost that right!" I scrunch my face in confusion, I thought Kane didn't know Davina was alive?

"You took that right from me--"Davina sounds pissed, we

are missing something here and I'm pretty sure Kane has been lying to us about his wife's *death.*

"You chose wrong, not me, not my kids."

"They are mine!" Kane and Davina's bickering is cut off when a loud angry growl sounds out.

"You both may have made them, but they are just as much mine as they are yours. I love the three of them like they are my own, I raised them, clothed and fed them." My heart aches for Meg, this must be such a hard position for her to be in. "I am beyond disgusted in you right now, how you could lie to our children so easily is beyond me. We always swore we would never lie to the kids or each other in yet our whole marriage has been based on a lie. Fix this shit now Kane, I'm going after *my* sons and we will be returning to the boat so I can tell *my* daughter what we have discovered." I silently fist bump the air, yes Meg, get it girl. I love that she didn't let Kane or Davina walk all over her, she is damn right, she is the twins and Creed's mother, not Davina. Blood doesn't make you family, loyalty and love dies.

"Sweetheart wait--"

"No, you need to sort whatever the hell this is out. I need to find my sons." Meg comes out of the gate and spots me standing next to the hedges, I smile at her sheepishly when she cocks a brow. She nods her head for me to follow and I do, I don't want to be a part of whatever the hell is going on in there. We remain silent as we exit the property, I can feel the anger and frustration wafting off Meg in waves, whatever was said back there has really upset her. After we exit the big gates, I can't hold my tongue any longer.

"Meg?" Her steps falter but she doesn't stop walking, I reach out and grip her arm pulling her to a stop. She wrenches her arm out of my hold and glares at me, I stumble back a step at the hostile look in her eyes. I take a deep breath and steel my spine. "Are you okay?" She throws her arms in the air like I have asked the most ridiculous question.

"No Jess, I'm not okay. My husband has lied to me for years, both my sons have taken off, I need to find them before they become vampire food and on top of that I have to tell my daughter her...real mother is alive." I can hear the watery tone in her voice, her eyes fill with tears and my chest aches for her. I pull her to me and wrap my arms around her as the first sob tears from her chest. I can't imagine what's she going through, Kane lied to her from the very start and she probably thinks, Creed, Cole and Cali will forget about her now that their bio mom is alive. Gut wrenching sobs tear from Meg, I tighten my hold and let her know that I'm here for her. "I...I can't l-lose them, their m-my babies." She hiccups out between sobs; I open my mouth to answer but am cut off.

"She is not our mother." Meg tears out of my hold at the sound of her son's voice, she spins around and standing there is both Reeves brothers. They are a sight to behold, they each look like a thunderstorm, their faces are masks of pure fury. Cole's green eyes promise pain and Creed's hazel eyes bore into mine, the look he gives me tells me he is going to cause destruction. Meg pulls away from me to race over to the guys, they each wrap their arms around her and pull her in close while she sobs. I have never seen Creed like this, the way he holds his mother and how he whispers words of love in her ear surprises me.

"I-I... didn't know."

"Shhh, mom, we know." Cole tries to say in the most soothing way. I can hear the hurt in his voice, and I just can't imagine how hard this is for them. His brown hair flops forward onto his forehead as he bends down to engulf his mom in a hug. Creed breaks away from them and comes to stand next to me.

"Nothing changes, she means nothing to us. We make our way back to the boat and we leave, we'll figure this out on our own and deal with the council." The conviction in Creed's voice is astounding, Meg pulls back from Cole and turns worried brown eyes to her oldest son.

"We don't have the numbers." She stutters out.

"We'll get them, now let's go--"

"What about your father?" Even after the lies he told, Meg is still worried about him, she is a better woman than me.

"He can find his own way back."

Chapter Two
Jessica

Before I can voice my concern about leaving my brother behind, we hear the crunch of gravel behind us. I spin around and see Cairo storming toward us, tension flees my body at the sight of him. The five years we spent together with the pack has made me come to rely on him, he is the father figure I never had. Ro has made sure that Harlem and I have never gone without and made sure that Harlem has always been safe. I owe everything to him, after what happened with Josh, he didn't have to take me in but he did, even at the risk of his own pack. Killing Josh wasn't something that I had planned, and I knew there would be repercussions, Ro didn't care, he said he would protect me at all costs and he has.

Once he's close enough, I close the distance between us and wrap my arms around him, he returns my embrace.

"I'm okay, but we should get out of here." I pull back and stare up into his blue eyes, so much uncertainty shines in his eyes. I give him a stiff nod and turn toward the others. "Did you want to wait for Kane?"

"No." The three Reeves answer in unison, Cairo cocks a brow at me in question, but I just shake my head and mouth that I'll fill him in later.

We all begin to make our way toward the boat, we're not in a rush, so we take our time and take in our surroundings. How they came to make such a city like this on an island in the middle of nowhere baffles me. The people we do see aren't scared or helpless, they seem to...enjoy being here. I mean, I'm no vampire expert, everything I know about them is from Twilight, so my knowledge is limited to say the least. Even children roam through the town, I look and see people crossing the makeshift bridges that lead from one tree top to the other. This place is incredible; I'm shaken from my thoughts when my brother quietly asks.

"How does it feel to meet our dad's side piece?" Judging from the low growls coming from in front of us, both Reeves brothers heard Cairo's question, I cringe.

"Maybe now isn't the best time for that question." I mutter and pin my dopey brother with a look that says *shut the hell up.* He shrugs his shoulders and continues like nothing happened. Sometimes my brother can be so insensitive, example, when I was in labor with Harlem he kept asking if I needed to keep screaming and breathing like that. Five times, Sky and Callie, both slapped him upside the head. I love him don't get me wrong, but Ro can be so dense.

I don't really know what to say or feel at this moment, I'm really glad that I don't have to do this alone though. Meeting Davina for the first time was not what I was expecting when we came to this island. I have no idea how we are supposed to deal with the council now. Each of us went out on a limb and trusted Shelley, no one thought her secret weapon would be a *vampire.* When we make it to the boat Creed and Cole climb aboard and offer both Meg and I a hand to get in. When Ro hops aboard he pulls the small anchor up and nods to Creed that we are ready to go. Creed starts the engine and then kills it a second later before he jumps out of the boat and heads back to shore. Cole jumps out after him and Ro, Meg and I rush forward to see why when my gaze lands on a guilty looking Kane, I understand.

I really hope he has a good excuse for lying to his family

because I honestly don't think Creed and Cole will forgive him. I can't think of a good enough reason as to why Kane would hide something as big as their mother being alive from them. Creed's anger and hurt has stemmed from the loss of his mother, his emotions were taut, needless to say lying to me and seeking vengeance. Anger begins to burn inside me, if Kane had just been honest from the start, then maybe Creed and I would have met under better circumstances.

He loved her.

Loved who, Sheba?

Davina, he did what he thought was right because he loved her.

But he lied to his children and his mate. *Meg is his fated mate and yet he still lied to her to protect a woman who didn't love him enough to stay faithful.*

Sheba growls in frustration inside my head which just serves to annoy me.

If our mate was married to someone else for the good of the pack but he loved you--

No, I wouldn't support it.

You would be okay with our mate making pups with another?

I close the link with Sheba in frustration, the thought of Creed and another woman together stirs a primal need inside me to stake claim on him. Sheba hums her approval inside my head, I need to control this urge to march over there and do something stupid. Ro, Meg and I all stand here and remain quiet, it's pretty obvious the three of us are shamelessly eavesdropping.

Creed and Cole stare at him defiantly as Kane stands there in shame.

"I have one question." Creed grits out, the anger that laces his tone sends a shiver down my spine.

"Yes." Kane breathes out.

"*Yes* what?" Cole snaps.

"Yes, I knew she was alive." Both Creed and Cole stumble back a step, Meg covers her mouth with her hand to try and muffle the sob that tumbles out of her, it doesn't work. Cairo wraps his arm around her and pulls her against his chest as she breaks down. Cole and Creed turn toward their mom and thanks to my shifter sight I see both of them have anger brewing in their eyes.

"Well, you should stay here and get reacquainted with *your* first wife. We will take *our* mom back to the ship so she can tell *her* daughter what a fucking lying piece of shit her father is." Kane doesn't say anything as Creed and Cole head back toward us. The look of utter devastation on Kane's face tells me Creeds words cut him deep--real deep.

CHAPTER THREE
Jessica

After we got back to the boat we are staying on, we sought out Sky and Callie, Ro and I thought it would be best to leave Meg, Cole and Creed tell Callie the news alone. We took Harlem with us, and Ro managed to find us some clothes and a bucket to wash in, not the best shower in the world but it beats smelling like ass for another day. I washed Harlem as best I could and changed him into the clothes Ro gave me, they are way too big but right now we don't have luxury of being fussy. I changed into the pair of jeans and a plain white singlet, I had to re-use the same bra and panties but at least some of the sweat and grime has been washed away. Ro even managed to snag us some toothbrushes and paste which I am eternally grateful for because I hate the feeling of having furry teeth, I know that's shallow but honestly, I cannot deal with people who have rancid breath.

"How do you think they're going?" I sigh and turn toward my brother, we're in the shipping box we slept in last night with Ro on one side and me and a sleeping Harlem on the other. I run my hand through my son's hair as I answer him.

"I don't know, Callie is a real daddy's girl and I think Kane keeping this from them is going to shatter her."

"At least she has Sky to help her get through it." I nod my head, before we can continue Zeke appears in the doorway and Ro releases a growl of warning. "How the fuck did you get back here?" Zeke cocks a brow at my brother like he's stupid.

"They have other boats dumbass, come on."

"We're not going anywhere with you."

"Cairo, I'm trying to help you here. Shelley has info--"

"I don't give a fuck about what Shelley has, she fucking

blindsided us back there and you knew!" Zeke shakes his head and raises his hands like he's surrendering.

"I knew about the vamps, but I had no idea that their mother was alive." Ro scoffs and rolls his eyes.

"And I'm just supposed to believe you? Fuck off Zeke, you have been lying to me for years." I can hear the hurt that laces my brother's tone, he trusted Zeke only to find out he betrayed him. Zeke has always been great toward me and Harlem and helped me whenever I needed it but since the day Creed showed up on pack lands, he went...funny. Almost like he was trying to portray he and I were more than friends; we never have been and never will be. I release a loud breath and face Ro.

"Creed and the others are clearly not there so it might be best if you go so then we won't be left out of the loop." Indecision wars in his gaze, he wants to know what's going on, but he doesn't want to leave me. "I'll come, you carry Harlem and try keep him asleep?" Relief crosses his features as he nods.

We follow Zeke as he leads us inside the ship, the halls are narrow, both guys have to turn sideways on some parts when there is a box or something attached to the wall. We go up a rickety looking metal staircase and at the top it opens into a room. There is a table with papers everywhere and a couple of bookshelves. Windows all around so we can see the deck and the ocean, the further we go in I can see bunk beds built into the wall. four of them in a row. Ro opens his mouth but snaps it shut when we hear someone else enter. I turn and see its Shelley, Dela and the man with an Australian accent. Ro growls and grips my arm yanking me behind him.

"The fuck is this?" I peer around him and see Zeke raise his hands, again.

"He is here to explain or answer any questions you have. We thought it might be better if you heard it from one of them instead of us." I look to Shelley; she seems on edge her brown eyes are imploring us to listen but why should we? The Australian guy steps forward and Cairo tenses in front of me, I nudge him, but he ignores me. The last thing I want is for a fight to break out while he has my son in his arms. The vampire doesn't look...like a vampire. He has brown hair, caramel eyes, and dresses like a normal person. I don't know what I expected them to look like but seeing how he seems so normal I begin to wonder if I have ever encountered a vampire before.

"My name is Vince; I am not here to cause any harm."

"Then why the hell are you here?" Vince ignores Ro's hostile tone and turns to look at Dela who nods his head. "To help you understand."

"Understand what, exactly?" I ask as I step out from behind my brother much to his dismay. Vince motions toward the table for us to sit, I follow the others over and ignore Cairo's groans behind me as we all take a seat. We sit in silence for a moment before Shelley breaks it.

"I never meant for this to seem like a set up, I brought you all here because Davina can offer us a safe haven and an army."

"Why would she help us?"

"Because Jess, her children's lives are at stake." I scoff.

"She didn't seem to care about them when she was faking her death." I shock myself with that outburst but make sure to keep my face blank.

"She didn't have a choice."

"We all have a choice Shelley, every single one of us. Davina chose to hide the truth from her children and as a mother myself, I couldn't imagine doing that to my son. Harlem is everything to me and there is no way I would be such a coward and hideaway on an island for how many years while my children navigated life without me." Shelley cringes but tries to mask it, what the hell was that reaction about?

"There are circumstances you are not privy to. Davina done what she did to keep her children safe, this was never about her." I glare at Vince; did he not just hear what I said. Davina is a coward in my book, she left her children behind and from what I saw on that island she has made a damn good life for herself without her children.

"I don't give a shit about her or any of you. We are leaving at first light tomorrow and we will take our chances against the council." I nod my head in agreement, Ro is right. The council will have to catch us first and even then, the world is a huge place so we can hide, right? But do I want that for my son, to constantly be on the run and never be able to call a place home?

"You don't even know what we can offer you." The sound of footfalls on the stairs alerts us to the fact people are coming, a moment later, Creed, Cole, Callie, Meg and Sky come into view. Creed looks like a pissed off beast, he snaps his gaze from me then to the others and growls. Callie's eyes are red and puffy, she is sandwiched between her mom and Sky. My heart hurts for her, I cannot imagine what she is going through right now.

"The fuck is going on here?" Cole demands, I can feel the

anger radiating off both Reeves brothers. I can also feel through the link Creed and I share that he is hurting and using his anger to cover his pain.

"We were just trying to--"Creed pins Shelley with a look that has her clamping his mouth shut.

"I don't give a fuck what you *think* you are doing." Creed marches over to us and stops beside Ro, he motions his arms for Harlem to come. My brother turns to me asking me silently what he should do. I feel Creed's anger soar through the bond and subtly shake my head, Ro tightens his grip on his nephew and looks at Creed.

"Calm down, then I'll give him."

"Fuck you, give me my son now."

"Creed--"He cuts me off.

"No, you don't get to pick and choose when I have my son. You will never take him from me Jessica, *never.*" I recoil at the harshness in his voice, Cairo tenses and then shifts toward me to pass over Harlem. I take my son and cradle him against my chest as my brother pushes back from the table and stands to face off against Creed.

"I get your pissed, I know your hurt and angry but don't *ever* speak to my sister like that again. You so much as think of taking that baby from her and I will fucking kill you where you stand Credence, do not push me." An evil smile cuts across Creed's face, he leans in to whisper in Ro's ear but has gaze pinned on me as he says.

"Push me and I'll take *her* and *my* son from you." I gasp, Cairo shoves Creed back a step and cocks his arm back ready to sock Creed in the face but in a flash, Vince is between them and has his hand wrapped around Cairo's fist, stopping his punch. Ro struggles out of Vince's hold and Cole rushes forward to haul Creed back. Harlem stirs awake from the commotion, and I grit my teeth in anger as I stand, the four guys stop their struggles and turn toward me. I pin them all with a filthy look as Harlem begins to cry in my hold. Creed deflates and I make sure he can see the anger brewing in my eyes as I say.

"Stay the fuck away from me and Harlem until you have dealt with your shit. I will not have people fighting around my child and arguing like this."

"Princess--"

"Shut up Creed." Harlem begins to wail so I make my way toward the stairs but stop when Meg blocks my way.

"C-can I hold him? I'll follow you out." The look she gives me has my heart sinking. The way she stares at me tells me she wants as much time with Harlem as she can before she is pushed aside from Davina. I hand Harlem over and he immediately begins to quiet down as Meg whispers sweet words of love in his ear. I place my hand on her shoulder and wait for her to meet my gaze.

"You will always be his grandmother. Creed and I will bicker and fight but that will never change your place in *our* son's life, Meg. You are and always will be Harlem's grandmother." Tears stream down her face; she wraps her free arm around me and we hug awkwardly while Harlem is stuck between us.

CHAPTER FOUR
Credence

I stand there stunned and watch as Jess leads the way out of the room with my mom and son following them. Sky motions for Callie to go with them and tells her she will catch up shortly. I gulp when Sky turns around and pins me with a look that promises pain., I'm man enough to admit that Skylar Cage scares the living hell out of me. She moves like a tiger ready to strike at any minute, she stops in the middle of the four if us and pins Vince with a look. The vamp is smart enough to drop his hold on Cairo and step back.

"If I ever and I do mean *ever* Credence catch you antagonizing my alpha again I will come for you. You won't know when or how but just know you will *feel* it." I nod my head but remain quiet. "And if you ever do anything to harm Jess or the monster, I'll take you apart piece by piece. No one will ever find you but rest assured though I'll hold your sisters' hand while she and your family search for your body." I nod.

Holy fuck.

"I think Creed is about to piss himself." I glare at Cairo, fucker needs to keep his mouth shut right now. Sky spins around and pins him with a look, the smile drops from his face and now I stare at him with a toothy grin. Fucker deserves to have his ass chewed as well.

"You have done some dumb shit, really dumb shit, before but coming up here with Jess and monster alone is one of the dumbest--"

"Sky--"

"I'm not done Cairo, we do shit together, *always.* Don't ever pull a stunt like this again or I'm out." Cairo pales and his mouth drops open in shock. I dart my gaze to Cole and find him staring at Sky like she is some alien. What the fuck is going on? Ro steps forward and places his hands on her shoulders with a guilt ridden look on his face.

"Never again, I swear. I won't lose you Sky."

"My time is coming, Ro." A gut-wrenching growl tears from him.

"No, we'll change it. Destiny isn't written in stone Sky, we'll fix it, I swear."

I left after Cairo and Sky's cryptic as fuck conversation, Indecision wars inside me. Should I find Jess or give her space? When Corbin whines inside my head I know my decision is made, I have to find them and fix this shit. I had no right to take my anger out on her, but she also can't keep telling me *no* when it concerns Harlem. He is just as much mine as he is hers. I try to scent the air but can't fucking smell anything over the salt water, I will find her the old-fashioned way. I search each container and by the tenth one I'm ready to give up until I hear my mom's voice. I follow the sound to another row of boxes and the fourth one in I find the girls and my son inside. They all snap their gazes to me and the easy going look on their faces quickly disappear.

"We'll leave you two be." My mom says but Jess reaches out and stops her.

"No Meg, Creed can wait. You don't need to be alone after

what you've been through; he can either join us and stop being an ass or go somewhere else." My mom bites her bottom lip to stop herself from smiling, I roll my eyes and decide talking to Jess can wait till later, she's right mom needs us right now. I enter the box and drop down next to Callie and lean back against the cool metal, my sister rests her head on my shoulder and mom smiles at us lovingly. A small whimper from Harlem shatters the moment and Jess surprises the fuck out of me when she gently lifts him from the mattress, stands and then brings him to me. I stare up at her in shock not sure what the hell to do.

"I said no before because I could feel how angry you were, not because I don't trust you." I hold my arms out for my son, she places him in my hold and he snuggles against my chest as she reclaims her spot next to my mom. Callie leans over and runs her fingers along his cheek and sighs.

"You both really do make a gorgeous baby." I hum my approval as I stare down at the best part of me. He is so innocent and carefree and I love that, I don't want him to be tarnished by the world that we live in. I'm pulled from my thoughts when Cole and Sky walk in and drop down beside mom. We all sit there in comfortable silence lost in our own thoughts until Cole ruins it.

"He looks so innocent when he sleeps but when he's awake he's a goddamn monster." I glare at my brother. "If he was my son--"Jess groans and I dart my eyes between them feeling like I'm missing something.

"I told you before--no!"

"Told him what?" Cole and Jess share a loaded look, her

cheeks begin to turn pink and I grind my teeth together to stop myself from snapping at them. Patients is not one of my virtues.

"It's nothing, Cole is just being...Cole."

"Clearly it's something if it wasn't a onetime conversation so I would like to know." She groans at my response, but Cole just chuckles which earns him a pointed look from me.

"I told Jess if he was my son, he wouldn't be such a monster, but because he's your son he didn't have a choice in being a little shit." I try, I swear I tried but Corbin surges forward and I can't stop him. He's displeased the thought of Jess being with Cole and the growl that reverberates inside the metal box lets everyone know how displeased Corbin and I are at the idea. I'm about to lose my cool, Cole and I haven't had a chance to talk about his little *crush* on my mate and the more I find out shit like this the harder it is to be around my brother. I will not lose Jess, and I sure as fuck will not let my brother get near her either.

"Can I speak to you all for a moment?" All eyes turn toward the entry, Vince stands there with his hands stuffed in his pockets and a pleading look on his face. Why can't he just fuck off back to the mistress of bullshit I share DNA with?

"Sure." All eyes turn toward my mom who just shrugs her shoulders and motions for Vince to come in. I grit my teeth and try to calm myself; I begin to breathe through my mouth because he reeks of rotting flesh.

"I don't know your past or what Davina's reasoning behind her deceit is, but I want to help and so do many of the others."

"Why? Why would any of you want to help us?" Vince smiles sadly at my sister, Sky being the badass that she is glares at him and pulls her upper lip back in warning. Ah, so Skylar Cage does have a weak point, good to know.

"Because most of us didn't choose this life. We have been hiding out here for years until the time is right."

"Time for what?" Mom asks, he meets her gaze, and I can see regret in his eyes but also vengeance.

"Revenge."

Chapter Five

Jessica

Revenge.

That one word holds so much pain and anguish that no matter how hard Vince tries he cannot mask his hurt. I dart my gaze to the others to see their furrowed brows, at least I'm not the only one who can pick up on his pain.

"We weren't always like this--"Oh my god, I gasp and pin Vince with a knowing look. The sad smile that crosses his face lets me know that what I am thinking is right.

"What's wrong princess?" I ignore Creed and ask Vince.

"You were all shifters, weren't you?" Gasps sound out.

"Yes." I slouch back against the metal wall and try to process this new information.

"How?"

"When?"

"Why would you change to *that?*" The others bark questions at Vince but don't give him time to answer. I can't focus on anything aside from this new information, they were shifters. Why would they change to vampires? There must be a reason, there has to be for them to change their whole DNA make up. I lift my gaze back to Vince to see him staring directly at me, the look in his eyes is unsettling almost like he is imploring me to understand.

"Keep staring at *my* mate like that and you won't make it to sunrise." Creed grits out, I sigh clearly his jealousy knows no bounds.

"Ignore Creed, we all do." We all chuckle as Creed pins Cole with a frosty look.

"If you were all shifters- "Vince cuts me off.

"Not all, most of us were." I nod and continue.

"If *most* of you were once shifters why change? There had to be a reason behind it, right?"

"Yes, you see the council--"

"That's enough." Vince clamps his mouth shut and we all freeze when Davina appears at the entryway, we're all on our feet within seconds growling and glaring. In her defense she doesn't wavier or recoil, she takes it all on the chin and holds her head high. Davina is beautiful there is no denying that, long brown hair, pale hazel eyes that make you think they can see inside you. Davina's gaze runs over everyone but settles on Meg, Creed and Cole both growl and shift so they can block their mom from...their mom?

"You don't get to look at her!" The venom in Cole's voice gives me pause.

"I won't hurt her."

"You won't ever get the chance to touch her. Get the fuck out of here now, Davina." Cole sounds more beast than man right this moment.

"We don't want you here!" Creed tacks on. Callie pushes past her brothers much to their dismay and just stands there staring at the woman who gave birth to her. Davina's left eye twitches but other than that her face remains an emotionless mask.

"As a little girl I never missed you. I never had the chance really because there was never a void to be filled. My mom is Meg, she raised us, loved us, fed us and was there. She has always been there for us, my brothers and I don't need you, Davina. We would rather go to war with the council than ever be in any kind of debt to you. Blood doesn't make you family, love, loyalty and trust does." Davina nods her head and clasps her hands behind her back she steps forward and is now standing shoulder to shoulder with Vince.

"I didn't come here to fight; I came here to speak with Meg." The three Reeves siblings release growls.

"California--"Meg shoves through the boys and grips Callie's hand yanking her back. Meg stands there staring Davina down.

"You do not get to speak to *my* daughter. I don't give a shit if you birthed them, they are *mine*. We owe you nothing and I swear to the gods above if you try in any way to harm my children, I will gut you where you stand!" A slow smile begins to spread over Davina's face.

"You Meg are much, much more than I could have ever hoped for. I would never try to sway them from you, you are their mother. I was just the vessel that gave them to you and what a marvelous job you have done at raising them." I can feel trepidation creep through the link Creed and I share.

"If you're not here to claim them, then why the hell are you here?"

"I'm here Meg because I can offer you all a safe haven. I can give you the numbers you need to go against the council and take them down once and for all but before that can happen you all need to put your anger with me aside and learn the truth."

"The truth about what?" Meg asks, Davina doesn't get to answer, she is cut off when a sheepish looking Kane rounds the corner and speaks.

"Why I lied about Davina being dead. Nothing is what it seems and when you all learn the truth behind why I did what I did, you will understand then."

"So, you're going to explain why you broke our mom's heart and lied to all of us? You are not the fucking man I thought you were, you mourned for her and let us all believe she was dead. You made me become what I am because you said it's what she wanted, I allowed you to mold me into who I am because I pitied you for the loss of your wife. Your fated mate is standing right fucking *here*! You lied to her and hurt her to protect that lying bitch who was fucking around on you--"Both Kane and Davina flinch, I cut Creed off.

"That's enough Creed." He turns and pins me with a look that sends dread pooling in my belly.

"At least now you know lying runs in the family princess, watch out I might fuck around behind your back just like my egg donor over here." I recoil back at his words, that fucking hurt! Cole moves to stand beside me and glares at his brother.

"If you weren't holding my nephew, I'd punch your fucking teeth down your throat. You don't fucking get to lash out at her because your feelings are hurt about your mommy." Creeds eyes change to the blue of his wolf as he growls long and loud, Meg turns and quickly plucks Harlem out of his hold and shuffles to the back of the container with Sky and Callie, I move to follow them so I can retrieve my son, but Cole stops me.

"You're only defending her right now because you want to fuck my mate!" I gasp and so do the others, Creed points toward Harlem and says. "He is mine, not yours and she will always belong to me, never you little brother. If I want to fuck her and put another baby in there I will!" My eyes widen in shock, Creed has gone way to fucking far now!

"Keep treating her the way you are and see how long she keeps you around. You ruin everything you touch, you're just like him!" Cole shouts and points at their father, Kane drops his head in shame. I shove behind Cole and grab Harlem from Meg; she pats my cheek and smiles sadly before she moves and stands in the middle of both her sons. She looks to each of them and shakes her head.

"You're both angry and hurt. You don't mean any of this-_"

"He keeps trying to play dad to my son!" Creed roars which startles Harlem awake.

"I fucking raised him!" Cole volleys back while pounding a fist against his chest. "I stayed up with her, I changed the diapers. I helped her through her grief and pain. I fucking helped her give birth not you because you're a lying piece of shit just like your daddy!" Creed moves so fast, he steps around Meg and slams his fist into Cole's face, Cole recovers quickly and both of them trade blows as they fall to the ground. Sky ushers Callie and me further into the corner and stands in front of us like a shield. Harlem is screaming at the top of his lungs in fear, his cries don't even seem to snap Creed out of his rage. Anger thrums inside me, how dare they do this while my son is present. I tuck his head into the crook of my neck so he doesn't see the fight happening between his uncle and father. Meg, Kane and Vince even Davina try to break them apart, after struggling to get a good grip on each of them they finally manage to tear them apart, Kane and Meg have Cole while Vince and Davina have Creed pinned to the other side. Both men are bleeding and have cuts on their faces, their breaths are coming in short rapid pants. If looks could kill they would both be dead, they look at each other with so much malice.

"You are nothing to me, you're as dead to me as she is." Creed snaps, Cole flinches but masks it. I dart my gaze to Davina and see her eyes cloud with hurt before she quickly masks it. Harlem is still crying; I tap Sky on the shoulder, and she moves to let me past. I make my way to the exit but stop at Creeds words. "Run with my son again princess and I'll hunt you down!" Tears blur my vision at his cruel words.

"And we'll mask her tracks making sure you will never find her, you piece of shit! Come near my sister again and I'll tear your fucking throat out." I rush toward my brother and Zeke; Ro wraps his arm around my shoulders and Zeke grabs a screaming Harlem from me ignoring Creeds growls and shouts. Ro leads us inside the boat and back up to the room where we were earlier and locks the door behind us, he turns to me and I break down. I let my brother hold me as I cry, Creeds words stung so bad and hurt me more than he will ever know.

Chapter Six
Credence

I shove Vince back and glare at the beefy fucker, Cole does the same to my dad. We each take a step forward but stop when mom and Callie jump in the middle of us, Callie's back is to me as she faces Cole, mom faces me with her back to my brother. Sky steps forward and eyes both of us as she pulls 2 blades out from her thigh sheath.

"Either of you hurt my mate and I won't use words; I'll just show you." I can hear the threat that laces each of her words.

"I am so disappointed in you both."

"He started it!" Cole screeches like a little bitch.

"You're just salty cause I'm fucking her and you're not." Mom, Callie and Sky both gasp, Dad and Vince groan but don't say a word. Davina just stands there stoic as ever; Cole pins me with a look of disgust.

"You don't deserve her. She isn't someone to sink your dick into, she is the mother to your fucking child, treat her with some fucking respect." Cole shoves past dad and Vince and leaves, good riddance. Callie spins around and the look on her face has me cringing internally, tears rim her eyes.

"You have no idea the hell she went through, I am so angry with you Credence." Callie storms out after Cole; Sky goes to follow her but stops and turns to pin me with a look that promises pain.

"You will never understand why Cole and Jess are so close, because none of us that know trust you enough to tell you the truth. I'm not telling you this because I trust you, I'm telling you this because I want you to feel half the pain she did! Harlem is a twin Creed." I recoil and smack against the wall. "You had a daughter."

Had.

"Where is she?" I whisper. She ignores my question as she says.

"Jess is the way she is with Harlem because of what she went through you insensitive fucking prick. Cole, Callie, Cairo, me and even Zeke were there for her. She gravitated toward Cole more because he reminded her of *you*. The next time you want to talk about having another kid, think again you dumbass."

"Why?" I grit out as she walks past.

"Because there were complications when she gave birth to the twins, you will never put another baby in her you stupid boy."

Sky threw my own words back at me, I slide down the wall and drop my head into my hands.

I had a daughter.

Silent tears leak from my eyes, I had a baby girl and she died. I didn't even know her or get to see her; my heart is breaking inside my chest for the loss of my little girl. It all makes sense now why Jess is so overprotective with Harlem; there's always someone watching over him and she gets anxious whenever he is away from her. She's scared she will lose him like she lost our little girl. What the fuck have I done? The things I said about her to Cole, I spoke about her like she was some common whore not the mother to my child... children. We have kids together, two not one. A hand lands on my shoulder and I snap my gaze up to see my dad looming above me. I look to the side to see my mom is crying, I accept the hand my dad offers me. Davina and Vince are gone I notice, I shove past my dad and wrap my mom in my embrace. She sobs into my chest while tears silently fall down my cheeks.

"I'm so sorry son." I stiffen at my dad's words. Mom pulls back and cups my face between her tiny hands and stares up at me.

"Fix it, don't wait. Go find her and fix this Creed, things were said and you can't change that, but that poor girl has been through so much and you have to stop hurting her. Stop pushing her away and punishing her for *your* mistakes. Jess is innocent in all of this, none of this is her fault."

"She hid my son from me, mom"

"Not out of spite but out of fear Creed. She was probably scared you would try to take him from her and after the loss she went through... I don't blame her." I hang my head in shame, I am fucking things up with Jess because I'm hurt about Harlem. I'm projecting my anger from dad and Davina onto her and it's not fair. Fuck, I even hit my baby brother! I grip my hair and tug on the strands in frustration, what the fuck am I doing? I'm hurting all the people I love and pushing them away!

"I-I'll fix this mom." She pats my cheek and smiles sadly.

"I just hope it's not too late son. Now go find your mate and your brother and fix this. Your father and I need to have a discussion of our own." I see dad flinch out of the corner of my eye.

"You sure? Do you want me to stay?" She shakes her head.

"No, you go and fix your mess while I fix mine." I nod and place a kiss to her cheek and head out but pause when I'm shoulder to shoulder with my father.

"You hurt her again and I'll never forgive you."

"Understood."

CHAPTER SEVEN
Jessica

I peel my eyes open and roll over, I can feel how swollen they are after all the tears I spilled last night. Zeke, Ro, Sky, Callie, Cole and I slept in the bunks with me and Harlem last night. I look around and spot the others seated around the table with Harlem bouncing on Cole's knee and I smile. Everything was so simple before Creed came barreling back into our lives, we were all content to just be and live how we wanted. I won't lie a part of me always yearned for him but as time went on the pain of his absence started to lessen. I don't think it would have ever gone away, but time heals everything.

"You're finally awake." I nod and smile at my brother as I sit up and stretch. "We have a surprise for you."

"If it's another hiking trip I'll pass." Ro playfully glares at me, a couple years back he was trying to cheer me up and thought a four-hour hiking trip would work, it didn't.

"No smart ass, follow me." I stand and follow him to the other side of the room where he opens a door, I didn't even see that yesterday. He motions for me to enter and when I do I squeal and launch myself at him, he catches me and laughs.

"You're the best brother in the world."

"Damn straight I am, go on. Callie left some clothes in there for you and a toothbrush. Cole showered Harlem." I peer around Cairo and mouth a thank you to Cole who just smiles. I shove my brother out and shut the door, the shower is tiny it reminds of one you might find in an RV. I don't waste time as I strip my clothes off and hop in. The water cascades down my body and I sigh, the water helps wash away some of the tension and stress. I find the pocket size shampoo and conditioner and begin to wash my hair; I look down and see the brown liquid swirling around the drain and cringe--gross. I use the soap bar to scrub my body twice, by the time I'm finished my skin is red and my fingers are prunes but by God does it feel good to finally be clean again. I make quick work of brushing my teeth and changing, then I run my fingers through my shoulder length hair. A knock sounds at the door.

"Breakfast is ready." I smile and shout my thanks to Callie and quickly finish up in here so I can join the others. I take the vacant seat next to Cole and place a kiss on the top of my son's head.

"Has he eaten?" I ask Cole.

"Yeah, two whole bowls of cornflakes and even ate a protein bar as well. His appetite is getting bigger." It really is, he is a shifter after all and let me tell you wolves eat a shit load! I dig into my toast and cereal, once I'm finished, I'm still not full. We need to think of something fast or we are going to have starving shifters on our hands, wolves need red meat, and we haven't had any in days.

"I think we need to go to the island." All eyes turn to Cairo. "Hear me out, we're all hungry and there must be something to hunt there surly?" Zeke clears his throat and meets Cairo's gaze.

"Yeah bro, there is." Zeke, Cairo and Sky break off into their own conversation and devise a plan of going to the island. Cole, Callie and I sit on the floor and watch as Harlem walks around the room exploring. It still stuns me each day how this incredible boy is mine, Harlem is such a clever kid and I never want him to go through half of the things I've been through. I know my mom did her best but constantly moving all over the country was hard for me, I want Harlem to have somewhere to call home. I want him to go to school and make friends with kids his own age.

"Penny for your thoughts, sweetheart?" I don't know how to tell Cole what I'm thinking.

"It's just...A lot. So much has changed and there is no stability for him."

"Home isn't a place love; home is where your heart is, and his heart is with you--always." Cole's words spread warmth through me, I never thought of it like that, but it doesn't mean I want to raise my son on a boat.

"I just want him to have a home, a room where he can have his own things. Go to school and just be a kid. I don't want him to worry about all of this shit."

"We will get there--"A knock sounds at the door and has all conversation stopping. We can't scent who it is thanks to the salt water, Cairo bends and turns Harlem around so he will come to me, which he does. Ro and Zeke move to open the door, a growl tears from my brother.

"You're not welcome here, now fuck off." You don't need to be a rocket scientist to know who it is.

"I want to see her." The dejected tone of his voice doesn't sway me to feel sorry for him or even the remorse I feel through our bond.

"Well, she doesn't want to see you, now get lost Credence." Cairo tries to shut the door, but Creed slams his arm out to stop him. Harlem wrenches out of my hold and runs toward the door, Zeke spots him and is about to catch him when Creed shoves Cairo out of the way and bumps Zeke with his hip and sends him toppling to the side. Creed drops down and grabs Harlem then throws him up and catches him before holding him against his chest. I jump to my feet and begin to panic; Creed could turn around and run out of the room with Harlem before I could even stop him. His gaze swings to me and the happiness he displayed a moment ago at seeing his son vanishes, guilt and shame war inside his hazel eyes. I dart my gaze from him to the door and whatever he sees in my eyes has him deflating.

"C-can I just spend some time with him, please. I promise I'll stay out of your way, and not even talk to you I...I just want to be with my son." I stare at him with my mouth hanging open, I'm stunned at the sincerity in his voice and the fact that he isn't demanding that I allow him time, he's actually asking me. I nod my head and he smiles his thanks as he makes his way toward the table, Harlem in hand. Cairo pins me with a look, but I shake my head, I may be pissed at Creed, but I will never use Harlem against him. There's tension in the room but I know Creed is choosing to ignore it. Harlem giggles and squeals when Creed tickles his sides.

"Want to play hide seek?" Creeds smirk morphs into a full-blown smile.

"Yeah, of course." Harlem turns toward us and asks.

"You all want to play?" Each of us exchange glances but all agree, there isn't any good hiding spots here, but we made it work. Ro and Zeke left mid-way through the game to try come up with a plan for food. It was only me, Sky, Harlem and the Reeves siblings in the room. We all sat down for some lunch and ate in silence; Harlem begins to yawn, and I can see in his eyes that he is ready for his nap. I push back from the table to lift him. Creed jumps to his feet with a look of concern on his face.

"What are you doing?"

"Putting him down for his nap?" It sounded like more of a question than I wanted it to, he relaxes his shoulders and moves around the table to stand in front of me.

"Can I do it, please?" I'm shocked he asked instead of demanded and also, I'm taken back that he said please. I nod and pass a tired Harlem to him; Creed cradles him against his chest and places a soft kiss to his head. I motion him over to the bed Harlem and I shared and grab one of his books from the bag Zeke packed.

"He likes this one, read it to him and he'll fall asleep." Creed nods and gets comfortable on the bottom bunk bed with Harlem as he begins to read to our son. I turn back toward the others and see Callie's eyes mist, I got to admit, I'm a bit choked up as well.

CHAPTER EIGHT
Credence

I'm halfway through the book and my boy is already snoring. I close the book and smile down at him, I just put my son to sleep! I know to most that isn't something to be celebrated but this is a first for me and I'm excited about it. I gently pull my arm out from under his head and slide out of the bed, I pull the throw blanket over him and just stand there watching him. What would it have been like if his sister survived? Would she look like me or Jess, would she be full of life like Harlem? I shake my head to clear those thoughts away; it's hard to understand why I feel so hollow.

I wasn't there but that doesn't change the fact that it fucking hurts like hell to know I lost a child. Life fucking sucks, why couldn't she survive? Why the fuck do people pray to a god if he takes the lives of children? I grit my teeth and spin around to find four sets of eyes on me, I run my gaze over each of them but when I land on Jess, I get mad. She had no right to keep this from me! I march over to her, and she stands from her chair, I see the others stand out of the corner of my eye but ignore them. Jess lifts her gaze to mine and I ignore the hurt in her blue eyes. I reach out and grip the back of her neck and clench tight enough to force her gaze higher but not hurt her. Cole growls in warning, fuck him, I growl back but don't take my eyes off her.

"Creed--"

"Stay out of this California. This is between me and my deceitful baby momma." Jess gasps at my words and her eyes harden.

"I haven't lied to you about shit." I laugh but there is no humor to it.

"You princess are a dirty little liar, yet you stand here on your high horse and look down your nose at me. Yeah, I lied and tricked you, but my lies will never amount to the shit you lied to me about." She tries to pull out of my hold, but I don't release her, I pull her closer and relish in the way her eyes darken and growl tears from her throat.

"I have no idea what you--"

"What's her name?" Her brow furrows in confusion and her growling cuts off. I see the others sharing looks of confusion amongst themselves.

"Who's name Credence? I have no idea what--"

"My daughter!" I scream at her. "What's my daughters' fucking name Jessica?" I'm vibrating with rage, but when her eyes begin to fill with tears and her bottom lip begins to tremble my rage flees. I drop my hold on her and step back, Callie and Sky move around and stand behind Jess, each of them rest a hand on her shoulders in silent support. "What. Is. My. Daughters. Name?" Silent tears trek down her face as she shakes her head.

"I...I c-can't." I narrow my eyes at her.

"You can't or you won't?" She drops her gaze to the floor. "I fucked up and I owned my shit princess. I have said sorry more times than I can count, but you hid something ten times worse from me. You hid my fucking kid from me and failed to mention that I had a fucking daughter!" I yell the last part and cringe when I hear Harlem startle awake, I glare at Jess when she tries to go to him. "I got it." I snap as I make my way over to my son. I ignore Jess's sobs as I rock Harlem back to sleep, I tuck him back in and then move back toward the table where Jess sits between my brother and sister and Sky sits next to her mate glaring at me, I glare right back.

I drop into a chair opposite Jess and glare at her. I know I'm being an asshole but right now I don't give a fuck, my heart is fucking aching and I need someone to take my anger out on.

"Calm the fuck down." I turn and glare at my brother, we may not be twins but we look so much alike except for the fact Cole's eyes aren't hardened but the trials of life. Dad and I made sure to keep Callie and Cole as sheltered from pack politics as much as we could.

"Don't Colton, I know you.... Care about her but right now I need the truth. It wasn't just her that lost a child, I did to, and I have a right to know what the fuck happened to my daughter. You owe me that much princess."

"Sweetheart you don't have--"

"I know." She cuts Cole off and lifts her gaze to meet mine. The brokenness in her eyes guts me but I make sure to not display any emotion on my face. "I got Hyperemesis Gravidarum, it's like extreme morning sickness and very rare. I also developed Anemia and went into labor early because I went into kidney failure, we tried everything. I didn't even know I was pregnant with twins--"

"How could you not know?" I wasn't asking to be an ass, but I am genuinely curious as to how she didn't know.

"They were mirrored, it means they were back-to-back, and we couldn't see two babies or even hear two heartbeats because of them being mirrored. I was sick the whole pregnancy, we tried everything to hold off, early labor, but nothing worked. I went into labor at 36 weeks, Harlem came out and he was fine, he was early, but we didn't see anything medically wrong with him, five minutes later more contractions came and then Cole said he could see another head which scared the crap out of us. I gave birth to the most beautiful baby girl... Her name is Katharine Tennessee Reeves, she had beautiful blonde hair and hazel eyes. She was...perfect." Jess breaks down into uncontrollable sobs and I snap. I jump up and move around the table, I shove Cole aside and pick Jess up and then take the seat she was sitting on and hold her in my arms as she breaks down. I bury my head in the crook of her neck and just hold her. My heart breaks for her and the child we lost, for the child we will never get to know. Jess continues to sob into my chest as I pull back and look at my brother.

"Can you guys give us a minute?" Cole darts his gaze between Jess and I, I can see he is hesitant to leave her with me so rather than going off I grit my teeth and remain quiet.

"Colton, she's his mate. Let's go." I turn and thank my sister, the three of them leave the room and when I hear the door click shut behind them, I move Jess until she is straddling my lap and clasp her face between my hands so she will look at me.

"It's not your fault. You didn't know, you couldn't have stopped this." She shakes her head rapidly.

"She didn't die at birth Creed." I reel back in shock, I assumed she was a stillborn. "She survived for two months."

"W-what happened?" Jess lowers her gaze; I grip her chin in my hand and lift until she meets my gaze. "Please, I-I need to know." She exhales a loud breath and nods.

"Katy died from SUDI."

"The fuck does that mean?"

"I thought she died because of how sick I was through the whole pregnancy, but she didn't. I blamed myself for a really, really long time until I read the report from the hospital. SUDI means, *sudden unexpected death in infants.* I had no idea about it, I never even knew that was a thing until it became a thing. I did everything right I swear, I fed her, bathed her and kissed her goodnight. Harlem woke and I got up to feed him, I always woke the other, so they didn't wake at separate times but when I went to Katy... She was... She was so cold. I tried everything, I screamed for help and the others came but no one could bring her back." A horrible gut-wrenching sob tears from inside her. "They couldn't bring her back; my little girl was...gone." Tears leak down my face, I'm so numb. I should have been there for my daughter I could have... I could have done something, anything! Instead, now I just have to sit here and hear the story of my daughter's short life.

Corbin whines inside my mind, he's in pain as well. Losing a pup is something so rare, why the fuck did this have to happen to my daughter? Is this Karma's way of punishing me for all the bad things I have done, for the lies I have told to the mother of my children?

Chapter Nine

Jessica

My chest feels like it has been ripped open and my soul has been laid bare for all others to see. I don't know who told Creed about Katy, I had planned on telling him, but we never got a chance. Talking about her brings back all the guilt and pain, I still blame myself for losing her. No one could tell me why, they just said it happens sometimes. Katy was a fucking shifter! How the hell does a shifter baby die of SUDI? Another sob wrenches out of me, Creed hauls me against him, and I bury my face in the crook of his neck. Seeing the look in his eyes when I told him how she passed guts me, seeing him cry breaks me anew. Creed is such a strong alpha male and to see him breakdown, it shatters me.

He runs his hand up and down my back, I wrap my arms around him and hold him close. When I lost Katy, he was the person I longed for, he was the one that I wanted to hold me and tell me it wasn't my fault. He wasn't there so I latched onto the next best thing--Cole. Cole held my hand through it all, when I would wake at night screaming, he would come and hold me until I fell asleep in his arms.

"We'll get through this Princess. I am so sorry for what I said last night, I don't want to keep hurting you. I know I fuck up a lot, but Jess please don't push me away, don't take my son from me, I am begging you." I pull back and stare down at him, how could he think that?

"I would never take him from you Credence, you're his father." Irritation flares in his eyes before he quickly masks it.

"I know losing our daughter has made you so protective over him, I understand now. You may not intentionally mean to, but you do keep him from me." I try to cut in, but he places his finger against my lips and shushes me. "I shouldn't have to ask to spend time with him, if you and I disagree you always take him. I may have ruined my chances with you Jess and I hate what I have done to you, but I swear to God I will never fuck up with him. I want to be his dad; I want to love him and show him the goddamn world. I don't want him to be like me, I want to end this shit with the council so he can be free of this life." I recoil in shock.

"I-I... Wow." Creed smiles sadly and reaches up and cups my cheek in his hand, I nuzzle into his touch and his eyes spark with heat at my acceptance of his touch.

"You're it for me Jess." The sincerity in his eyes is my undoing, I close the space between us and smash my lips against his. Fire spreads throughout my body, I don't think that will ever go away. Whenever he touches me, I begin to heat, it's like he's the match to the fire inside me. Creed grips the back of my neck and holds me in place as he devours my mouth, I release a moan when his free begins to squeeze my ass. He thrust upward and I can feel how much he wants me; he moves his hand to my hip and begins to guide me so I'm rocking against his hardness. Heat emanated from his body; I was awash with the scent of him. Another moan tears from me, fire explodes in my veins. His hands begin to roam all over my body, my breast's, my back, my ass, he touches everywhere except the place I want him to touch most. He breaks our kiss and we're both a panting breathless mess, he pushes me back so I'm sitting on his la with my back flat against the table.

He runs his hands down my chest and tweaks my nipples

through my shirt and I moan. I'm so freaking turned on I can smell my own wetness; his hands roam lower and then he pops the button on my jeans and slides the zipper down slowly. He taps my ass so I'll lift up, he peels my pants from my body.

"Fuck princess." I lean up on my elbows and bite my bottom lip. "Where's your panties?"

"There isn't exactly a washer here, so I had to go commando." His only answer is a growl as he stares down at my bare pussy, I haven't been able to shave so I'm a bit self-conscious. Creed lifts me by my ass and pushes me back until I'm lying on the table, I sit up to ask what he's doing but clamp my mouth shut to keep from crying out when he lowers his head and begins to lap at my pussy. He spreads my legs wider and parts my folds, exposing my clit to him. He flicks his tongue out and I shudder. He licks me from my clit to my opening and moans tumble out of me, he stops and I sit up to glare down at him but stop when I see him pull his shirt off and chuck it at me with a smirk on his face.

"Bite down on that and keep quiet or you'll wake our son." I freeze, I totally forgot Harlem was sleeping mere feet away from us. Creed must see the horror on my face because he adds. "If you're quiet he will never know, or I can stop now and leave you wired and tense?" I glare at him as I ball his shirt up and hold it against my mouth. "Good choice." He drops back into his chair and dives back between my legs, all thoughts of being self-conscious fly out the window when I feel my impending orgasm rise, its right there but I can't reach it. Creed must sense this because he pushes a single finger inside me, and I have to bite down on his shirt to stop the cry from sounding out and waking Harlem. Four pumps later and I'm muttering Creed's name into his shirt, he withdraws his finger and doesn't give me time to come down from my high before he's undoing his pants and sliding them down exposing his rock-hard cock. I can't tear my eyes from it, has it grown? "Shirt off princess." Reality comes crashing down on me, I shake my head and Creed cocks a brow at me. I remove the shirt from my mouth and look up at him.

"Creed, my body.... It isn't the same.... It's changed--"He leans down and smashes his lips against mine, this kiss steals the air from my lungs.

"You're beautiful Jess. This body of yours gave us the greatest gifts, never hide it from me. I love you regardless." Tears cloud my vision, he grips the bottom of my shirt and slowly lifts it over my head, my bra goes next. I lay here naked with his heated gaze on me, I have stretch marks now on the sides of my hips and some on my lower stomach but the way he is looking at me makes me feel beautiful. He leans down and captures my lips in a heated kiss, he's pouring all of his love into this kiss, and it melts me. He pulls back and looks me directly in the eyes. "No more lies, no more secrets."

"Okay." I whisper, he moves his hips forward and I can feel the tip of his cock at my entrance and stiffen.

"Relax little alpha, I got you." I do as he says and relax, he nudges forward and inches inside me slowly, a moan comes from me. He places his hand over my mouth as he slams the remainder of his cock inside me, and my cry of pleasure is masked by his hand. His eyes change to blue, and a small growl sounds inside his chest. He gives me time to adjust to him before he begins moving inside me, oh my god. I forgot how good this felt. "Fuck, you're so tight princess." His pace picks up and I start to feel my orgasm building again, he leans back and lifts my legs, so my ankles are on his shoulders and bends forward so I'm folded like a staple.

Holy fuck!

This angle is definitely hitting the exact spot I need. I feel around with my hand and grip his shirt then shove it in my mouth as he begins to slam inside me. the look on his face tells me he is loving being inside me as much as I love having him in me. He leans in closer to me; my legs are nearly flat against my chest. He slams into me again and then I'm seeing stars as I scream into his shirt. I watch as he pumps into me two more times before his forehead creases and his eyes slam shut and he bites his bottom lip to stop himself from making any sound. I feel his cock swell as he cum's inside me, he pushes my legs from his shoulders and slumps forward resting his forehead against my chest. Our loud breathes fill the silent room, my chest is rising and falling rapidly, that was amazing! I reach up and stroke the back of his head, my heart begins to swell with joy. I open my mouth to utter the three words I know I feel for him but then clamp it shut when I hear Harlem stir. Creed leaps off me like I just burnt him, I scurry off the table and drop down to the ground beside Creed, we both frantically search for our clothes and try to dress as quick as we can, so we don't get caught, I chuck him his shirt as he throws me my jeans. We both change as fast as we can and jump to our feet, I look to Creed, his gaze is already on me, then we lose it. We both break out into fits of laughter, Creed hunches over laughing.

"Mommy?" I snap out of my fit of laughter and head toward my son. I feel like a teenager who just about got caught having sex in their parents' house.

After Creed managed to get his laughter under control, we decided to take Harlem for a walk to find the others. We find them near the back of the boat, Cairo, Zeke, Callie, Cole and Meg all stand around laughing. They all halt in silence as we approach, everyone seems happy to see my hand clasped in Creeds, except Cole. Cole glares at our joined hands, he pushes off the side of the boat and storms past us. I exhale a loud sigh.

"Just give him some time." I snap my gaze to Callie and nod before turning to look up at Creed who has Harlem on his shoulders. His eyes narrow when he sees the look on my face.

"I have to talk to him."

"You don't have to do shit, princess." I sigh, I knew he wouldn't take this well.

"I need to fix this Creed." I don't give him time to answer, I pull my hand from his and chase after Cole.

I searched the boat but couldn't find him anywhere, so I decided to check the room we stayed in last night and sure enough, there he is gazing out the window. I make my way inside and gently shut the door; I don't make it two steps before he speaks.

"Outside I may not be able to scent shit but in here I can smell the both of you." He turns and pins me with a look that has my steps faltering. His green eyes shine with so much hurt and anger, I move toward him and meet his gaze.

"Colton--"

"No Jess, don't *Colton* me. What the hell are you thinking?" I reel back in shock at the anger in his voice.

"I don't think that is any of your business." He throws his hands in the air and glares at me.

"It is my business, after everything we have been through together you just toss me out. Why?" I deflate, Cole was there for me when I needed someone, and I love him for that, but he has no right to behave like this.

"Because--"Cole doesn't let me finish, he closes the space between us and smashes his lips against mine. I stand there stunned for a moment, when my brain finally registers what's going on I shove against his chest until he moves back. "What the hell Cole?"

"Yeah, what the hell Cole?" Both Cole and I spin toward the door to see Creed standing with a look of rage on his face. I go to move toward him, but I'm yanked back when Cole pulls my arm. Creed growls and storms toward us, I wrench my arm free and jump in the middle. I turn to face Cole, pleading with my eyes that he does not antagonize Creed. I feel Creed press against my back like a second skin and it takes everything inside me not to lean into him.

"Cole, you should go." Cole's eyes widen in shock.

"Me? You're not serious." I jump when I hear Creed release a warning growl. He wraps his arm around my waist and holds me against him.

"The only reason I'm not punching your face right now is

because of what you did for her. She is my mate Cole and I will not give her up, aside from being my mate she is the mother to *my* children--not yours." It fills me with pride that Creed said children instead of child.

"She could have been if you just stayed away!" Cole yells, I see the hurt in his eyes and it guts me.

"Yo, we need to go now!" We all turn to see Cairo in the doorway with a look of panic on his face.

"What happened?" Creed asks.

"Shelley and Davina called a meeting and your dads with them."

"Fuck them, I'm not going to that island!" Creed snaps.

"We don't have a choice, Shelley got word from one of her guys. Jacob knows we left on a boat."

Chapter Ten
Credence

I don't know how I let Jess convince me going back to that stupid Island was a good idea. We all stand in the middle of Davina Reeves yard waiting for the woman to come out. A part of me hopes she can't because its daylight, well late afternoon but still the sun is out and aren't vampires supposed to burn in the daylight? I snap out of my thoughts when I hear Harlem whine to Jess. I didn't exactly relish in the idea of bringing him ashore with us, but we didn't have a choice, my family, Sky, Cairo, Zeke, Shelley and Dela came with us. I smile down at my son and ignore the heat of my brother's gaze; it took more control than I have not to beat the shit out of him when I saw him kiss Jess. I know he loves her, but she doesn't love him, she's mine.

"I want to go dad, Mommy." Hearing that three-letter word out of his mouth melts my heart. I don't think I will ever get tired of hearing it, I reach over and pluck him out of Jess's arms, he squeals in delight. I grip him under his arms and chuck him into the air and he laughs. He grips my face between both his hands and places a wet sloppy kiss against my cheek. "Again!"

"I thought only Ro-Ro was allowed to do that?" I turn and grin at Cairo while waggling my brows.

"Dude, I'm always gonna be the first choice, live it, love it and learn it." Cairo narrows his eyes and glares.

"You're on my shit list Reeves, don't think I don't know what you just did with my sister." I see Jess cringe; I can't help the laughter that bubbles out of me. Cairo storms over and steals my son from my arms and places a kiss to the top of his head. "You do realize what I just did with your sister made that baby that you're carrying and kissing right?" Ro freezes, he darts his gaze between me and Harlem and then turns to glare at his sister who smiles up at him sheepishly.

"Parlay?" Ro's face scrunches in confusion, the rest of us get what Jess is asking and laugh. Zeke, Sky and Ro are the only ones who don't.

"I have no idea what that means, Smalls."

"It's a pirate saying for like...peace?" Ro shakes his head.

"You could have had a kid with anyone in the world and you chose him? We have good DNA and you muddied that with his."

"Hey!"

"Asshole." Both Callie and Cole say in unison as I laugh and wrap my arms around Jess and tug her back against my chest.

"You should be thanking me."

"Why in Gods good name should I thank you? You're a fucking cradle snatcher!" I bite my lip to stop myself from laughing.

"Dear lord, if you reply with something about having a big penis I will hurl." I glare at my sister.

"I do have a big dick!" I retort, I don't miss the snort that comes from Jess and my mom. "Laugh all you want princess, but I wasn't the one who asked, *'did it grow?'* or *'will that thing fit?'*" Jess pulls out of my hold and turns to slap me on my chest and storms off to stand with my parents, Sky and Callie.

"I swear I raised him better than that, I blame his father for his huge ego." My mouth drops open in shock as I stare at my mom. I glare at my brother and dad when they begin to laugh uncontrollably.

"Wasn't that funny." I mutter as I glare at my mom.

"Sorry to keep you all waiting." I spin around to find Davina, Vince and another guy standing there. The stench of rotting flesh fills my senses and I have to stop myself from gagging. I take deep breaths in through my mouth. "I see that you have--"

"Eww, something stinky." All eyes turn toward Harlem, the vamps remain silent while the wolves try to hide their laughter. Clearly Harlem has the nose of a shifter already and that makes pride swell inside me. My laughter dies in my throat when Davina moves forward toward Cairo and Harlem, I step in front of her blocking her path.

"You stay the hell away from my son." Hurt flashes in her gaze before she quickly masks it, she gives me a stiff nod then steps back by her men.

"Why are we here Davina?" Dad asks, I see Shelley and Dela move from the corner of my eye and come to stand by Davina. I move back until I'm shoulder to shoulder with my dad.

"Because I just got word Jacob tracked your scent to the seaside."

"How?" Her eyes dart to me as she answers.

"I assume he followed your scent until it disappeared and decided to keep going and see where it led? I honestly don't know; I guess he gathers you all fled by boat. With all that being said, it is not safe being where you are so I'm inviting you all to reside on the island with us." She has to be joking, right? There is no way in hell I will stay on this island with her and her minions.

"That's very kind of you, we appreciate it." I spin around and stare at my traitor of a mate. She must have lost her goddamn mind; either that or I fucked the sense out of her.

"Jess is right, tension on the boat is ramping up and we don't have the supplies we need. We also don't have the facilities for everyone to use, it's our best option." I throw my hands in the air, Shelley has lost the freaking plot as well.

"I'll have my men arrange adequate accommodations for you all. Everything should be set for you by morning--"

"How can you stand out in the sun?" Fucking hell, that's seriously all Cole can think about right now?

"Vampires are not like what you see in movies, we don't burn in the daylight."

"Well, I guess you'll have to tell us all about that and what your weaknesses are and how to kill you." Callie chokes on air at our brother's comment.

"Colton, that's rude."

"It's fine Meg--"

"With all due respect Davina, don't butt in when I'm speaking to *my* son. I will handle *my* children the way I see fit. Now, thank you for allowing us to stay here but my children and I will be getting back, my grandson is hungry."

Mic drop!

Mom just served Davina a can of ass whooping on a silver platter. Everyone is staring at mom like she is some strange being, she nods her head and leaves-- we all follow like sheep.

We're all sitting around the table that Jess and I fucked on, I glance over at Jess, and she blushes. A smile stretches across my face at the memories of her body and what it felt like to be inside her. Shit, now I'm hard as a fucking rock.

"This is the best option for us, all our wolves are restless, and we need to shift."

"How do we know they won't kill us, Dad? They're vampires!" Dad runs a hand through his hair, Cole has been an ass since we got back and honestly, I don't blame him. I don't like the idea of staying on that island anymore than he does.

"Colton, there isn't enough food here for all of us. This won't be easy, but we have to do it, this won't be forever. We just have to work out our best plan and the take the council down, then we can all go home." Well, when mom puts it like that.

"Meg's right, I don't relish in the thought of raising my son on an island, but I also don't want to spend the rest of my life looking over my shoulder either. We need to stop the council and all their corruption. The day we went to the summit, I saw a woman with Jacob and the look in her eyes was utter fear. She doesn't want to be there, but she doesn't have a choice, we have to do this not just for ourselves but for every other wolf who isn't being treated right." I turn to my mate and smile, she sounds like a true alpha and judging from the looks on the others faces they all agree with me.

"In order for that to happen Jess, you need to stand up and take your place as the rightful alpha. There will be backlash and men who don't want to live under a women's rule, are you prepared for that?" Jess meets my dad's gaze and the determination in her eyes tells me everything I need to know.

"Yes. I will not raise my son to think he is better than any man or woman. If taking down the council means I have to step up and claim my birthright, then so be it."

We spent the rest of the evening planning and plotting what we should do, numerous disagreements broke out. Too many alphas in one room isn't a good idea but for the most part we all made it work and came to the conclusion that we *are* in fact going to the island tomorrow, much to my dismay. Jess offered to let me sleep up here with them, Harlem is sleeping with Ro tonight so Jess and I can share her bed. Her back is to my chest, and we're stuck sleeping on our sides thanks to the bed only being a single. I don't notice the lack of space, I'm just grateful to be laying here with her in my arms. She let me in on their little secret, having a shower never felt so good and I even got to brush my teeth. I tried to con Jess into joining me, but Cairo stormed over and picked her up bride style and refused to let her go.

Chapter Eleven

Jessica

My body feels like its smoldering, I try to move away from the heat but I can't. I snap my eyes open and see an arm wrapped around my waist and that's when I remember, the heat is coming from Creed. I turn and peer over my shoulder and melt, he looks so peaceful when he sleeps. The harsh lines on his face are smoothed out, his full lips are parted slightly as he snores softly. I roll over as smoothly as I can, so I don't wake him and then run my fingers through his hair, a soft moan falls from his lips at my touch.

I trace my finger down his face and cup his cheek, something shifted between us yesterday. My anger and resentment aren't as prominent, talking to him about Katy broke down a wall I had up to keep him out. We have hurt each other enough, and I don't want to continue to push him away. I love Creed and it's about time I let him know how I feel. I lean forward and place a featherlight kiss against his lips, his hand slides up before I get a chance to pull back his hand snaps up and holds the back of my neck so he can deepen the kiss. All thoughts about morning breathe fly out the window when his tongue invades my mouth, my veins begin to feel like lava, as he devours my mouth and cups my ass at the same time.

"For fuck's sake!" Creed and I jolt apart, I peer over his shoulder and feel my cheeks flame when I see my brother and Zeke standing there, Z shakes his head and smiles while Ro glares at us. He points an accusing finger at Creed who just chuckles and cocks a brow. "From now on you sleep on the floor." Ro darts his gaze to me, and I bite my bottom lip to stop myself from smiling. "And you, I liked it better when you didn't like him." I lose it, I laugh and not a second later Creed is laughing with me and wrapping his arm around my waist again pulling me against his chest, I burrow my face in the crook of his neck, to avoid looking at my brother. "Fucking Reeves."

"I wish she was fucking a Reeves, but you ruined it when you opened your mouth." I gasp at Creed's crude words.

"I fucking hate you." Creed chuckles and rests his chin on top of my head.

"Be a good uncle Ro and feed your nephew so I can get lost inside your sister." I hear a growl and cringe; Creed is pushing Ro to the limits this morning.

"Fuck you, get up and get dressed you dick. We leave in half an hour to go see your egg donor." At the mention of Davina, Creed stiffens before nodding.

Half an hour later we are on the boat and heading to the island, Davina has organized for her men to ferry the rest of the pack over on some of her small boats. Creed and I are standing inside our so called new...house. Wolves are pack animals so it doesn't bother us to share, Cairo, Callie, Sky, Cole and Zeke are sharing this house with Creed, Harlem and me. It's a two-story house and has plenty of space, Davina tried to offer us a play gym for Harlem, but Creed flat out refused. Davina organized clothes, food and other necessities to see us through, even Harlem has his fair share of essentials. Thank the heavens that we all have individual rooms, the house is plain, but at the end of the day it's way better than living on a boat. We were given permission to do what we like and make it our own, but I don't see any of us putting personal touches on the house.

We all agreed to take the day and night to ourselves and then we would all gather tomorrow so we can discuss a plan. Kane and Creed didn't let on that we had already discussed a plan, they want to find out what Davina has up her sleeve before they tell her anything. I understand their caution, but if we're going to work together then we at least need to try trust each other. I release a sigh and decide to look around our room and notice a walk-in closet, filled with clothes, behind the other door is a private bathroom with a tub, Harlem is going to love that.

I'm stunned at how they are able to make houses like this on an island, it's so intriguing to me how they have all built a comfortable life here. I snap out of my thoughts when two arms wrap around my waist, Sheba growls her approval inside my head. I shrink back into Creed and sigh, having him near me and not fighting is new and I love it.

"Is it wrong that I'm excited to be able to sleep in a proper bed and shower whenever the hell I want?" I chuckle and turn in his embrace wrapping my arms around his neck. His hands grip my waist as I stare up at him and smile.

"No, there's even a bathtub Harlem is going to love that." He leans down and places a soft kiss against my lips.

"I can't wait to finish this shit. When everything is done, I want you and Harlem to come back to Rosewood with me." I drop my arms and step back, a look of hurt flashes in his eyes before he quickly masks it.

"I... What about my brother?"

"If you take over as alpha, you will have no choice but to

return to Rosewood and lead both packs, Princess." I know what he is saying is true, but I guess I just thought--. "Cairo can return with us, if he chooses."

"How will that work though? Ro is an alpha and so are you... I will be as well."

"Your brother loves you; we can figure something out."

I must admit it's so nice to be sitting around a table and eating a meal together--A proper meal. Steak, mash potatoes, corn, carrots and beans, it's been so long since we've had a decent meal. Sky and Callie cooked for us, and I tell you what, they are amazing cooks.

"That is the best meal I have ever had."

"Preach Z, you girls out done yourself." Callie beams at Zeke and Cairo.

"I had no idea you could cook."

"Well, there is a lot of new things you don't know brother."

"I want to know all about these new things Callie." Callie stares at Creed in wonder and nods her head jerkily.

"Daddy?" It still shocks me to hear that name come out of Harlem's mouth. Creed beams every time he says it.

"Yeah?" The love in Creed's voice fills me with warmth.

"I want you to have a tub-tub with me." Creed turns to me and cocks a brow in question, but I don't get a chance to answer.

"He wants you to have a bath with him." Cole says as he pushes back from the table and stands. I stare up at him and find his gaze on me. His green eyes shine with so much hurt; I don't know how to fix this between him and I. I had no idea Cole even had feelings for me!

"Can I talk to you for a minute?" Cole is slow to pull his gaze from mine to look at his brother. The hurt in his eyes is quickly replaced by anger.

"Whatever you got to say, you can say it here." Creed nods and takes a deep breath.

"I'm sorry, I shouldn't have lashed out at you and said the things I did--"

"So, what, because you say sorry, I'm supposed to forgive you?" Creed tenses and I can see he is trying to control his temper; Cole is acting like an ass.

"No, I'm just trying to say that I don't want to fight with you. You're my brother and I love you, but Jess is my mate--"Cole slams his palms down on the table and glares at Creed, Cole's eyes change to the yellow of his wolf. I have to give Creed credit, he doesn't react and remains calm, Ro and Zeke sit forward ready to intervene if they have to.

"I know! We all know, you don't deserve her."

"You're right. I don't deserve her Cole, but what makes you think you do? I know you love her brother, but I will never let her go. I'm trying to right my wrongs here and I don't want to be at odds with you. This is my one and only warning little brother, you ever and I mean *ever* kiss her again or make a move on her, I won't hold back."

"You kissed Jess?" Callie snaps.

"And if she chooses me?" I stand, I'm sick and tired of listening to these two battle over me like I'm not even in the room. I pick Harlem up and turn to leave, but stop and turn to Cole.

"Don't ask me to choose Colton."

"Why?"

"Because it won't be you, it will be him. I love you Cole but not the way you want me to love you. You're my best friend and I couldn't have gotten through losing Katy without you, please don't ruin what we have."

CHAPTER TWELVE
Credence

After Jess left to bath Harlem, I helped the others clean up and I've been sitting on one of the loungers out the back since. I know she meant it in a brotherly way, but she told Cole she loved him and not me. Does she not feel the same way about me as I do her? Have completely ruined things between--.

"You frown any harder and your face will stay like that." I peer over my shoulder and glare at Cairo, he and Zeke make their way over to me and drop down into the other chairs. We sit in silence for a while, each of us lost in our thoughts. "Why are you here and not with my sister?"

"I'm not sure she wants me around." Zeke scoffs and I pin him with a look. "Got something to say?" I snap.

"Actually, yeah I do. Pull your head out of your ass and stop feeling sorry for yourself for fuck's sake."

"The hell is that supposed to mean?"

"It means don't be dumb Credence. Jess loves you; you can sit there and deny it, but we all know that's why you're out here sulking."

"Am not!" Zeke rolls his eyes.

"You've been quiet ever since she told Cole she loved him." Am I that obvious? I have never been insecure before; women came and went, and I liked it that way. Ever since meeting Jess no women has even caught my eye, my dick won't even get hard unless I'm thinking about her! "She didn't mean she loved him like *that*." I glare at Zeke; he is the last person I want to be talking to about any of this. I know he harbors feelings for Jess, and it pisses me off.

"You don't think I know that?"

"Then why are you so pissed, Creed?" I swing my gaze to Cairo, his question has me stumped. Why am I so pissed that she told my brother she loved him? I run my hand through my hair in frustration. "You're pissed because she hasn't said it to you." A whoosh of air rushes out of me, Cairo is right I drop my gaze to my lap. We sit in silence and get lost in our own thoughts, again. I should be worried that we are on an island of vampires but instead my thoughts are plagued by a beautiful blonde woman who manages to set me ablaze by just looking at me. I know Jess cares about me, I can feel it through the mate bond. Feeling it and hearing it are two totally separate things though, those three words spilled out of her mouth so easily tonight when she was talking to Cole. I've told her that I love her, but she hasn't said it back, she just smiles and that's it.

"You know Cole loves her, right?" I don't bother to look at Zeke, I just nod my head. "Cole bent over backwards for her after she had the twins. We were all there with her--"I snap my gaze to Zeke and growl; Corbin and I don't appreciate the reminder that we weren't there for the birth of our pups. Zeke raises his hands as if surrendering. "Easy, Alpha. There is a point to all of this." I nod my head and sit there stiff as a board as Cairo leans back and closes his eyes. "When she went into labor, she was so scared and all she wanted was her mom and...you." My eyes double in size.

"Why?" I whisper, Zeke smiles at me sadly.

"Because as her due date neared, guilt ate at her that you wouldn't be there. She felt ten times worse after she gave birth knowing that you missed not one but two of your children's births."

"Why are you telling me all of this?"

"Because the whole fucking time she has been away from you all she wanted was *you*. Jess may not have known it then, but she was in love with you before she ran. Cole and I both tried, we care about her, but she never saw us. All she ever sees is you Credence, you think because you lied and used her that she will do the same to you? You're dead fucking wrong, she loves Cole because he reminds her of you. She used to pretend he was you; she thinks none of us know that, but we saw it. Jess has eyes for only you, don't throw away what you have with her because she's tight with your brother." I slouch back in my seat and ponder over Zeke's words; he is so fucking right but it isn't Jess who I need to go to right now.

I find Cole in one of the rooms upstairs, when he sees me standing in the doorway he growls and narrows his eyes. I take a breath and look at my little brother, I owe him more than I can ever repay, and I have been nothing but a dick to him.

"Thank you, brother." Cole's brows furrow in confusion.

"For what?" I uncross my arms and let them dangle at my sides.

"For everything. You were there for her when I wasn't--"

"I didn't do it for you!"

"I know. I'm still grateful to you though, you protected her, and my children and I can never repay you for that Cole. I know I have fucked up a lot and done shit that I shouldn't have, but I am trying to make up for all of it now." Cole sighs loudly and his whole body turns stiff as he meets my gaze. The look in his eyes is pure anger, I feel Corbin pushing against my ribs urging me to shift.

He's, my brother!

He is challenging us; we need to assert our domin--

No! I will not hurt him.

I close the link between Corbin and I and focus back on Cole. I know without a doubt what he is about to say is out of hurt and anger and I try hard to brace for the impact of his words.

"I never betrayed you. I told them all that if it came to a fight, I would never stand against you, I could never do that to you. But the other night you went a step too far brother, you can blame me and take your shit out on me all you want, but you can never change the fact that I slept with your mate." I stumble back a step and stare at him.

Jess and Cole slept together!

She lied to me.

I see his mouth open, and I can't for the life of me hear a goddamn word he is saying, the ringing in my ears is too loud. My chest feels like it has just been broken in half, I turn and stumble the whole way out of the house. I don't know where the hell I am going I just know I need to get away from my brother before I do something I will regret. Corbin is urging me to shift and allow him to take over so he can deal with my pain.

Creed, let me take over

He slept with her, Corbin!

He lied.

I stumble to a stop.

No, I saw the look in his eyes he was telling the truth.

If he slept with her, I would know.

How?

Shift and I'll tell you.

I move toward the palm trees and head toward the beach, I look left and right and when I see that the coast is clear I begin to strip and lay my clothes in a pile on a random piece of driftwood. It used to be painful when I first shifted, I could feel every bone break and I would cry out and beg for someone to make the pain stop. Now, the pain lasts a fraction of a second and then it's over. I allow Corbin the control he craves and within a few seconds I go from standing on two legs to standing on four. Corbin doesn't hesitate, he spins around and begins to run back toward the way we came.

Where are you going?

To deal with your brother.

Oh shit, don't get me wrong I am furious and confused as fuck about what Cole just said but no part of me wants my brother dead. I try to wrestle for control back, but Corbin puts a block in place and now I'm locked in the back part of his brain. Corbin and I always work as a team, we have never *not* seen eye-to-eye, so for him to do this to me means he is beyond pissed. I try with all my might to get control back, but Corbin is strong, really fucking strong. He isn't the alpha wolf for nothing. I see through his eyes, and I notice our house in the distance, the scent of Cole assaults our nose and Corbin releases a loud howl. Everyone on the island will be able to hear that, all the shifters are aware of what that howl means.

Corbin has just issued a challenge against my brother. When a challenge is laid out, two wolves will fight for the others role in the pack and the fight won't end until one of the challengers is dead.

Corbin skids to a stop at the front of the house and snarls loudly before howling again. I hear others approaching from every direction and when footsteps come pounding toward the entry of our house, I try again to wrestle control back.

Corbin!

He must pay for his crime.

He was lying!

His heart rate remained the same and his pulse didn't falter.

I know he's right, a wolf can tell when someone is lying, if you lie your heart rate will change or your pulse will speed up. Coles didn't change, he wasn't lying about sleeping with Jess.

I will never forgive you if you do this to my brother.

So, you would allow him to bed our mate?

I--uh, no.

You are becoming weak Creed. We are not weak-- I am not weak.

We are the fucking alpha--

We don't have a pack; we have no pack lands because you are weak and didn't claim our mate. You let your humanness cloud your mind and now we have no reign or land to rule over.

I don't get a chance to answer, the front door swings open, and my sister comes barreling out, tears trekking down her face. She drops to her knees a couple feet away and bows her head in submission before meeting our gaze, her eyes hold so much heartache and fear.

"Please, I am begging you Creed, don't do this." Being the alpha gives me the privilege of being able to speak into the minds of those in my pack.

He defied me, he will fight or be banished.

Callie reels back in shock, her eyes dart side to side before settling back on us.

"Corbin?" She has just realized it isn't me in control. Corbin releases a growl, letting her know it is him in control. "Let Creed take over."

You will mind your tongue and step aside California before I order it!

The look in my sisters' eyes guts me, she knows she will have no choice but to follow Corbin's wishes if he orders it. A commotion inside the house snags our attention, I lift my gaze to see Zeke and Cairo holding each of Cole's arms as he struggles to free himself. Jess walks out of the house behind them, Cole is glaring daggers at her, but her gaze is focused on me-- Well me in wolf form.

"Callie, Sky is inside with Harlem can you please go watch him for me." Callie looks from me to Cole and then to Jess, whatever she sees in Jess's eyes has her nodding her head and heading inside closing the door behind herself.

"Sweetheart--"I release a loud growl at the pet name Cole uses for her. "Please, don't do this." Jess turns to Cole and shakes her head.

"It's already done." She turns back to face me, and I can tell from the stubborn set of her shoulders and the tilt of her chin she has something up her sleeve. "Colton Reeves will not be accepting your challenge Corbin." Corbin growls and is about to open the mind link to Jess but stops when she speaks again. "I will fight in his place; you will not harm him. If you wish to take your anger out on someone then do it to me, not your brother."

CHAPTER THIRTEEN

Jessica

I have no idea what has set Creed and Corbin on this war path, but I refuse to let them take their anger out on Cole. I know things are tense between Cole and I right now, but it still doesn't mean I won't have his back. Creed should know that I'm so angry at him for doing this, I thought he was passed this, I guess I was wrong.

"Corbin, do you accept the substitute, or do you wish to retract?" I ask, I feel the mind link open and wait.

Stand down, Mate. I want Colton not you. Let us settle this as wolves and step aside.

I glare at Corbin. *Credence, he is your brother don't do this to him!*

Credence isn't here, he has no say in this.

Shock ripples through me, Corbin has locked Creed away and taken control. I need to find a way to get Corbin to release Creed, he wouldn't want to fight to the death especially not against his brother. I peer over my shoulder and see Zeke and Cairo struggling to hold Cole back. My brother shoots me a warning look, if it comes to it, I know he won't let me fight Corbin-- he'll take my place. I refuse to lose anyone else I love.

I will not let you harm him.

You laid with him!

I reel back in shock, the hell does he mean I laid with him?

You have no idea what you are talking about Corbin-

He told us; you dare to disrespect me by laying with another.

You need to calm the hell down Corbin, let Creed out now so we can sort this!

Credence has grown weak and bows to your charms, but I will not. I am an alpha and will not allow you to treat me as less than I am.

You need to calm down, I never slept with Colton!

Corbin releases an angry growl and stalks toward me, I hear growls sound out from the three guys behind me, but Corbin doesn't even bat an eye at them. Before he can get within five feet of me Kane and Meg jump in front and block me from his view.

"Stop, whatever it is we can work this out son." Corbin releases a vicious growl that sends trembles through everyone except me. He is using his alpha power to cower his pack into submission. I try to brush past Kane, but he snaps his arm out and shakes his head. I spot movement out the corner of my eye, I notice its Davina moving toward us. She looks angry, Kane ushers me to the middle of him and Meg and stands tall as he faces her.

"I will not have this here; we do not fight or sort our troubles with violence." She turns toward Corbin; his cheeks lift in warning. "This may be how you did things with your pack, but you won't do it here on my lands. You have a problem, then use your fucking words not your fist or teeth. We have all lost enough because of violence and I refuse to allow you all to fight amongst yourselves on my island." That... Was not what I was expecting her to say. Corbin begins to shake his head and blow out harsh breaths, I can tell he and Creed are fighting internally. I don't know what has gotten into the pair of them but whatever it is they clearly are not seeing eye to eye on the matter.

"Son, shift back please." Meg begs, I see Davina flinch, but she quickly tries to mask it. I stifle my gasp; she does care about her kids-- so why act like she doesn't? I hear bones snap and quickly turn back toward Corbin; within a few seconds Creed is back and braced on his hands and knees. Sky rushes past us and chucks a pair of sweats beside him, he takes a few deep breaths then heaves himself up and pulls the pants on, I would be lying if I said I didn't just check him out. He lifts his gaze to mine and I see so much remorse in his hazel eyes, that look guts me! I break away from Meg and Kane and move to him, I stop when there is only sliver of space between us. His hands go to my hips, I don't hesitate to wrap my arms around him and pull him to me, he buries his face in the crook of my neck.

"I'm so sorry princess."

"Shhh, we can talk about it later."

"Someone want to tell me what the hell is going on here? I offered a safe haven, not for you and your pack to come here and shed blood." I pull away from Creed and interlock our hands together as we both face his bio mom.

"We meant no harm; this won't happen again." Shelley says as she comes to stand beside me, I didn't even know she was here.

"You know what will happen if it does Shelley, see to it that it doesn't come to that." Davina eyes us all before turning and stalking away, I have no idea what the hell she just meant! Shelley moves to stand in front of us, the scowl on her face pisses me off. She has no right to look down her nose at us, we are wolves and have been living in a confined space for days, of course tensions will be high!

"You do realize what could have happened right?"

"Take the bass out of your tone when you speak to me!"

Creed snaps back at her.

"You nearly caused a war between our two factions Credence!"

"What the hell are you on about Shelley?"

"If you had of drawn blood, what do you think the vampires on this island would have done?" I stiffen and dart my gaze around, I never thought about that. We could have just put both packs in danger because of a family feud, how could we have been so stupid and selfish. I feel Creed stiffen beside me, he looks around at the growing crowd and each of our onlooker's wear masks of fear. Living with vampires is new for all of us and this is going to take some time for us all to get used to. Creed tightens his grip on my hand and brushes past Shelley, well yanking me along behind him, he ignores his parents as we pass them and doesn't stop until we are standing in front of Cole, Zeke and Cairo. Cole glares at his brother but says nothing, tension thrums through me as the silence between them stretches.

"You went too far tonight brother, way to fucking far." Creed doesn't wait for him to respond; he moves past them and leads me inside.

I tuck Harlem into bed and turn to face Creed, he sits on the end of the bed with his head clasped between his hands. He looks do defeated and I don't like seeing him like this, he and I have to talk things out because this divide between us is doing more damage than good. We have a greater enemy to fight and in order for us to take the council down and figure out what part Davina plays in all of this. I move toward him and sit down making sure there's space between us, I can't think whenever we touch. The heat that overtakes my body whenever he touches me consumes all my thoughts. We remain in silence for a while, as I try to think of a way to break it and broach the subject but I'm honestly at a stalemate. Cole is his brother and this rift between them only started because of me!

"I had no control tonight." I lift my gaze; he looks at me with a solemn face. So much anguish shines within those stunning hazel depths. "I have never not had control, Corbin locked me out Jess and because of that I nearly killed my brother!" I reach over and grip one of his hands and hold it between mine.

"But you didn't. You stopped him!" He shakes his head rapidly denying my claim, he yanks his hand from my grasp and begins to pace in front of me. He tugs on his hair, and I cringe when I see some of the strands pull loose.

"You don't get it! If it wasn't for my mom and dad I...I don't know if I would have stopped. Corbin had me locked down Jess, I couldn't break free of his cage-- I was trapped in my own mind. Corbin's rage toward Cole was something I've never felt before, Corbin wanted to kill him Jess, my own fucking brother!" The anguish in his voice is nearly my undoing.

"What made you think I had slept with Cole?" I whisper, his head whips toward me, I ignore the look of betrayal in his hazel eyes making sure not to back down.

"Colton told me the two of you fucked." I reel back, my

eyes widen at the implication.

"You seriously think I had sex with Cole?" His eyes narrow in suspension.

"That's what he said!" Creed grits out. I stand and place my hands on my hips as I glare up at the stubborn bastard.

"Well did it cross your mind that he was lying? No, of course it didn't because you assumed the worse of me! I love your brother Credence but not in the way you think." His shoulders slump forward, and he drops his chin to his chest.

"I did believe him." He whispers.

"Why?" His gaze slowly lifts to mine.

"Because it makes no sense for you to be with me. Colton is the better choice, I'm damaged and will not relent to you, Princess. I will challenge you on everything, I will never bow to you, but Colton will. He will obey everything you say and he has never lied to you."

My heart bursts inside my chest, he has no idea what he means to me. Yes, we had a rocky start, and we have both put each other through hell but that is in the past now. I don't like this divide between us, I reach out grip his arm and swivel us so his back is to the bed, I push against his chest until he finally relents and sits. I don't give him a chance to question my motives, I straddle his lap and relish at the shock in his eyes. I weave my arms around his neck, and smash my lips against his.

Chapter Fourteen
Credence

Shit.

She uses my moment of confusion to slip her tongue inside my mouth. My hands automatically grip her waist and haul her closer against me. She moans into my mouth when I push her down harder on my growing erection. She scarps her nails through my hair and I groan into her mouth, I run my hands up and down her back then squeeze her ass and grind her against my cock. The way she purrs and tugs on my hair spurs me on, I grip the bottom of her shirt and yank it over her head then reclaim her mouth. I feel Corbin push against my ribs and try to rise up but I lock him down, he will not be showing himself anytime soon after what he did. As soon as I unsnap her bra it becomes a race to see who gets undressed quicker, I grab her and throw her on the bed as I marvel at her body. I see doubt creep into her face as she tries to shield her body from me. I climb on top of her and yank her hands away from her stomach, she has faint marks from where the twins stretched her belly, I place tender kisses to each of her stretch marks. Tears start to dwell in her eyes.

"You are beautiful princess, don't hide these from me. Your body is something to be proud of, these marks represent the lives you brought into this world." She smiles and for a moment all the tension dissipated from my body. I slide down her belly and pause at her navel, my tongue lashes out as I push her thighs apart, yearning for a taste of her, a gasp tears from her as I blow on her enlarged clit. I dart my tongue out and moan at the taste of her, her pussy tastes like heaven. I lap at her clit as I push a finger inside her, I look up and smirk, finding her eyes glued to my hand as it pumps in and out of her. "Your pussy is dripping, what a dirty little princess you are." I don't wait for her to answer, I dive back in and eat her like she is the last fucking meal I will ever have. When her moans get louder, I pull my fingers out and reach up. "Suck on them and stay quiet or you'll wake our son." Her eyes widen in shock as she darts her gaze to our sleeping boy, she forgot he was even in here. I continue to indulge in her clit and relish in the way she bites down on my fingers, I suck her clit into my mouth and a seconds later she shatters beneath me, while clamping her teeth down on my fingers, I hiss at the pain but love it at the same time. She unclamps her jaws and I pull my hand free, I run the fingers that were just in her mouth through her slick folds and grin when she trembles.

"Creed..." She moans.

"Hmmmm?" A fire burns in her eyes as I cup her breasts, her nipples are already as hard as granite when I tweak them.

"Fuck me." I snap my eyes to hers and smirk, I grip her under her thighs and hoist her legs up, her wet pussy is on full display, my cock twitches at just the sight of it. I don't delay this for either of us, I line myself up and slam into her. We both cry out at the feeling and I quickly clamp my hand over her mouth as I pump inside her, I bite down on my bottom lip so I don't make a sound. I move my hand from her mouth and capture her lips, I try to tell her without words that I love her. She wraps her arms around my neck and locks her legs around my waist and hauls herself up until I'm sitting back on my hunches with my cock buried balls deep inside her. I deepen the kiss to muffle our moans, her pussy has swallowed my cock whole and the way she begins to clench around me I know she won't last long at this angle. I break our kiss and cup her face locking my gaze onto hers.

"I love you Jess." Her face softens and her eyes begin to cloud over, our hands are cupping each other's faces.

"I love you to Creed, have done for a while now." I stare at her in shock, hearing those words from her lips is everything. She slams her mouth against mine and then begins to rock her hips I groan at the feeling. I grip her hips and then lift her up before slamming her back down on my cock, she cries out and I quickly cover her mouth with mine. She bats my hands away and takes over, I grip the back of her neck to keep her mouth on mine while she rides me like a pro bull rider. I feel her begin to clench and know she is about to come, again. Gripping her hips, I lift her off me, she glares at me but I ignore her as I move us to the side of the bed and position her so she is on all fours. I grab a pillow and shove it in her face and push her head down.

"Bite down on that, don't make a fucking sound or I will pull out and not let you come." She turns and glares at me over her shoulder, so I slap her exposed cunt. She gasps and leaps forward, a red hue begins to coat her cheeks. Ahhhhh, my little alpha has a kink. I yank her backward and shove her head down into the pillow before slamming my cock inside her. The pillow does its job and muffles her moans. I rear my arm back and slap her ass, she jumps but not from pain, her pussy flutters and I know she loves this. I slap her ass again and again until its bright red, I shit you not, her cunt is dripping from being spanked, the little princess isn't so innocent after all. She turns her head and the glassy look in her eyes tells me she is close; she opens her mouth to say something, but I grip the back of her hair and slam her face into the pillow and fuck her so hard the bed begins to shift along the ground. My balls begin to tighten as I feel her pussy clench, I quicken my pace and just when we're about to come Corbin forces a partial shift and without warning I lean forward and clamp my teeth down on her mate mark, we both cry out as we explode into euphoria.

Corbin recedes and my teeth retract from her mark, guilt gnaws at me instantly. I claimed her for a second time without her permission, I pull out and she rolls over and stares up at me. My mouth opens but no words come out, I don't know why I was so rough with her and why the hell I had no control over Corbin, I want to explain this to her, but nothing seems to be coming out of my damn mouth! She begins to sit up and I just stand there, I don't know what to say or do, I'm afraid if I say something it might piss her off. She pushes me back and climbs off the bed, she stands before me naked and the only thing I can focus on is the mate mark with small droplets of blood on her shoulder. I drop my head in shame, I hear her sigh and watch as her feet move away from me, the sound of her voice has my head snapping up to look at her as she stands in the doorway to the bathroom.

"The sex was amazing..."

"Just amazing?" Of all the fucking things to finally say that's what comes out!

"Fine, mind blowing. The first time you marked I had no idea what it meant, but this time I do. I know we are already mated Credence but next time...at least give me a choice." I just stare at her as she turns and closes the bathroom door behind herself quietly. I growl and fist my hair, fucking Corbin!

I did what I had to!

You claimed her again without her fucking consent you jackass!

Renewing our mark means our scent on her will be stronger, you need to think clearly.

I am goddammit. You are ruining everything Corbin--

You are not in control Credence; I can feel irrational anger inside us, and I don't know where it stems from. What happened with Colton tonight shouldn't have, but I couldn't control the rage and bloodlust inside me.

I stumble back and drop down onto the side of the bed, I can feel the anger inside me now, still. I was rough with Jess tonight and that isn't how I normally fuck. I wanted to worship her and take things slow but then something came over me and I just needed to...hurt her. I flinch at my own thoughts-- something is wrong with me!

We need to figure out what this is Corbin, I won't harm Jess or my son. We nearly hurt Cole tonight and I will never allow that to happen, again.

Agreed, I think it has something to do with this island.

Fan-fucking-tastic, so you want me to talk to Davina, don't you?

She would be my first choice, yes.

I close the link between Corbin and I when the bathroom door opens, and Jess walks out. I can't get a read on her emotions, I need to fix this divide between us that I just created, again. I keep fucking things up with her and I don't mean to. I stand and quickly locate my sweats, I pull them on and move toward her, she has a white silk robe wrapped around herself and I can see her nipples pebble as I draw near, I fight the smirk that wants to break free. I clasp her face between both my hands and lean down to plant a soft kiss against her lips. She stiffens from the shock but relaxes almost instantly into my hold and kisses me back. I pull back and rest my forehead against hers.

"I'm sorry princess, I don't know what has gotten into me." I drop my hold on her and spin her around yanking the back of her robe up, she gasps and tries to pull away, but I won't allow it, her ass is red and has angry handprints all over it. I pull back in disgust, she turns around and meets my gaze, she tries to come closer, but I step back and shake my head. I see hurt gloss over her eyes before she quickly masks it.

"I'm fine Creed."

"You're not fine Jess! Look at your ass!" I shout then flinch when I hear Harlem stir, Jess and I both remain quiet and watch to see if he will wake, when he doesn't, I focus back on her. "Something is wrong with me princess; Corbin thinks so too, ever since we came to this island, for some reason my anger keeps spiraling. I don't know what it is, but all I can think about is hurting people and wanting to relish in their pain." She flinches and I don't blame her, I just fucked her like a common whore. I hate myself for what I just did, I'm a piece of shit. I took her virginity and walked out on her and then I fucked her on a table and just now I shoved her face in a pillow and fucked her like a dog. I growl low in my throat.

"What the hell is going on Creed, I enjoyed it--"

"You enjoyed me fucking you like a whore?" I scoff and

begin to pace; she has no idea what I'm saying. "Tonight, I couldn't control Corbin, that has never happened before, *ever*! Corbin couldn't control his need to hurt Cole and just five minutes ago I couldn't control my need to claim and hurt you. I am telling you princess something isn't right with me!" She marches over to me and blocks my path until I'm forced to look at her, she reaches out and cups my face, her eyes search mine, for what I don't know.

"Okay, tonight we sleep and tomorrow we find out what the hell is going on with you and Corbin."

Chapter Fifteen

Jessica

Creed and I woke early thanks to Harlem deciding that our bed is a great trampoline, Creed didn't mind though. He and Harlem both decided to jump on the bed while I took a shower. I changed Harlem and made the beds, I'm on my knees putting Harlem's shoes on when his question has my movements halting.

"Are you gonna marry daddy?" My mouth open and closes but nothing comes out.

"Yeah, big guy, daddy just has to man up and ask her first." Shivers travel down my spine at his words, I'm too much of a coward to turn and meet his gaze so I keep focusing on tying Harlem's shoes as he answers his dad.

"Good, I don't want you to leave and fight the bad men again." As soon as I finish tying his shoes, Creed leans over me and scoops Harlem into the air. I stand and watch as he blows raspberries on our sons exposed skin, he lowers Harlem until he can look him in the eyes and says.

"Never again, daddy will never leave. Do you know what a heart is?" Harlem nods and places his hand over his heart and smiles triumphantly.

"Good boy, well you see my heart is yours and you can't live without a heart can you?" Harlem's brows furrow, my eyes begin to mist. "What I mean is you are my heart buddy, and I can't live without you so, I'm not going anywhere." He clutches Harlem to his chest and nuzzles his head. My heart swells, seeing how well Creed has taken to being a dad still surprises me. I honestly never thought he would take to the role as well as he has.

We make our way downstairs, when we hit the landing

Harlem takes off toward the others and launches himself at Cole, he catches him with ease and chucks him into the air and catches him. He places Harlem on a stool beside Callie as she ruffles his hair and snickers while patting his hair back down, he really needs a haircut.

"What are you having for breakfast monster?"

"I want loop-loops Co-Co please."

"Froot loops it is." Cole begins to pour him some cereal, Sky, Callie, Zeke and Cairo turn toward us and smile. The tension in the room is stifling, I hate that there is this divide between everyone, and I have no idea how to fix it!

"I'm sorry." Creeds blurts out, all eyes turn to him except Cole's. Cole places the bowl in front of Harlem adding the milk and places a spoon in his hand before slowly turning to face us. The cold look in his eyes has me stiffening, I'm annoyed that Cole told Creed we had slept together. I have no idea why he would say something so hurtful when nothing has ever happened between us except for him kissing me on the boat.

"For what exactly?" I narrow my eyes at Cole, he is being an ass and it's not cool.

"For going off at you last night. What you said...sparked something inside me and I plan to figure out what's going on with me today."

"What does that mean?" Callie cuts in.

"Ever since we stepped foot on this island something hasn't been right with me. Corbin and I have been disconnected and last night he locked me out, to the point of no control. When I did shift back, something happened last night and I didn't mean‐ ‐‐ "

"The fuck did you do to her?" Cole shouts, I step forward and meet his angry gaze. Creed done nothing wrong last night and what happens in the privacy of our bedroom is none of anyone's business.

"Nothing, Creed thinks this island is changing him and I believe him. Creed can explain it to the rest of you but Cole, I think you and I need to have a chat--privately." Cole nods his head and makes his way to the backyard; I turn to follow him but am stopped when Creed grabs my elbow.

"You don't have to do this." I smile up at him.

"I know, but this has to be sorted. This is not about you, he's upset at me and you're in the firing range." Creed releases my arm and nods his head.

"If you need me, I'll be right here with the monster." I nod and pat him on the chest as I follow Cole out the back and close the door behind myself. I find Cole sitting on one of the couches with his elbows resting on his knees, he lifts his head and when his eyes meet mine a sigh escapes me. I move toward him and drop down in the couch opposite him, the look in his eyes has my stomach twisting into knots. He looks so defeated and the accusation in his gaze tells me everything, he heard Creed and I last night.

"You just gonna let him waltz back in and forgive him for everything?"

"What do you want me to say Cole?" I steeled myself for his response, He glares at me and throws his hands into the air.

"That you're better than that, you're not a doormat sweetheart and that's how he's treated you!"

"It's my choice!"

"And you're making the wrong one!" I stand and so does he, we glare at each other, neither of us willing to back down.

"It's my mistake to make Cole." I whisper. He reels back like I slapped him and shakes his head.

"I expected more from you sweetheart--"

"No!" I shout. "You do not get to do that; he is the father to my kids--"

"I fucking know." He roars while pounding his fist against his chest. "I was there! Me. Not him, I was the one that was there for you and the twins." Tears flow down my cheeks; Cole and I have never fought like this and the fact that he is throwing what he did for me and the twins in my face is breaking my heart. "Shit." He mutters as he steps forward, I put my hand up to stop him, but he knocks it out of the way and wraps his arms around me. I sob into his chest; he drops his chin on top of my head. I feel my tears soaking his shirt and I can't bring myself to care, he holds me as I breakdown.

"I-I'm sorry." I hiccup, he sighs, and I feel him shake his head as he pulls back and cups my face. He smiles down at me sadly, he runs his thumbs under my eyes to dry my tears, but they continue to flow.

"You haven't done anything wrong sweetheart; I don't know what's gotten into me. I love you don't get me wrong babe, I know he is your mate, and your love lies with him. I want you to be happy and if you can look me in the eyes right now and tell me Creed is it for you, then I'll back off and try to deal with whatever this is thing between you and him." I hold his gaze as I say.

"I love him Cole, I know we started out shit, but I want to make things work with him. I want Harlem to have his dad--"

"But what do you want?" He cuts in, the hope in his voice guts me. I steel my spine as I take a breath and say the words that I know will destroy him.

"I want *him* Cole, I've always wanted him, I was just in denial about it. I never meant to hurt you or give you the wrong impression I swear, but I had always held out hope for Creed. He and I aren't perfect, and we still have a lot to figure out, but I want to figure it out with *him*. I love you Cole but not in the way you want me to, I'm so sorry." He inhales sharply and nods, a slow sad smile spreads across his face as he looks down at me. His thumbs stroke across my cheeks in an intimate way but I don't have the heart to bat his hands from my face.

"Then.... I won't stand in your way. I want you to be happy sweetheart and if my brother is the one to do that for you then so be it. You and I will always be good and don't expect me to change the way we interact because of him." I smile hopefully up at him and my heart swells when I see nothing but the truth in his eyes.

"Never." He leans down and places a kiss against my forward and pulls back, he wraps his arm around my shoulders as he leads us back inside. All eyes turn to us as we enter the room, Creed looks at me questionably, I smile with a nod, the tension in his shoulders flees.

"Just so we are clear, Jess said I'm hotter and if it wasn't for the mate bond, she would have gone for me." I choke on air while the others snort and laugh at Cole's stupid statement. My eyes meet Creed's and I'm shocked when I don't see anger in his gaze, I just see mischief and happiness. I really hope these boys can fix their bond because I know they love each and would take a bullet for the other.

"Brother, she was not screaming your name last night." I freeze and my eyes widen in shock, my brother begins to choke and Zeke smacks him on the back while chuckling. Callie lifts Harlem from his seat and motions for Sky to stay here. I look over to Cole and expect him to leave, but to my dismay he remains seated, a wide grin splits across his face and he wraps an arm around my waist and hauls me into his side.

"Babe, how many times have I told you it's not nice to fake an orgasm?" I feel the blush coating my cheeks, I turn my head toward Ro, I swear if my brother were a bull, you would see horns literally growing out of his head, he points an accusing finger between Creed and Cole and scowls at each of them.

"You fuckers! Shut up now or I swear to Christ I'll make your faces beat up my hand!" Both Cole and Creed break out into uncontrollable laughter. I pull away from Cole and head toward Sky but pause at my brothers' words. "If I ever and I mean *ever* hear you moan anyone's name or make fuck me eyes from across the table, I'll kill your mate and his demented brother." I smile sheepishly and decide to quickly scurry out of the room to find my son, the guy's laughter follows me out, but warmth fills me as I hear Sky's words.

"Keep it up, she will kill you dickheads while you sleep, and I'll be the one to help her bury you."

Chapter Sixteen
Credence

Jess and I stand outside the black container home with Jess's hand clutched in mine, Cole, Cairo and Zeke are with us. I didn't want Harlem to be here, so Sky and Callie offered to watch him and take him over to my parent's house. Cole and I still have a lot to work out, but for now we've decided to put our shit aside so we can figure out what the hell is going on with us. Cole mentioned his temper has been rampant and his wolf has been on edge as well since we came ashore. Dread pools inside me but is immediately replaced by anger.

"Ouch!" I snap my gaze to Jess and quickly release her hand when I realize I was nearly crushing it.

"Fuck, I'm sorry princess I didn't mean to--"

"I know, it's okay but how about I just stand beside you and not hold your hand I kind of don't want you to break it." I nod my head still annoyed at myself for hurting her again, it appalls me that I'm standing outside the entrance of Davina's house, but I have to figure out what the hell is going on with me. The worst part is, I didn't have the heart to tell my mom that I was meeting Davina today. I know she doesn't say it but being near Davina makes her feel insecure and she worries we will choose our egg donor over her.

"Let's get this over with, being here is giving me hives." Jess scoffs but doesn't rebuke Cole's claim, we make our way around the back and find Davina sitting at the table with a pitcher of...Lemonade, really? "Wow, I feel like I'm 4 and mommy has made us lemonade for being good boys." I smirk, Cole hates Davina as much as I do and neither of us are willing to give her an inch. Vince narrows his eyes slightly but remains quiet, Davina motions for us to claim the empty seats around the table.

Cole and I position Jess, so she is between us, Ro gives me a thankful nod and sits at the end of the table opposite Zeke. I lean back in my chair and sling my arm around the back of Jess's chair. We sit in tension filled silence for a long while, with Davina darting her gaze between me and Cole, Jess releases a sigh when Davina's gaze lands on her.

"Since the guys won't say anything, I will. Is there something on this island that could mess with a shifters temperament?" Davina looks to me and cocks her head to the side, her eyes assess me, making me feel vulnerable, The way she's gazing at me makes me feel like she can see straight into my soul.

"It's possible."

"Can you elaborate please?" Davina tears her gaze from me and focuses on Jess. She remains silent as Jess becomes tense, a growl escapes and everyone turns to her, her eyes are narrowed and her lip pulled back in a snarl. "I'm asking you to help your son, not me! For once in your life put your kids before yourself and help him."

"I am the only one that can help save you and your son Jessica Cruz." Jess cringes at the use of her birth name, which she still refuses to change her name from *Hastings*. Her hands clench into fists atop the table, her gaze laser focused on Davina.

"I will never put my son's life in your hands, I mean you did an amazing job of raising your own--."

"Enough! We didn't come here to trade insults, Davina something is going on with Creed and we wanted to know if you could help? Also as far as saving Jess and Harlem goes, we won't discuss those matters until the others are present, and I think it best we start planning that tonight." Davina nods then turns to Vince.

"Set up the meeting hall and make sure the first line is there."

"Yes, ma'am." Vince rises and claps Zeke on the shoulder as he exits the yard.

"What's the first line?" Ro asks her.

"It's what we call the trainers of our army, you all might benefit from training with them. I'll get word to Kane and Shelley to let them know about the meeting toni--"

"How can you walk in the daylight?" Cole blurts out, I groan and slouch back into my chair. Have we not been over this already? Davina reluctantly answers.

"Not everything you see in movies is true, we don't burn in the light of the sun. We do however get sunburnt faster than most, we also don't thirst for blood like the movies and books make you believe."

"So, you don't drink blood?" Cairo questions.

"We do, but it doesn't have to be human, animal blood is sufficient. When the change commences, our hunger is at its worst, we crave blood like air but after a couple of months the urge to drink hourly dies down, and we are able to focus a lot clearly."

"How exactly do you turn?" Jess asks. Davina darts her gaze between me and Cole, and I can see the hesitation in her eyes, but she answers anyway.

"You have to die with vampire blood in your system." That.... Wasn't what I was expecting to hear.

"How did you have vamp blood in your system?" I ask, Davina has her gaze laser focused on Jess as she answers.

"Austin told me the night he died to drink it, he said it would save me. I think he knew he would die that night and wanted to make sure that I survived." The longing in her tone pisses me off.

"Wow, so our father chose to save you instead of us, what a fucking--"Cole cuts Jess off.

"Eggplant?" Cole and I both laugh at the glare Jess shoots him.

"I said that one freaking time, let it go man!" Jess huffs and slouches back into her chair, Cole slaps my arm away from her shoulders and replaces it with his, I growl but he ignores me and hauls her closer into his side.

"Never sweetheart, even on your tombstone it will say *"here lies the eggplant"* it's your tagline now babe." Jess pulls out of his hold ignoring his laughter and leans closer toward me.

"What am I missing?" Zeke asks.

"Jess got pissed at Creed and called him an eggplant, it's stuck ever since." Jess glares at Cole and shakes her head.

"Anyway, like I was saying. Our dad is a dick, he chose you over me and Ro." Davina shakes her head rapidly.

"No. He had three vials, he made sure you and Cairo had one each. I think the third was meant for him but because I snuck out to meet him that night, he had no idea I was coming, and I took his failsafe from him. I'm sorry about your father, if I had of known what was going to happen, I would never have gone that night. I never thought Jacob would be ballsy enough to rise against him."

"I was there that night and so was Creed, we watched you

and my dad die." Davina turns toward an angry Cairo.

"I did die, but when I woke later on and saw Austin I panicked and ran." Cole jumps to his feet and slams his hands down on the wooden table, he leans forward and glowers at our egg donor.

"You left us! You chose dick over your own fucking kids, our dad loved you and you treated him like shit."

"I helped her escape." We all spin around to see dad walking toward us, shock ripples through me, dad knew and helped her. He manipulated me my whole life and molded me into the man I am now because he said he never wanted someone else to die like my mom. Dad claims the seat Vince vacated, he darts his gaze between me and Cole. "We should talk--privately." Both Cole and I growl.

"Fuck. You."

"Charming Colton--"

"You do not get to make demands of us, you are no longer my alpha and at the rate you are going you won't be my father either come week's end." Dad sucks in a harsh breath at Cole's words, I hate to say it, but I agree with my brother. I eye my dad warily, I used to look up to him and want nothing more than to impress him and make him proud, I never had freedom like the twins. I always had to train and learn politics and make sure that when the time came, I was ready to lead the pack. Thinking on it, that was all for nothing. I have no land, most of my pack is dead and we're on an island controlled by vampires.

"Look, I think it would be best if we give the four of you some time to talk. We will meet you all tonight, I have one request though Davina." Davina turns to Cairo and nods her head. "I don't think this island is just affecting Creed, I think it might be doing something to Cole as well, so if you could look into that we would appreciate it."

"You have my word; I'll deal with it." Ro nods and stands; Zeke follows his lead and Jess prepares to leave, Cole and I snap our hands out and place them on her shoulders. She looks to each of us and cocks her brow at me, I shake my head and say.

"Not you, they can go but I want--No, I need you here with me Princess." Her blue eyes soften, and she nods her head. Cairo and Zeke exit the back yard and we all sit there awkwardly for a few seconds before dad speaks.

"California is on her way; we should wait for her."

"No, I don't want Harlem here for this." Jess interjects.

"He won't be, he is staying with Meg while Sky and Callie join us."

"Why is Sky coming?" Cole asks. Dad frowns and asks.

"Did you want to deal with *hurricane Callie*?"

"No thank you." Cole says as he slouches into his chair.

"Exactly, hence why I asked Sky to join us so she can handle her mate." Us three guys chuckle at that, my sister may be small but when you piss her off, she is a fucking natural disaster and will destroy shit.

Chapter Seventeen

Jessica

Callie made a dramatic entrance; she dragged her chair from the end of the table all the way to the other end and dropped it between Sky and Cole. I had to hide my smile by biting my lip, Sky looks annoyed that she is here, but I know she would do anything for Callie even if it means suffering silently through this *talk*. I feel awkward, like I'm intruding on their private conversation but judging from the hostile vibes all three Reeves siblings are giving off none of them want to have this chat. I stifle a gasp when I hear Creed's voice in my head.

Thank you.

For what?

For staying and being here with me, I don't think I could get through this without you by my side.

I reach under the table and interlace my fingers through his and squeeze.

I wouldn't be anywhere else; I'm worried about Cole though.

Me to, he will need...you.

I turn to stare at him, I know how hard that must have been for him to say. I have no idea how they could go from trying to kill each other to being able to joke and sit so closely. Before I can answer him, Kane speaks.

"Ask us what you want to know."

"How about you tell us why the hell you lied?" The anger that laces Cole's tone doesn't surprise me. Finding out your parents lied to you your whole life isn't a great feeling, I should know after all. Kane drops his gaze causing his brown hair to flop onto his forehead, his hazel eyes shine with remorse. Davina on the other hand just looks stoic and resigned to whatever judgment her children give her, she is so put together, her long brown hair is slicked back and tied into a high ponytail, her eyes are bright and all seeing but you can just tell she holds so many secrets.

"I did it to keep you lot and Davina safe--"Callie scoffs cutting Kane off.

"Paaalease! You're so full of shit, your eyes are turning brown. You didn't do this for us, you did it for yourself and for her, you just didn't want the pack to know your wife was fucking around on you." I gasp, Sky places a comforting hand on her mates' shoulder, Kane's eyes widen in shock. Both Cole and Creed remain quiet, Davina doesn't say anything, the only movement that she gives away is that Callie's words stung, her eyes crinkle at the corners.

"California--"Callie slams her hand down on the table and releases a loud growl, Kane stiffens, and I can tell from the strain on his face that he is fighting his wolf for control. "Drop your gaze now!"

"Or what? You gonna act like I'm dead as well?"

"My wolf doesn't like your challenge California." Kane grits out through clenched teeth.

"Then tell your wolf to calm the fuck down or it will be me you face in battle not your daughter." Oh my god. I swear I swoon internally at the way Sky jumps to her mates' defense; she is one badass chick!

"Skylar, this is between me and my daughter, please stay out of it." A devious smirk crosses Sky's face as she eyes Kane.

"What concerns her concerns me, here is my warning to

you. Hurt my mate or cause her any harm and I will kill you where you sit without any remorse. You will sit there and take her anger because you deserve it, you lied and thought you could get away with it. You have hurt her, and she will say what she needs to in order for her to heal, now sit the fuck back and listen." If looks could burn you alive Sky would be burnt to a crisp. Kane leans back and crosses his arms over his chest while glaring at Sky.

"Answer me this, why did you flee Davina?" Her gaze cuts to Creed, his face is an emotionless mask.

"Because the blood lust was strong, I feared I would kill you children. Despite what you all may think of me, I never wanted to cause any of you harm."

"But you did! We grieved for the mother we didn't know, we longed for a memory of you. All we had to go on was what Creed told us about you, Dad would never mention your name or even tell us stories about you." My heart aches for Cole and the pain he and his siblings suffered.

"I'm sorry."

"Save it Davina, we forgot all about you when mom came along. Meg may not be our blood or our bio mom, but I am telling you now, you will never be half the woman she is. She loves us and has always treated us as if we were her own. I don't care if you and dad fuck off, as long as we have our mother, we will be fine."

"I'm glad you all have Meg, Creed."

"Fuck you! How can you sit there and act like this doesn't hurt us? My brothers and I deserve to know why you fucking chose Jess's dad over us. You abandoned us for some dick, you could have come back once you figured out how to control your urges, but you didn't you--"

"I couldn't!" Davina shouts, this is the first time she has displayed any emotion, her eyes hold so much pain and sorrow in their depths. "I wanted to come back but if the fucking council knew I was alive they would have hunted me. Kane had to act like I died in order to keep the three of you safe, they threatened to kill you all to get to me. They think I knew what Austin was hiding but I didn't, Jess's mother is the only other person who knew his secret."

"My mother is dead.... Both of them." I answer. Davina narrows her eyes, and a sly smirk splits her face.

"Is your mother really dead though?" I wince.

"What do you mean? I watched as Jacob broke her neck!"

"Not your aunt Jess, I mean your real mother, are you sure she is really dead?" Creed stands and hauls me to my feet by my arm, the others stand as well but I can't tear my gaze from Davina's, is my mom really alive?

"We're done here." Creed snaps as he drags me away, but I turn and watch Davina over my shoulder, her gaze is still locked onto me.

"Find me when you want to know the truth Jess." She says as we leave the backyard.

I'm quiet the whole way back to our house, once inside I head straight toward the lounge and plonk down on the sofa next to my brother. His gaze swings to me and his forehead creases with concern, he wraps an arm around my shoulders and pulls me into his side, I rest my head on his chest and just breath him in. Should I tell him about what Davina said? Creed

comes in and drops into the vacant seat beside me,

He places his hand on my leg and I reach down and interlace my fingers through his, I should be the one comforting him not the other way around. Cole, Zeke, Sky and Callie come in and occupy the other sofa's, we all sit there silently lost in our own thoughts for the longest time until a knock sounds at the front door. Callie rises but is stopped when Sky grips her arm and shakes her head, she lets out a huff but drops back down and allows Sky to answer the door. A familiar voice sounds out and I can't help the smile that splits across my face Harlem barrels into the room with the biggest grin, when his eyes land on me and Creed he pauses then lets out a squeak of joy before running toward us and jumping into Creed's arm, I pull away from Ro and plant kisses all over his face as he laughs. Meg follows Sky into the room, everyone is focused on Harlem and smiling at him. This boy brings so much joy and happiness to us all.

"Daddy we play trains?"

"Sure thing big guy." Creed hops on the ground and sits with Harlem on the rug, he pulls the basket over which Davina had dropped off. It's full of trains and wooden tracks, Harlem loves it, and it keeps him amused for hours. I look to Meg and see tears shining in her eyes as she watches them play, I will never tire of seeing the two of them play together, Harlem has already bonded with Creed and just adores him.

"So, any of you want to tell me what happened back there?" The moment of bliss is shattered by my brother's question. "Not trying to push or anything but its better we know so we don't get blindsided tonight at the meeting."

"You didn't miss much, dad talked shit and Davina tried to pass the buck by claiming your mom was still alive." Ro's brows jump as high as his forehead at Cole's words, he turns to me, and I shrug my shoulders.

"Nah-uh, you do not get to just shrug your shoulders and act like that wasn't an epic as shit bomb drop." I sigh in defeat, squaring my shoulders I turn and tuck my legs under me as I face my brother.

"Davina suggested that our *real* mother was still alive."

"Do you believe her?" I ponder his question for a moment, do I believe she is alive? I mean stranger things have happened after all, Creed's mom turned out to be alive and well, except for the fact that she's a vampire. Wait, if our real mom is alive does that mean she is a vampire as well? "Jess?"

"Sorry. I don't know what to believe and if she is alive why would she hide?" Cole scoffs and rolls his eyes.

"Bio moms tend to love hiding from their kids and living a life full of freedom." I cringe, yeah, he does have a point.

"What else did she say?"

"Just that if I wanted to know the truth to come find her, do we really want to venture down that road Ro? I mean Davina hasn't exactly given us a reason to trust her so why should we believe her about this?"

"From what Shelley tells me, Davina may be a lot of things,

but a liar isn't one of them."

"What else does dear old Shelley tell you Zeke?" Zeke glares at Creed but doesn't comment.

"I think maybe it is an avenue that you both should think about exploring." Everyone turns to Meg in shock.

"Mom--"

"Hear me out California, I don't think much of the woman as you all know." The three Reeves sibling's chuckle. "If *she* can come back from the dead who is to say that Jess and Cairo's mom can't as well."

"If she is alive then she is just like Davina, I will not have anything to do with her if she chose to leave us because she wanted to be with someone else." The anger in Ro's voice startles me but if I'm being truthful with myself, I agree with him. If she is alive then she better have a damn good reason as to why she hid from us.

"I still think you two should talk to Davina tonight." I shake my head.

"Creed and I don't want Harlem near her- "

"He won't be, I refuse to attend that meeting, I'm more than happy to stay here and amuse my grandson." I smile at Meg and thank her; Creed does the same as he stands.

"We better start getting ready then." Before we exit the room, Creed stops us with a question. "Zeke, I need to know where your loyalty lies." Zeke glares at Creed before turning to look at my brother.

"I may have been sent to you, but I have always been loyal to you. I did what I did so I could protect you and the pack, I will never go behind your back again Ro, I swear."

"You need to prove that to me Z and win my trust back." I'm proud of my brother, Sky walks forward and slaps Z on the chest then gives him a cold callous look that sends shivers down my spine.

"Fuck him over again and I'll kill you, I won't hesitate either." Zeke swallows but nods his head stiffly. "Good boy."

CHAPTER EIGHTEEN

Jessica

We follow Zeke to the meeting hall, I expected it to be a dingy looking place but it isn't. It reminds me of a school cafeteria, tables are all set out in rows and a buffet is set up to one side, Cairo being the bottomless pit that he is has already dished up a plate and eats noisily beside me. Creed hasn't eased his grip on my hand, he's been very reserved since we left the house, the more shifters and vamps that fill the room, the more tense he becomes. We managed to snag a table in the middle near the front, Creed and Ro are uncomfortable at the fact that their backs are exposed, I spot Shelley, Dela and Kane as they enter the hall, Shelley's gaze lands on me and they begin to make their way over. No one offers to shuffle down and make room for them, but I think our group is stating a point. I watch as Dela drops his chin to try and hide his smirk, I don't know much about him from my minimal interactions with him, he actually seems like a nice guy.

"Davina has filled me in on your…. Problem Credence--"Creed snaps his gaze to Shelley and growls.

"Shut your mouth." Shelley's eyes narrow to slits and her upper lip twitches.

"I am not your pack Alpha therefore I do not answer to you, it will serve you well to remember who you are speaking with." Creed scoffs, the others around the table snicker.

"Look around Shelley, there is no council here and none of us have any pack lands thanks to you and the council taking them from us."

"I didn't do a damn thing Creed, I tried to help you all, but you couldn't tell the damn truth. We are all here because of your lies, if you had of just been honest with Jess--"

"That's enough!" I cut in, I dart my eyes around the hall and notice we have caught the attention of the others and they really don't need to know that we are not united. Shelley follows my gaze.

"We will discuss this matter later, tonight." I nod and watch as the three of them walk away.

"She isn't wrong you know." I stare at Sky with my mouth agape, she just shrugs her shoulders.

"You don't think I know that? I never meant for any of this to happen, I had no idea the amount of control the council really had. We need to figure out what they have over everyone so we can take them out and finally free all the packs around the world from their control." I open my mouth to reply but snap it shut when I spy Davina and Vince entering the hall, she is flanked by other men I haven't seen before. I make the mistake of inhaling through my nose and cough to mask my gag, ever since being on the island we have all been trying to get used to this feral stench but its freaking hard. So, we have resorted to breathing through our mouths unless we are at home, smelling rotting flesh everyday isn't something I want to get used to. Davina moves toward the front of the room, she scans the hall but pauses on our table, her gaze jumps to each of her kids, and I find it odd when I see her shoulders relax. The worry lines that crease her face have me on edge, but she quickly smooths her features and straightens up as she nods to Vince. He places his thumb and index finger in his mouth and lets out an ear-piercing whistle that has my ears ringing, all the shifters in the room turn and glare at the smirking asshole.

"Now that I have your attention, Davina would like to say a few things." Vince steps back and I focus on Davina, Creed squeezes my hand a tiny bit harder, and I cringe, if he tightens his grip any more, I fear he will break my hand. I try to flex my fingers so he will get the hint, but he doesn't.

"I'm afraid what I have to say isn't good news, I had planned to fill you all in on how we do things here and integrate everyone slowly into our way of life but that isn't the case." Murmurs break out around the room but are quickly stopped when Vince whistles again, this time growls follow.

"Shut up and listen to what D has to say, you will all have a chance to ask questions soon." Something is off, Vince seems tense, even his off siders seem taught and on alert.

"Thank you, Vincent, as I was saying something has happened. Two of our boats haven't returned from the mainland, we have had zero contact from them for 48 hours--"

"Merv isn't back?" A lady asks, Davina shakes her head, and her eyes take on a hollow look.

"We are going to send out a search party for them, best case they are stuck at sea, worst case the shifter council is on to us."

"But they don't know about Vampires." Callie states, Davina swings her gaze to her daughter and the look she gives tells us everything. Of course, the council knows about vampires, how did we not see that one coming.

"They do know about us; your council is vile and will stop at nothing to get what they-- "

"And what is it that they want exactly?" Creed growls out.

"Our submission Credence, they have wanted that for years, but we will not yield to their demands. We have the numbers and they don't, why else do you think the council is taking control of all your packs?" Holy crap! This was never about any of us, this was about the council trying to amass an army so they could take control of the vampires but why?

"Why?"

"Because we have something they want Colton."

"Which is?" Davina narrows her eyes at her youngest son.

"Something which I am not at liberty to discuss right now. We need volunteers that are willing to go in search of our missing brothers, I know this a lot to ask but we need to find them and get the supplies back here." People begin to stand and chorus of *yes's* sound out around the room, I'm shocked to see even some of the shifters have agreed to join the search. "Thank you, could you all find Vince after the meeting and he will prep you for the search tomorrow. Now to address the other matter, as you are all aware, our guests are present, I have invited the Reeves pack and their alpha Credence as well as the Cruz pack and their alpha Cairo to join us. They like many of you once were and are now being hunted by the council, we have the space and the means here on our island to help them. Many of these shifters have lost family members as well as their homes and their land, with their help we may finally be able to take down the council--"

"Why now D? We have been asking this for years and all of a sudden they show up and now we go to war!" I turn and stare at the pale skin man who spoke, he is thin and willowy with russet hair, he seems angry.

"The time wasn't right Michael--"He cuts Davina off and

shouts.

"Bullshit! You're hiding something from us Davina--"

"Mind your tongue Michael, you speak to her like that again and I'll tear it out." So much for the whole no violence thing.

"Ah, of course you would know the real reason, Vince. Meanwhile the rest of us have had to wait and hold onto our revenge because Davina had other plans." Michael sounds really pissed, but I can't help but wonder why Davina didn't claim her revenge years ago. What made her hold off, if it was Creed that had died, I would have gone after them straightaway so why didn't she? Davina squares her shoulders and stares at the man, there isn't a hint of anger in her hazel eyes.

"Michael, I know it has been hard for you to wait all these years, I really do, but we needed to make sure--"

"You're a fucking Liar!" He roars, Cole slams his hands down on the table top causing us to jump in fright. He stands and lets loose a loud angry growl as he faces Michael, his eyes change to yellow and I shiver, his wolf is close to the surface.

"She said she had her reasons, now shut the fuck up and sit your ass down!" Michael pulls his upper lip back and I have to stifle my yelp when I see his fangs! The man really has freaking fangs, it hits me then-- vampires are real!

"You know nothing pup." Cole lets out a humorless chuckle that sounds more like a gruff laugh thanks to his wolf being so close to the surface.

"Test me and I'll show you how much of a *pup* I really am."

"Enough!" Davina shouts, but the guys keep hurling insults at each other, I turn to Creed to find his gaze already on me.

"Stop them please, we can't be fighting amongst ourselves."

Creed stares at me for a long moment and when the others join in screaming insults across the room, I fear Creed won't intervene to stop them, until he gives me a stiff nod, drops my hand and stands. He steps back and walks toward Davina, the four men stand, they are failing terribly to calm the vamps. Davina eyes Creed warily as he approaches her, but doesn't say anything when he stands beside her and turns to face us, he motions for Vince to do something and when I see Vince lift his fingers to his mouth, I quickly cover my ears as he lets out a loud screeching whistle. The noise begins to dwindle down and for that I am grateful.

"All my wolves will sit their asses in their seat and shut the hell up." Creed then turns toward Michael and narrows his eyes. "You will shut the fuck up and sit the hell down as well."

"Fuck you, you are not my alpha." Oh no, Creeds eyes begin to sparkle as he makes his way toward Michael, I attempt to stand but all of sudden Ro is claiming Creeds vacant seat and placing a hand on my shoulder.

"Let him do this, I have a feeling I know why him and Cole are so out of sorts and if he does what I think he is about to, then we will have our answer." I stare at my brother in shock for a moment but snap out of it when I hear Creed speak and swing my gaze to him, he stands a foot away from Michael.

"Last chance."

"Kiss my ass *pup*." Creed strikes so fast I don't even see it coming, one minute Michael is standing there smirking then the next minute Creed has punched him and is now sprawled out on the floor. Creed spins around in a slow circle with his arms out wide and yells. "Anyone else got something to say?" When no one answers they all begin to take their seats, I can see how tense he is as he fights to suppress Corbin, we need to figure out what the hell is going on with his wolf, in case we have to shift, let's hope he considers what's at stake, because if he doesn't, we're all as good as fried eggplants.

"Thank you, Credence." Creed glares down at Davina.

"I didn't do it for you." His gaze meets mine and I'm stunned, I see so much love and longing in his gaze that it steals my breath.

"Okay, now that we have that settled. The next thing I want to discuss is all of us training together before, everyone goes off and starts shouting again, let me explain first. If we train and work together it will help us get to know one another's tactics, this way when it comes time to take down the council, we will all be well-oiled machines, I know there'll be mishaps along the way which is why I am asking members from the Reeves and Cruz pack as well as my first line to teach the others how to coexist and fight as one." Hate to say it but Davina has a bloody good point.

"I'll have six of my men ready, my family and I will help train them as well." I look at Cairo stunned that he willingly offers to help, he is up to something, and I want to know what.

"I will do the same, we can meet back here tomorrow at ten to discuss a training schedule. Any of my pack joining the search party will be brought up to speed as soon as they return." Davina nods and thanks both Creed and Cairo before turning to address the room.

"I know this is going to take a lot of getting used to, but if we all work hard it will happen. We cannot go after the council and all the packs around the world halfcocked, we need to be ready and smart about this or we will all end up joining our loved ones earlier than we had planned." I zone out after that my mind can't get passed what Michael had said, why has Davina waited all this time. It's not like we have thousands of pack members here with us, we would be lucky if we had 300. Davina is hiding something from us, and I want to know what it is, she is preaching for us to amalgamate, but if we can't trust her then what is the point?

CHAPTER NINETEEN
Jessica

I lay next to Creed unable to sleep, when we got home everyone was wiped out from the meeting, so we decided to regroup in the morning. I roll over and stare at him, he looks so peaceful and relaxed when he sleeps. Feeling rather parched I decide to get up and get a drink of water, stepping as quietly as I can so not to wake Creed or Harlem. I sigh in relief when I exit the room without waking them. I tip toe down the stairs and head to the kitchen, I grit my teeth to stop the squeal that wants to break free when I spot Ro and Z sitting on the stools in the dark, both their gazes turn to me.

"Couldn't sleep either?" I shake my head and grab a glass then fill it from the tap, I drain the entire cup before answering my brother.

"Too much crap on my mind." He nods stoically but doesn't say anything.

"I trust Shelley, but I feel like we are missing something, I spoke to Dela on the way back here and he thinks the same."

"What do you mean?" Z turns to Ro as he answers.

"Davina is hiding something from us and it's something big. She refused to tell Cole why the council is after them and she won't let Shelley or Dela know what it is."

"I agree, but why hasn't she attacked the council either? She has the numbers from what Creed has told me and it's not like we exactly have a large amount of shifters to contribute." I say.

"I thought the same thing. It doesn't add up, we need to find out what the council is up to, if Jess is to take over being alpha of the Michelson and Reeves packs." I drop my head and release a long sigh.

"I know you're right Ro, but I think there is more to this than meets the eye."

"What do you mean Jess?"

"What I mean Z is that this is bigger than me becoming alpha. I will gladly accept the role if it meant the council and Jacob would back off and let us go home, but I don't see that happening. I also don't believe this whole big war thing is over me being alpha, I think it has something to do with Davina and we are all just pawns in this big game of chess." Zeke and Cairo remain silent for a while mulling over my words. I truly believe what I just said is the truth, if it's all about me becoming alpha, then the task should be an easy fix. But they won't, because they are after something. "We need to find out what it is that our dad told our mom, Davina said she was the only one dad confided in. If that is true and she did flee, her reasons for leaving us might just be acceptable."

"Jess I... Shit, you might just be right. I think we need to speak to Davina." I cringe.

"Creed wants me to stay away from her, he thinks she will corrupt me, or brain wash me." Both Z and Ro chuckle as they shake their heads.

"He's asleep, right?"

"Uh yeah, why?" The twinkle in my brothers' eyes has me groaning internally.

"Well, there is no time like the present. Let's go pay Davina a visit." I gasp.

"You're joking right?" Ro smiles and shakes his head. I motion with my hand gripping my singlet and sleep shorts. Z snorts and then stands; he exits the room and I stare at Ro who just shrugs his shoulders and heads toward the door. Z comes back to the kitchen a minute later and chucks a large hoodie at me.

"Put it on, it will cover your sleep wear." I nod and thank him as I slip his hoodie on and follow the boys out the door, I just hope Creed doesn't find out about this visit.

We all remain quiet on the walk to Davina's house; you can hear voices and laughter in the distance at the same time still and quiet. This island is a hidden paradise and so beautiful, I think I might take Harlem exploring tomorrow while Creed and the others gather for the training program. As the gates to Davina's house come into view, my heart begins to gallop at a thousand miles an hour, a part of me feels like I am betraying Creed by doing this. Before Z can even push the button for the intercom the gates open, we all share a look but remain silent and continue trekking up the drive. We make our way around the back; we see a light flicker on and the sound of the ranch slider opening lets us know someone is awaiting our presence. When we enter the back gate, I'm shocked to see both Davina and Shelley standing there. I look to Shelley, and she gives a subtle shake of her head, what the hell is going?

"What brings the three of you here at this time of night?" None of us answer, Zeke pulls out a chair and drops down into it, he motions for Ro and I to do the same. Davina releases an irritated sigh and takes a chair opposite us, Shelley claims the seat in front of me. Her attire is the same as earlier, but Davina is in a silk black robe and her long brown hair hangs loose down her back. I'm woman enough to admit that Davina is stunning, to no surprise though, her genetics were passed down to her children.

"We have questions."

"Then ask what you want to know alpha Cairo."

"I'm not an alpha." Davina cocks her head to side and eyes Ro.

"But you have a pack that follows and answers to you, do you not?"

"I am not their alpha; I'm not one to rule over people. Everyone is entitled to do and live as they please. They have a choice, and if that choice is to stand against the council, then I will stand with them. I'm not like your son." Davina purses her lips and then steeples her hands resting her chin on top of them.

"I see. You are a better man than most of the shifter men I know Cairo, now what is it that you came here to ask." I quickly intervene.

"Why is it that Creed and Cole are at odds with their wolves." Davina smiles broadly and that look sends shivers down my spine.

"Wolves are born to lead; therefore, they will always want to outrank their parents. Since coming to this island both my sons are unaware that their wolves can sense the shift in power here. Their wolves are trying to stake a claim at dominance over each other."

"But why? Creed is the alpha not Cole." Davina shakes her head.

"You don't get it, Creed is alpha of the pack, yes. But here on this island I rule, so to break it down for you, my son's wolves are trying to fight each other because they want the power I hold. If Creed had succeeded the other night and killed Cole, his wolf would have demanded him to challenge me for my role. It's all a power game for males, and that is why they will never succeed without a woman." I slouch back in my chair shocked silent.

"That isn't everything though, is it?" I furrow my brow at Ro's question.

"Very perceptive you are Cairo, no it isn't. Creed is used to leading and his wolf not having the power of ruling over everyone is making him angry. I will not relinquish my leadership of my people, I want everyone to train together so their wolves can get used to the shift in power. Creed and Colton will have to work out their struggles themselves."

"Okay, now what are you not telling us?" Shelley releases a long exhale and stiffens at Zeke's question.

"I don't know what you mean Zeke." Z scoffs and rolls his eyes.

"Let me spell it out for you then, why are the council coming after us?"

"Because they want Jess, I assume of course."

"Cut the shit Davina, what the hell did my dad tell our mom, and why the hell are the council really coming after us? It's not because of my sister, if it was, they would have backed off the moment she accepted the role as alpha to both packs." Davina cuts her gaze to Shelley and cocks a brow.

"Did you want me to tell them...or?" Shelley growls low in her throat.

"Shut up Davina." A cruel smirk graces her face as she tuts Shelley.

"Tell them or I will, I will not risk my people because of you!"

"Fuck you, this is all your fault! They would have been safe if it wasn't for your fucking son pulling Jess back into all of this shit!" Huh, what the hell are they talking about?

"He did what he thought was best in order to deter the council and Jacob from destroying his pack."

"His bullshit led her here and brought Cairo back, he was fucking free Davina. I did everything to conceal them after Austin died and your son ruined everything, all my hard work..." Shelley snaps her mouth closed and turns shocked eyes to me and Ro, my mouth hangs open. I can see out of the corner of my eye how stiff Ro is, low growls begin to tumble out of me but stop when a dark chuckle escapes him.

"It's you, isn't it?" Shelley shakes her head; tears begin to cloud her brown eyes.

"I can explain--"

"You gutless swine." His dark words leave me shaking.

"I did it to protect you." My breaths are coming fast, for the first time in a long time Sheba stirs inside me and she's begging for me to let her out.

"Oh, do tell us how you protected us. We are dying to know how ditching a baby with their aunt and letting a small child fend for themselves is protecting us, *mother*." I spit the word mother at her like it burns my tongue. This whole freaking time Shelley was right under our noses, sitting here and staring at her I feel nothing but anger and disgust. "You know, you and Davina are a piece of work, you both fucked the same man and abandoned your kids for your own gain. Mothers of the year the pair of you."

"I did all of this to protect you! I made sure Cairo was safe and that you and Katharine got away. I kept the council from finding both of you." Ro slams his fist down on the table causing Shelley to jump and clamp her mouth shut.

"You did that for you, not us. You left us behind and let us believe that you were dead!"

"I did that to protect you both, Cairo there is so much you don't know--."

"Then explain it to us, because right now I have the right mind to get my son and mate and get the hell off this island. What the hell is it with wolves and lying, just tell the freaking truth for once goddammit!" Shelley releases a whoosh of air as she stares at me and nods.

"Please just hear me out first Jess. The night your father was killed he came to me and told me to have both you and your brother ready to run. He said he needed to meet with Jacob first and if he wasn't back within the hour I was to take the both of you and run. I did as he asked but before the hour was up Dela and Phillip showed up with tag a longs, I sent Cairo to his room and put you in your crib, I thought if I was to die that night then I didn't want my children to see it. Dela slipped me a note and told me if I went with the others, he would make sure that you and Ro got to your aunt and uncles safely. I did as he said and left, the council tried to get information from me for months, but I wouldn't say a word. I thought I had lost everything, Dela got word to me that Cairo wasn't in his room and that Kat had fled with you. I was also informed that there was a car wreck on the news and it was Kat's car, years later I learned that she had staged the whole thing so the council would believe she had died. I had no idea that Cairo had gone in search for your father that night to get help."

"Why join the council then?" Cairo asked the question that had been burning a hole in my mind.

"They didn't give me a choice; it was either I join them, or stay their prisoner, so I thought to take them down it was better for me to be on the inside. I learned a lot by staying quiet and just watching as they worked. I was never allowed to attend their meetings nor did they keep me in the loop on the plans they discussed, but Dela was my saving grace. He was there for me when he didn't have to be, he was the one who helped me track your where abouts. We watched over you both for years, as time went on, I began to gain the councils trust so I was given permission to attend pack meetings and go to packs to visit. Well, I was there Dela, and I would meet with members of the pack that hated the council and get information and try to build our own army."

"What changed?" Her eyes begin to turn sad as she stares at me. "Credence Reeves changed everything. I did everything I could to get him to give up on the myth of the alpha destined to lead both packs. He is persistent I give him that, I knew he and Cairo were searching for you and I couldn't let them find you. I would get word to Katharine, and she would pack you up and move, but luck ran out when Creed found you and gave Kat no choice but to bring you back to Rosewood."

"You did nothing to save her!" I snap, my chest begins to ache at the memory of my mom on her knees and her head clutched between Jacobs hands. Shelley drops her gaze and that just pisses me off. "Look at me!" She snaps her gaze back to mine. "You did nothing as he killed her, you could have saved her."

"No Jess I couldn't, if I had of saved her it would have put your life on the line, and I guarantee you Kat wouldn't of wanted that. I know Kat loved you." A sob tears from my throat and tears trail down my cheeks. "I am truly sorry for your loss Jess." I can hear the truth in her words, and it just angers me further.

"Why do you all lie? All these lies have done is cost innocent people their lives, just tell the truth!"

"Ask me what you want to know then Jessica, I will not lie to you." I ignore Cairo's scoff as I face Shelley, now that I know she is our mom I see so much of Ro and I in her features. I've never seen my dad, but my mom always told me I looked like him.

"Do you know why our father was killed?" She takes a deep breath and nods. "Are you going to tell us?" Her gaze cuts to Davina before focusing back on me. The look she gives me tells me she isn't willing to disclose this information in front of the vampire queen, Davina scoffs and rolls her eyes.

"So, you still refuse to tell me?"

"I'll tell you what Austin said if you tell me why the council is after you?" They glare at each other; I admit I am glad to know that we aren't the only ones who don't have all the information. Clearly these two don't trust each other enough either, interesting.

"You both are ridiculous, this will never work if the pair of you can't disclose all the information. We are all risking our lives here and going in blind because you two refuse to tell us the truth!" Both of them turn to Cairo, he pins them both with a harsh look. I sigh, I have an idea and if this doesn't work, I don't know what else we can do.

"Davina?" I wait for her to meet my gaze before continuing. "If I can get Creed, Callie and Cole to meet with you, will you tell them the truth?" She doesn't hesitate as she answers.

"Yes, but on one condition?"

"What?"

"Meg and Kane attend as well, and Creed brings Harlem." I stiffen but don't get a chance to answer because Cairo cuts in.

"You can meet with everyone but the monster, my nephew won't be used as a bargaining ship!" Davina shakes her head and looks at each of us like we are thick and missing the whole point.

"You still don't get it."

"Get what?" I grit out.

"None of this is about any of you anymore! You are no longer the rightful alpha to lead both the packs." I reel back shocked.

"W-what?"

"The day you gave birth to a male heir Jess is the day your right was given up. Harlem is born from two generations of leaders; he is the true alpha and the rightful heir to the packs."

Terror drags through my chest like barbed wire.

"The day I let you near my son is the day I die." I stand so fast my chair topples over, standing at the gate in nothing but a pair of gray sweats is my pissed off mate. His gaze is glued to me, and I can see so much anger and hurt in his eyes, I open my mouth, but he narrows his eyes and I clamp it shut. He moves toward us and that's when I notice everyone else is standing as well. He doesn't come to me, he stands at the head of the table and runs his gaze over the three of us, when he sees the hoodie I'm wearing, a growl sounds out and I flinch, he turns to Davina and Shelley and looks at them like they are nothing but shit beneath his boot. "You both disgust me. My siblings and I will meet with you, if mom refuses to join then you better fucking respect that. My son isn't coming near you, either of you. We'll meet with Davina, Shelley you will meet with your children and tell them the truth." Shelley opens her mouth but Creed growls and she slams it closed. "Once we have the information, we decide whether or not to share it with each of you. You have both had ample enough time to come clean and make this shit right, but you didn't, so now it is our turn to hold all the cards."

"And when will this meeting take place?" Davina asks, Creed is grinding his teeth so hard I worry he will break them.

"Tomorrow after the training meet." Creed turns to me, and I can tell from the look in his eyes it's time to go. Ro and Zeke lead the way out, Creed doesn't touch me as we walk side by side, we all pause when Creed turns back to the women and speaks. "Oh Davina?"

"Yes?" Her brow is furrowed in confusion.

"My brother and I will always fight; I am alpha and would never want to double rule."

"I don't understand." Creed chuckles but the sound sends shivers down my spine.

"It's not me you have to worry about coming for your throne, word of advice. Watch your back because you will never see Colton coming." Her mouth drops open in shock, Creed turns and brushes past Z and Ro. We all quickly follow him out the gate, the walk home seems like it takes hours. None of us have said a single word but I can feel Cairo and Zeke looking at me and then looking at Creed. I got to be honest I'm shitting myself; Creed is so angry at me, and I don't know how to fix it. When our home comes into view he stops at the edge of the lawn and turns to us. "Jess and I will join you shortly." I gulp, oh boy.

"Not gonna happen bro." Creed turns his angry gaze to Ro; his eyes are blue now. Corbin is right there below the surface and if I don't defuse this quickly, we are going to have a fight on our hands. I grip my brother's forearm and tug until he looks at me, I can see the concern in his eyes but I shake my head.

"I'll be fine, can you check Harlem for me?" I can see he wants to argue but he knows this is between me and Creed, so I urge him. "Please."

"You got, ten minutes and then I'm coming back." I nod and smile my thanks; Ro turns back to Creed. "This was my idea." Creed doesn't even look at him, his gaze is on me as he answers.

"Don't care." Both Zeke and Ro head inside, each of them drags their feet hoping I'll change my mind. When the door finally closes behind them, I lift my gaze to meet Creed's and cringe.

"I'm sorry." I whisper, he closes the space between us and reaches out to tuck a strand of hair behind my ear, I shiver at his touch and immediately start to feel my body warm.

"For what?" I lose my train of thought when he bends down and runs his nose against the side of my neck, I tense when I feel his lips against the shell of my ear. "Are you sorry for going to Davina's or are you just sorry you got caught?" I reel back and push against his chest, he wraps his arms around my waist and holds me in place. I growl up at him, he growls back, neither of us are willing to back down and I feel Sheba pushing against my ribs, the longer Creed holds eye contact. I feel my vision shift and know my eyes have changed to my wolves, Creed smiles wickedly down at me.

"Let me go!" The smile vanishes from his face.

"Why so you can run to mummy dearest or run inside and steal more of Zeke's shit?" Ouch, that was a freaking low blow.

"It's not what you think--"

"Then tell me how it is princess, I wake up and you're not in *our* bed or even in the house. Then it hit me, my deceitful mate went behind my back when I asked her not to. I find you at Davina's of all places and in another man's clothes to top it off!" I scoff.

"I learnt how to bullshit from the best baby, so I guess I should thank you?" He narrows his eyes, and his upper lip pulls back in a snarl. Is it wrong that I'm getting turned on by how angry he is?

"I had to track your scent; do you know how hard that was

when all I can smell is rotting fucking flesh?" I cringe but refuse to back down.

"Aww baby, that must have been awful for you." He moves one of his arms from around my waist and uses it to grip the back of my hair, he pulls until my neck is craned back at an awkward angle. I won't give him the satisfaction of hissing my annoyance.

"Don't patronize me princess, I'm about--"

"About to what? What are you gonna do Creed, ground me, forbid me to see her, or are you gonna spank me?" A devilish glint enters his eyes as I say the word *spank*, oh shit. I gulp and struggle in his hold, but he won't budge. He releases my hair and I sigh in relief but its short lived, before I can comprehend what is happening, he lifts me and throws me over his shoulder I squeal as the front door slams open. I turn my head and see a seething Cairo standing there with Zeke and Cole right behind him.

"Unless you want to see me fuck your sister, I suggest you fuck off back inside." I gasp and immediately feel the blush that begins coat my cheeks, I drop my head and growl when I smack my nose into Creeds hard back.

"The fuck you are asshole! Put her down now."

"Fuck off Cairo and go watch my son." I gruff at the audacity of him, before I can say anything Creed is moving at a brisk pace away from the house, I lift my gaze and watch as my brother struggles to free himself from Cole and Zeke's hold.

Chapter Twenty

Jessica

Creed doesn't stop walking until we hit the sandy shore by the beach, my head is going fuzzy from being carried upside down for so long, but I refuse to speak. He is behaving like an asshole, but my body and mind are not on the same damn page. My body is thrumming with need, and I know I'm wet for him, but my mind is still pissed at his macho man display! Creed rounds a bend and then finally comes to a halt; I expect him to put me back on my feet but that isn't the case. I yelp when I feel his hand connect with my ass, the hoodie has ridden up my back and there is nothing but my thin sleep shorts covering my ass.

"Credence!"

Smack! I yelp again and begin to squirm in his hold.

"Jessica." I growl in warning and all that does is earn me another smack to my tender ass, I bite down on my lip when a moan escapes me. I jiggle in his hold when he begins to laugh. "Scream and yelp all you like princess, no one can hear you out here."

"You've had your fun now put me down." I grit out.

"Or what?"

"You're such a freaking--"

"Eggplant?" I groan and drop my head against his back, they will never let me live that down!

"I was going to say asshole." I mumble into his back, his hand lands against my ass again but this time I'm not quick enough to stifle my moan. I have no idea why I am getting turned on from him spanking me.

"I can smell how turned on you are princess." I still in his hold, how the hell can he scent anything? I take a risk and inhale through my nose; I can still smell rotting flesh, but it isn't as potent out here.

"Can you put me down now?"

"What's the magic word?" I grind my teeth together.

"Please!" He maneuvers me until I slide down his front and I don't miss the fact that he makes sure I can feel his erection the whole way down. Once on my feet I try to take a step back, but he quickly snaps his arm out and grips my waist hauling me back against him, he glares down at me and then grips the hoodie I'm wearing and literally tears it off me! I gasp as he grips the ruined garment and hurls it over his head. He grips my chin between his hand and lifts my gaze to his.

"Don't ever let me catch you wearing another man's clothes again. I will not have another males' scent on my mate. You are mine princess." I gape at him but remain silent, he spins me around, so my back is to his chest and wraps an arm around my waist and uses his free hand to travel up my chest, he tweaks my nipple through my shirt, and I gasp. "Hmmm, no bra I wonder...." He wraps a hand around my neck tight enough to hold me in place but doesn't restrict my airway, he moves his arm from my waist and surprises the hell out of me when he slips it beneath my sleep shorts and moans. "No fucking panties either." I stand there and do nothing because truthfully, I am loving every freaking minute of this. He trails a finger through my folds, and I drop my head back against his chest and moan, he parts my folds and then uses another finger to push inside me. "Fuck, you're so fucking wet princess." My only response is to moan as he pumps his finger inside me, moans tumble out of my mouth. He releases a growl and then withdraws his hand, I'm about to protest until he spins me and captures my lips in a heated kiss, before I can deepen it, he pulls back and pushes me till I'm lying on my back in the damp sand. He wrestles his way between my legs and stares down at me.

"Why did you stop?" He cocks a brow at me with an arrogant smirk on his face.

"Because you are going to learn that you don't get to go behind my back." I open my mouth, but he quickly shushes me by placing a finger against my lips. "I'm going to eat your pussy while you tell me everything that was said tonight, if you stop talking then I'm gonna stop eating." He can't be serious?

"You're joking right?"

"Oh, princess I would never joke about feasting on your beautiful pink pussy." I feel the blush coating my cheeks at his crude words, but I can also feel more wetness gathering between my thighs at his crass words. He grips the sides of my sleep shorts and yanks them off, my eyes widen in shock, he really is serious. He pushes my legs further apart and just stares down at my dripping pussy like it's his last meal, instead of feeling self-conscious I feel...Confident and desired. He shuffles back and rests on his elbows then stares up at me. "Now, what did you and Davina discuss?" My brain short circuits when he drops his face between my legs and parts my folds with two fingers blowing on my swollen clit at the same time. Holy fuck! how on earth does he expect me to remember what Davina said when he's down there having a feast.

"Uh, we..." I moan when he darts his tongue out and swipes it over my clit. "Talked.... oh god." He hums his approval as he continues to eat me out. "About what my dad had told Shelley....

Shit!" My mind blanks as pleasure rolls through my body, I moan his name and begin to thrust my hips up toward him needing more but he pulls back and clicks his tongue at me.

"You stop talking, I stop eating remember?" I sit forward and rest on my elbows and glare down at him, well I try to, but he just laughs at me. "Don't pout princess it's not becoming of you." My mouth drops open in shock. "Talk or you can sit here and watch me get off?" I huff, my body is so tense, and I need to release the tension or I might just go nuts.

"Fine! We talked about you..." Creed begins to swirl his tongue around my clit again but this time he inserts a finger inside me and pumps. It takes so much willpower to focus on talking rather than enjoying the beautiful torture he is inflicting on my body. "And Cole and why your wolves--shit, right there." I peer down at him and watch as he laps at me, tears begin to build, and I try to swallow them back. He pauses and looks up at me, the arrogant look in his eyes vanishes when he sees the tears dwelling in my eyes. He quickly reaches forward to cup my face between his large hands.

"What's wrong?" The concern in his voice is my undoing, tears trail down my cheeks and he pulls me against his chest, I wrap my arms around him and sob. "I'm sorry princess, I didn't mean to push you..."

"It's not you." I hiccup.

"Then what's wrong?"

"My mom is alive." He tightens his hold on me, but I don't want to be held right now. I pull back from his hold and he looks down at me with so much sadness. I reach down and grip the ends of my shirt and pull it off, his eyes go straight to my tits before he snaps out of it and meets my gaze again. "I want you to make me forget, I don't want to think right now. I promise I will tell you everything later but right now I just need--"

"Shhh, I got you princess." He leans down and captures my lips in a kiss that steals my breath, he uses his body weight to push me back into the sand. He holds himself up on one of his elbows and then tweaks my nipple with his other hand, I moan into his mouth and wrap my arms around his neck. He trails his fingers down my stomach and shifts his leg slightly so he can run his finger through my slit, he doesn't mess around as he pushes inside me, and I cry out breaking our kiss. He trails kisses across my jaw and then down to my neck, he licks a path toward my mate mark, and I stiffen. He doesn't stop finger fucking me as pulls back and speaks. "I'm so sorry I took the choice from you princess. I was an asshole and if you'll let me, I will spend my life making it up to you." It's so hard to focus on his words when I can feel my orgasm cresting. "When we fuck, I lose control over Corbin, he always wants to mark you because it sends us both into euphoric bliss and lets him assert his claim to you again."

"Make me come and then mark me while you fuck me." His eyes widen in shock, but I don't give him time to recover, I yank him down and cover his mouth with mine. He growls his approval; I can feel my orgasm building but I need more! Creed breaks the kiss and sits back yanking his sweats down and pulling his hard cock out.

"Wow." He chuckles but it sounds forced, the lust in his eyes boosts my confidence. He pumps his cock and I lick my lips in anticipation, not wanting to lay here like an idiot I try to think of a way to be sexy and then it hits me. He watches as I caress my nipples trailing my hand slowly down my body, his eyes blaze when a moan escapes me. I release one of my nipples and trail my hand down my body slowly, he watches me with laser focus and when my hand cups my sex I see him grip his cock tighter. Feeling embolden by the way he's turned on encourages me even more, I bend my knees and spread my legs giving him full view of my pussy. He darts his tongue out to moisten his lips, I run my index finger over my clit and gasp. It's so swollen and sensitive, Creed begins to pump faster as I circle my clit and moan, I keep tweaking my nipple and the sensations that are coursing through me is satisfying my every need.

"Fuck princess, make yourself come I want to see you come by your own hand." My eyelids feel heavy as I lift my gaze to his. His eyes are blue, and I can tell from the way he is gnawing on his bottom lip he is fighting for control over Corbin. I keep circling my clit and pinch my nipple as I begin to feel the pressure inside me build.

"Oh god, Creed I'm so close."

"Fuck!" He stops pumping his cock and slaps my hand away from my pussy, I glare at him, ignoring me he swiftly grips my hips and flips me onto my stomach. He positions me so I am on my hands and knees with my ass toward him. "I have to taste you, next time you make yourself come, but right now I need this." I don't get a chance to respond, he spreads my cheeks and I immediately clench and try to move forward but he holds me in place and yanks me back and fuck, I scream out when I feel his tongue inside my pussy. All thoughts of having my ass in his face are out the window when he begins to lick up and down my slit, I feel the orgasm and have no time to prepare for it. My climax is torn from me, and I scream out his name as I come all over his face, he doesn't ease me down from my high as he pulls back, I feel the head of his cock nudging my entrance. In one swift move he is inside me and we both cry out at the pleasure of being joined, Creed stretches my walls and I feel so full but God it feels so amazing. He begins to thrust inside me, I drop onto my elbows, so my ass is positioned higher.

Creed moans, and I yelp as he slaps my cheek, clearly something is wrong with me because I actually like the feeling of being spanked. He lands another two blows to the same cheek and then massages the sting out of it, I can feel my pussy getting wetter each time he smacks my ass. He smacks the other side three times and each time he does it I feel myself clenching around his cock. I can feel the orgasm right there on the horizon, but I can't quite seem to reach it. As if he can sense my needs, he picks up the pace and then I stiffen when I feel him spread my cheeks, I feel something wet slide down my asshole. I turn my head and look back at him to see that the wetness against my hole is his spit. I watch as he circles my hole with his thumb and try not to clench.

"Trust me princess, just relax and I swear you will come harder than you ever have." I nod and close my eyes trying to focus on the pleasure building inside me, he slows his thrusting and then begins to prod my hole with his finger, I take a lot of deep breaths and try to stay relaxed. When he pushes his thumb inside my ass I stiffen and begin to feel hot all over, he withdraws his digit and then pushes it back in, he does this a few times so I can get used to the feeling. "I'm gonna fuck your ass one day soon princess." His words draw a moan from me, and I'll be honest, the feeling of his cock in my pussy and his thumb in my ass is heightening everything. He fucks me and fingers me at the same pace and holy shit!

"Creed, oh god don't stop fucking me, please!"

"I need you to come princess." I shake my head; trying endlessly to savor this moment I feel his dick swelling inside me and know he is so close; he reaches around with his free hand and pinches my clit. Holy mother of God, It's like a bomb, one minute my orgasm seems miles away and then with one pinch to my clit, his cock in my pussy and thumb in my ass I come harder than I ever have screaming his name to the heavens above. Creed grunts behind me as he finds his release a second later, he releases my clit and pulls his thumb from my ass but keeps his cock inside me as he lazily slows his pace. Aftershocks wrack my body and no matter how hard I try I can't stop my pussy from constantly clenching and trying to milk his dick of more cum.

Creed finally pulls out of me and drops down on the sand beside me, he reaches out and pulls me to him. I snuggle into his side and rest my cheek against his peck. The only sounds I can hear is his heartbeat and the waves crashing against the shore. That was the most intense earth-shattering orgasm I have ever had, I'm a bit embarrassed that I enjoyed being spanked so much and I even loved that he was fucking my ass. I never in a million years thought I would ever be excited over the prospect of someone fucking my ass, if it felt that good with just a thumb imagine what his dick would feel like? "Princess." He groans.

"What?"

"How the fuck can you be getting turned on right now when you just milked my cock for all it was worth not two minutes ago." I bite my lip to stop myself from laughing, I'm too ashamed to admit to him what I was thinking about.

"Uh..."

"I can smell your need and so can Corbin." I stiffen.

"How?"

"It's a gift."

"How so?" He rolls over and pins me beneath him, he uses his knees to nudge my legs apart and settles between my thighs.

"Because I know whenever my mate needs me to relieve her tension and trust me princess, I will always be down to relieve you of any tension." I giggle as he playfully glares down at me.

"That was the worst pick up line I have ever heard."

"Stop stalling, what were you just thinking about?" I clamp my mouth shut and just stare up at him, he leans forward and places his hands in the sand either side of my face. "Did you enjoy what just happened?"

"Y-yes."

"Do you know why?" I shake my head. "Because you trust me to take care of your body and give you what you need. In order for us to continue having mind-blowing sex we need to be open and honest, so please tell me." I take a deep breath and blurt it out all in one go.

"*Iwantyoutospankmenexttime.*" His brows furrow.

"Say that again but *slower* please." I take another deep breath and fight off the blush that wants to break out.

"I want you to spank me again next time." His eyes darken and the concern in his eyes is quickly replaced with need. The sound of footsteps approaching has us both scrambling apart and quickly trying to find our clothes, we manage to get dressed in record time. I try to pat my hair down but it's no use there is sand all through it and I can feel sand in places that you should never feel sand. Creed grips my hand and begins to lead me back toward the way we came, I spot Zeke's hoodie and attempt to lean down and grab it, but Creed yanks me away. I try to hide my smirk, but he sees it and growls.

"It was a fucking ugly jumper anyway, serves the prick right." More laughter tumbles out of me, I ignore him mumbling about me being annoying beneath his breath. Creed screeches to a halt and yanks me behind him as he lets loose a loud growl.

CHAPTER
TWENTY ONE
Jessica

I peer around Creed and see Vince moving toward us with his hands raised as if surrendering. Creeds growls grow louder the closer Vince gets toward us, I place my hand on Creed's back, he stiffens but relaxes after a second.

"I didn't come here to cause trouble."

"Then why the fuck are you here Vincent?" Vince darts his gaze around as if making sure no one else is around to hear this conversation, odd.

"Because I know what D is hiding." Well, that is not what I expected him to say.

"And what? You're just going to tell us what that is?" The sarcasm is thick in Creed's voice, I move out from behind and stand next to him. Vince smiles kindly at me, and me being the awkward person that I am just waves like an idiot.

"Yes, but I need your help." Creed scoffs, but the look on Vincent's face gives me pause so I ask.

"With what exactly?" Vince reaches up and rubs the back of his neck, he's clearly uncomfortable.

"Are we able to maybe speak about this inside?"

"Why?"

"Because if I get caught Credence I am as good as dead." Creed stares at Vince, I have no idea what he is looking for, but a minute later he grips my hand nodding to Vince to follow us, the tension between Creed and Vince is suffocating. When the house comes into view I sag in relief, as we enter I hear the sound of voices coming from the kitchen, five sets of eyes swing my way and I freeze under their scrutiny. Cairo's gaze narrows to slits when I feel Creed behind me, Ro points an accusing finger at

Creed and snaps.

"You are a fucking piece of shit, don't ever do that to my sister again." Not wanting them to fight while Vince is here, I cut in and lie through my teeth.

"Ro, nothing happened we just…talked?" I mentally facepalm myself at how dumb that sounded. Ro scoffs and rolls his eyes.

"Your shirt is inside out and back to front and I'm pretty sure you were wearing Z's jumper when you left." Much to my dismay, he's right. Creed makes matters worse when he wraps his arms around my waist and pulls me flush against him.

"You do realize you were just babysitting our son?" If looks could kill Cairo would have burnt Creed alive. Everyone's attention is snagged when Vince makes his presence known. I couldn't be gladder to have a vampire in my house. Cole jumps to his feet, so does Zeke, Sky and Callie, Cairo moves toward the others and pins an accusing look at Creed.

"The fuck is he doing here?"

"He has something to tell us apparently Cole, so let's hear what he has to say and then he can fuck off." Cairo motions for us to have a seat on the stools at the counter, I sit while Creed stands behind me, Callie claims the stool beside me, and Sky takes the same position as Creed. Z, Ro and Cole choose to stand rather than sit, Vince sighs as he proceeds to tell us what he knows. This has to be daunting even for a vampire having seven werewolves staring you down.

"First, I need your assurance that what I am about to tell you doesn't leave this room." We all agree to his terms. "Davina told you how she was turned, correct?"

"Yes, now what the hell does this have to do with anything?"

"Everything Cairo. Unless you are born of the first of our kind your blood cannot change someone."

"Wait, so what you're saying is that you have to be turned by an original family or something?"

"Yes Callie."

"How very Vampire Diaries." I shake my head and chuckle at Callie.

"I'm not kidding!"

"What the hell does this have to do with anything Vince?"

"Davina has the last child from the first ones stashed and the council wants that child." Oh, now that makes a lot of sense.

"Why the hell would she have some kid? Where is the rest of the kid's family?" Cairo took the question right out of my mouth.

"I don't know the whole story, but the first family was hunted by the council and somehow Davina got the child. She isn't what you are all thinking, she is good and pure."

"She?" Both Cole and Zeke ask in unison.

"Yes, her name is Belle."

"And where might this Belle be?" Vince narrows his eyes at Ro.

"Nice try." Creed growls.

"Get to the freaking point Vince, I'm tired and have a big day tomorrow."

"Davina will not give Belle up; I don't know what she has planned but I will not stand by and watch as innocent people are hurt."

"Why are you really telling us this Vince?" I ask and he drops his gaze, something more is going on here and Vince seems to be the only one willing to give us the answers we need.

"Because if push comes to shove Davina will give you all up before she gives up Belle."

"Okay, so if you don't want us to harm this girl then why tell us about her?" He lifts his gaze back to mine slowly.

"Because Belle is special and if Davina finds out that you know about her, she will be less inclined to give you all up if it comes to it."

"Nah man, you don't strike me as the type to switch allegiance. You're telling us this to keep someone else alive, who is it?" Vince swings toward Zeke in shock, oh my god Z's right!

"My sister."

"Huh?"

"Who is she?"

"Is she a wolf?"

"Where is she?" Everyone is barking questions at him and not giving him a chance to answer.

"Yes, she is a wolf, I will not tell you who she is. I just need to make sure she is safe, and no harm comes to her." Everything makes sense, Vince is only helping us because his sister belongs to one of the two packs. If Davina gives us up to the council, then that means his sister will be caught in the crossfire. Would Davina really give up her own flesh and blood?

"Okay, so what exactly do we do with this information?"

"You use it Cairo, Belle is the last of the first family and the only one that can turn vampires. Your council is after Davina because they believe Belle is with us."

"Why the hell does the council want someone who can turn people into vampires?" Sky just asked the million-dollar question.

"Dear god are you all dense." Vince is met with growls, from all the guys but ignores them. "Your council is power hungry; they want Jess because she has the blood of two alphas, and they want Belle because she can create them an army. With these two powerful women they are able to take control and be the superior race." Sky snorts but doesn't say anything further.

"So, Davina is protecting this Belle because she doesn't want the council to create more vampires?"

"Yes Colton. When Shelley reached out and let her know that she had Jess and Cairo with her D was relieved."

"Why?" I can hear the accusation in my own voice.

"Because then you were out of reach of the council. Cairo and Harlem were factors we didn't anticipate, with Harlem he is now the rightful heir to both packs, not you. Cairo was thought to be dead; the council knew from a young age that Cairo is unable to be lead which is why they wanted him exterminated." I flinch and dart my gaze to my brother; he doesn't seem shocked by this revelation.

"So, to sum it all up the council wants power and Jess, Harlem and this Belle can give it to them?"

"Yes." Vince seems uneasy as he stares at Ro.

"Okay, so then it's simple. We take Jess, Harlem and Belle out of the equation and then we devise a plan to take them down from the inside."

"What the hell are you on about Ro?" Cairo turns to me

and the look in his blue eyes gives me pause.

"I'm going to the council and pledging my allegiance." Chaos erupts and everyone begins to shout and talk over each other, I stare at my brother unable to believe what he just said. "Enough!" everyone begins to quiet down at Ro's request, I can't wrap my mind around this! "If I go, I can play the jealous brother and they will eat it up. They won't trust me, but they will try to make it seem like they do for information. If I do this then that means we will get a man inside and then we will be able to prepare and take them down." What he is saying makes sense, but I don't want my brother to put himself in harm's way, I won't lose him!

Creed decides that we all need a break and sleep on everything we have learned. Waking this morning I feel so tired and restless, I tossed and turned most of the night, learning that my bio mom is alive and everything else in the mix played on my mind all night. Guilt has been eating at me, I had no idea the real danger my son is in because of me and now my brother wants to risk his life to help us. When did everything become so difficult? Why couldn't I have just had a normal life and been a normal human girl! I don't regret meeting Creed; thanks to him I now have my brother and our son, but I just wish he hadn't lied. I'm not blaming him, I know he hates what he did and truthfully, I know I should be mad with my mom for hiding all of this from me but how can I be mad at a ghost?

Creed and the others are at the meeting this morning organizing the search and training program, I honestly didn't have the energy to sit through that, so I decided to take Harlem down to the beach and let him play before meeting Shelley. I sit here and watch as my son giggles and runs around collecting seashells. Harlem has been the biggest blessing in my life, I don't know if I would have survived losing our daughter without him. He looks so happy and unaware of the danger that surrounds him.

We need to shift!

I jolt in shock; Sheba and I haven't been on good terms since the night she killed Josh.

No!

You weaken us by keeping me caged.

Whose fault is that Sheba?

I did what you couldn't, we need to shift Jess. If we don't shift, we remain weak and vulnerable.

I close the link between us and grit my teeth, she's right but I haven't been able to shift like before. Ever since I ran from Creed the night Sheba killed Josh, I have kept her locked up, I only shift when I have to. Each full moon I would stay locked up so Sheba wouldn't run and try to find Creed, I have never been on a pack run because of it. I have watched the others run together and envied them so much, I want to run with them and share in the excitement but I'm...scared. I worry that Sheba will attack someone and kill them, but in all honesty, I think I just need help to overcome my fears. Now that Creed is here, I will be able to go on my first pack run. Each time the full moon has come I watch and wait to see if Harlem will shift, I made sure my son knew exactly what we are from the moment he could understand. I never wanted him to grow up and be kept in the dark like I was, he needs to be prepared. Harlem hasn't shifted yet and Ro told me it isn't anything to worry about, he will shift when he is ready it's not something myself or anyone can force. The sound of footsteps approaching has me peering over my shoulder, I smile when I see Meg making her way toward us. Harlem spots her and squeals in delight as he bounds toward her, he wraps his arms around her legs and Meg rubs his head. She bends and whispers something in his ear that has his chest puffing up a bit and then he is racing back toward the water's edge. Meg drops down beside me and rests back on her elbows as we both sit and watch Harlem play. It warms my heart to see how much she loves him.

Chapter Twenty Two
Jessica

Meg and I have been sitting here chatting and laughing as we watch Harlem roll through the sand and make sand castles. He ran through the water and tripped over so he is soaked but refuses to leave the beach and change so here we are half an hour later sitting in the same spot because my son is having fun. It warms my heart to watch him laugh and play around like a normal child, that's all Creed and I want for him is to be free of the burdens we have placed on us.

"You have done an amazing job raising him Jess, you should be proud." I turn to Meg and smile; she will never know how much her words mean to me.

"Thank you, Meg, hearing that means the world to me."

"I see so much of his father in him." The sadness in her voice has me turning back to watch Harlem.

"Creed loves you Meg, being here with Davina won't change that." She sighs sadly, I can't even imagine what she must be feeling right now.

"It already has."

"How so?"

"I just found out my mate lied to me from the first moment we met." I snort.

"Yeah, I know exactly how that feels." Meg and I both chuckle.

"I heard about Shelley." A whoosh of air escapes me. "Callie told me you found out last night." Ro had filled everyone in this morning about what happened last night.

"Yeah, I wish I could say how I felt about it, but I honestly don't know how I feel. On top of everything that has happened I just don't think I have the emotional space to deal with that."

Meg reaches over and places her hand on top of mine.

"How about tonight you join us for a run, the packs need to shift, and I think a run will do us all some good." Excitement and fear thrums through me.

"I-I don't know if I can."

"Why not?" I drop my gaze to my lap slightly embarrassed.

"I've never been on a pack run before." I expect her to judge me, but she doesn't.

"Oh sweetheart, I'm sorry, may I ask why?" I keep my gaze on Harlem as I answer.

"Because Sheba would always try to escape and go back to Creed every time I would shift."

"Hmmmm, is that the only reason?" I deflate a little, how she knows I'm holding back I have no idea but I'm chalking that up to mothers' intuition.

"Sheba and I haven't seen eye to eye since...Josh."

"Ahh, I see. Can I give you some advice?" I turn to Meg, nothing but love and understanding shines in her eyes so I nod. "Let it go, let all of it go because in the end Josh is dead. It isn't Josh who is hurting by you not shifting, it's you. You can be mad at Sheba, but she did what she had to do to ensure your safety, she did her job sweetie. If you keep her caged, one day she will take over when you least expect it and won't allow you control back. You need to be one with your wolf, if the council were to attack now do you think Sheba would sit back and allow you to be defenseless?" I shake my head. "Exactly, shift tonight and let go of the past Jess. Creed will guide you through all of it, at least now Sheba won't run because she has her mate by her side."

I sit on the couch and wait for Creed and the others to get back; I enjoyed our day at the beach, and it was great that Meg joined us. I held out as long as I could before having to leave and bring Harlem home for his nap time, he went down so fast after I gave him a quick bath. I've been sitting down here for the past half hour making dot points in my head about everything we have learned.

- *My bio mom is alive*
- *Creed's mom is alive*
- *We live with vampires*
- *The council wants power*
- *Cairo wants to infiltrate the council*
- *There is a girl who can turn people into vampires*
- *Harlem will become a target if the council finds out about him*
- *Shifters and vampires are being made to train together*
- *We can't go home*
- *People from the island haven't returned and I'm sure it's because of the council*
- *I might actually get to go on my first pack run*

I release a huff and slouch down further into the couch. I

don't know if I'm broken or if I'm just getting used to people lying to me all the time, but I just can't make myself care about the fact that Shelley is my mom. I know I have to meet with her soon, but I honestly would rather eat soap than listen to her talk. If only I could turn back time just to be with my mom laughing on the couch while eating ice cream. Those times were the best, I was so carefree and didn't have to worry about a pack of power-hungry assholes hunting me down. I don't understand why they are after me, it's not like I have superpowers, so what if my bio mom was the alpha's daughter from the Reeves pack and my dad the alpha from the Cruz pack. I close my eyes and decide to try take a nap, maybe that way I might be able to shut off my thoughts and finally stop reeling from everything I have learned.

                       I'm having the most amazing dream, but I'm yanked from it when I feel something stab the side of my neck. I snap my eyes open and sit up placing my hand against the spot that stings, I attempt to stand but fall back into the couch. I feel woozy. I turn my head, but my movements are sluggish, something isn't right. My lids begin to feel heavy, my arms and legs start to feel like they weigh a ton, I roll my head to the side, and I see someone standing at the back of me, but my vision is so fuzzy I can't make out any features. I open my mouth but no sound comes out, I reach for Sheba, but I can't feel her. Panic begins to flow through me, what the hell is happening, I strain my hearing, but I can't hear anything over the pounding in my chest. I try to reach for the mind link Creed and I share but it feels...... I can't even feel him anymore. Oh my god, Harlem!

That's the last thought I have before I pass out and pray to God Harlem stays asleep.

Chapter Twenty Three
Credence

Sitting here listening to how the vamps plan to try and get their missing people back is entertaining. The hall is filled with the best of the best from the vamps and from the shifters as well as both alphas and our best trackers. What I didn't expect to see though is Shelley, Dela, Davina and my dad. I have no idea why they are here, but I can't stop staring, I watch the way my dad interacts with both the women and how he can be so easy going around both of them baffles me until realization finally dawns. My dad has known this whole fucking time that Shelley is alive, he knew Jess's mom was on the council and said nothing! I feel Corbin rise inside me; he has been so antsy ever since we got to the island. He and I have managed to control our anger and keep our self in check, you see being a shifter is fucking hard. We have two souls inside one body and sometimes getting along is harder than you might think.

"How the fuck can he be okay with her?" Cole makes sure to keep his voice low enough that only I can hear.

"I have no idea, if he hurts mom, I'll make him regret it." We have known our whole lives that dad loved Davina, what I don't get though is how he can still love her when mom is his mate! I couldn't imagine loving someone other than Jess, from the first moment I saw her, Corbin and I knew she was it for us. The scent of other women turns me off, even when I tried to piss Jess off by talking to Kayla it made my skin crawl.

"He doesn't even care! You know mom hasn't been staying at their house, right?" I turn to the side and stare at my brother, the look in his eyes tells me he isn't kidding.

"Where the hell has she been staying?" I grit out.

"With some of the packs, why do you think she is always at

our house?" It honestly never dawned on me, I have been so focused on Jess and Harlem I have slacked off on all my alpha duties. Guilt wars inside of me because right now my pack needs their alpha and all I have done is neglect them, I've been so focused on myself and my little family. That changes now.

"We don't have to talk to Davina today, we already know her secret. I'm going to round up the pack so we can join Cairo and his for a run, our pack needs to run so we can all bond again." Cole's wide smile is all the answer I need. I rise to my feet and the vamp who was just laying out the game plan clamps his mouth shut, I feel all eyes on me.

"So here's what's going to happen, Cole, Asher, Tommy and a few others as well as myself will accompany you all on your search."

"Why?" The vamp asks, I narrow my gaze at him. As the alpha no one gets to question my reasons why, I allow Corbin to rise up so he can see the wolf in my eyes. He tries to hide his flinch, but I notice how the other two vamps beside him step back slightly, good.

"Because I fucking said so. We are the best trackers in my pack, and we will find your people faster than any of you can." I move my gaze from the vamp to stare at my egg donor, the cocky bitch arches a brow at me. I lift my lip in a snarl, she may own the island, but I own the fucking pack and trust me I am better as an ally than an enemy. "My pack needs to run tonight, make whatever preparations you need, but we shift at eight." I don't wait for her to respond; I turn my gaze to my dad and make sure he can see the anger in my eyes. "You and Shelley aren't invited!"

Shock colors my dad's features but I ignore it as I turn and motion for my pack to follow me out. We head around the back of the hall to where Vince and a few others are waiting with Cairo and his pack members.

"Good timing, we were just going over what days' work for training." I motion for Vince to continue. "We will train Monday through Saturday and take Sunday off, each day we will train for 6 hours. We will learn to work together and fight as one, wolves will teach us to track, and vamps will teach wolves how to fight without their wolves."

"What does that mean?" Vince doesn't look at Callie like she asked a dumb question.

"It means that if the council is to subdue your wolf, you will be defenseless so you all need to learn how to fight without your wolf."

"How can they do that?" Cole took the words right out of my mouth.

"It is rumored that the council has made a concoction that can nullify a wolf, from what I have heard it is a mix or Mercury, Rohypnol and Ketamine. It will knock you out and keep your wolf senses out of action for at least 4 hours." To say I'm shocked is a bloody understatement, Corbin growls inside me and I can feel the anger of my pack through our pack link.

"How do you know this?" Vince looks uneasy as he answers, his shoulders are tense, and he won't meet Cairo's gaze as he answers.

"Because we were the ones to design it." Gasps and growls sound out around the group, the vamps start to back up and drop into a crouch ready to fight. I push forward and call my pack to stand down. Cairo must do the same because his pack falls back behind us as we face off to the vampires.

"Why the fuck would you do something like that?" Ro snaps. Corbin is riding me so hard that I am fighting to stay in my skin and not shift to fur.

"Because we had to be prepared in case the council came for us."

"How the fuck did they get the drug Vince?" My voice is more wolf than man right now.

"We were betrayed by one--"

"That's enough Vincent!" I glare as Davina moves toward her vampires, the way she looks at me pisses me off. "All you need to know is that they now have the formula for the drug and will use it."

"And we're just supposed to take your word for it?" The sarcasm is thick in my voice.

"Yes, you are, we could have withheld the truth and told you that there was no drug, but we didn't. Now if you will excuse me, I have preparations to make for your run." I glare at her as she turns to leave, the fact that she thinks she is safe to turn her back on me is comical.

"We won't need to meet with you either Davina." That gets her to falter in her step, I keep the satisfied look from my face as she turns to face me. She tries to search my face for any clue as to why I would give up knowing the truth, but she won't find a chink in my armor.

"Why?"

"Because we don't want to hear your bullshit, now piss off

so your men can train and figure out a way to protect their gutless leader." Davina glares at Cole but says nothing, the vamps hiss at my brother and move a step forward but stop when I drop to a crouch and release a deafening growl.

"Stand down!" The vamps snap their gaze to Davina in shock.

"But D--"

"I said stand the hell down Maurice." The looks of confusion on their faces tells me they have no idea who we are to Davina. Good, I would rather everyone think that my bio mom is dead because to me, she is.

After we all agree on a a plan for the training and what we would work on, we decided we may as wells start today. Cairo refused to leave and meet Jess so they could go and see Shelley, the fact that she was hanging around to watch us train tells me Jess didn't meet with her either. I stand back and watch, seeing a shifter in combat with a vampire is something I never thought I would ever see in all my life.

Vampires may not be able to shift but that doesn't mean they are weak, they're fast, and their agility to jump is unbelievable, as well as strength, speed and healing abilities. We are at our strongest when we are in wolf form so to see them not shift but have the same abilities to us is astounding. So far, the vamps haven't caused any trouble, I can see majority of them are at odds with us being here, but the others seem okay. We even had a couple of pack members reunite with missing family members, apparently Davina rescues anyone who is hunted by the council and offers them a safe haven here. I asked Vince if it is a requirement to be changed into a vamp, but he said no, it's a choice that they have all made willingly. I wonder how Davina does it though, if you have to use the blood from this first family how has she been able to do it if this Belle kid isn't even here?

"Vince!" We all turn to see a young boy running toward us, he screeches to a halt when he sees Callie, she shifted into her wolf so the vamps can practice taking us down in four legs. The kid can't seem to pry his eyes from my sister, I hear a small growl and fight to keep the smirk off my face, Sky doesn't like him eyeing out her mate.

"Unless you want me to remove your bloody eyes you will take them off my mate!" He snaps his gaze to Sky, instead of fear all I can see is wonder.

"You're a wolf?" The kid sounds like he is in awe. "You're beautiful." Now Callie growls at the little shit, he raises his hands as if surrendering. "Sorry! I've just never seen a wolf before, and I mean...I thought that.... Ladies don't change but then you're a girl and you're here and I mean you must be one because--"

"Caleb for fuck sake shut up!" The kid slams his mouth closed and smiles sheepishly at the girls before turning to an annoyed looking Vince. "What are you doing here Caleb?" The kid stands taller and tries to puff out his chest a bit to make himself look bigger.

"I wanna fight with you guys." Vince releases a loud exhale and shakes his head, the kids shoulders slump slightly before he quickly stiffens his spine.

"Caleb, you're sixteen. You are way too young to be involved in this, let us fight so you don't have to kid."

"Fine, I'll prove to you that I can handle myself." Vince shakes his head but before he can speak the kid spins toward us and when his gaze lands on me, I can't fight the smirk that breaks free. He raises his pointer finger at me and speaks. "He looks like a wolf; I'll take him down and when I do you have to let me fight."

"Caleb, no he is--"

"Deal kid." I say cutting Vince off, he darts his gaze to me pleading with me to not do this but I'm a wolf, an alpha wolf can never back down from a challenge. The kid closes the space between us, and I brace for him to attack, I can sense everyone's gaze on us now. The nosey fuckers have stopped training to see how far I'll take this. Instead of striking at me like I expected him to, to my surprise he offers me his hand.

"Hi, I'm Caleb and I'm a new blood." I cock a brow at him in question. "Oh, a new blood means I have just turned, so you know.... I'm new to all of this." I place my hand in his and shake it as I say.

"I'm Credence Reeves, alpha to the Reeves pack." The kids eyes double in size and he turns pale, I swear he is about to piss his pants. He yanks his hand out of mine and this time I let the smirk break free, Caleb rubs the back of his neck and darts his gaze around. The kid has spunk I give him that, he isn't big for his age, he's skinny and his hair is in bad need of a cut, it hangs down to his ears and he's constantly blowing the strands from his forehead, his brown eyes are full of life and mischief. I don't know what it is about this kid, but I like him already.

"So…" I can't stop the laugh that breaks free, the kid smiles up at me sheepishly. I see Vince out of the corner of my eye and watch as he relaxes slightly, now that he knows I won't hurt the kid. I may be an alpha and never back down from a challenge, but I will never hurt a kid for trying to prove himself.

"Dude, how about we teach you a few skills, and maybe in a couple of weeks you try your luck at taking on the big bad wolf?" Caleb smiles up at Cole like he hung the moon for him, I hear Vince curse and mutter beneath his breath which causes me to smile. If training this kid is going to ruffle the vamp's feathers, then I'm all for it.

"Deal!"

"Alright, you can go with Sky and Callie, they will help you out." Cole motions for him to go to an angry looking Sky but the kid shakes his head, my brow furrows in confusion.

"I would love to but--"

"No wolf will harm you kid; you have my word." My voice drips with my alpha tone as I communicate through the mind link that they take it easy on the kid.

"It's not that- "

"Then what is it?" I snap, Caleb flinches but doesn't back away.

"I mean I want to train, but I have to tell Vince something first, if that's okay." I grit my teeth and nod; he spins toward Vince and says. "I may have broken into a house!" he rushes to say, well that was…unexpected. Vince turns a bright shade of red and I can see the anger swirling in his eyes.

"You did what?" Caleb at least has the decency to drop his

gaze and seem remorseful.

"I had to Vince!"

"Look at me now, Caleb." He lifts his gaze slowly and stands tall. The kid has balls I give him that. "Why?"

"Because I heard a kid screaming and when I looked in the windows no one was there! I couldn't leave him Vince!" Ice fills my veins.

"What house?" I can barely get the words out over the fear choking me.

"The one that backs onto the woods, the two-story house." I snap, I dart forward and grip him by his shoulders lifting him off the ground, so we are eye level. I ignore the hissing and the growls around me as I stare at the kid. "Where is my son?" His eyes double in size and fear begins to fester in his brown gaze.

"I-I took him to Davina." I drop the kid and sprint toward my house, I know the others are following me but I don't care. I run as fast as my two legs will carry me, and when I see the house come into view, I try to feel for Jess...nothing! I burst through the front door and run straight up the stairs to our room, I search the whole upstairs, but she isn't here. I race back down to find Cairo and the others scanning the area as well, he looks at me and shakes his head.

FUCK!

I take off again and head toward Davina's, maybe she went there. Maybe someone told her Davina had Harlem and she went to get him? I hear the others following me again but don't stop, I don't slow my pace even as I see the gates. I bolt straight around the back and screech to a halt when I see Davina, mom and Harlem. I sprint toward my son and pluck him from my mom's lap crushing him against me.

"Daddy." He wheezes out, shit. I relax my hold on him but keep him close to my chest as I turn to my mom who is now standing.

"Where is Jess, mom?" She reaches out and places her small hand on my arm, tears fill her eyes, and my heart begins to pound inside me. Fear starts to choke me from the inside, I start to shake my head then a sob breaks free from my mom. I stumble back a step, Cairo dashes in front of me and grips my mom by her shoulders.

"Meg, where is my sister?"

"She was taken." I snap my gaze to Davina. "Caleb brought Harlem to me, so I called for Meg and went back to your house. Your mate wasn't there, I have sent out an alert to check for any boats missing."

"I was just with her, she said she was taking him for a nap." I can hear the devastation in my mom's voice but none of their words are registering. I don't hear or even notice as two men enter the gate and move toward Davina, one whispers something in her ear and then her gaze snaps to mine.

"One of the boats is missing and someone has taken the keys to the others. One of the men at the dock saw your mate being carried aboard a boat." My knees give out, I drop to the ground with my son clutched to my chest, my heart aches. Corbin is going nuts inside me; I throw my head back and release the most gut-wrenching howl.

Chapter Twenty Four
Jessica

I open my eyes, but everything is fuzzy, I try to push myself up when I feel a sting in my neck, and everything goes dark again.

Chapter Twenty Five
Credence

2 days!

2 fucking days since Jess was taken!

I am holding onto my sanity by a thread, Corbin has broken free so many times and hunted the whole fucking island. He even tried to swim! We tried to hot wire the boats and that's when we realized that the fuckers had not only taken the keys but cut the fuel lines to ensure we don't follow. Cairo and Zeke swam out to the cargo ship to see if we could use that instead, it'll be slower, but at least it's a start instead of sitting around doing fuck all. The bastards had broken the propellers and cut the wiring for the engines; we're stuck on this fucking island! I haven't been able to focus on anything aside from getting Jess back, when I find out who fucking took her, I will kill them. The tension between the vamps and shifters has risen, vamps deny it was them and the shifters swear they never did it either but someone did, and I'll find out eventually who it was. It's so fucking hard to track her over the scent of rotting flesh, fucking vamp stench. I tug on the strands of my hair and growl. I won't fucking lose her, not again.

Davina has tried to say Jess left willingly, I leapt across the table and nearly tore her fucking throat out for that comment. I would have if it wasn't for my mom stepping in front of her, Jess wouldn't leave me. I know shit has been hard between us, but I just know with every fiber of my being that Jess wouldn't walk away from me this time, and there is no way she would leave our son. Harlem has been searching for her and it breaks my heart when he screams for his mother. We have done everything we can to distract him, he has never been without her before. I hate that I have to rely on the twins, Cairo, Sky and even Zeke to know what my son wants. They know how to comfort him, they know what he likes and doesn't like, I fucking hate that I'm in the dark with this shit!

"Vince thinks he is able to get the boats up and running by the morning. If he succeeds then, we leave for the mainland." I shake my head to snap me out of my thoughts and focus on the discussion happening around me. Cairo, Vince, Davina, Dad, Callie, Zeke, Cole, Sky, Mom, Shelley, Dela and some other vamps I don't know decided it was better to hold this meeting in the hall. I look over at my mom and watch the way she gently rocks and taps my sons bum to soothe him. Since Jess has been gone, he won't sleep unless he's in the arms of someone. I haven't slept a wink.

"And go where Ro? We have no idea where the hell they would have taken her!" I know Cole is only lashing out because he is angry that Jess is missing. I have taken my anger out on everyone and anything I can hit.

"We go to Rosewood." All eyes turn to me, my voice is hoarse from lack of use. I haven't spoken much these past 2 days, every time I try to talk, I just snap, so it's better not to talk at all.

"Why the hell would we go there?" I turn toward my brother and meet his gaze as I answer.

"Because that's where Jacob will kill her." Everyone begins to yell and scream over the top of each other. Harlem startles and begins to scream for his mother, hearing him cry for his mother is what makes me snap. I slam my fist down on top of the wooden table and hear it splinter. Everyone goes dead silent, Cairo has a death glare directed at me and I relish in the challenge in his eyes.

"The fuck do you mean kill her?" He sounds more wolf than man, and right now Corbin will take any excuse he can get to release his pent-up anger. If Cairo so much as hints at a challenge Corbin won't hesitate to shift and take him down. You see with a wolf we are all about pack, fucking and fighting. Those three things are the most important things to any wolf.

"He will take her to the summit where she killed Josh, if my count is correct, we have 7 days till the six-year anniversary of his son's death. He will do it then; they will know we are coming so we don't have the element of surprise. They also know we have the backup of the vampires and will expect them to come with us."

"But they need Jess--"I shake my head and cut my sister off, I dart my gaze to my sniffling son and my anger subsides when his eyes meet mine.

"Not anymore, whoever took her knows she has a son. The council will come for Harlem but not Jacob, all he wants now is revenge for his son's death."

"What are you saying Creed?" I pry my eyes from Harlem and turn to my father.

"The council has someone watching us, as soon as we leave, they will come for my son and Davina. They only allowed Jacob to take Jess to distract us." I see the moment my words register; dad looks to Davina, then my mom and I growl. "You are more fucking worried about your *dead* wife than you are about your own fucking mate?" Dad doesn't even flinch at my outburst.

"Don't you dare judge me; I did what I had to--."

"Fuck off Dad, you hid the fact that your cheating wife was alive and to top it off you lied to my fucking mate." That last part has his brow furrowing in confusion.

"I've never lied to Jess--"

"Yes, you have! You knew her mother was alive this whole fucking time and did nothing. You knew my best friend was packless and being hunted by the council and still you did fucking nothing. I begged you to help Cairo, all you could fucking say was it wasn't our business because he isn't pack." I move around the cracked table and don't stop until I am toe to toe with my father. "News flash old man, he is my fucking pack, but you aren't any longer, I Credence--"

"Son, please stop don't--"I ignore my mother and continue.

"Reeves hereby banish you Kane Reeves from my pack." My dad stumbles back a step and his hand whips up to cover his heart, I feel the link that binds him to my pack evaporate inside me. He will no longer be able to mind link the pack or be welcomed on our pack lands again. I hear my mom sob behind me, and spin around dropping to my knees in front of her. Tears flow down her cheeks as she looks down at me while she clutches my son to her chest. I place my hands on the tops of her knees. "He may be banished but you aren't, Meg Reeves you are now and forever will be our mother with or without him. You don't need him to be our mom, given a choice we would always choose you, mom. He doesn't deserve you after what he has done." Sobs wrack my mom's body, Sky moves over and gently peels Harlem from her arms, I feel my brother and sister at my back, mom looks to each of them, and the tears flow faster.

"You may not have given birth to us, but you are our mom

in every sense of the word. We need you mom." Mom smiles up at Callie.

"Fuck Kane, fuck Davina. All we need is you, they never raised us, you did. We are who we are today because of you." I stand and help her to her feet, the four of us stand there in a circle and hold each other, everyone is silent. We pull apart and mom pats each of us on the cheek and smiles lovingly.

"I love the three of you more than anything, there has never been a day where I don't consider you, my children. Thank you for loving me and making me a mom and now a grandma." I chuckle and wrap her in a hug, I know shit has been hard for her as well. I only banished my dad because I overheard them arguing the other night. Mom caught him kissing Davina, but the worst part was hearing her agree to stay with him because she was scared to lose us.

"You know I used to envy Creed." I spin around and watch as Cairo moves toward my dad. "I thought he was so lucky to have a cool dad, I always wondered why Creed never invited me inside. I thought it was because I was the homeless packless rat that you didn't like, but I was wrong. You never wanted me near your son because you knew my mother was alive and she would have told you that the council was after me because I can't be led." Ro looks my dad up and down in disgust. "You're a pathetic excuse for an alpha, and most of all, a father. Oh, in case Creed wasn't clear, you are banished from ever being near my sister or my nephew." Davina motions for two of her men to come forward, they each grab an arm, as he struggles and turns pleading eyes to my mom.

"Meggy, please don't do this." Mom scoffs.

"You made your choice Kane, you're only sorry because Davina didn't want you back." Davina nods again, and the two guys drag him out of the hall kicking and screaming. Davina moves toward us, and I see Cole and Callie stiffen as she approaches, we move in unison, to block our mom from her view. Davina stops and sighs as she looks to each of us.

"I would like to speak to Meg, please." Mom pushes between me and Cole and steps out much to our dismay. Davina doesn't look smug or even gleeful, she looks at mom with... sadness. "I hope you know that when Kane attempted to kiss me, I didn't allow it. I may be a lot of things, but I will never tear your family apart Meg. Kane is an idiot for how he has treated you, he was a very lucky man to find someone like you. Not many women would have stepped up and raised three kids that weren't hers. I apologize for any part I may have played in you and your mate... Parting." I stand here stunned and stare at Davina, I never expected that to come from her.

"I have always known Kane was still in love with you, but I thought over time it would lessen, it never did. I couldn't compete with a ghost, so to speak. I only stayed because I was afraid, he wouldn't allow me to be a part of the kids' lives." Mom moves toward Davina and surprises the fuck out of everyone, even Davina when she clasps both her hands in her own. "Thank you." Davina reels back slightly in shock.

"Uh, for what?"

"For giving me the three greatest gifts in the world. You may have carried them, but I have loved them their whole lives. I can't promise you that they will forgive you Davina but over time the anger will lessen, if you try to mend the bridges you broke and be honest with them." For the first time since meeting Davina, she finally drops her mask and I see the longing and regret in her eyes. "They are great kids, they love hard and fight even harder for what they cherish most. You may have made wrong choices, but you can try to make things right by being the best freaking grandmother to *our* grandson." Hearing mom refer to Davina like that has me fighting back my emotions, I may not like it, but my mom wouldn't be extending this honor to Davina if she didn't think she was worthy of being in Harlem's life.

"I-I would like that very much." Mom shocks us again when she drops Davina's hands and pulls her into a hug. Davina's shocked eyes dart to the three of us, it takes a lot of my control not to laugh at the horrified expression on her face, after a moment she reaches up and pats mom on the back like one would pat a dog. Cole and Callie don't even attempt to hide their laughter, I spy Vince out of the corner of my eye concealing his laughter behind his hand.

"As touching as all of this is, I think we need to formulate a plan and work out numbers of who is staying here and who is going." Dela is right, I move toward him and notice Shelley is staring directly at me. I search her gaze for a challenge but there isn't one, I can see she wants to say something.

"Whatever it is, just say it because I don't have time for your bullshit." She takes a deep breath and nods.

"The night Austin was killed he told me that the council was after him because they knew he was in touch with the first family."

"As in the first family if vampires?"

"Yes Colton, Austin had stumbled upon the vampires when he was out hunting. He formed a friendship with Alexander, the leader of the family. Austin found Alex when he was traveling abroad after college--"

"Wait, so this was before you and him were even together?"

"Yes Creed. I only found out about Alex the night Austin died, I had never met him. Austin would talk to him all the time on the phone, and I never had a reason to question it, I thought at least if he's here on the phone he's not--."

"With me?" Davina finishes for Shelley and she nods.

"So why were they after Austin?" I ask.

"Jacob followed Austin when he went out of town and saw him with Alex. I don't know how he knew what Alex was, all I know is that Jacob told the council in a bid to get rid of Austin so they would name him alpha of the Cruz pack. Austin knew Jacob was trying to overthrow him, Dela was the one who warned Austin that Jacob was coming for him, the kids and me as well. He met with Jacob that night knowing that he would try to kill him, but he told me he had a way to make sure that never happened."

"He gave the blood to me instead of taking it himself." Shelley nods sadly.

"Yes Davina, Alex had given Austin a vile of his blood. Austin and Alex were trying to broker a truce so vampires could come out of hiding, but the council didn't want that. They didn't like the idea of another race being out in the world that they couldn't control. So, they set Austin up, he left to meet Jacob and the council came for me and the kids, except Cairo had escaped. Jess was just a baby, Dela told me if I went willingly, he would make sure the kids weren't harmed, so I did. Except Dela couldn't find Cairo. The only way to ensure the kids safety and even know if they were alive was to play dumb and eventually join them. Dela helped me get Zeke to Ro and he kept tabs on Kat and Jess. Eventually I managed to find both my kids and make sure they were kept off the radar and that the council still believed they both died the same night Austin did, but that changed--"

"When I brought Jess back to Rosewood."

"Yes Creed."

"Where is this Alex now?" Cairo asks.

"I-I don't know, like I said I've never met the man only your father did. Cairo I am so--"

"Save it."

"Cairo, please--"

"He said to save it! You don't get to waltz in and spin a sad story and then think all the years of pain and suffering he went through will just vanish. You are fucking pathetic." Shelley stares at Sky in shock, everyone who knows Cairo knows that if you fuck with him, you have Sky to answer to.

"He's, my son." Sky scoffs and Ro doesn't even attempt to intervene or stop Sky.

"No, he isn't. I found him and nursed him back to health, I made sure he was okay and safe. I did all of that, not you, so don't you dare claim that he is your son. Your story may be true, but it's too late, the boy you left behind is gone, he died the night his mother left, and his father was killed. You ever try to push him for more than he is willing to give, I will fucking gut you like a pig!" The hall is deadly silent that you could hear a pin drop. After a minute Ro steps forward to break the staring match between Sky and Shelley by placing his hand on Sky's shoulder. Sky looks up at him while he smiles down at her, I can see nothing but love and respect in his gaze when he looks at her. I have always wanted to know how their strange relationship works; it intrigues me.

"I'm okay, we're okay. Reign it in now, deep breath killer." I look at them in confusion then dart my gaze around to see everyone else is just as confused, I look to my sister who is holding her nephew and she seems to be the only one who knows what the fuck is going on.

Chapter Twenty Six
Jessica

I feel so dizzy, my head is pounding, and my mouth feels like it is full of cotton. I reach up and rub my head hoping that it will take the headache away, I'm glad Harlem isn't awake yet, that means I can lay in bed longer. I roll over to reach for Creed, but my hand cuts through the air and slaps against the cold hard ground. That's when I remember I'm not at home in bed next to my mate! I peel my eyes open, and the florescent light above has me slamming them closed again, the headache begins to throb against the base of my skull. I open my eyes slowly this time, the light is harsh against my eyes, and it takes me a couple seconds to adjust. I sit up and it's a struggle, I feel so tired, and my limbs feel like they are being weighed down with bricks. Once I'm sitting, I dart my gaze around and begin to panic when I notice I'm in a cage! I reach inside myself for Sheba but.... I can't feel her. I try to reach for Creed through the mate bond, but I can't feel him either! I start to panic and wrack my brain trying to figure out what the hell happened, then it hits me. I was on the couch, and then felt a sting in my neck, I reach up and feel the spot where I was injected with something. I have a sinking feeling I'm not on the island anymore, I remember seeing someone and hearing murmurs before I passed out.

Oh my god!

Harlem, what if whoever has done this to me has taken him too? Oh god, a sob tears from my chest. I'm not religious but right now I'm praying to God that Harlem stayed asleep and whoever took me didn't harm him. I push myself to my feet and grip the cage bars to steady myself, my head isn't just throbbing now it's also spinning. I use the bars to maneuver my way around the cage, I pull on the bars and yank on the chain that is wrapped around the door hoping beyond hope that I can snap them. There's no way I can do that without my wolf, I know Sheba and I have been off lately, okay for a few years now but not being able to feel her inside me petrifies me! I feel incomplete, like I have lost half of myself and I fucking hate it! Whoever has done this will pay, I just need to remember to keep my cool and not mention Harlem. If whoever took me is working with the council and they find out I have a son, they will take him. But if I don't ask, how the hell will I find out?

I look around and thanks to not having my wolf with me I can't see anything past the cage. It's so dark and the light above me only shines in the cage, clearly it was designed this way so I'm not able to see my surroundings. I hear a bang and then voices; I take a breath and give myself a mental pep talk. I release the bars and move back to the center of the cage; I will not allow whoever it is to see me as weak. It's harder than I thought to stand here and not sway, I try to ignore the dizziness and the pounding headache but its freaking hard when I feel like someone is bouncing a basketball around in my head.

It feels like minutes have gone by before someone appears but really its only seconds. I have no idea who the hell this woman is, but she keeps her gaze on the ground, I have to squint because of how dark it is, I can only tell it's a woman because of how short she is and the fact she is tiny. I can't see what she is doing but I do notice that she has stopped moving and just stands there, I may not be able to see her, but I can feel her gaze on me. I feel like I'm on a platform almost like I'm on show for everyone to see, I ignore how uncomfortable I am and focus on everything Z and Ro taught me.

If you are ever captured, never show weakness, never break the silence, and never ever beg.

I keep replaying those words repeatedly in my head, Cairo and Zeke made sure to train me in case the council ever found me. They were shocked to learn that from a young age my mom made sure I learnt martial arts and self-defense. I hear more footsteps, but I refuse to take my eyes off the shadow in front of me, I feel more eyes on me but ignore them. I see two more shadows approach the woman and they too are conceded by the darkness. More footsteps approach and time ticks by as more and more shadows surround the cage, I can feel their eyes on me, and my skin begins to crawl, but I still refuse to look anywhere other than the first woman that came in. I can feel that I am surrounded and with no wolf, I have to rely on my basic human fighting skills to help me if they all decide to have a go.

Just when I think this can't get more eerie the light above me goes off, I bite back my scream. I stand here still as a statue and make sure to keep my breathing even so they don't know how terrified I am, I hear movement, and the chain jiggles, they're opening the gate. I push all the pain away and block it out, I crouch down low and get into a fighting stance with my hands raised in front of my face ready to attack or defend myself. I hear feet shuffling against the concrete floor, but I can't keep track of where they are moving. I never realized how much I depended on Sheba until now, I regret keeping her locked up and shutting her out. I slam my eyes closed when the light flickers back on, I quickly blink them open and try to adjust to the light as fast as I can but it's too late. The first fist connects against my cheek, and I stumble back, I spin around and see that I am surrounded *inside* the cage now. I have no idea who these men and women are, but they all look pissed! I can hear my brothers voice inside my head.

Never go down without a fight even if you know you will lose. Always fight back until you can't!

And I do, as each of them lashes out at me I fight back. I kick, punch, scratch, bite, I do whatever it takes to inflict as much pain as I can, but it doesn't last, there is too many of them, I go down like a lump of flour when one of the men punches me directly in the face, they don't stop, the blows keep coming and when a kick lands against my ribs I swear I feel them crack. I try to curl into a ball and cover my head but still...they don't stop. The pain is so intense that I bite into my bottom lip because I refuse to give these bastards the satisfaction of hearing me scream, I welcome the darkness when I pass out.

When I wake, I wish I hadn't, my body aches and everything feels like it is broken. I try to open my eyes but only one of them opens partially because the other is swollen shut. I feel woozy and I have a headache from hell, thanks to being beaten. I can already tell that Sheba isn't here because if she was my injuries would have healed, I don't know how long I was out but I can't feel any eyes on me so that's a good sign. I decide to sit up so I can check my injuries but as soon as I move a horrible scream tears from my throat, tears roll down my cheeks. Oh my god, I have never been in this much pain, I dart my tongue out to moisten my lips and then flinch in pain. My lips are split, and I can taste my own blood on my tongue, I need to block out the pain and try to find a way out of here, if I don't I fear whoever has taken me will kill me.

I take some deep breaths to prepare myself for the pain I'll be enduring when I move again, excruciating pain thrums through my body as I grit my teeth to stop myself from screaming. It takes me so long to climb to my feet and I have to use the bars of the cage to help, I'm panting and sweating from exertion by the time I'm on my feet, I take deep breaths and cringe every time. My ribs burn and fresh tears trek down my cheeks with each breath I take. I know damn well my ribs are broken, I notice pinky finger is broken on my left hand, using my right hand to gently pat my face for injuries and hiss instantly. My whole face is swollen, I feel gashes on the front and back of my head, I look at the ankle that is causing me pain and attempt to put weight on it, it hurts but it isn't broken so I'm thankful for that. I wrap my arms around myself to stabilize my ribs as I move slowly across the cage toward the door. I glare at the padlock and chain, how nice of them to remember to lock up after they beat the shit out of me. After searching for any weak points in the cage and not finding one, I decide to go back to the middle and sit down--well drop down. More time passes and my stomach growls, my throat is hoarse and I'm beyond thirsty, but I would rather eat shit than ask for food or water from these assholes.

I must have fallen asleep; I wake to the sound of footsteps, and I get the feeling they're *not* here to talk. I refuse to take a beating lying down, I am Jessica freaking Hasting, I am the first female alpha, and I would rather die than give these bastards the satisfaction of seeing me break. I push to my feet and bite through my bottom lip to stop the screams that want to tear from me, I feel the blood dripping down my chin as I stand and face off against the shadows. I turn around slowly and let a dry humorless laugh escape me, I may be broken and in the worst pain of my life, but I won't back down. I have every reason to fight and make it out of here alive, I refuse to die and let my son grow up without a mother!

"Come on you pussy's, is that all you got?" They don't make a sound or even move from what I can see. Then the light goes out, I brace myself for what I know is about to happen. I hear the chain clink and the squeak of the door opening; I send up a little prayer hoping someone is listening. When the light flickers back on they're all in here with me, I don't wait for them to attack, I let out a strangled battle cry and launch myself at the nearest women. I last a minute before I'm thrown to the ground and once again, I'm curled up in a ball trying to protect myself and my already battered body from more injuries, when my vision begins to turn black, I welcome the darkness once again.

CHAPTER
TWENTY SEVEN
Jessica

My body is broken beyond repair, my limbs refuse to move, I can barely wiggle my toes or move my fingers. I have no idea how much time has passed or how many beatings I have endured. I'm given a bottle of water and two stale bread rolls once a day, I'm only guessing its daily because I have no idea what the time is or how many days I have been in here. Every part of me aches, even my fingernails are in pain. Each time they come down I always make a show of pushing through the pain and getting to my feet but the last time no matter how hard I tried I just couldn't manage it, so instead I stayed on the ground and ran my mouth. Truthfully every time I wake up, I just cry from the pain and the loss I feel inside me, I miss Sheba so much and without her I know I am going to die down here. My hair is crusted and mattered to my face and neck from the dried blood, I've even lost control of my bladder. It didn't bother me before to just squat in a corner of the cage but now that I can't move, I had no choice but to pee myself. I cried the whole time, I have never felt more powerless in my life.

Each time I wake, I try to reach for Creed through our bond, whatever they used to get me here took away my wolf and my mate link! Is he even searching for me? Does he know where I am? Is Cairo coming? I push those thoughts from my head and try to open my eye, yes eye because my left one is sealed shut, I can only open my right one a tiny sliver. I roll my head to the side and groan in pain, right there on the other side of the cage is two bread rolls and a water bottle. A brittle laugh escapes me, even if I wanted the bread and water, I don't have any energy to reach it. I close my good eye and get lost in my own head. I think back to the times Harlem and I played outside, I think about when the twins were first born and how happy I was. I think about Creed and how much I miss him. My heart begins to ache when reality settles in, I will never have a future with my son or with my mate. Creed and I will never get to make love again, I'll never get to see my son have his first haircut or watch him get married. I know deep down inside myself that I am never going to make it out of here alive.

"Pssst." My eye snaps open, well as far as it can, and I lull my head to the side trying to scan the cage for whoever made that noise, I can't see anyone. "Jess." The voice is right beside me, but I still can't see who it is. "Don't talk just listen. When they come down again tell them you give up, if you do, they will leave. This is what my father does, he pushes people until they break." It hits me then; I know who the voice belongs to.

"Kayla?" I wheeze out, my throat is dry and coarse.

"Shhhh, I'm trying to help you out here."

"W-why?" She is the last person who I ever thought would help me.

"Because a few weeks ago I was you, when the council and my dad took over the Reeves pack then I was punished. My father enjoys breaking people, let him think he broke you and he will stop. I can hear how slow your pulse is and your heart rate is slowing, you will not survive another round."

"Why is he doing this?"

"You killed my brother Jess, he wants revenge." It all clicks into place; Jacob is behind this torture, and this is his way of punishing me for taking his son from him.

"My wolf is gone."

"No, she isn't, she is just subdued. They keep injecting you with this drug that subdues your wolf, you have to stop this so they will stop injecting you and then your wolf will come back, and you can heal." I hear voices in the distance and Kayla curses quietly. "I have to go, trust me Jess." I hear her move and before I can think twice, I call out to her quietly.

"Kayla?"

"Yeah?"

"Thank you."

"Don't thank me yet, we still have to make it out of here alive once you heal." Hearing those words from her sends a renewed sense of hope through me. I might not need a prince charming to rescue me after all, giving up goes against everything I was taught, but if that is what it takes to live then so be it!

I don't know how much time passes but I'm startled awake by the sound of footsteps. A war stirs inside me; my rational side knows that Kayla is right, I don't think my body can survive another beating. But the other half of me being the alpha side, detests the idea of rolling over and giving up. I feel them surround the cage and know I only have mere minutes before the lights shut off and they come in, I grit my teeth and take deep breaths as I push the words out through clenched teeth.

"You win, I give up." Saying those words hurts me more than I want to admit, tears of frustration leak from my eyes. I'm battered and bruised and slowly dying inside, but my pride is wounded beyond repair after uttering those words. My head pounds and the base of my skull is throbbing, my eye drifts shut, and sleep claims me. If they decide that another beating is what

I need then I would rather be unconscious, so I let the darkness take over.

Chapter Twenty Eight
Credence

Vince was able to fix the boats the next morning. We made sure to leave men behind on the island; I needed to make sure that my son is protected and safe before I left. My mom decided it was safer for her and Harlem to stay at Davina's house, Callie offered to remain behind with our mom for extra protection, , Zeke, Cole, Sky, Vince and I are in one boat, we spilt the shifters and vamps into another 2 boats. The trip to the dock where we boarded, lasts two and a half days, then one day's drive back to Rosewood. By the time we get to the outskirts of town all the shifters are antsy and need to shift, our wolves hate being confined.

"We have to hide the cars and travel on foot, the vamp's scent will mask ours." Cole is right, we were damn lucky that the cars we used to get to the dock were still there and started without any trouble. Vince directs his guys to stash the five cars we brought with us in the woods. When they return, we gather to hatch a game plan, none of us can agree on anything. My frustration begins to build the longer we stand here and do nothing!

"We shift, the vamps lead, and we follow their trail. We need to head toward Jacob's pack lands, he won't be moving her yet."

"How can you be so sure?"

I grit my teeth and answer Vince. "Jacob will want to break her before he kills her." Growls sound out around me, even the vamps look pissed. Since arriving on the mainland, I have tried to reach Jess through the mate link, but I feel nothing, Corbin has been going nuts and thrashing against my ribs to be free so he can chase after his mate.

Shift!

No, we can't fuck this up Corbin. If any of his pack catch our scent, he won't hesitate to kill her.

I'll kill him.

Yes, but we need to get Jess first.

I close the link with Corbin and join the others as we start to undress. Nudity isn't something shifters worry about; modesty is something only humans care for. Vince and the other vamps take our pants and place them in a bag, I turn to Sky and cock a brow.

"You're not shifting?"

"No."

"Why?" Sky doesn't answer this time, Cairo does.

"Because she needs to stay on two legs to communicate for us." I don't buy what he is saying for even a second, but I don't push it. Instead, I focus on letting Corbin take control, we shift within seconds. Corbin shakes out our duel-colored coat and chuffs a couple times, I see Cairo and Zeke have shifted as well. I can feel the alpha power rolling off Cairo in waves, he may have fled his pack at nine years old and without an alpha, but you wouldn't think so with the amount of power radiating from him. Cairo taught me a lot about being a wolf, he would have been the best alpha for the Cruz pack. Thanks to Jacob he never got that chance, he fled the night his parents were killed hoping one day he could come back and lead, but Jacob forced him to go rogue thinking that he wouldn't survive.

"I can see here on the map that the town is surrounded by woods, we need to stay in the shadows." I turn to see Vince has his phone in his hands, he must have looked up the town on Google maps. Corbin growls his understanding.

"Cairo wants to split up, surround the town so that we can block them in if they flee."

"Okay, we go in groups. Mike will go east; you and I will go west, Tommy and the others will stay here to block off this exit point." I open the mind link to my pack.

Colton is with me, Asher you take three with you and Tommy you stay here with the others.

Yes alpha.

Yes alpha.

If anyone tries to flee you take them down, no one is to leave here.

Everyone agrees and I turn to Cairo and nod.

"We're ready to roll out, Cairo and Zeke will come with us, and the others will split off." Vince nods and barks orders at his guys, I turn to my brother.

We are here to get Jess, if we can get in and out without being seen we do it.

We need to take Jacob down!

I release a growl and step forward, Cole tries to fight against submission, but he can't, I'm the stronger wolf and if I have to make him submit to me I will.

We need to find my mate, then I need to get back and make sure my son is safe. We will deal with Jacob another time.

Yes.... alpha.

I can hear the strain in his voice, but I'm not sorry for making him submit, Jess is my only concern right now. I plan on killing Jacob slowly, he doesn't deserve a quick death, I'll pro long it for as long as I can.

Chapter Twenty Nine
Jessica

The sound of voices has me stirring awake, I come to with a groan, I try to blink my eyes open but only one of them opens to a tiny slit, the light above me beams so bright. I hear voices, but I see nothing but darkness. I try to lift my hand, but my body ignores me and refuses to move an inch, I don't feel any new wounds so maybe Kayla was right. I mean I'm still alive so I guess they didn't beat the shit out of me after all, I hear whispers again, but I can't make out what they are saying. I hear feet scuff along the ground and remain as still as I can and close my eye so they think I'm still out cold. I make sure to keep my breathing and heart rate steady, I can feel them right beside me, and I remain still.

"If they get any closer, we have to move her."

"To where?"

"Dunno, alpha just said to be ready to move her at a moment's notice."

"You got the sedative?" One of them snorts, men are such arrogant pigs!

"Look at her, she's half dead anyway so no point wasting it on her."

"Is she really an alpha?" I can hear the wonder in this guy's voice, and it makes me sick. "If she is, I'll take her as my chosen mate." The other guy laughs.

"Why?"

"Dude, that would mean I would be alpha."

"Huh, I never thought of that. Wonder what it's like to bang an alpha bitch?" Bile begins to rise up my throat. I can deal with getting beaten but being raped is something I couldn't deal with.

I feel tears building through my swollen eyes and I try to think of something that will help me focus on something other than the prospect of me being raped!

"Did you know that her brother is Cairo Cruz?"

"The fuck, no way!"

"Yeah, I heard Jim and Kyle talking about it the other day."

"Wait, so the border breach might not be her mate, it might be Cairo?" I perk at the mention of a border breach.

"Dude did you know the council is trying to recruit him?" What the hell?

"No, why?"

"Cairo is a legend. He was exiled from his pack and thought to be dead for years but turns out he is the alpha to all rogues' but check this, he can never be led!" The awe in their voices when they speak about my brother is worrying.

"Why did he come back?"

"According to some of the pack, he only came out of hiding for *her*." The '*her*' they are referring to is me, guilt gnaws at me. My brother would still be safe and living his best life if it wasn't for me. They both go quiet for a moment and then I hear them shuffle around as the guy says. "Shit, we need to move her now." I remain calm and allow them to think I'm still unconscious. I physically don't have the strength to even lift my own arms let alone fight off two shifters. The chain clinks and the door squeaks as they open it, I try to let my mind wonder to a happy place hoping that when they drag me out of here I'll be too lost in my head to feel any pain. No such luck though, they each grip one of my arms and yank me up. I scream and this time I can't stop the tears from streaming down my face. They grip the top of my shoulders and hold each of my forearms as they drag me from the cage, I can't even get my shoeless feet under me to walk. These two air heads literally drag me out of the cage and through the darkness, neither of them seems to care that I keep hissing or moaning in pain. I can't see anything, granted I can only peer out of the tiny slit of my eye. They drag me up a flight of stairs and each of my feet slap against the stairs. I hear a door open but they're moving too fast for me to scan my surroundings, plus my head feels like it's on a merry-go-round and I feel like I might hurl whatever tiny amount is in my stomach.

"Take her to the car and head for the mountain!" A woman snaps, we pass through another door and that's when I realize I must have been kept in a basement of a house. The fresh outside air hits me as I'm dragged along the grass, we come to a stop and the guy on my left releases me and I nearly crumble to the ground, but the one of the right holds me up in a bruising grip that has me biting into my lip again to stop the scream that wants to tear free.

I'm pushed forward and grabbed immediately then I'm lifted and scream out when the grip on my ribs tightens, I'm thrown into what I assume is the trunk of an SUV and before I can do anything the door slams shut, I hear four doors open and then slam closed as the car peels away, I'm powerless to stop myself from rolling around, and smacking into the backs of the chairs and the trunk door. I have no idea where the mountain is, but I'm thankful to be out of that cage!

It hits me, they must be moving me because they've heard that Cairo and Creed are coming for me. I send up a silent prayer to whoever may be listening and just hope and pray that they find me, even I admit I know I can't hang on like this much longer. I'm snapped out of my thoughts when the car screeches to a halt and I slam into the back of the seats with a groan.

"Shit, they blocked the exit!" I hear the panic in the woman's voice, and it thrills me. My pack has come for me!

"Turn around B and go the back way." I recognize the man's voice as one of the guys that dragged me from the basement. The car is put into reverse and I try to stop myself from rolling but fail and slam into the boot. I'm so over feeling this powerless and at the mercy of some asshole people, I have never felt this powerless in my life except for when I lost my girl. I suppose at least if I did die, I could be with my daughter again and Harlem would have Creed and the others. I snap myself out of that downward spiral, I can't let myself think like that. I may not have been able to save my daughter but I refuse to leave my son, he needs his mother and I won't stop trying until I really am dead. The car screams to a stop again and I'm thrown forward into the backseat again, I growl in anger.

"Shit, they blocked this one as well!" The woman shouts.

"Go the long way to the mountain, there is no way Cairo knows about that route." I'm mentally picturing all the ways I am going to kill this guy from the basement.

"And what if it isn't Cairo?" The woman snaps.

"Oh shit, Reeves knows all the exits." A new male voice says. "If it is Reeves, he will kill us without mercy for touching her." Hearing the fear in his voice as he talks about Creed warms me inside.

"We have no choice Kane, if we don't do this the alpha will

kill us." The woman hisses.

"Kacey, we are surrounded. They have all the exits blocked and there is no way Reeves didn't come, she's, his mate." I hear a scoff come from the back seat.

"Run them down, I ain't dying for no alpha bitch and Jacob will kill us so run the fuckers down!" It's the other guy from the basement. We sit here in silence for so long, I begin to wonder if they have changed their minds.

"Kane...."

"I see them B." I growl inside my head at the fact I have no idea what they are talking about. "They know she's here." The tone of the guy Kane's voice has my skin prickling with awareness, it only ever does that if Creed is near, hope begins to build inside.

He came for me!

CHAPTER THIRTY
Credence

Ro and I stand shoulder to shoulder as we stare at the blacked-out jeep, I know she's inside. Her scent is faint and being masked somehow, but I know it's her, and judging from the looks of the two people in the front seats she's definitely inside. They look around and check their mirrors for an escape route, but they won't find one, we have them surrounded. We have a circle formed around their vehicle, all the pack is still in wolf form except for me, Cairo and Sky, Vince has his vamps fanned out around the car and he and the others are slowly moving closer. I can scent that the four in the car are shifters, I'll kill them all! Ro moves forward a few steps, he stands there in nothing but his shorts, his tats on full display for all to see.

"You have five fucking seconds to hand over my sister or I'll kill each and every one of you--slowly!" The authority in his voice even has me wanting to obey him. I look at him in shock, I have always known Cairo is a strong alpha but it's almost like his power has increased. I tear my gaze from him when the windows of the car start to wind down, the driver and the passenger put both their hands out the window to show they are surrendering.

"What the fuck are you two doing? He will kill all of us if we don't take her to him!"

"Fuck up Garrett, we are dead either way and I for one would rather die quickly than be tortured by Jacob!" I eye the woman in the driver's seat, she opens her door and the guy in the passenger seat follows her lead. They both move toward the front of the vehicle with their hands in the air they both looked scared shitless. "We had nothing to do with what happened to your sister--"I growl and move forward till I'm next to Cairo.

"What the fuck happened to my mate?" The man and woman exchange a look before turning back to me, I hear the guy gulp.

"Jacob had her... broken in." The woman mumbles and my body begins to vibrate with unbridled rage.

"Open the fucking trunk now!" I snap, Ro and I follow them to the back of the jeep, Ro motions for Vince and two of his men to retrieve the other two from the backseat. The woman is hesitant to open the trunk and that causes me to panic. I strain my hearing and I can hear her faint heartbeat; I scent the air and I smell.... blood. I shove them out of the way and yank the trunk open snapping the clip but freeze when I see her.

Oh god no!

I black out as Corbin forces a partial shift, he spins around and grips the man and woman by their throats and digs his claws in, Corbin relishes in the fear in their eyes.

"You feared the wrong alpha." He snarls as he tears their throats out, blood spurts all over my naked chest as they drop to the ground, the sound of them gurgling and choking on their own blood doesn't even satisfy the beast inside me, Corbin wants to end every single one of Jacob's pack. I fight for control, and he reluctantly relents as I take over, I need to help Jess. I move toward the jeep and brush past Ro, he stares at his sister with a blank look on his face, I gently bend over and cup her cheek but yank my hand back when she hisses in pain.

"Princess?" I whisper, I feel tears building behind my eyes. I can't even see the color of her skin; her whole body is covered in cuts and bruises. I see some deep gashes on her face, her hair is mattered to her face from the crusted blood and her clothes are torn. I can smell urine all over her, some of its hers and some of it isn't. I clench my fists at my sides and try to reign in my anger, I want to break every single one of these cunts.

"Bring those two here!" I know what's about to happen, I can feel the rage rolling off Cairo. Those other two guys will be dead in seconds.

"We didn't touch her!" His pleas are falling on deaf ears, Cairo's wolf is too close to the surface for him to be reasoned with.

"Why the fuck isn't she healing?" Its then that it sinks in, Cairo is right. Sheba should have been able to heal all of Jess's wounds. I know this is gonna hurt her, but I have to hold her, so I reach into the trunk but before I grab her out, I say.

"I'm so sorry princess, this is gonna hurt." I pull her out of the trunk and cringe when a gut-wrenching scream tears from her, I cradle her shaking form against me and that's when I notice that both her eyes are swollen shut. I grind my teeth together and turn to face the two fucking cowards. "You spineless pieces of shit, I will fucking kill you all for what you have done to her!" Cairo and I don't get a chance, Cole's wolf leaps past us and his jaws clamp around one of the guy's neck and takes him down, his scream is cut off when Cole shakes his head and rips his throat out. Cole isn't done, he spits the flesh from his mouth and turns to the other guy with blood dripping down his jaws. The guy is shaking like a leaf and so close to pissing himself, he raises his hands in the air and tries to plead his case but is cut off when Ro speaks.

"Why the fuck isn't she healing?" He darts his gaze between me, Cole and Ro.

"I-it's the sedative." That's all we needed to hear, Cole takes him down and he's dead within a minute. Cole shifts back and stands in front of me with blood still dripping down his chin and chest. He runs his gaze over Jess, and I see the war in his eyes, he wants to help her but he doesn't know how.

"Sweetheart, we'll kill every last one of them." Jess is still a writhing mess in my arms, her heart rate is low we need to move now and get her help.

"We have to go, she needs a doctor." I snap.

"We have to take her back to the island; Al will treat her."

"That's a four fucking day trip Vince, look at her she doesn't have four days!" Cairo is right, I can hear how slow her heart is beating and her pulse is slowing. She needs help now; we will never make it to the island. Cairo turns to Sky, and they share a loaded look before Ro sighs in relief and turns to Vince. "Cole, you drive. Creed, you and Sky in the back, Vince you and the others get the cars and meet us at the boats we're taking her to your doctor." I open my mouth to protest but Cairo cuts me off. "Trust me Creed, I would never let my sister die." The conviction in his voice gives me pause, I look down at Jess and nod. I move toward the back of the car and each step I take she whimpers or flinches in pain, I fight the urge to tighten my hold on her. I slide into the backseat and cringe when she shouts in pain from the movement, Cairo closes the door and hops in the front as Sky gets in beside me and Jess. Cole jumps in whilst pulling up his pants and we speed toward the docks. I keep my gaze on Jess the whole time, guilt eats away at me, I should have been there to protect her! My mate lays here dying in my arms and I can't do a fucking thing about it!

"Hold on princess, don't leave me, I need you." A tear drips down my cheek as the reality of the situation kicks in. I was so focused on finding her that I didn't even begin to think about what she had to endure in her time away from us. She was with them for nearly a week, and this is what they did to her! Cairo turns in the front seat so he can see both Cole and I, the look on his face makes me uneasy. "You said to trust you and I am, now how the hell are you going to help her?"

"I'm not."

"The fuck does that mean, Ro?" Cole yells.

"It's because of how much I love my sister why I am about to let you both in on my sacred secret. If either of you two breathe a fucking word about this to anyone I will slit both your fucking throats and help my sister search for your killer." I stare at him in shock.

"The fuck is wrong with you?" I snap.

"All of you shut up, if you want her to live you will agree to his terms!" I look at Sky then meet my brothers gaze in the rearview mirror.

We don't have a choice; I won't lose her Cole.

Agreed, we keep their secret in order to save her.

I close the link between us and both Cole and I agree to Cairo's terms, he looks to Sky, and she nods her head.

"Thank you."

"I won't do this again Ro, do you understand."

"Yes, I swear this is the one and only time Sky, I swear."

"Fine." Sky turns in her seat and lifts her hands placing them on either side of Jess's head, Jess flinches. "I'm sorry Jess, I'll make it all go away I promise." I watch Sky in confusion, her mouth is moving but no words come out her eyes close for a second and then snap open. My eyes widen in shock, her eyes are completely white, I feel pulses of energy coming from her. I feel Jess begin to relax in my arms and her jaw finally starts to loosen. Sky continues for at least twenty minutes, and everyone in the car remains silent, Cole keeps sneaking glances in the mirror to see what is happening. I see a strain begin to spread over Sky's face, her forehead furrows and her brows begin to pinch together as her eyes begin to blink rapidly. Jess hasn't stirred once even as we hit bumps or potholes in the road, whatever Sky is doing it's taking away Jess's pain.

"Reign it in Sky." Cairo has his gaze laser focused on his beta; he waits for her to stop but when she doesn't he firms his voice. "I said stop!" Sky shakes her head and a moment later I feel the energy that was pulsing from her body start to fade. Another minute passes and she drops her hands as her eyes return to their normal muddy brown color. She slumps forward and rests her head between her knees inhaling deep breaths. Everyone remains silent as we wait for Sky to speak. After five minutes I look to Ro and see his gaze is still focused on Sky, I see the worry in his eyes, and it sparks so many questions inside me. "Skylar?"

A whoosh of air escapes Sky before she answers. "I'm okay.... just give me a few more minutes." Ro growls and reaches over to place his hand on her shoulder blade.

"Siphon me now."

"Cairo, no."

"I said *now*." Sky slowly lifts her head and slouches back against the seat and stares at Ro. "Sky, you exerted yourself, now take it from me." I can't help but stare at the pair of them, Sky searches Ro's gaze for what I'm not sure, but whatever she sees has her nodding her head. She leans forward to clasp Ro's face between her hands and speaks.

"This is the last time, I mean it." Ro nods, and what happens next is not what I fucking expected. Sky smashes her lips against Ro's and.... kisses him! I meet Cole's gaze in the mirror and see he is just as fucking shocked as I am. I expected them to stop after a minute but when they don't I clear my throat a couple times to give them the fucking hint to stop! When they finally do, they both break apart as if something shocked them, both panting and breathing hard. Ro turns around and stares out his window, Sky does the same and the tension in the car soars to new heights. I don't have the emotional capacity to deal with what just happened so instead I focus on Jess; I reach down to cup her face in my hand. I try to feel for our mate bond, but I can't locate it, it's like it's not even there anymore.

We reach the docs before the others, we only stopped for fuel and that was it. I tried to get Jess to drink some water, but each time I tried she either spat it out or choked. I fucking hate this, nothing I seem to do helps her, I only seem to make shit worse. She choked and coughed that hard it caused her nose to bleed, she hasn't stirred or even muttered a single word!

Chapter Thirty One
Jessica

I can feel his body heat.

I hear his voice.

I hear his heartbeat against my ear.

But I'm so exhausted, my eyes refuse to open, and I can't seem to get my voice to work. I keep drifting in and out of consciousness, when I feel the darkness coming to claim me again, I let it, but before I fall into a dreamless slumber, I hear him whisper.

"Come back to me princess, I can't live without you please fight baby, our son needs his mother."

Chapter Thirty Two
Credence

I can see the cargo ship in the distance and sigh in relief, we didn't wait for the others. Cairo mind linked Zeke and told him we will meet him on the island. Jess hasn't moved or even stirred; Cole has pushed the boat to its limit. Instead of it taking us three days, its only taken us two and bit to get back. Jess is so dehydrated and needs to be on an IV stat, we have tried to get fluids into her, but she won't take it. The stench of rotting flesh assaults me as we draw near the cargo ship, and I quickly change to breathing through my mouth. As we approach the island, I notice guards lining the shore and my hackles start to rise. Cole docks the boat and Ro quickly jumps out to tie us off, but before we leave the boat Sky blocks our exit. She pins Cole and I both with a stern look before saying.

"What you saw never happened, what happened after what you *didn't* see also didn't happen." Cole and I both nod and she steps aside, Cairo reaches out for Jess, and I reluctantly pass her over. As soon as I'm on the dock Ro shoots off toward the island, he snaps at the guards lining the beach to get the doctor. The guard takes one look at Jess and motions for us to follow him, we keep pace with the guard as we run. I cringe when I see Jess jostling in Cairo's embrace but at least she isn't screaming in pain.

"What the fuck...." I turn toward where Cole is looking, the outside of the hall is littered with injured bodies on stretches with both vamps and shifters administering aid to them. My stomach sinks, when the guard motions for us to enter the hall and that the doctor is inside, I turn to Cole and Sky.

"I need you two to find Harlem, he should be with mom and Callie." They both nod and take off toward Davina's house.

I follow Cairo inside and gasp, more bodies line the inside of the hall, it's been turned into a makeshift hospital.

"I need a doctor, now!" Cairo roars above the noise, his tone bleeds with his alpha power and I watch as shifters bow their heads, even members from my pack bow their heads. A man pushes through the throngs of bodies, he looks like he is close to my age. Blond hair, dark blue eyes that are hidden behind thick black framed glasses. He clicks his fingers and motions for a woman to follow him, he stops in front of Ro and pulls out a slender pen looking thing, he clicks a button and I realize then it's a torch. He tries to open her left eye but its swollen shut, he moves to the right, and it only opens slightly, he flicks the torch side to side and places fingers against her neck timing her heartbeats at the same time.

"Jackie set up a bed and get me some IV bags and some morphine. She will need a CT scan and an X-ray to check for internal bleeding."

"Yes sir." Jackie scurries away as the guy stands there running his gaze over Jess.

"Has she been conscious?" He asks.

"No, she hasn't said a word or even drank."

"Right, follow me." I remain silent as the doctor leads the way; I can't seem to get any words out of my mouth. I run my gaze over the injured as we pass by, What the fuck happened here? "Place her down on the bed." Cairo does as the doctor says and places her on a hospital bed. "Now stand back and stay out of the way." I grit my teeth at his order, Cairo growls in warning. The doctor pins Cairo with an angry glare. "You may rule shit out there, but in here I'm the boss. You get in my way, and I will have you removed, am I clear?" I look at the man in shock, he has some big balls talking to us like that. Cairo and I both nod and stand back as we watch the doctor and Jackie place monitors on Jess, he pulls a metal tray table over and grabs a pair of scissors. I grind my teeth together and fight back the growl that wants to break free as I watch him cut my mates shirt open.

"Sir, I have her IV fluids and morphine drip set up."

"Good, get Gene and Chloe and let them know we need to transfer her to the clinic."

"Yes sir." Jackie leaves and I stand there stiff as shit as I watch him begin to cut her pants from her body. I slam my eyes closed and take deep breaths, I'm a wolf and wolves fucking hate watching another male touch their mate. I keep reminding myself that he isn't touching her in that way, he is trying to help her.

"Shit." I snap my eyes open in worry.

"Shit? What the hell do you mean shit?" Cairo barks.

"She has mass infections, and her pulse is dropping, we need to put an intubation tube in. Jackie, I need you here now." Jackie and another lady rush in, we stand by and watch as the doctor prods her with another needle and the two nurses move toward her head, the new nurse holds her head straight while Jackie has this metal reaper looking thing in her hand and opens Jess's mouth, that's when I lose it.

"What the fuck are you doing?" The doctor snaps his gaze to me and then shouts.

"Dylan, Brock, I need you to remove these two immediately." I glare at the doctor and open my mouth to give him a piece of my mind, but he cuts in. "Unless you want her to die, you will get the hell out! We will do everything we can to save her, but we can't work with you lot hanging around, now leave!" I turn to Jess and my heart breaks; her body is on full display and every inch of it is covered in bruises and cuts. When the machine starts to beep and the doctor curses, I decide to trust in them to save the love of my life. I grip his arm and spin him around ignoring the two goons he called over when they try to grab me.

"Do whatever you have to, make sure she lives, or you are the first one I come for." I release him and shoulder check the two vamps on my way out, fuck them! I hear Cairo behind me but don't stop, I need to occupy my mind, or I'll go back inside and tear the docs fucking throat out. The rational part of my brain knows he is doing his job, but the other part of me that doesn't give a fuck, wants him to work faster and tell me she will be okay, it's the not knowing is what's killing me.

Creed, you need to come to Davina's now.

On my way

The urgency in Cole's voice has me sprinting the whole way there with Cairo right beside me, he doesn't ask questions just follows. When we get to Davina's I see the front door is wide open and hanging off its hinges, I burst through and follow the sound of voices, we pass a living room and an office and then emerge into a sterile looking kitchen.

"Daddy!" I turn to the left and smile wide; relief washes over me when I see that my boy is unharmed. Mom puts him on his feet and he runs as fast as his little legs will carry him, I scoop him up and hold him tight. I look around and notice that it's only Davina, mom, Cole, Callie and Sky here, my mom and my sister look like shit, and I'll even admit that Davina looks a bit rough.

"What happened?" I ask, no one seems to want to look at me and that pisses me off. "Someone better start talking, I don't have the patients for this shit right now!" Davina is the one to meet my gaze, I note the dried blood on her lip and how her brown hair is out of place almost like someone had pulled it.

"You were right, they attacked the night that you left." A growl escapes me and Cairo.

"How did the council get here?"

"The council didn't Creed."

"The hell does that mean Davina?"

"It means that we were betrayed by our own men. People from both the packs and even some of my own men done this, they came for us--"

"They tried to take my son?" I roar, Harlem whimpers in my hold, shit! Mom rushes over and reaches out for him, I turn, and a crestfallen look over comes her features. Fuck!

"He doesn't need to hear this son; he has already seen enough, please let me take him." I look at mom in silence, her eyes are saying so much but I just can't seem to let Harlem go. I begin to shake my head but stop when Cairo gently eases mom out of the way and stands in front of me.

"Hey monster, come give Ro-Ro some love my man." Harlem wiggles in my hold trying to turn so he can go to his uncle, I glare at Cairo. "Creed, he isn't my sister, and you clinging to him won't change anything. Let him go with your mom so we can deal with this, then you have to shift and sort your shit out before going to see my sister."

"Mommy! I wanna go see mommy, now!" Shit, Harlem begins to wail and struggle against my hold, Cairo reaches out and pulls him from me. He turns around and places Harlem on the countertop and bends so they are eye level.

"Monster, mommy needs to rest okay. The doctor is making mommy better--"

"I want mommy Ro-Ro!" It shatters my heart to see the tears fall down his cheeks and devastated look in his eyes. Cole moves toward them and clucks his nephew on the chin, Harlem turns watery eyes to Cole.

"Tell ya what, if you go with grandma, I bet she will make those cookies you like."

"I don't want it; I want my mommy." Sobs begin to wrack Harlem's body; I have no fucking idea what to do or say.

"I'll make you a deal, if you go with your grandma and bake cookies and be a good boy, I'll go see doc and ask if he will let you see your mom." All eyes turn to Davina; even Harlem is smiling at her.

"Promise?" Davina's features soften as she looks at my boy.

"I promise, I'll call doc as soon as I finish talking to your dad." Harlem nods and smiles his thanks; my mom picks him up and pats me on the chest as she leaves with my son. I know I'm not father of the year and I really am trying to learn how to care for my son, but I would be so fucking lost if I didn't have my family and friends.

"They took Shelley, Dela and your.... father."

"How the fuck did they get off the island?"

"It was an inside job Creed; I couldn't stop them!"

"Why the fuck not Davina?" This is the first time I have seen any real emotion from her, I can see her anger shining as bright as the sun in her hazel eyes.

"Because I was protecting your mother and son, that's why! I made a choice, and I don't fucking regret it. If it wasn't for me your mother and son would be gone as well." I stumble back a step in shock. I look to my sister who nods, confirming Davina is telling the truth.

"Why didn't they take Harlem?" Cairo utters.

"Because I told them he was my son and the monster confirmed it when they asked. He stuck to the same story we taught him." I hate that my son had to learn from birth that he can never be honest about who his parents are, but right now I am so fucking thankful. "Whoever they are had no idea what they were doing, almost everyone on this island knows Harlem is Jess's son but these idiots didn't."

"Who were they?"

"I don't know Cole; they all wore masks; it was their scents that gave them away." I grind my teeth together.

"Why the hell did they take those three?" I voice allowed and I'm surprised when Davina answers me.

"Punishment, they will take Shelley and Dela back to the council where they will be punished. They took your father to lure you out, it's a trap." She isn't wrong, I look to Ro and see he has his fists clenched at his sides. He may not be okay with Shelley lying and hiding all these years but at the end of the day it's still his mother.

"We have to do a head count, figure out who is missing from both the packs and your men. We'll find out then who betrayed us, we will also need to move because this location is now compromised." I'm in awe of Sky right now, she sounds like an alpha in her own right.

"Agreed, then we need to look into how many numbers we have left. With Shelley and Dela gone, we can't rely on the people she had on land to help us." I turn to Cairo and quirk a brow, he sighs before continuing. "If they have more numbers than us then we need to reach out to the other packs."

"The fuck would we do that for?" I grit out.

"Because some of them may feel like we do, if we can convince them to join us, we will begin to build numbers and maybe have a chance of fucking winning this war." As much as it pains me to admit it, Cairo is right, we need numbers if we are we are going to take the fight to them.

"Who absorbs the packs?" That is the million-dollar question Colton. You see if an alpha challenges an alpha, and one dies in the battle, then the victor automatically to claims his pack.

Chapter Thirty Three
Jessica

I feel like I've been living in a bad dream, a dream where my wolf is no longer with me. My chest aches at the thought of losing Sheba, we may not have been getting along but she is a part of me!

Beep, beep, beep.

The sound of something beeping nearby rouses me from my slumber and I regret it immediately. My whole body is aching and every breath I take burns, the pain I'm feeling is so terrible I can't even describe it. Then it all comes back to me, it wasn't a nightmare it actually happened me! I push those thoughts away as I try to open my eyes I manage to open my right eye halfway but my left eye is still swollen shut. I scan the area and notice I'm in an old...office but it's been turned into a makeshift hospital room. I try to lift my head but end up gagging, that's when I notice there is a tube shoved down my throat and begin to cough and splutter as I try to figure out how the hell to get this thing out before I choke to death.

"She's awake!" I look to the side and see a middle-aged woman rushing toward me, she grabs my hands and pins them on the bed either of side of me. "Jess, you need to stop." I narrow my eye at her. "The doctor is coming now to remove it, if you pull it out it can cause you harm and damage you internally." A man comes into view and I shrink away when he raises his hand, his brow furrows but he doesn't stop undoing the straps on this thing down my throat.

"Jess, my name is Al, and I am the doctor here on the island. Gene is going to let go now but I need you to remain still so we can remove the tube, can you do that?" Island? I furrow my brow at the doctor and the expression on my face is a clear indication of what I'm asking. "You're back on the island Jess, you are safe, but I have to take this out now, okay?" I try to nod as best as I can, he finishes undoing whatever it is and then begins to slowly pull the tube out, I try not to gag but it's a losing battle. As soon as he pulls the last bit of tube out the woman Gene wraps her arm around my shoulders and lifts me into a sitting position as I gag and spit all over myself, the pain in my ribs burns but I'm powerless to stop myself from gagging. The doctor hands me a plastic cup of water after I finish my gag fit, I gulp the liquid gold but wind up coughing it up everywhere. "Slow sips Jess, your throat will be raw for a few days." I nod and attempt to swallow, when I don't choke, I take another few sips until the cup is empty.

"Well done, Jess, I'm gonna incline your bed to a 90-degree angle so you'll be able to lean back." I nod my thanks to Gene as she pushes a button on the side of the bed and within seconds, I'm able to lean backward. My ribs protest the movement but its better leaning back then hunched over and putting pressure on them.

"Okay Jess, if it's okay with you I'm gonna check you over?"

"Y-y." I clear my throat and wince, Al smiles as he waits for me to try again. "Yeah." I know he is about to approach me and I try to prepare myself for the examination but as soon as he raises his hand toward my face I shrink back, he drops his hand immediately and sits in the chair beside my bed.

"You have been through hell, and I empathize with you, I really do Jess. But in order for me to make sure everything is functioning I'm gonna need to touch you, I swear I'll limit skin to skin contact as much as I can." Gratitude fills me, tears cloud my eye as I nod for him to proceed. I sit here stiff and tense, waiting for him to begin, I jerk when I feel a hand land on top my mine and turn toward Gene, she has a warm smile on her face but I can see recognition in her eyes.

"It gets easier honey; it'll take a while, but it will get easier to stand the touch of another." I furrow my brow at her.

"I-I don't understand." I wheeze out.

"You went through a traumatic ordeal; it will take time to heal not only physically but mentally hon. Don't push yourself, take each day as it comes." I blink back my tears and nod my head; I clutch Gene's hand in mine and close my eye as Al continues. Gene squeezes my hand reassuringly. "Just breath honey." I do as she says and focus on my breathing.

In and out, in and out.

"All done." I pop my eye open and stare at Al, the checkup didn't even hurt. "Sorry, I meant all done with your facial check, I just need to check the cuts on your arms and legs and the binding around your ribs." I nod my head and watch as he checks the cuts on my arms, I refuse to let Gene's hand go as she stands there pacifying with me. When he moves to my legs I begin to tremble, I try to fight it but I'm powerless in my own body! "I only need to check from the knees down Jess."

"O-okay." I remain stiff and tense until he pulls the blanket back down over my legs. Al and Gene share a look of concern I can see the hesitation in her eyes.

"Jess, I have to check the binding around your ribs so for me to do that your gown has to be lifted. I can help you with that while Al steps out?" I hold her gaze for a long moment unsure if I can do this or not. I know I wasn't raped, but a part of me knows that was the next step if I didn't take Kayla's advice and surrender. I take in lungful's of air and ignore the searing pain in my ribs as I nod. I hear the door click shut when Al leaves, Gene helps me lift the gown and I pause to see the binding covers my breasts as well, Gene see's the panic on my face. "I did the binding hon; Al doesn't do that side of it." A whoosh of air escapes me and I smile my thanks as she calls out to Al. He enters and I focus on my breathing as he nears, he raises his hands so I can see them, and I am grateful for that.

"Okay Jess, this might be a bit painful but please try and bear with me, you have broken ribs on both sides, and I just want to make sure that the binding is secure."

"Okay." I flinch when he touches the ribs on my left side, a hiss escapes me, and I bite down on my bottom lip. The door opens and a loud growl sounds out, my eyes double in size when I see a shirtless Creed standing there brimming with rage. I spot my brother and Cole behind him, and my heart starts to beat faster than normal. Creed swings his gaze to me, and his growls stop immediately, his eyes change from his wolf's back to his normal hazel color. He moves to enter the room and I tighten my hold on Gene's hand, fear grips me, because I know he wants to touch me, and right now I can't handle the thought of his hands on me.

"Stop!" Everyone turns to look at Gene. "You three need to wait outside until we are finished."

"Fuck that, she's, my mate!" I look back to Creed and freeze, he makes his way toward me, but Al blocks his path. "Unless you want me to fuck up that pretty boy face of yours, I suggest you get the fuck out of my way!" The anger in his voice causes me to shake, I can't take this right now.

"This is my clinic and so long as she is in my care what I say goes. Now the three of you need to leave before I have you escorted out."

"You son of a--"Ro cuts Creed off.

"Enough, if smalls wanted us here, she would have said something. Give her some time, we're here if you need us sis." Al blocks my view of the guys, but my heart warms at my brothers understanding. Another growl sounds out around the room, and I know Creed is pissed.

"I'll be back in an hour." Then I hear him storm out and the door slam closed behind him.

"Your mate is a real.... charmer." I snort at Al's attempt at a joke.

Chapter Thirty Four
Credence

I pace back and forth in the stupid waiting area; it's been two days since Jess woke up and she still refuses to see me. I brought Harlem here yesterday, but the know-it-all nurse Gene refused to allow us in because he shouldn't see his mother in this state, I don't care if she is right, she won't leave Jess, which means I have had no chance of sneaking in there to see her. The doctor said if I kept threatening him or his staff, he would stop treating Jess, that earnt me a fist to the face from fucking Cairo. Cole has been riding my ass as well about giving her space and being the fucking alpha. I know my pack needs me, but so does Jess, half my pack was injured in the chaos that erupted on the island. Thankfully everyone from my pack lived, but Davina's guys weren't as lucky, she lost at least twelve. We managed to learn from some of the others that four boats came with wolves, Davina is trying to locate another residence for us to reside, but it is proving harder than she thought.

I stop my pacing at the sound of a door opening and wait with bated breath, I fight back a growl when I see Gene. She narrows her eyes at me and shakes her head as she approaches, she motions for me to follow her over to the waiting room chairs and sits down. I want information on Jess, so I do as she says and sit down.

"You need to give her time." I glare at the woman.

"I need to see her; my wolf won't rest until we can be with her."

"She isn't ready for you yet Creed--"

"The fuck is that supposed to mean?" She rolls her eyes and takes a steadying breath as if I'm a pain in her ass which just pisses me off. Corbin protests at this woman is acting like she has a right to look down her nose at me.

"She went through something that no person should ever have to endure, she has PTSD and is plagued by nightmares." My chest constricts, Corbin growls in my mind. "She needs time to heal, at this very moment the thought of someone touching her scares the living daylights out of her. I'm not trying to keep you from her, she has requested that Al and I keep everyone away. You have to respect her wishes, if you go barging in there you will set her back. She will call for you when she's ready, let her deal with this how she sees fit." I hear everything she is saying and as much as I want to ignore it and give into Corbin's demands about storming in that room and taking our mate, I can't. I sigh and drop my head into my hands, how did things get so fucked up? I never wanted any of this, all I wanted was to unite the two packs and live my life. Finding out Jess is my mate was a shock, but I don't regret it and I don't for a second regret my son, but when is it time for us to finally live freely and not have to go through anymore fighting. I snap out of my thoughts when I feel a hand on my shoulder, I turn to see Gene smiling at me sadly. "Can I give you some advice?" I nod my head jerkily. "Distract yourself, go be an alpha and a dad. I promise you I will look after her."

"Thank you." Gene pats my shoulder and stands to head back to Jess, but I call out to her, she turns to me. "Can you tell her...I love her and...I'm sorry this happened." She nods and continues on her way. She's right, I need to deal with my pack and help Davina find somewhere safe for us to move.

I summon for my wolves to meet me at the beach, I stand here and stare at all of them in front of me. They all wear looks of fear and anger, I don't blame them, I have let them down time and time again since Jess went missing five years ago. I have to make this right, I spot my mom and the twins at the back, mom smiles reassuringly at me. I left Harlem with Cairo; I didn't want him here in case the pack decided to turn on me. I clear my throat a couple of times hoping for their attention, but when that fails, I open the mind link to my pack.

Enough! Silence descends as they all stare at me, I scan each and every one of them. My heart aches when I see for the first time how many members we have lost, some of my pack fled with the traitors and now only thirty or so of us remain. Cairo has about eighty wolves with him, I think last he checked, but it isn't enough for us to take out the whole shifter population if the council decides to call for war.

"I know shit has been bad, I'm trying to fix it--"

"Bullshit, all you have done is chase your mates' tail. You abandoned us Creed!" I turn to Chris; he is one of the older shifters in our pack. He may be right, but I am the alpha, and I cannot let that slide.

"If you think you can do a better job, then challenge me!" Gasps and murmurs break out, I spy my brother out of the corner of my eye making his way toward me. I quirk a brow at Chris taunting him, I have so much pent-up rage inside me I will welcome his challenge. When he doesn't respond I release an impatient growl, Corbin is bristling inside me and demanding that I shift and put my pack in their place but all he will do is scare them and I don't want to be *that* alpha who rules in fear rather than respect. Chris drops his gaze and then reluctantly bows his head in a show of submission, as do the others. I take a deep breath and square my shoulders; my pack is in dire need of me to lead. "My mate has been through hell, and I will continue to be there for her, but I want you all to know that from this day forth the pack will not suffer because of my lack of attention."

"Alpha, may I speak freely?" I nod my head to one of the women to speak up. "Is it true that your mate is the true alpha to both packs?" I bristle at her words, but I can't deny that she speaks the truth.

"Yes, Jess is the rightful alpha to both the Reeves and the Michaelson packs. When and if my mate is ready to take over, I will guide her and help her to be the best alpha she--"I stop speaking as murmurs break out and glare when I see that none of the pack are even looking at me, I turn and follow their gaze, my mouth drops open in shock. Jess is walking--limping toward us with Cairo, Zeke and Sky forming a sort of blockage around her. It takes everything inside me not to run to her and whisk her away so I can check her over myself, but the look on her face tells me it would only set her back further. I may not like Gene but looking at Jess right now tells me everything she had said is right, Jess needs to do this on her own and I can't be the one to fix this for her. I wish I was able to take all her pain and suffering away, the four of them stop within a few feet between us, Cairo steps back and stands beside his sister, keeping a foot of space between them, Sky and Zeke do the same on her other side. The murmurs stop and everyone stands there and stares at Jess with wide eyes, bruises still mar her beautiful face, the short sleeve shirt she wears displays the bruises on her arms, her face is littered with cuts and bruises as well but at least her other eye is open slightly now. I run my gaze down her body, but her lower half is covered by jeans, she trembles as she takes each breath which tells me her ribs are hurting.

Corbin, why isn't she healing?

I...I can't sense Sheba

What the hell does that mean? Anger and worry begin to soar inside me.

I can't sense her wolf...at all.

I close the link and stare at Jess, Sheba should have been able to heal all her superficial wounds. Any broken bones would have taken a couple of days to heal but Jess isn't healing at shifter speed, she's like a...human.

"My name is Jessica Hastings, I'm Creeds...mate." I detect a bit of hesitance in her voice admitting she is my mate, the pack look at her with pity and anger. They're angry that someone they consider pack was taken and none of us could stop it. I'm so proud of her for doing this, I know leading isn't something she ever wanted to do but watching her stand there with her head held high and the determined look on her face has pride swelling inside me. "I haven't come here to demand anything of you, I will not force anything upon any of you. I may be the rightful alpha but that doesn't mean I am the right alpha. I...I just want us all to be able to live in peace, I know some of you have guessed and some don't even know but Creed and I have a son." Murmurs break out and I release a growl of annoyance making all of them clamp their mouths closed. "I want to raise our son in a real home, I want him to go to school and have a normal life. But in order for that to happen we need to put an end to the council and their reign of terror. I know some of you are fearful and unsure at what happens next, honestly so am I. But if we have any chance of reclaiming our lives and pack lands, it's imperative we work together, visiting other packs and asking for their help will be a start."

"Why?" I can't see who asked that question.

"Because we don't have the numbers, I won't lie to you. With Shelley and Dela being taken we don't have the numbers Shelley had promised us, even with the vampires fighting at our side, it still isn't enough. If we can get other packs to join us, maybe it won't have to come to a fight--."

"The council won't back down, no one has ever done it. We may despise what they have done, but they are stronger as a whole than any pack." Jess doesn't seem angered by April's question.

"No, they won't, but we won't either. They took our homes from us; they took our loved ones from us, and I don't know about any of you but I sure as hell will not let them take anything from me again. This I promise, I will reclaim my father's pack from Jacob and the council will be stopped even if it is the last thing I do. You all have a choice, fight with us or don't. If you do, I cannot guarantee that you will make it out alive, if you choose not to, then all I ask is that you help the others by taking over their daily duties. When this is all said and done, everyone will be welcomed back to pack lands, not just those that fought for it." Jess was born for this. "One more thing, if anyone and I mean anyone, shifter or vampire tries to use my son against me or his father to bargain their freedom from the council, I will kill you. I will not offer second chances when it comes to my son's safety." Corbin growls his approval and so do my siblings as well as Cairo. Cairo steps forward and eyes my pack with a fierce look.

"My pack will fight with you, so will the vampires, training is a must. We have six weeks before we leave this island, there will be round the clock guards scoping the area every second until we can get a ship here big enough to move everyone. You have until tomorrow morning to make your decision, if you choose to fight, then we meet behind the large hall." When Jess and the others turn to leave, I quickly follow her, but Cole slaps a hand on my shoulder and shakes his head.

"Let her go brother, she will come back to you when she is ready." Then it hits me.

"If Cairo was here then where the hell is Harlem?" Cole and I both take off after the four of them.

CHAPTER
THIRTY FIVE
Jessica

"Princess!" I halt in my tracks with my back to him, I feel Zeke and Cairo move in closer to shadow me. I hate that I feel the need to hide from him but I'm scared. "Where's Harlem?" I open my mouth, but words fail me.

"Davina is watching him." Cairo answers, Creed releases an angry growl and I flinch.

"That wasn't your fucking call!" I stay still as he moves toward us, shivers run down my spine, I'm shocked when I see him and Cole running right past us in the direction of Davina's house. Guilt begins to gnaw at me, I sigh and follow after them at a much slower place. My body is begging for me to stop and rest but I refuse to give in, anger begins to build inside me. I refuse to lay in that bed any longer, I want revenge for what Jacob did to me. I will not let him break me, seeing Cairo today gave me the courage to face my demons head on and take back control of my life. Jacob didn't break me, and I won't let what happen to me dictate the rest of my life, I'll face my fears and conquer every bloody one of them!

By the time we reach Davina's house we can hear shouting from the inside, Zeke doesn't bother knocking as he pushes the front door open and strolls in. We follow him in and head toward what I assume is the living room. The closer we get I can now distinguish that the two raised voices belong to Creed and Davina, I brush past Zeke when he stops to scan the room. Creed and Davina are standing at either ends of the room glaring at each other and Cole stands in the middle against the wall with Harlem clutched in his arms.

"He was perfectly fine with me!" Creed scoffs and rolls his eyes.

"How the bloody hell would you know how to look after a kid? Tell me Davina what experience do you have exactly?" I cringe, Creed is really angry and even if he is right, he shouldn't be speaking to her like that in front of an audience. This conversation should be just the two of them.

"Cole, can I please have my son?" I can feel Creed's gaze burning into the side of my head, but I keep my gaze on his brother. I can see he is hesitant and unsure, he heads toward me but is stopped when Creed blocks his path. I have no choice but to meet his gaze and when my eyes meet his something inside me cracks. I make sure to keep my face blank of any emotion.

"You are not taking him anywhere." His words hit me like a whip.

"Creed--"

"No Jess, you want time to yourself then that's fine, but you are not taking my son from me as well." If I wasn't in so much pain I would stomp my foot, instead I clench my fist and snarl at him, it is taking every bit of strength I have to remain standing.

"I just want to see him Creed."

"Then see him, but he isn't hiding away with you." Zeke and my brother both release growls of anger.

"I'm not hiding!" I try to defend myself, Creed scoffs.

"Bullshit, you've been hiding since the day you woke up." My mask falters, I feel tears begin to build in the back of my eyes. "Why the fuck are you hiding?"

"I am not, I came--"

"Don't you dare lie to me! I know Cairo has been coming to see you, I am going to ask you again Jessica. Why the fuck are you hiding from me?" The heartache in his voice is my undoing, tears cascade down my cheeks. Creed mutters a curse and then closes the space between us, he cups my face gently and tilts until I meet his gaze. His hazel eyes swim with so much hurt and pain, I never wanted to hurt him. "Princess, please don't shut me out, I need you." My resolve cracks and the words start to tumble out.

"I gave up, I fought as long as I could but then I just...gave up. I felt so fucking helpless, I just wanted the pain to stop. I did everything Ro and the others taught me, I baited them, and I never made a sound as they tried to break me but the last time...I knew I couldn't take anymore. I thought if I let go I could be with Katy and Harlem would be okay with you." Creed stands there staring at me like I'm demented, I grind my teeth to stop the sobs from breaking free.

"You didn't give up. You fought back; you chose to stay with us because--"I cut Creed off.

"I didn't, I would have let them finish me off if Kayla hadn't of warned me what was coming next." Creeds sharp intake of breath tells me he knows exactly what I am insinuating.

"What the fuck was next, smalls?" I plead with my eyes for Creed to answer my brother, he drops his hands from my face and gently pulls me against him. I wrap my tired arms around him and breath in his scent, he smells like home. "What was next?" I stiffen in Creed's hold at the anger in my brother's voice.

"He wanted to break her, clearly beating her wasn't working so he wanted to break her in another way." The disgust in Sky's voice is so prominent.

"I'll fucking kill that slimy bastard!" I ignore my brother as Creed pulls back and stares at me, he runs his thumbs under my eyes brushing away my tears.

"Are you hiding from me because... did they?" It takes a second for me to understand what he is asking.

"No, something happened and then I was moved from the cell to a car and then I blacked out." Relief crosses his features.

"Why are you hiding from me Jess?" I search his gaze and when I see nothing but love I know I need to come clean.

"I thought if you knew that I gave up you wouldn't want... I thought--I mean I thought you wouldn't want me as your mate anymore, and I assumed staying away would make it easier for you to end things." Anger crosses his face, and his eyes begin to turn blue, I try to pull away, but he holds me firm. I hear Ro and the others step forward, but Creed releases a growl in warning.

"You listen to me now and you listen fucking good, okay?" I nod my head stiffly. "I will never, and I mean never reject the mate bond between you and I, I meant what I said. I love you Jess, and I will never fucking let you go, I will annihilate anyone who tries to come between us, you fought fucking hard. You endured more than most men could ever handle, you Jessica Hastings are one bad mother-wolf and don't you ever forget it!" This time I can't stop the sob that tears out of me, I wrap my arms around him and cry into his chest. I know he meant every word, I felt it in my bones. I'm crying because I'm scared to tell him that I don't know if I'm a wolf anymore, I haven't felt Sheba inside me, no matter how hard I try to pull on the thread we share. I have seen Ro a couple of times, I thought he would be the easier one to voice my darkest thoughts to about what might happen if Sheba isn't with me. Creed pulls back after I've pulled myself together, How about I go deal with the pack and finish up with them and you take Harlem home, I'll meet you there as soon as I finish--"

"I want to train and fight as well." I cut in. Creed sucks in a sharp intake of air and darts his gaze over my head to my brother, I despise the fact that he looks to Cairo for permission. "I don't need my brothers blessing, it wasn't a question, I was just letting you know what is about to happen." Creed gnaws on his bottom trying to fight a smile, I glare up at him.

"As you wish princess."

I've been sitting outside in the lounger since Ro, Zeke, Sky, Harlem and I got back to the house. It fills my heart with joy that my little boy isn't scared of me even though I look like crap, his concern melts me. He touched my face gently and when his eyes met mine, I swear I heard a growl escape him. I'm still too sore to play out in the yard with him, but Zeke and Cairo didn't mind taking on that task, it brings me joy to see my son so happy. I smile wide when Harlem squeals and tries to run away from Z pretending to be a monster who eats little boy's, Cairo pretends to die when Z playfully punches him in the stomach. I forgot Sky was sitting by me until she shuffles in her seat, I turn to her, and I can see it in her face that she has something to say. I know this has been hard for her, she doesn't like being around people and from what Ro has told me Callie plans to asks Creed if she can leave the Reeves pack and stay with Sky. I honestly don't know how Creed will handle that, he is a control freak and letting his little sister go will be hard for him.

"Sky, please just say whatever is on your mind." She keeps her eyes on the guys and Harlem as she speaks.

"In order to go against the council, we need the other packs to help us." I furrow my brow not understanding why she seems so riled up about this. "Which alpha do you think will take the packs?"

"I don't understand what you're asking me?" She finally turns to face me and the look in her eyes sends a shiver down my spine.

"Creed is an alpha; you are an alpha heir, but Cairo is also an alpha. Who exactly will the packs bow to and follow?" I mull over her words for a moment, I never actually thought about that. I don't want to be alpha, never have. From the way things are now I doubt anyone will care about the fact that Cairo and I are both from two different alpha lines. I gasp and my eyes widen when I get what Sky is actually saying.

"You want me and Cairo to take over the packs, why?" A sly smile graces her face.

"Cairo loves you and he would go to hell and back for you, and I believe you would do the same for him." I nod my head firmly; I would do anything for my brother. "If you both lead the packs, and the council is taken down then there will never be a battle over land or power again. If Creed becomes alpha to the packs and one day decides he wants Cairo to submit to him, what do you think would happen?"

"That's enough Sky." We both turn to face my brother; he

is standing mere feet from us, She climbs to her feet and pins my brother with a determined look, Cairo holds her gaze and I'm surprised that he isn't bristling at her holding eye contact.

"You know I'm right; I will not risk your life Cairo. Creed needs to back down and let you and Jess lead the packs like it has always supposed to have been." Ro darts his gaze to me briefly before focusing on Sky, again.

"Now isn't the time--"Sky cuts him off.

"It is, you have to do this Cairo. If you don't, it will cost us both more than we are willing to give up right now." I see a look of shock cross my brothers face before he quickly masks it.

"I'll do it." I turn around to see Creed, Cole, Callie and Meg standing in the doorway. "I'll stand down so Jess can lead."

CHAPTER THIRTY SIX
Credence

Jess looks at me like I've grown a second head, Sky has a knowing smirk on her face and Ro just looks...weird. I dart my gaze around them to see Zeke and Harlem making their way over to us, Harlem squirms in his hold and Zeke places him on the ground so he can run over and sit next to Jess. I'm in awe of how gentle he is when he places his small hand on Jess, normally he would have jumped in her lap, but he knows he isn't able to do that at the moment. He gives me a big toothy grin and I can't help but grin back at my handsome boy.

"Why?" I look back to Jess.

"Why what princess?"

"Why would you give up being alpha? You love being alpha." She really doesn't get it; I walk over to her and crouch down cupping her face between my hands I don't miss the way she flinches;. I want her to see the truth in my eyes when I say this.

"My priorities changed the moment you re-entered my life, I love being alpha but being a mate and father is more important to me. I will help you and your brother anyway I can, all I want is to be with you and our son, nothing else matters to me." Tears cloud her vision, and her mouth opens and shuts but no words come out. I release her face and stand to face Cairo; I look him up and down and there isn't a shadow of a doubt in my mind that Ro and Jess will lead our people fairly and never put their own needs above the pack. The council has ruled for decades, and everyone only follows them because they fear their wrath and the damage they can cause.

"I won't take your pack from you." The conviction in Cairo's voice tells me he means what he says.

"Thank you, then as alpha of the Reeves pack I, Credence Reeves herby pledge my loyalty to the Cruz pack. My pack is at your service and will fight with you." Jess climbs to her feet and looks to her brother, she seems terrified, and that look has me reaching for her, but she backs away. I drop my arm and stare at her, her gaze is still locked on her brother, I dart my gaze between them and when Cairo gives her a stiff nod, I hear a whoosh of air escape her.

"I-I can't lead the packs; I don't want to be an alpha." Oh, she's scared because she thinks she can't do it.

"Sweetheart, you will be an amazing alpha." I nod my head in agreement with Cole.

"The pack listened to you this morning, they will follow you Jess." Jess shakes her head at my mom, I turn to Cairo hoping he will clue me in on what the hell is happening, but all I see is anger in his features.

"What's wrong princess?" She still won't meet my gaze; she claps her hands in front of herself and interlocks her fingers.

"I can't be alpha."

"Yes, you can, I'll help you princess." She finally meets my gaze and I try to smile reassuringly but it doesn't seem to help ease the tension from her body.

"We'll all help you."

"Cole's right, we will all help you Jess." I appreciate my brother and sister so much right now.

"You don't understand! I can't lead a pack." She snaps, then the first tear rolls down her cheek. She quickly swipes it away and squares her shoulders as she looks at me.

"Why not?" I push.

"Ever since I was taken, I... it's like..." She swings her gaze to her brother pleading with him to help her, Cairo moves toward her and stands by her side.

"Jess hasn't been able to access her wolf since she was taken, all the drugs are out of her system but still she has not been able to feel Sheba." My eyes widen as I stare at her, is that the real reason why she has been hiding from me?

"Princess?" She ignores me, so I move forward but keep a small amount of space between us, as much as I'm dying to touch her, I know she wouldn't appreciate me doing it. "Jess, will you look at me please?" She remains staring at the ground for so long, I think she won't but then she finally lifts her head and tears roll down her cheeks, her eyes blaze with anger and I'm struck stupid as to why she is angry with me.

"I don't have a wolf now, so I guess you can go find a new mate and rule a pack with her." Her words have me stunned silent; her eyes narrow as she stares up at me. "Kayla's probably free, go find her and mark her as your mate!" My mouth drops open and with nothing to say I watch as she turns and clasps Harlem's hand in hers and brushes past me as she makes her way inside. I try to get my feet to move but my brain and body isn't on the same page, I hear the roller door slam closed and cringe. My thoughts are reeling, Jess can't access her wolf, what the fuck did Jacob do to her? That explains why her wounds and bones are taking so long to heal, with her shifter healing she should have been back to her normal self by now. I'm snapped from my thoughts when I'm shoved backward, I glare at Cairo and release a growl of warning, he does the same and bares his teeth at me.

"The fuck is your problem Ro?"

"You are Reeves, why the fuck did you stand there like an idiot and say nothing?"

"What the fuck could I say? She is the one who is ready to throw away what we have because she assumes shit. Your sister never gives me the opportunity to explain myself.

"You selfish prick! She is fucking hurting because she thinks you won't want her anymore because she may have lost her wolf!" I stand there and just stare at him, fuck! Does she really think that little of me?

"I would never give her up, she's mine!" My voice comes out gruff thanks to Corbin riding me so hard, he and I agree that we will never let Jess go even if she doesn't get her wolf back. Why does she always doubt me? I just told her that I would love her no matter what at Davina's, it feels like she is trying to find any excuse to push me away.

A month has passed, and Jess still avoids me, I have tried to make small talk and bridge the gap between us, but she refuses. We go to bed every night and she refuses to face me, she tries to sneak off to bed and be asleep before me every night. We're only dignified when it concerns Harlem but other than that, she gives me the cold shoulder. I don't know what else to do, Cairo, mom, the twins, fuck even Zeke have tried to talk to her and tell her that I don't give a shit about her being wolf less. The little minx even went as far as asking Davina if she knew of a lawyer on the island that will help her with custody papers. When Davina told me, I lost my shit and blew up at Jess, she just stood there and stared at me, it was like she wasn't even seeing me. All she could say was *'are you done?'* I'm at a loss as to how I'm supposed to fix things, when she won't even give me the time of day. I know what she went through was fucking hard and messed her up a bit, but all I have done is try to be there and help her through it. Jess is self-sabotaging and there isn't a goddamn thing I can do about it.

My mom has been trying to be there for Jess as help her however she can but I also know my dad being taken is weighing on her. The council has made no contact, we don't even know if Shelley, Dela and dad are even alive at this stage. I have been working closely with Vince and Davina to try and formulate a plan to get them back, we leave here in 2 weeks to another safe location. My pack has been training daily, as the other shifters and vamps have. Jess trains with them in hand-to-hand combat whenever they shift to practice fighting in their wolf form she escapes to the beach with Harlem, he seems to be the only thing that is holding her together. Mom and Davina have bonded which is weird as shit for me and the twins, I had to rein in my temper when I found out Mom had taken Harlem to Davina's house for dinner. When I confronted her, she said that Davina and I may have our issues, but Harlem is innocent, I have to say her words hit their mark. Ever since then I have allowed Davina to spend more time with Harlem but never on her own, thanks to Cairo insisting on my mom training with them today I'm stuck at Davina's house so she can spend time with Harlem.

It still makes me feel weird watching Davina sit on the floor and play trains with him, a part of me hurts at the view. I remember when I was younger, she would play with me like this, losing her not only broke me but it hardened my heart. When dad came home and told me that he had found his fated mate I was apprehensive, but meeting Meg changed everything. She didn't need to have my blood; she loved the twins from the start and even when I tried to push her away she never left. I cried every night for the mother I thought I lost and after the second week of Meg moving in with us, she gave up sitting outside my door listening to me cry. She pulled me out of bed and took me out into the woods into a clearing and told me to look up at the stars. I did as she asked, and she told me not to weep for my mom because she was the brightest the star in the sky and would always watch over me and the twins. From that night Meg became my friend and then before long she became the mother, I never thought I needed. If Davina thinks just by her being alive that we will ever desert our mom for her, she is fucking wrong.

"Creed!" I shake my head to clear my thoughts and look at Davina, from the frown on her face I can tell this isn't the first time she has tried to get my attention.

"What?" That came out harsher than I intended but I don't care, I didn't want to be here today. I know my mom only agreed to train with Ro because everyone else was busy even Jess doing who knows what, which meant I was stuck with staying with Davina. She keeps her emotions from her face and tries to act unbothered by my tone, but I can tell from the way her shoulders droop forward slightly that she is hurt. Mom thought I was mad at Davina because she is a vampire but that isn't it at all, I'm pissed at her because I don't understand how she could abandon us–her kids! I could never leave Harlem.

"I'm going to put him down for his nap." I look to my son and can see his eyes drooping shut; a yawn escapes him. I stand and Davina does the same, I quirk a brow at her in question, but she raises her hand to stop me from speaking. "He can nap in the spare room here; I have something to discuss with you about the move and the council." I stare at her for a moment wondering if I'll be able to tolerate being alone with her, but my need for information wins out and I nod. She picks Harlem up but before she can disappear to the room, I stop her and place a kiss on his head.

"Have a good nap monster, I'll see you when you wake up." He smiles tiredly at me and nods his head.

"Love you, Daddy." My heart swells, I don't think I will ever tire of hearing him say that to me.

"Love you too." Davina heads down the hallway to put Harlem down so I reclaim my seat and wait for her to return.

She won't harm him.

How do you know that Corbin? Corbin growls in annoyance.

I would sense if the pup was in danger, I can scent her emotions. I must be a sucker for punishment, but I ask anyway.

What does she feel for him?

Love.

Before I can question Corbin more Davina returns and sits on the opposite sofa facing me, she crosses her legs and clasps her hands on her knee. The way she is holding herself makes me apprehensive.

"I can help you with Jess." I reel back slightly shocked.

"I'm not here to talk about Jess, you said you have information on the council and our transport." I grit out, but Davina isn't being deterred.

"I lied." I release a growl and narrow my gaze. "Hear me out, I can help her get her wolf back." I want to tell her to go fuck herself but honestly... I'm out of options on how to help Jess so instead I find myself asking.

"How?" It pisses me off when she smiles triumphantly.

"Trauma caused her to lose her wolf, so she needs a damn good reason to push through her barriers to bring it back."

"What are you saying?"

"I heard that you have agreed to let the Cruz siblings lead the packs?" I nod still unsure where the hell she is going with this. "Well, if you don't get your mates wolf back in the next 2 weeks Cairo will be the sole alpha of all the packs." I bristle at that; I may have relented to Cairo and Jess leading but Corbin hates the idea.

"What's your point Davina?"

"My point is that I will help you get your mates wolf back." I scoff.

"I wasn't born yesterday, what's in it for you?" Her smile widens, shock of the year of course she wouldn't do this out of the kindness of her cold dead heart.

"When the council is defeated, I want my people to be able to live on the mainland."

"No!" I growl out.

"Why not?" She must be kidding?

"I will not allow you to return to civilization so you and your people can feed on the innocent." Davina stares at me for a moment and then shocks the hell out of me when she begins to laugh like a nut case. I don't see how what I have said is so fucking funny, I release a growl warning her, she raises her hand and tries to get her laughter under control. It's weird to see her laugh and look so... normal.

"Creed, we don't eat people. Well, some of the older generations did but me and my people don't, how do you think we have survived on this island for so long?"

"Fucked if I know." I don't like that I'm not the one with all the answers, it pisses me off.

"We can eat red meat, live off the blood of animals; we don't need to feed everyday like the movies tell you. We can drink from an animal and go two weeks without feeding again, we have had to push it to a month a few times when shipments were late, but we weren't desperate enough to sacrifice a whole town." This news surprises me, it goes to show even though I have been living with them for weeks, I really don't know much about them.

"So, you can personally guarantee that no human will be killed by a vampire?" All traces of humor vanish from her face.

"I would love to say yes but the truth is I can't. My people are loyal to me, but the vampires that left to be with the council I cannot guarantee that they will not feed on humans." It irks me to even think it, but it isn't her fault that her vampires jumped ship and decided to switch sides. Even as much as I dislike her, I couldn't hold her responsible if those other vamps killed a human. I release a frustrated sigh and run my hand through my hair contemplating if I should help her or not.

"Before I can agree to this, I would have to run it pass Cairo and Jess--"

"No, your word is enough."

"Why?"

"Because even if Jess leads, you will still be the alpha male to the packs." I open my mouth but then close it, I never thought about it like that. If Jess accepts this responsibility that still means that as the alpha mated pair, I remain with the same stature. "You didn't consider that did you?" I shake my head, no point in lying to her my look of shock already told the truth.

"*If* I agree to this, what will need to happen for you to help Jess?" Her face changes and she straightens in her seat, her eyes take on a harsh edge which makes me uneasy.

"No harm will come to your mate, I swear it. All you have to do is trust me, you may not like my methods, but I promise you, I can help her." I mull over her words for a moment, is trusting Davina really a good idea? "No one can know, not even your siblings or your mother." That raises my hackles.

"Why?"

"Because they will need to buy what I'm selling in order for Jess to believe it." Something inside me is telling me this is the only way to help Jess but the sane part of me is telling me to tell Davina to shove it up her ass. We sit here in silence; I'm still mulling it over and trying to weigh up the pros and cons of this. What if I don't agree and Jess never gets Sheba back? What if I do agree and it doesn't work and only pushes Jess further away from me? If it was anyone else offering this to me, I would have said yes already, but my anger toward Davina is making me second guess this.

"How do I know I can trust you?" She sucks in a deep breath and meets my gaze; I can't tell from the look in her eyes what she is thinking.

"You don't, but you can trust that I want what is best for Harlem, and that is having his mother whole again." If Corbin hadn't told me what she felt for Harlem earlier, I would never have believed her.

"Fine, but if anything happens to Jess or she gets hurt in any way I will be coming for you. My mother won't be able to save you from my wrath, are we clear?" It shocks me when I see a look of pride cross her features before she quickly masks it.

"I wouldn't expect anything less." I hope I don't live to regret this decision.

CHAPTER
THIRTY SEVEN
Jessica

These days I'm up before the sun, I roll out of bed and try to be quiet as I head toward the adjoined bathroom. I close the door softly, so I don't wake Harlem, I strip my clothes off and head for the shower but pause when I see my reflection in the mirror. I no longer have to wear the wrap for my ribs, they are healed but still slightly tender. My bruises have faded and the stitches from my head are out, my eyes are open and I'm thankful that they are no longer red and bloodshot. It scared Harlem when he saw my eyes like that, I hated that he feared me. The bruises and broken bones may have healed but the memories haven't, every time I close my eyes, I feel their blows and kicks. I've been trying to bury myself in training; it's the only thing that helps me keep my mind off what happened. Sky has been trying to help me with finding my wolf, but I don't even feel a flicker or a spark from her. I broke down last week when Vince tried to push me to shift, everyone has been pushing so hard to try but I can't! they don't understand that every time it doesn't work it breaks me all over again, we leave in five days to a new location on the mainland.

I hear everyone talk about the up-and-coming battle as we eat dinner each night, but I refuse to get involved. I am of no use now; I can't shift so I can't even help defend my family or get vengeance for what happened to me. I sigh and pull my gaze from the mirror and hop in the shower. As I wash my hair my mind drifts to Creed, he won't leave! I have tried to push him away and tell him to find someone else, but he won't. The truth is I don't feel worthy of him anymore, without Sheba I'm just... Jess. I'm so scared that in a few years' time Creed will get bored and tire of me not being able to shift and then break my heart. I feel the tears leaking down my cheeks, I don't brush them away as I stand here silently and cry. I never wanted this life or to be a wolf but now that I've lost Sheba all I want is for her to come back. I'm snapped out of my thoughts when I feel arms wrap around me, I snap my eyes open and stare up into Creed's gaze. His hazel eyes shine with so much hurt and sadness that it physically makes me ache. He has been nothing but kind and supportive, but I don't want him to be tied down by me. I try to push him away, but he tightens his hold, I go limp in his embrace and narrow my gaze.

"Come back to me princess." The rawness in his voice saddens me, I want nothing more than to curl into him and let him hold me while I break down.

"I can't." A growl from him is all the warning I get before he slams me against the tiled wall and lifts me, my legs automatically wrap around him, and I rest my hands on the top of his shoulders as he squeezes the globes of my ass. I glare down at him; he narrows his eyes and glares back.

"For the past five fucking weeks I have let you push me away, I have taken your bullshit silent treatment." I open my mouth, but he growls again so I snap it closed. "I'm done with your shit!"

"Good! That's what I've been trying to convey to you, now put me down." He moves one of his hands from my ass and reaches up to wrap it around my neck, my body trembles in fear but he doesn't relent.

"Never! I'm done with your shit, but I will never be done with you little alpha. I'm going to give us both the release we have been craving for weeks." I feel his cock begin to harden beneath me, I stare at him in shock and shake my head. "Try deny it all you want princess, but I scent your need, I bet your pussy is wet for me already."

"Put me down." He drops his hand from my throat, and I think he is about to obey me when he shifts slightly then tightens his hold on my ass and gently begins to lower me. I feel triumphant until I realize he isn't lowering me to the ground he's lowering me onto his cock. I feel his head prod at my hole, and I open my mouth to protest but then he slams inside me, and a moan slips out as my head falls backward against the wall.

"I want you in every way, with a wolf or without a wolf I want you. I love you Jess, and I'll never stop fighting for you because you." *Thrust.* "Are." *Thrust.* "Mine." He continues to move inside me, and I grip him tighter with my legs pulling him closer, my mind is screaming at me to push him away, but my body is begging for more from him. He reaches up keeping one hand on my ass and grips the back of my hair then pulls me to him, he rests his forehead against mine, the look in his eyes is too much for me so I close the gap and smash my lips against his. The kiss is messy and angry our teeth clash and I bite his bottom lip until the tang of his blood hits my mouth. He doesn't stop, he picks up the pace and continues to destroy my pussy. I can feel how close I am, and moans keep tearing from me, I don't give a fuck if the whole house can hear me come because I want this. My body has been so wired and Creed is the only one who can relieve this tension. My orgasm is right there but I can't reach it, I stare down at Creed and can see from the strain on his brow he is close.

"I need...more." I moan out, he shocks the hell out of me when he pulls out and then lifts me until my legs are over his shoulders and I need to bend to the side, so I don't hit my head on the roof, he doesn't give me a chance to question him. He buries his face in my pussy and eats me like it's his favorite meal. He pulls back and stares up at me licking his lips, that sight alone has more wetness dripping out of me.

"You taste so fucking exquisite princess." He buries his head back inside me; I moan as he flattens his tongue against my clit. I rock my hips back and forth riding his face like a pro bull rider trusting him not to let me fall. He squeezes my ass and pulls me closer to his face, how he is able to breathe right now I have no idea. I feel his thumb begin to circle my other whole and a fire ignites inside me. He starts to prod my ass with his thumb while simultaneously eating my pussy. He finger fucks my ass and eats my pussy like there is no tomorrow, after a minute I feel my orgasm slam into me and I cry out his name, he doesn't let me ride it out. He pulls me down to him and slams his cock inside my pussy covering my mouth with his to quite my screams. Creed is merciless as he slams into me over and over again, this isn't make up sex, this is pure unadulterated hate fucking and I love it. A minute later I feel another orgasm brewing and before I can scream my release, he covers my mouth with his again and we both come together, that second orgasm has me seeing stars.

Creed places me on my feet after I stop trembling from the two-mind blowing orgasms. I expect him to hug me or try to talk or something, but he doesn't, he just stares down at me for the longest time with water dripping over the both of us. His eyes scan me from head to toe and I begin to feel self-conscious, until he sighs and runs a hand through his hair before he turns and leaves. I stand there and just watch as he grabs a towel and walks out of the bathroom without saying another word.

What the fuck just happened?

I dropped Harlem off with Meg on my way to training with Sky, Creed was already gone by the time I was ready to leave which was a first. Training has been grueling and hard, but my body has started to thrive from the efforts of training. I chose to train with Vince rather than with Creed and Cairo's group. One, I am avoiding Creed, two my brother would go soft on me and that isn't what I need right now. Vince on the other hand has been pushing me and doesn't handle me with kid gloves. He earned my respect the first week I started training, he never pitied me or told me to take it easy, he pushed me as hard as he pushed the others. I know Cairo thinks he is smooth and that I don't know, but I knew from the moment Sky joined me on Vince's team that Ro had put her up to it. I mean, why the hell would she train with me when she could be training her own mate?

"I want you all to pair off and work on your kill shots. We only have a couple more days before we head out and I want to make sure you are able to handle yourselves." We do as Vince says and break off into pairs and naturally Sky and I pair off together, we get into our fighting stances. I'm not new to fighting, my mother had me trained as a young kid in Martial arts, so I am well versed on how to handle myself. That being said Martial arts isn't exactly going to help me when fighting something supernatural now is it? I bend my knees and raise my hands; I make sure to keep my face blank of all emotion. Vince told us that showing emotion is the quickest way to give your enemy the upper hand. I have become a pro at keeping a blank face these past few weeks, I learnt to hide the strain walking would cause me when my ribs were still broken or hiding the longing from my gaze when I would stare at Creed.

"You ready?" I nod my head in answer to Sky's question; Sky is a skilled fighter and the best opponent I have faced. I have only been able to take her down a couple of times, she always manages to find a way to hand me my own ass on a silver platter. We circle each other trying to find an in, Sky is well versed in not leaving herself open to attack. Between training with Ro and his pack for five years and all the training my mom had put me through as a child it has helped me with training. I watch and the moment Sky lifts her left arm high enough to leave her side exposed I strike; my fist connects with her ribs and I jump back narrowly avoiding her fist. We continue to do this dance for five minutes before Sky finally finds her opening, unlike me she doesn't back out she continues to land blow after blow until I'm a hot mess on the ground. I stare up at her in frustration, she reaches down to offer me a hand up and I accept it. I start to dust myself off as she speaks. "Stay out of your head Jess, I can see the moment you begin to think."

"I'm trying!" I snap, I cringe slightly as its not Sky's fault I'm so distracted today. I meet her gaze and see nothing but understanding in her eyes which just confuses me.

"Sleeping with Creed would distract anyone." My eyes double in size, she has the biggest grin on her face.

"H-how did you know?" I made sure to scrub myself three times before getting out of the shower to rid myself of his scent.

"I think the whole house heard." I feel the blush rise up the back of my neck and I drop my gaze. Sky reaches out and places her hand on my shoulder. "Don't ever be ashamed of loving him, he is your mate."

"No, he isn't, I don't have a wolf anymore Sky." Before Sky can answer we hear a commotion and turn to see what's happening, that's when I notice Davina and a large number of vamps, I haven't seen train with us come into the center. Vince makes his way over to her, but she raises her hand to stop him, her gaze then lands on me, and I shiver. There is a sinister look in her eyes, and I don't like it, I spot Cairo, Zeke, Creed and Cole making their way toward us. What the hell is going on and why are they here?

"Detain them." I stare at Davina in shock as the vamps around us hustle to follow their leaders' instructions. They all rush toward the guys and Sky breaks away from me to go help my brother, I try to follow her, but I'm yanked backward. I dart my head from side to side to see two vamps holding each of my arms, I struggle in their hold as I watch my brother and the others try to fight off the vamps. There are too many vamps for them to possibly fight their way out of this, I watch as Colton is pushed to the ground by four vamps, Zeke is next roaring out his promise of killing them all slowly. Sky manages to get two of the seven off my brother but then Davina sends more men to help.

"What the fuck are you doing Davina?" She doesn't pay me any attention, I turn back to my brother and Creed, Creed's gaze is locked onto mine and my breath stills. He stops fighting and drops to his knees with his hands above his head. "What the fuck are doing Credence? Get up and fight now!" I feel the tears stream down my cheeks and confusion and anger wars inside me, the vamps pin his arms behind his back and drag him to his feet as they pull him away to stand next to Cole and Z who are both on their knees. I turn back to Sky and my brother and watch as they both struggle to fight them off.

"Subdue her or you will never get the alpha alive." Davina sounds so cold and deadly; I stare at my brother with my heart in my throat.

"Skylar, you run--"

"Fuck off Cairo, I go where you go." The conviction in Sky's voice tells me she will never leave my brother. Sky would lay down her life for Cairo, he is stupid to think she would ever run when he is trouble. Six more vamps move toward them, and I notice that they wedge themselves between the two, they are now divided. Ro fights hard and fierce as fuck but with eight of them on him he doesn't stand a chance, why won't he shift? Cairo is brought to his knees, and I see the moment Sky notices him too, her arms swing out wide and her head lulls back as the wind begins to pick up around her...

"Sky, no! submit to me now and drop down, don't fucking do it!" Sky swings her gaze to my brother with her chest rising and falling in rapid succession, she looks side to side at the vamps that are stood still around her. "Skylar?" She turns back to my brother with her fist clenched at her sides, anger radiating off her in waves. "Submit, no matter what, you fucking submit do you hear me?" Ro and Sky stay locked in a stare off for a long tense moment before Sky drops to her knees and locks her arms behind her back, the vamps rush forward and secure her before dragging her over toward Creed and the others. Creed remains on his feet with his gaze on Davina while the other three remain on their knees, the vamps drag my brother toward the center and my stomach begins to sink.

Oh my god, Davina plans to harm him.

CHAPTER THIRTY EIGHT
Jessica

My breaths come in rapid pants; my hands are getting clammy as I watch Davina move toward my kneeling brother. She stops in front of him and stares down at him like he is nothing but shit under her designer boots. She reaches out and grips Ro's hair yanking it back until he stares up at her. He doesn't make a sound; I can't see her face because her back is to me, but I can see my brothers. The defiant glint in his eyes tells me he won't give up without a fight, I have no idea what the hell happened to cause her to do this. We have done nothing but respect her rules and train, I even let her have time with my son!

"You are going to pay for what you have done Cruz."

"The fuck are you on about Davina? I haven't done shit to you or your people!" Why didn't he shift and rip out the vamps' throats?

"It's time to pay for your sins, Cairo Cruz I hereby sentence you to death." Gasps and shouts break out, I struggle against my captors hold and see that the others are doing the same. I watch as Sky fights harder than I have ever seen her do before.

"Kill me, I did it not Cairo. I'm the one you want!" Davina lifts her head toward Sky and shakes it.

"Knock her out, she lies." I scream when I watch one of the vamp's punch Sky three times before she is finally knocked out. Anger burns inside me and my hatred for Davina grows, I will burn this bitch alive if she takes my brother from me.

"The fuck is wrong with you! Don't you cunts fucking touch her." I hear the pain and anguish in my brother's voice, he can't see Sky, but he must know what just happened to her. Growls slip out of him, but he still doesn't shift.

"Ahhhh, you see I had your water spiked this morning at your training camp. None of the wolves aside from Jess and Sky will be able to shift." Fear courses through me, I look to the others and see concern on their faces, Sky hangs limply in the pathetic vamps hold. Four guys on one girl that hardly seems fucking fair to me! Anger soars inside me, I can feel the heat of it coursing through my veins as I stare at Davina, I want nothing more than to wipe that smug look off her perfect face. I tear my gaze from her and face Creed, he isn't fighting against the vamps hold but his face is pure anger, why isn't he saying anything?

"You fucking bitch, I'll kill you for this!" Davina tsks Cairo as she moves toward him, the crowd that has gathered around us does nothing! They all stand there with their mouths agape watching this shit show, I look around and see only a handful of wolves' present.

"Why the fuck aren't you lot doing anything?" I scream at the wolves, the six of them refuse to meet my gaze and I watch as the vamps around close in, they are as trapped as we are. Desperation claws at me when Davina grips my brother's hair and yanks his head back, so he is looking up at her. A whimper escapes me, I'm powerless again and there isn't a damn thing I can do to stop this crazy bitch from killing my brother.

"Any last words?" Her voice holds no emotion she sounds so cold, tears stream down my cheeks and the lump in my throat grows when Cairo yanks his head free and faces me. His gaze holds no fear, but I can see the look of worry in his eyes but it's not for himself it's... for me.

"Ro..." I choke out past the lump in my throat.

"Close your eyes smalls and look away." I shake my head unable to speak. "Do not watch this, close your fucking eyes Jess." Sobs break free as I thrash against my captors hold.

"I'll take his place, take me not him!" Zeke yells out. Davina ignores Zeke's plea as she grips my brother's hair again and yanks his head back. One of the vamps closest to her hands her a dagger, the silver of the blade taunts me as it shines in the sunlight. She lifts it to Cairo's throat; my gaze is still locked on his as he smiles sadly. I can hear a scream echoing around us and it takes me a moment to realize that the scream is coming from me.

"Davina that's enough, if you do this, we will never fucking forgive you!"

"You will never forgive me anyway Colton." It's as if time moves in slow motion, I see her arm stiffen as she prepares to slice the blade across my brother's throat...then it happens. I feel Sheba thrash against the mental barrier between us, I don't get time to rejoice in finally feeling her again and knowing she isn't lost to me. She forces the shift upon me, and I don't fight, I welcome the pain, I relish in the burn of my muscles tearing and reforming, I thrive on the feeling of my bones breaking and reforming. I feel the guards hold on me drop as I land on all fours. I shiver at the feeling of my coat being shook out and how sharp my senses become in my true form, Sheba doesn't hesitate she leaps from the ground and dodges the guards that try to step in her way, when we are mere feet from Davina she jumps back from my brother and drops the blade to the floor with her arms up surrendering. Sheba crouches low ready to pounce on her, she releases a growl of pure terror, its long and loud and filled with so much power that I can feel it ricocheting around us. Sheba tenses and then launches into the air with her jaws open ready to clamp them around Davina's throat and tear it out but then suddenly we're knocked sideways and sailing through the air and land with a hard thud. Sheba uses the sliding momentum and rolls to her feet growling but stops when we see *who* knocked us away from Davina.

What the fuck? I snap to Sheba.

He will pay for that!

Sheba moves forward and begins to circle the gray and white wolf as anger thrums through her at the fact that her own mate interfered in her fight. Before she can advance on him, he shifts back, Creed stands there stark naked with his chest rising and falling rapidly.

"This isn't what you think." Sheba opens the mind link and releases an angry growl; she is pissed Creed interrupted her kill shot. I'm more confused as to why he is protecting Davina after what she just did to us! That crazy bitch nearly killed my brother.

You dare to stop me?

It isn't what you think Sheba.

Then what is it? She tried to kill my pack and yet you defend her.

Shift back.

No!

I need to talk to Jess and right now your emotions are running way too high to see reason.

Sheba releases another growl and refuses to even entertain Creed's urge to shift. She turns back toward Davina who is now surrounded by vampire guards which just pisses us off, I spy Ro out of the corner of my eye trying to shake Sky awake. Cole and Zeke just stand there glaring at Davina and the other vamps, good at least they aren't on her side and trying to stop me.

We can't take out eight guards to get to her Sheba.

I want her blood on my tongue Jess. The anger in Sheba's voice is so potent.

I know, but we can't take her out now, we need to be smart about this, please.

What do you suggest?

I don't want you to leave me again though! I can hear the sadness and worry in my own voice.

I will never leave you.

But you did!

No, I didn't, your trauma and the drugs just locked me down for a while. You and I are one in the same Jess, we are bound together.

If we shift back, you will still be with me, right? Sheba doesn't answer, she relinquishes her control over our body and then I begin to shift back. I don't enjoy the shift this time I'm too wired from what happened and fearful that Sheba will be gone again. Having her back and hearing her voice made me feel complete again. Once I'm on two legs I remain crouched with my head bowed slightly to give myself a minute.

I'm still here, Jess. Relief rushes through me, renewed determination charges through my body now that I have her back. I rise to my feet not caring that I'm standing here naked as the day I was born in front of all these people. I keep all the emotion of my face and make sure that no one will be able to read the way that I'm feeling.

Chapter Thirty Nine
Credence

I can't tear my eyes from her she looks so destroyed but stronger than ever at the same time. She holds her head high and squares her shoulders as she stares me down, I can see her fighting inside herself. She wants to rip me a new one but is holding back, I spy Cairo helping Sky to her feet and Zeke and Cole watching me and Jess. Davina has the right idea about staying as still as a statue not saying a single word, the vampires around us all stand stoically and watch. I step forward to try close the space between Jess and I so I can explain but she steps backward making me halt. When I agreed to Davina helping me unlock Jess's wolf, I didn't think this would be her solution.

"You knew this was going to happen, didn't you?" The accusation in her voice is clear.

"I didn't know she was going to do *this.*" I try to defend; she narrows her eyes and places her hands on her hips. I know this must be hard for her standing in front of all these people naked, but she is doing a good job of acting like them seeing her post baby body doesn't affect her.

"But you knew she was going to do something, didn't you?" A whoosh of air escapes me, I can feel my brother and the others watching me and the weight of their stares is heavy.

"Yes." A low growl escapes Jess as she moves toward me, she leaves enough space between us so I can't reach for her.

"Why the hell would you agree to something like this?" I try for humor.

"Because I'm an *eggplant?*" Her face remains blank, but I can see the anger swimming in her blue eyes. "I was just trying to help."

"Help? You think your psychotic mother trying to kill my fucking brother is going to help? How would you like it if I took a knife to Cole's throat?" I tense and dart my gaze to my brother; he looks like he wants his hand to beat up my face. "The thing is, I would never ever do that to someone you love. Cairo is supposed to be your friend and you used my brother as a pawn to manipulate me into shifting. You know what?" I pull my gaze from Cole to stare at Jess. "You are more like Davina than you think, you truly are your mother's son." I stumble back a step at her harsh words, I don't get a chance to reply, she turns away from me and heads over to Cairo and motions for Sky and him to follow her. I'm a bastard, I watch her ass sway side to side until I can't see her anymore. I grit my teeth when I see my brother and Zeke approach me, I don't need Cole's shit right now.

"How the hell could you do this to her? She went through something so fucked up and you let your mommy over there literally scare the wolf out of her." I glare at my brother; he is still beneath me, and he clearly needs a reminder of that.

"You don't get to judge what the fuck I do with *my* mate. I just helped save her fucking life, she wasn't going to stay behind when we approached the packs, did you really think they would follow her without scenting her as a wolf?" Cole's reply is cut off when Zeke's fist connects with my face, the punch fucking hurts but I don't let it show before the two of us can get into it Cole steps in the middle. Zeke points an accusing finger at me and glares as his chest rises and falls in rapid succession.

"You son of a bitch! You never change, you did this for yourself not her, you agreed to Davina's help and never once thought to ask what her plan was?" he doesn't let me answer as he continues his tirade. "You Credence don't fucking deserve her or your status as alpha, Cairo and Sky could have been killed today and you couldn't give a shit! You're a selfish prick--"

"I did it to protect her! I didn't know this is what Davina had planned, I just wanted Jess to have Sheba, so she wasn't unprotected. Jess hasn't been herself for weeks since she thought she lost her wolf; she has pushed everyone away. She won't even spend much time with Harlem because she doesn't think she is worthy of him without her wolf, call me whatever the fuck you want but I did this for her and our son, now get the fuck out of my way." I nudge Cole out of the way and shoulder check Zeke as I pass, that fucker needs to learn to keep his nose the fuck out of my business. I still don't trust him after he hit on Jess. I ignore Davina as she calls my name and shift, I let Corbin take control knowing he will take us to Jess I don't know what I'm going to say to her, but I have to fix this. I never thought Davina would go as far as she did, but am I sorry? *No*, I would do it again if it meant Jess got Sheba back.

I shift back as soon as Jess, Cairo and Sky come into view out front of the house, they all scowl at me when I approach. Cairo looks like he wants me six feet under, and I honestly can't blame him, I stop and leave a good amount of space between us knowing that the closer I get the more pissed off they'll be. I raise my hands and focus on Jess, she is grinding her teeth so hard I think she may actually break them.

"Davina offered to help get your wolf back, she never told me what her plan was, only to trust that what she had planned would bring her back. I never meant for any of this happen--"

"How did you shift?" I turn to Sky and quirk a brow. "She said that only Jess and I could shift, but you shifted and stopped Jess."

"I... I don't know." I can see they don't believe me, so I press on. "I honestly don't know, I just shifted."

"What did you think would happen?" The sarcasm in Jess's voice tells me she is going to hit me where it hurts. "Did you think because we fucked this morning that I would drop to my knees and worship you because your mommy figured out how to free Sheba?" I flinch and she scoffs. "You never learn, this isn't a dictatorship it's a partnership Creed--"I cut her off with a growl.

"Bullshit Princess, this hasn't been a partnership since you shut me the fuck out, you never gave me a choice! You chose to try and end things with us and shut us all out, you left me no fucking choice!" I scream at her; I want to stop but the words just keep flowing. "You made decisions without me, you put words in my mouth and doubted my love for you. I tried to be there for you ever since we got you back and you have done nothing but push me away and you have even started to pull away from our son." She recoils but I'm not done yet, I bend so we are eye level. "I don't fucking regret what happened, maybe now that you have your wolf back you might actually start to be the Jess I fell in love with. Until you can be her again, I'll be taking Harlem with me to my mom's." I don't stick around; I brush past her but stop when Sky and I are shoulder to shoulder. "I'm sorry for what they did to you." I head inside to pack me and Harlem some things for a couple days. I think it's best for all of us if Jess and I take some time apart, I won't push her anymore. If she wants to be with me then she needs to show it, my chest aches and Corbin is howling inside me at the idea of leaving her, but I don't see any other way. Once in the room I pull on a pair of jeans and forgo a shirt, I start grabbing clothes out of the draws for me and Harlem. The bedroom door slams open, If the smell of rotting wouldn't assault my nose, I would scent air rather than peering over my shoulder to see Jess standing there in another man's shirt--again. I growl my disapproval but say nothing as I continue to grab clothes out.

"Relax, it's my brother's shirt."

"I didn't say a word."

"You didn't need to, the growl said it all. You are not leaving with my son--"That does it, I slam the draw shut with more force than needed and it slams back against the wall. I spin and face her seething with anger, my hands are clenched into fists at my sides as I stare her down.

"He isn't *yours* he is *ours*! I get to make decisions for him as well, we have had this same argument repeatedly, and I am tired of it. I'm tired of fighting Jess, all my life I have had to fight to prove myself to my father and the pack. My dad's gone, the pack has turned to shit and I'm not even really an alpha anymore, you are not the only one who has lost shit. You walk around and act like you are the only one who has suffered, we all have Jess. I'm asking you now to step aside and let me leave." Seeing the tears gather in her eyes guts me but I can't back down, we need space-- I need space. Her and I living like this for the past month isn't healthy for us or for Harlem, I drop the clothes on the bed and move toward her cupping her face between my hands.

"Don't go." A loud exhale escapes me as I see the tears trailing down her cheeks.

"I have to little alpha; you need time to process shit and I need time to think. I'm sorry that Davina did what she did today, but I would do it again if given the choice." I release her and grab a duffle from the walk in and stuff mine and Harlem's clothes into it, Jess stands in the same spot unmoving. I zip the bag and sling it over my shoulder, I can't bear to look at her as I head for the door, just before I can exit her words have me halting.

"I'm sorry, I swear I never meant to hurt you."

"I know, princess." Hearing her sobs nearly breaks me but I know this is the best thing for us, I spot Sky and Cairo in the kitchen and decide to speak to them first before leaving. Both of them look at me like I am shit under their boots and I don't blame, they would have heard everything that was just said upstairs.

"She needs you and you decide to leave?" That isn't what I expected Cairo to say.

"I have to, we have been living like strangers for weeks and it isn't healthy for us or for our son. I think a few days apart will do us the world of good--"

"We leave this island in a few days, what then?" My shoulders droop.

"I don't know... I love her Ro, but I also can't live like this. I'm not like my dad; I can't live with a mate that doesn't love me." Saying that out loud hurts more than I ever thought it would.

"Men are so dumb." Both Ro and I glare at Sky. "She loves you so much, she is just in a dark hole after what happened. You leaving will be the best thing for her."

"How?" Ro asks.

"Because then she is forced to face her trauma head on in order to get her family back. Jess isn't good to anyone let alone the packs being in this depressed state, don't give up on her Creed."

"Never, I'm sorry you were both caught in the crossfire today. I swear I had no idea Davina was going to pull a stunt like that." They both nod and I take that as my cue to leave.

CHAPTER FORTY
Credence

My mom ripped into me as soon as I stepped foot in the door, apparently news of the morning's events travelled faster than I thought. Mom is still seething at me and won't give me a chance to explain, I suppose I should be glad she hasn't kicked my ass out. She cooked dinner for us, I offered to help but she just glared and told me to bath Harlem. I didn't argue, I was glad for the excuse not to be around her while she was wielding a knife. Dinner was eaten in silence except for when Harlem spoke, I'm just finishing up the dishes when a knock sounds at the door, I rush to answer it before they knock again because mom just put Harlem down and I don't want him to wake. I swing the door open, and I'm shocked as hell to see Cairo standing there.

"You gonna invite me in or just stand there staring like a dick?" I shake myself out of my stupor and step aside to let him in.

"Is Jess, okay?" Ro scoffs and rolls his eyes as he drops into one of the single chairs, I'm too on edge to sit right now.

"Do you really think I would be sitting here if my sister was in some form of trouble?" Yeah, he does have point there, I drop into the other seat and open my mouth to speak but snap it shut when my mom walks in. When she spots Cairo the angry look on her face vanishes and is replaced by a tender loving smile-- I scoff.

"What a lovely surprise Cairo."

"Thanks Meg, just wanted to drop by and see Creed and check in on how the monster is doing?" Mom beams at the mention of her grandson.

"He has been such a good boy, even brushed his own teeth and sat still while Creed cut his hair--." Ro leans forward and cuts my mom off as he stares at me in shock.

"You cut his hair?"

"Uh, yeah why?" Ro shakes his head and slouches back.

"Dude, no one has been able to cut that kids hair since the day he was born." I furrow my brow for a moment and then something Jess said comes back.

"I didn't even think about, Jess did say that a while ago at your house, but I asked him today and he was happy for me to do it." Ro laughs and shakes his head; mom and I share a look of confusion before she mutters something about boys and being silly, then leaves.

"Wait till I tell Jess; she is going to flip it." I tense.

"I didn't do it to piss her off--"

"Calm down Romeo, I meant she will flip it as in a good thing. She has been dying to cut his hair for so long and I honestly think she will thank you for that." Pride has me puffing my chest slightly, but when Cairo's face changes and the laugh lines disappear from his face I sigh and ask.

"Why are you really here Ro?"

"Because I wanted to make sure that you and the monster were okay." Guilt eats away at me as I stare at him.

"After what happened today you came here to check on me?" I can hear the doubt in my own voice, Ro shrugs his shoulders as if he doesn't give a shit.

"You didn't know what she was gonna do, I'm pissed you had a plan and didn't tell me, but I can't exactly blame you for what Davina did now can I?" Holy shit, Cairo is a bigger man than me, I would be salty as fuck and holding a grudge for years!

"Thanks..."

"Don't sound so shocked, not everyone is an asshole like you." Both of us chuckle, sitting here with him feels like old times growing up when he would come back for a visit. Back then neither of us had to worry or stress like we do now, we were young and carefree and just enjoyed running wild in our wolf forms. A sense of longing and sadness hits me as I think about how our lives might have turned out if my mom and dad didn't lie and I didn't trick Jess into coming to Rosewood.

"How did we get here, Ro? Things used to be so easy and none of the shit with council ever mattered to us, things were so different back then."

"We grew up, life isn't all sunshine and rainbows Reeves, the council didn't matter to us then because we didn't understand what they were about. Don't live in the past brother all it will do is eat you up, focus on the here and now."

"That's a bit hard to do right at this moment."

"Look my sister is stubborn and hardheaded--"

"I wonder where she got that from?" Cairo scowls at me playfully. He leans forward and rests his arms on his legs and meets my gaze, the look he gives me tells me that we're about to have a serious talk.

"Look, when Jess first came to me, she was scared and unsure, she didn't get a lot of time to deal with what had happened. When she found out she was pregnant that was all she focused on, and she poured her energy into that and blocked everything out, until she couldn't. After the twins were born it was like that sparkle was back in her eyes and she even smiled more but then..."

"Katy died." It's a lot harder to say that out loud than I thought.

"Yeah, after that, it was like she went backward again, she blamed herself for what happened. The doctors told her that it was a horrible thing that can occur, but she became fixated, she read through so many books to see if any other shifter babies had gone through this--"

"Were there any others?" He drops his gaze and I already know the answer before he voices it.

"Not that she could find, no." My heart sinks. "She gravitated toward Cole... a lot. We all knew why she was dependent on him and why he was the only one she wanted near her, when she would wake in the middle of the night screaming. She seemed to get better over time with Cole being around--"

"Why?" I try to keep the anger and jealousy out of my voice, but I fail.

"Why do you think Creed?" I give him a blank stare and can't stop the growl that slips out, it pisses me off when he laughs. "He looks like you, we all knew, even Cole did, that she was using him as a crutch because she...wanted you." I thought as much but hearing Cairo say it hits differently, I really didn't realize how much she needed me. With how much I love Harlem already in a short amount of time the fear of losing him haunts me. Jess and I both lost Katy and her loss leaves me with a hole in my chest and I didn't even get to gaze upon her or hold her. The loss of her must of destroyed Jess. "God strike me down for saying this...but," The watery tone of his voice gives me pause, I see tears gathering in his eyes and that shocks me Ro never cries! "It was harder for her to lose Katy because she got to raise her for a small measure of time, I hate myself for thinking it but I sometimes I think that if she were a stillborn it would have been...easier." My mouth hangs open in shock.

"I...uh..."

"I've never told anyone that before. Watching my sister break apart and mourn for her daughter destroyed me." I feel like there is a double meaning here.

"Why are you telling me this?"

"Because I feel like I'm watching her lose Katy all over again."

"How?"

"Even when she was angry at you for showing up, her eyes still lit up with life. She wasn't living before you showed up Creed she was surviving, she smiled more often as well. But ever since she was taken the spark in her eyes and her smile has vanished. She has never pulled away from Harlem before until now, I don't know how to help my sister and it is fucking killing me." I growl and jump to my feet and pace the small space between us, I tug on the strands of my hair in frustration.

"What do you want me to do Ro? I fucking love her and want to make this shit work, but she keeps pushing me away, I won't force her to be with me but I... can't let her go either. What the fuck am I supposed to do?" He stands and approaches me, then places both his hands on my shoulders and looks me straight in the eyes.

"Don't give up on her Reeves, everyone she has ever loved

has left her or died. She is pushing you away, don't let her push you out brother. She loves you and is just dealing with shit in her own way."

"I get that, but I just need some...time to sort shit out for myself." He nods and steps back and I release a breath.

"I have something else to ask."

"Ask away, you seem to be on a roll for talking today." Ro glares but I just laugh.

"I don't want to lead any of the packs, I've never wanted to be an alpha." I stare at him, dumfounded that he doesn't want to lead the packs.

"W-why not?" Ro drops his gaze from mine, and I drop into my seat and watch as he begins to pace.

"It's hard to explain, but ever since I fled after my dad was killed, I made a vow."

"What vow?" He quits pacing and pins me with a look that has me straightening.

"I vowed to never lead a pack; I don't rule over the rogues they all sort of just... found me. They view me as their alpha, and I guess I have sort fallen into that roll and I'm okay with that. But as far as leading any other packs, I don't want that. All I want is to stay with the pack that I have built over the years and be free from the rest of the political bullshit that comes with leading the others." I hate to admit it, but I envy him, I wish I had the freedom that he does to choose. Unfortunately for me I'm not wired the same way, I thrive on the leadership and crave the control.

"What do you want from me then, Ro?"

"I want you and Jess to lead the packs. I'll help you both

achieve this goal, but when all of this over I want to return to my pack lands and live amongst my people."

"What about Jess and Harlem?" He drops his head and his shoulders hunch.

"I love my sister and that monster more than anything, but she and I can never run freely together, her wolf is just as dominant as mine and I would never forgive myself if we fought. Plus, she has you brother and weather she wants to admit it or not, you are enough for her. You both need to work your shit out and remember that you have a kid together, do better for him Creed, he deserves to grow up in a place where he isn't looking over his shoulder all the time." I stand and reach my hand out to him; he stares at it for a moment and then finally places it in mine as he meets my gaze.

"Once all of this is over, I will help you rebuild your lands, I vow to you here and now that I will help Jess lead these packs the right way."

"She doesn't want to lead brother; she will hand it all over to you. So, I expect you to do shit the right way and make a difference and be an alpha we can all look up to-- scratch that, be the alpha your son wants to grow up to be." Well shit, that really hits home.

I didn't get much sleep after Ro left last night, I spent most of the night just staring at my son or glaring at the ceiling. Thoughts of Jess have plagued me all night, even when I did manage to catch some sleep, I dreamt of her. Waking this morning I told myself that I was going to shut any and all thoughts of her from my mind today and just focus on the pack and my son. After breakfast I decided to bring Harlem with me to help with the pack and get them ready for what's next.

I stand here with Harlem on my shoulders and let the pack get their fill of him. I know this must be a shock for most of them, when we first boarded the boat, I let them all believe that he was Jess's son and not mine. Now there is no point in hiding him, they are risking their lives after all to save him. Harlem doesn't squirm under the pressure of their gazes if anything the little monster loves the attention. I have no idea where he got that trait from because his mother and I don't thrive under the attention of others like he does.

After they get their fill, they break away and go about packing their houses, I instruct them to move whatever belongings they are taking with us to place it all in the garage of George's house which is the closet to the beach. After we finish I ask the pack to help anyone else who needs assistance, Harlem and I make our way toward the hall to see if there is something I can do. Truthfully, I just need something else to focus on, so I don't sit around and think about Jess. Harlem talks the whole way, and I can't help but laugh when he pronounces words wrong, it's so cute, just as I'm about to answer his question he tears his hand from mine and takes off yelling.

"Co-Co!" I follow where Harlem is running and see my brother and Zeke standing near the entrance to the hall, Cole scoops Harlem up and chucks him into the air, my boy squeals in delight as Cole catches him. I give Zeke a nod hello and wait for Cole to acknowledge me, I expect him to be pissed at my decision to move out and leave Jess, but when his eyes land on me I see no anger.

"Ahhhhh, the runaway bride is here." I glower at my idiot kid brother; Zeke chuckles and tells Cole he'll meet him inside. Before he turns to leave, I stop him with my words.

"Do you think you could take Harlem in with you for a bit?" Zeke looks at me in a weird way. "I just need to talk to Cole and then I'll be in."

"Yeah, of course, I can do that." Z reaches out and Harlem willingly goes with him, maybe I need to let 'by gones be by gones' where Zeke is concerned.

"What's up brother? You seem tense." I take a deep breath and I motion for Cole to follow me so we can have some semblance of a private chat, that is hard to do when there are so many shifters around. We stop out the back by the palm trees, this place still astounds me. I wish I knew how they got these little huts in the trees and how they even managed to grow any other type of tree aside from palms here. Cole clears his throat which snaps me from my wondering thoughts.

"Cairo doesn't want to lead any of the packs." If Cole is taken back by my statement, he doesn't show it. Clearly my little brother knows more than I do about Cairo's wants.

"I figured."

"How so?" He sighs and runs a hand through his hair.

"Ro has never seen himself as an alpha, everyone knows he only took on that role to keep the rogues safe. If it was up to him there would be no leader, and everyone would just do whatever the hell they wanted."

"It doesn't work like that with shifters, we need an alpha or there will be anarchy amongst the pack." He gives me a dry stare.

"We know that smartass, hence why Ro took on the job. What's the big deal if he doesn't want to lead?" It's my turn to stare at him like he is dense. "Ah, Jess doesn't want to lead either, right?" I nod my head. "Well then as her mate that job then falls to you." There it is, the root of the problem. I refuse to meet his gaze and don't reply. "Oh shit, you don't want to lead either, do you?" I stare out at the trees and let his question roll through my mind for a bit before I finally answer.

"I'm scared Cole." I hear his sharp intake on breath and cringe internally. I have never ever shown or let my brother know my feelings before.

"W-why? You're Credence fucking Reeves, nothing in this fucking world scares you." His confidence in me is inspiring.

"I'm scared I will end up like dad." There, I said it.

"You're nothing like dad, brother." I turn to face him and meet his stare.

"Dad molded me into who I am today, he never let me be a kid or have any fun. I started training to be alpha since I was 4 years old Colton. I never fucking want to do that to my son!" His eyes soften and he reaches out and places his hand on top of my shoulder.

"Then don't be dad." I growl in frustration, but he ignores me and continues on. "You are not him Creed, yes we had mom, but you helped raise Callie and me as well. You will never be him; dad has always been hard on us because he wanted all three of us to be the best we could be. So, what if you lead all the packs, that doesn't mean you have to make your son a solider like dad did to you. Break the cycle brother, if anyone can do it, it's you." I stare at him for a moment in awe, since when did my little brother become so wise?

Chapter
Forty One
Jessica

Our time on the island is officially up, its moving day. These past few days have been so hard not being able to be with my son as much as I would have liked. I haven't spoken to Creed since he left, I see him out and about but whenever he spots me, he turns and goes the other way. I only see Meg when I visit Harlem and spend time with him, Creed let me do bath time and put him to bed last night. I was hoping with me being at his house later that I might have run into him and had a chance to talk, but I never saw him when I left. As much as it burns me to admit it, Creed is right, I did pull away from Harlem and pushed him away. I have been in such a black hole, and I have no idea how to pull myself out of it. Jacob broke something in me, my anger and hatred has been the only thing fueling me since I got back. I pushed Creed away because I thought I was less than him due to not being able to shift but I was wrong.

"Ready to go?" I shake my head to clear away my thoughts and head downstairs. Cole smiles and claps me on the shoulder as we head out the door to follow the crowd to the beach where the boats are waiting for us. But as soon as we step outside the both of us freeze, Davina, Vince, Cairo, Creed and Zeke stand there huddled around each other and whispering in hushed tones. Creed lifts his head, and he locks his eyes on me, instead of the usual lust that shines in his gaze when he looks at me it is replaced by... worry. Cole grips my elbow and leads me toward them, by the time we reach them all of them are looking anywhere but at me. Panic begins to seep inside me, I can tell from how ridged they are that whatever they were discussing isn't good.

"No point in hiding shit, what were you all talking about?" Bless Cole for not beating around the bush. Vince looks to Davina and cocks a brow as if pushing her to answer Cole's question.

"Just tell her D, the letter is for her anyway." Cole and I share a look of confusion before I ask.

"What letter?" I expect Creed to cut me out of whatever this is, but he nudges my brother and motions for him to give me the piece of paper in his hand. Ro glares at Creed before handing me the paper, Cole shuffles in closer and peers over my shoulder so he can read it as well.

> *You don't know me and have no reason to trust what I say.*
> *I hope you do heed my warning though as your life depends on it.*
> *Do not attack the council!*
> *All shifters have fled Rosewood, return there, and fortify your lands because they are coming for you all, especially.*
> *H.E.R.*
> *I wish you all well,*
> *Gabrielle Wilder.*

I re-read the note twice, who the hell is this woman and how could she possibly know any of this. Cole snatches the note from me and waves it in the air as he growls at the four people in front of us.

"Who the hell sent this? How do you even get mail on a bloody island?"

"It came in with one of the ships captains, Cole."

"Oh, so that is just supposed to explain everything is it, Vince?"

"Colton calm down--"

"Nah, fuck that Creed. Who the hell is this woman?" The anger that laces Cole's words is tangible.

"You need to listen to your brother--"Cole turns and glares daggers at Davina.

"This is an A and B conversation now C your way out of it Davina." Ro and I both snort and try to mask our laughter but fail miserably when Davina turns her ice-cold gaze to us.

"You need to grow up Colton."

"And you need to stop thinking you have any say in what the fuck I do Davina. I may have popped out of your messy cunt, but you are not my mother!" Cole screams at her; people begin to slow down around us and stare. Cole is vibrating with rage and if he doesn't calm down his wolf will force a shift and he will attack his bio mom. I reach out and place a hand on his shoulder, he turns to me with his upper lip pulled back in a snarl. I see Creed out of the corner of my eye pressing in closer to me in case he attacks.

"Cole, ignore her. We have to figure out this letter before we leave here, I promise I will help you deal with all this rage toward her *after* we figure out what we're going to do." His eyes flicker back and forth between him his and his wolfs. he takes deep breaths and I know it is a struggle for him to gain complete control of their body, but he manages to do it after a couple minutes. I feel terrible that the three Reeves siblings are having to deal with all this crap with Davina, none of them have really had the time to properly process or figure out their emotions where she is concerned.

"She is to stay the hell away from me, from now on." Cole grits out between clenched teeth, I squeeze his shoulder and nod reassuringly.

"For now, she needs to stay so she can fill us in on who the hell sent this letter." Hearing the command in Creed's voice sends shivers down my spine, he truly is an alpha in his own right. Creed motions for us to follow him inside, we all stand around in the kitchen. No one has uttered a word; I open my mouth to speak but snap it closed at the sound of the front door opening. Callie, Sky and Meg walk in, I smile and move toward them so I can pluck my son out of Megs hold. I clutch him against my chest and just breath him in, I feel Creed press up against my back and it takes everything inside me not to lean into him. He reaches around and ruffles our son's hair; Harlem tries to bat his father's hand away but fails.

"Daddy no, Gammy, dad ruined my hair." Meg turns and glares halfheartedly at Creed, I try to fight my smile.

"Credence, don't touch his hair he spent a long time doing it."

"Oh no way!" Everyone turns toward my brother who has a shit eating grin on his face.

"What?" Creed snaps. Ro shakes his head and smiles as he reaches out and steals my son from my hold, I release a growl on annoyance but don't fight him.

"I think my nephew has a crush on some young lady." Harlem stills in his hold his chubby cheeks turn pink; my mouth drops open in horror. Creed and Cole begin to cackle like girls, so I ram my elbow into Creed's stomach and relish in the grunt that tears from him.

"As amusing as this is we do not have time." Everyone's laughter dies off at the seriousness in Vince's tone. "D, I think it's time you told them the truth." Davina being the emotionless statue that she is, gives nothing away, she moves her gaze across all of us before finally settling on me.

"Would you prefer your son be present or not for this?" I open my mouth to answer but Meg beats me to it.

"It's okay, I'll take him out." Meg moves to grab Harlem from Ro, but Creed reaches out and grips his mother's elbow stopping her.

"My mother stays and so does my son, just make sure to keep anything graphic to a minimal if the need arises." It warms my heart to hear him say that, he has fallen into the role of being a father like a natural.

"Very well, Gabriella Wilder is someone very special to my kind. She is the last living decedent of the original bloodline." Gasps ring out around the room.

"She's the girl, isn't she?" Ro asks Vince who nods, Davina spins toward her second and narrows her eyes. Whoops, cats out of the bag that Vince snitched and told us already.

"Clearly you all have been informed--"

"Some of us haven't." Meg interjects, Davina locks eyes with her and I expect to see annoyance or irritation but instead she shows empathy, Davina looks to Meg as an... equal, wow.

"Of course. Gabrielle also known as Belle is the last of her kind. Meaning that as vampires we cannot change anyone at will, that can only be done by one of the originals."

"This sounds like The Vampire Diaries." Davina ignores Callie's jib and continues to explain to Meg who Belle is.

"Okay, so why would this girl send a note to Jess? If she is a vampire, why would she be willing to help a shifter?" For the first time since coming to this island Davina's mask slips for us all to see-- fear, hope, longing, loyalty all shine in her eyes.

"Belle isn't like us."

"The hell is that supposed to mean Davina?"

"It means Creedence that Belle has no idea who or what she really is." I am completely astounded by this, anger courses through me which makes Sheba leap inside me. As someone who has gone through this myself, I'd hate that another young woman is living a lie like I did. A growl escapes me, and I feel all eyes on me, but I am only focused on Davina.

"How dare you do that to her; she has a right to know who she is and what she bloody is!" Davina's eyes spark with anger and within a split second she is directly in front of me thanks to her vamp speed. Creed, Cole and Sky move closer, but I raise my hand to stop them and meet Davina's angry look with one of my own.

"You have no idea what you are speaking about!" I roll my eyes and scoff.

"Please spare me the bullshit. I lived a lie for 18 years, if it wasn't for my baby daddy tricking my ass, I still wouldn't know who and what I really am, so save your bullshit lines. Belle deserves to know everything, it's her goddam right!"

"No!" The anger in her eyes evaporates and is replaced by

utter fear. "No one can know about Belle. I will not let her die at the hands of those that wish me dead." I stumble back in shock and swing my gaze to Creed who is staring at his bio mom like he is finally seeing her for the first time. Silence encompasses the room; Davina is shaking and quite frankly I'm worried I have never seen her so... rattled. Vince moves toward Davina and places a hand on her shoulder in comfort.

"D, we won't let anything touch her I swear." Sky shocks the shit out of me when she snorts and begins to laugh like a mad woman. Callie stares at her mate as if she has lost her ever loving mind.

"Skylar, enough!" She stops laughing and turns toward my brother.

"Don't Cairo, you have no idea."

"Then tell us Sky, what did you--what happened?" I hate that Ro and Sky have these cryptic talks, it irritates me, even Zeke seems like he is out of the loop most of the time and he was one of their closest friends. Sky looks to Davina with this knowing look in her eyes.

"Why are you so protective over this Belle?" Davina opens and closes her mouth a few times, but no words escape. "Tell me!" Sky yells. "If you're hiding this from them and it puts my mate in danger, I will kill you." Davina's mouth stretches into a cruel smirk as she stares at Sky.

"I'll tell them my secret if you tell them yours." A growl erupts from my brother as he steps in front of Sky, He passes Harlem off to Meg as he glares down Davina. Vince saddles up next to D and has his fangs on display, hell no! I cut across to stand next to my brother, none of them will touch him if I have any say in it! Creed and Cole jump in the middle of us and stand back-to-back with Cole facing us and Creed turned toward the others.

"This is not helping anyone! Take it down a notch Davina-

-"I can't bite my tongue; the words fly out of my mouth without consent.

"Oh, so you protect your *mother* even after what she did to me and my brother?" As soon as the hurtful words are out, I can't take them back, I slap a hand over my mouth and turn to Meg who is now staring at her feet like they are the most interesting thing in the world. "I-I, Meg I-I'm--"Creed spins around and in one swift move has his hand around my throat and slams me against the wall, chaos breaks out around us, but Creed and I are lost in an angry glaring match. Growls are tearing out of both of us, I can tell my eyes have changed to the color of my wolf and so has his.

"You want to hurt me, go for it, but *my mother* has nothing to do with any of this. You can yell scream and hate me all you like, but I will not let you tear her down on your way to self-destruction." I recoil internally and yank Sheba back so I can be in full control.

Don't Jess, we need to put him in his place.

No Sheba, he's right. I am lashing out at him but in doing that I am hurting others, that is not who I am.

Then be true to your feelings and face them instead of hiding behind them.

I growl, not at Creed but at the truth that my own wolf's words hold. I can lie to everyone else, but I can't lie to her, we are the same person after all. Creed drops his hold from around my neck and steps back, Ro breaks out of Vince's hold and shoves Creed away from me.

"You ever do that shit to my sister again and I--"The sound of Harlem wailing cuts off his reply. I turn toward my son and see Meg has him clutched against her trying to soothe him, what the hell is wrong with us? We just did that in front of our own son! I break away from the wall and move toward Meg, but Creed cuts me off and glares at me as he grabs our son from his mother and begins to whisper words of love in his ear.

"It's okay monster, mommy and daddy were just playing I didn't mean to scare you." Harlem pulls back and when his eyes lock onto mine I gasp.

Sheba?

I think you're right; we need to see the letter again.

Creed's brow is furrowed as he stares at me, I spin away from them and face Davina.

"I need to see that note again."

"Why?"

"Please Davina, I need to." She hands me the note and as I scan it over my stomach plummets. I look to Creed, and I can feel the tears threating to spill.

"Princess, what's wrong?" The gruff tone of his voice tells me that he may be mad at me, but he still cares enough to worry about what is upsetting me.

"They aren't coming for me Creed." I whisper.

"What?" the weight of that one-word grounds me and gives me enough strength to say what I need to.

"Belle wrote, *they are coming for H.E.R.*" His forehead creases as he tries to grasp my meaning.

"Oh shit!" I turn to Cole and from the look he gives me he gets exactly what I'm trying to convey.

"Can someone fill me in here?" Callie snaps. I don't take my eyes off Creed as I answer.

"Belle doesn't mean *her*, as in me. She wrote H.E.R which I believe stands for our son." Creed stumbles back a step and stares at our boy in his arms as he whispers.

"Harlem Edward Reeves." Gasps sound out around the room, and everyone begins to shout and demand things, but my soul focus is on my mate and our child. Meg rushes over to us with Callie in tow, Meg wraps her arms around me, and I can't contain the sob that breaks free.

"I am so sorry Meg, I never--"

"Shush, that is enough of that. We can talk about what is going on with you later, but right now we have to work out what we are going to do and how we are going to protect my grandson and get Kane, Shelley and Dela back from the council."

Chapter Forty Two

Jessica

I don't recall feeling seasick on the way to the island but right now I don't feel so good. This boat is much nicer than the one we come over in, this is an actual cruise ship, so everyone has their own rooms and there is actual food on board. We were told it would take a few days before we dock. Davina put me, Creed and Harlem in the same room and honestly the tension between the two of us is suffocating. I'm sitting next to Harlem rubbing his back as he goes down for his nap and Creed sits by the window refusing to even look at me. I'm not used to being the one that has to do the making up, I have spent so long being the one in the right that I have no idea how to be the wrong one for once. Everything he said earlier is right, I had no right to hurt Meg the way I did, and I feel sick just thinking about it. Once Harlem is finally asleep, I stand and move toward Creed, leaning against the wall and staring out the same window he does. The silence is tense and uncomfortable but at least we are in the same room for a change. Neither of us speaks, we just gaze out the window lost in our thoughts for a long while.

"I have never had to worry about a woman or their feelings before." I turn and face him, but he continues to stare out the window. "As eat ass as it sounds women always wanted to please me," An irrational surge of jealousy spikes inside me. "They just wanted to bed the alpha and hope I would choose them, but I never wanted that. I have been following you for years, ever since I saw a picture of you for the first time, I think a part of me always knew, that you would be it for me. When you came to Rosewood I had a plan, albeit a bad one but a plan none the less. But that all went to shit when I first laid eyes on you and Corbin uttered that word." He finally turns to look at me as he says. "*Mate.* I knew then that I had to have you and no matter the cost I would never let you go." The longing and love in his gaze steals the very breath from my lungs.

"Creed--"

"Let me finish please, I need to say this, or I never will." I nod my head and drop into the other chair as I wait for him to continue. "That day at the summit when I watched you break because of your mom, something shattered inside me. It was the first time in my life that I wanted to take away another's pain and make it my own. Then when I realized you had run I...I lost it, I searched everywhere for you Jess, I knew Cairo had helped you in some way, when I reached out to him, he refused my calls, and when I learnt that the twins fled with you as well, I died a bit inside, my own blood chose to run with you because I fucked up so badly. Every time I got a lead on where you might be, hope spiked inside me, then when it turned out to be a dead end, another part of me would fall away and die. I became angry and bitter that my own mate fled, little did I know she fled while she was pregnant with my children." Guilt rears its head inside me. "I slacked off as alpha because my only focus was on getting you back, dad had to step up and help. Me being distracted meant that I wasn't on my game when Jacob and the council started to take away our land and in turn some of the pack begun to switch sides and I honestly... didn't blame them. I mean how could I? When Shelley called and told me she had a ping on your location and had spoken to you, I was already on the road searching--"

"Searching?" He smiles sadly.

"I searched for you every day, two days a month I would spend with the pack and help with issues and then the rest of the time I was on the road trying to find you." An incomparable amount of guilt swarms inside me, Creed put his life on hold for five years scouring the country trying to find me. I stand and then kneel in front of him, his eyes widen in shock as I grip both his hands in mine and stare into his hazel eyes. I didn't realize I could feel more for him than I already do but I was wrong, I misjudged him and held so much of my past anger against him. I have to let that all go if we are to ever move forward and try to make things work between us.

"I fled because I thought I didn't have another choice. I had no idea who or what I was to you, I wish I could have trusted you then, like I do now." He drops his gaze from mine, so I reach up and cup his cheek forcing him to look at me. "I am so sorry that you missed meeting our daughter or seeing our son grow. I wish I could say that if I had of known that day at the summit that I was pregnant that I would have stayed but I won't lie to you. I would have still run, we both made mistakes, and we will spend years trying to make up for it. I don't want to be away from you anymore and I sure as hell don't want to stay away from our son. I know I have been reserved and pulled away from not just you but Harlem as well, everything you said is true. I have a lot of trauma I need to work through and I'm going to do it. But please be patient with me, I need you--." He doesn't let me finish, he bats my hand away and cups my face and smashes his lips against mine. This kiss isn't soft or slow, this kiss is his way of branding me as his own and I'm not even mad about it. He yanks me up and settles me in his lap so I'm straddling him, I can feel his erection growing beneath me and moan into his mouth. Before I can deepen the kiss, he pulls back, both of us are panting and breathing hard.

"This can't be like the other times Jess. If we do this, we need to be all in, no more bringing up the past or blaming each other for shit. I-I can't do it anymore, I won't be shut out or second guessed. I want you to be straight with me and tell me if you can do this or not?" The way his voice wavers as he gives that ultimatum breaks through my last wall of defense.

"I promise, I won't shut you out or drag up shit from the past. I also swear that I won't second guess you as a father, you're an amazing dad Creed." I smash my lips against his and explore his mouth while I grip the strands of his hair and pull. A growl reverberates in his chest sounding out his approval which just bolsters my ego. I grind down on him and moan into his mouth, he runs his hands down my back and grips my waist keeping me pressed down on his hardening cock. Creed stands and I wrap myself around him without breaking our kiss, he presses me against the nearest wall and presses into me, electing a moan of pure pleasure from me. The heat that has always been present since the first moment Creed touched me is nowhere to be found, I'm pulled back to the here and now when Creed breaks the kiss and begins to lick a trail down my neck.

"You're wearing way too much clothes for my liking." I wheeze out between pants. I feel him smile against my neck before he pulls back and meets my gaze.

"That can be rectified in about point two seconds." He grips his shirt and hauls it over his head without dropping me, the eagerness he is displaying is turning me right the hell on. Without being a shifter I'm sure any human would be able to scent my arousal, the ache between my thighs is growing to be unbearable. He grips the end of my shirt and pulls it off chucking it over his head with a triumphant smirk on his face. My bra is the next to go, he places me on my feet and it's like a race between us to see who get their pants off first. Once we are both standing here naked, he grips the back of my thighs and lifts me, I wrap my arms and legs around him. My back is plastered to the wall and my gaze is locked on his, we don't move as we get lost in each other's eyes. I reach out and cup his cheek, I feel my tears begin to build as I look into his eyes.

Mate.

Yeah Sheba, he is ours.

"We can stop, I didn't--"He goes to pull away and set me on my feet but I hold on tighter and shake my head. "Then why are you about to cry?" he sounds so perplexed.

"Because I just realized how madly stupidly and crazily in love with you I am." His face breaks out into the biggest smile, I feel his hard cock pulse against my ass. He positions himself at my opening and begins to push inside me slowly as he says.

"I have loved you from the first moment you called me an *eggplant*" The fact that his dick is pushing inside me is the only reason I don't sass him back about that comment. Ripples begin to roll through me as he finally sheaths himself balls deep inside my pussy. We both moan in bliss at the feeling of being connected again, he maintains eye contact as he begins to move. My eyes roll back, God he feels so good inside me, he hits that elusive G-spot without even trying.

"Eyes on me princess." I snap my eyes to him and without letting them waiver, a loud moan comes from me, and he quickly seals his lips against mine to hush my cries of pleasure. If not for him being able to maintain rational thought my moans would have woken our son that I forgot was asleep in the room. I break the kiss and throw my head back biting my bottom lip to mute the sounds that want to escape me. Creed licks the mark on my shoulder and an inferno builds inside me, I feel my orgasm cresting and I try to latch onto it, just as I think I'm about there, it keeps moving out of reach.

"Creed--"

"Oh, you want to come, do you?" I meet his stare open mouthed, he didn't?

"You're doing it on..." I moan. "On purpose."

"You can come when I tell you to come, not before princess." The command in his voice has more liquid gathering between my thighs, the growl that comes from him tells me he knows and approve of my body's reaction to him. He kneads my ass cheeks between his hands and memories from our night on the beach replay in my mind. As if he can sense where my mind has gone, he pulls out of me and walks us toward the chair he was sitting on, he places me on my feet, and I stare up at him waiting. "Brace yourself on the seat and spread your legs on the arms of the chair." Eager to please and see what is about to happen I do as he says and balance my legs on either of the arms and clutch the back of the chair. I feel Creed move in behind and shiver as he runs his hand down the backs of my thighs. With my legs spread wide and my pussy open I know he will be able to see how wet I am and a part of me loves the fact that he will know he is the reason for my growing wetness. He runs a single finger through my lips, and I lean down and bite the back of the chair to stop myself from crying out when he pushes that finger inside me. "Quiet!"

"I can't." I whisper shout, he growls then slaps my ass which elicits another cry from me. He reaches around with his free hand and clamps it over my mouth, he continues to finger fuck my pussy as he whispers in my ear.

"Keep quiet or I stop, and you can walk around on edge for the rest of the evening knowing it's your own fault why you didn't get to come?" I glare at him from the corner of my eye which just causes him to chuckle. Sheba on the other hand is enjoying the challenge he just laid down, I'm glad one of us has faith in our abilities to keep quiet. He pulls his finger out and runs it up to my puckered hole, I tense as he circles it, but manage to relax myself a little when I remember how good it felt with his finger in *that* hole while his dick was pounding away inside me. "When we have more time, I'm going to fuck this hole, I plan to fuck every hole you have princess so there will never be a doubt about who this body belongs to."

My mind is too focused on needing to come to even care about his stamp of ownership that he just made clear. I will let him say and do whatever the hell he wants right now as long as he makes me come. He pushes his finger inside my ass, and I bite down hard on my bottom lip to stop myself from crying out. He lines his cock up and slams inside me, the euphoria that blasts through me has tears in my eyes. His pace is relentless as he fucks me in both holes, I have no time to prepare as my orgasm slams into me. I go limp against the chair, but Creed isn't done yet, he pulls his finger out of my ass and then grips the back of my hair and yanks me up until my back is flush against his chest.

"Oh my god."

"Fuck you feel so good, princess."

"Hmmmm." I feel another orgasm building, Creed reaches around and pinches my clit which sends me plummeting over the edge with Creed following me a second later. Both of us are breathing heavy and panting like we ran a marathon, I guess in a way we kind of did.

"I would love to stay buried inside of you... but we both need to shower and clean up before the monster awakens." At the mention of our son, it snaps me back into reality, Creed ushers me into the bathroom and motions for me to shower first while he collects our scattered clothes.

After we showered and Harlem woke, we decided to take him out on deck and let him explore a bit. Creed and I follow him and smile when he waves to everyone, is it weird that I'm comfortable with vampires rubbing my sons head and being around him? I may not like Creed's birth mother but that doesn't mean I blame all vampires because their leader is a bitch.

Ah, speak of the bitch and she will arise.

"I didn't think I would run into the three of you." I hold

back the growl that wants to tear from me, after everything Creed and I just spoke about I don't want to ruin it by clawing his bio moms face off. So, I pull my hand from his and smile as sweetly as I can at him and say.

"I'm gonna go find Ro and the others." His brow furrows but he doesn't comment, I turn to walk away but he pulls me back by my elbow and plants a breath-stealing kiss on me. Davina clearing her throat is the only thing that has us pulling apart, Creed smirks and winks before he says.

"Go find your brother, I'll keep the monster with me." Every part of me is screaming for me to take Harlem with me but I made a promise, and I won't break it. So, I nod and place a swift kiss on my son's head as I head off to find my brother and the others. They aren't hard to find, you can hear their boisterous laughter and loud booming voices in the middle of the boat. I gasp as I round the corner and see sun loungers and a pool, a freaking pool! Shifters and vampires are meant to be mortal enemies according to movies and books but here they are laughing and swimming together as if we are...normal.

"Jess!" I shake my head and turn to smile at Callie as I make my way toward her. Ro slings his arm around my shoulders, but he quickly drops it and jumps back while glaring at me.

"What?" I ask, he narrows his eyes.

"You reek of Reeves." I feel the blush heating my cheeks, I can feel everyone's eyes on me. I spy Cole out of the corner of my eye next to Zeke and expect him to be angry, but he just laughs and shakes his head. Callie is making gagging sounds; Sky doesn't seem fazed at all by any of this.

"Uh, I um." I stop and take a deep breath; I haven't done

anything wrong! "So what? We are mated and have kids together Ro, how do you think the twins were created?" He flinches and shakes his head.

"My god, I think I liked it better when you hated him, at least then I didn't have to smell his stench all over you." Z claps him on the back and laughs as he says.

"Baby sis isn't a baby anymore bro."

"Thank you very much for that useless bit of information Zeke." We all bust out laughing at my brothers clear un-comfortability with this situation. Callie, Sky, and I break away from the boys and claim some free loungers, I feel very over dressed in shorts and shirt while the girls are in their swimmers. Before I can get lost in my thoughts too much, something slaps me in the side of the face, I turn and glare at Callie as she laughs. I pick up the garment she threw at me, and it's a pair of swimmers.

"Go change, there is a changing room behind the stairs." On closer inspection I notice it is a two piece and all my insecurities come rushing forward as I stare at the bikini. "Nah uh." I lift my gaze to Callie. "Don't you dare look like that, you are a hot as fuck mom and you are going to rock the shit out of that outfit, now go change or I'll make Sky do it for you." I look to Sky and cringe as she quirks a brow as if daring me to defy her mate. I groan and stand heading toward the changing room with Callie's laughter following me.

I take a few deep breaths after changing into the bikini, I ignore the mirror on the back of the door. The bottoms are more like a G-string and have my ass on display, the top is clearly for Callie's size boobs as the cups just cover my tits.

Ignore your inner thoughts and go out there.

I can't...

You can and you will, you do not hide from anyone. This is not who we are, tomorrow isn't promised Jess, and this may be the last time you can have with your friends.

The sobering reality of Sheba's words give me the confidence that I need to take a steadying breath and unlock the door and embrace my curves and the body that I have.

Chapter Forty Three
Credence

I glare at Davina, after what Jess and I just discussed, the last person we needed to run into was her. I reach down and haul Harlem up onto my shoulders, at least if he is up here then she can't touch him.

"What do you want Davina?"

"Nothing, I was just out here organizing for a team to go ahead of us on one of the speed boats." I make sure to keep the shock from my face.

"Why?" She rolls her eyes and puts her hands on her hips.

"Because I refuse to go in blind, I want to make sure what Belle said is true before my grands-- people walk into a trap." I ignore the fact that she was about to say *grandson*, I hate to admit it, but her plan is a good one.

"If you need men, I'm happy to send some of mine with yours." She shakes her head.

"No need, Cairo has offered to send some of his with Vince and the others."

He is not alpha!

Calm down Corbin, starting a war with our mate's brother isn't going to please her.

He relinquished his claim to being alpha.

Now isn't the time Corbin.

I close the link between us and focus on Davina. "If it's all the same I will send two of men with yours, they know the land better than any of the others."

"Very well, they will leave at first light tomorrow morning." I don't bother to say anything else; I turn around and go in search of my mate.

"Daddy?"

"Yeah monster?"

"I wanna see grandma." I blow out a breath but agree, I may talk a big game but when it concerns my son, I can't seem to find the balls to say *no* to anything he wants. We manage to find my mom on the lookout of the boat, Harlem started to shake on the way up the stairs, so I opted to give him a piggy-back ride instead. I think I just found out something new about my son, he is afraid of heights. "Grandma look, I big." My mom spins around with a broad smile on her face when she spots us, beside her is Connie and George. They both bow their heads in a show of respect, I nod and focus back on my mom.

"You are so big, look how tall you are!" The way my mom can act shocked and surprised on que is a skill in itself. She reaches around and plucks my giggling son from my back.

"Now I not big." Mom frowns and places Harlem on his feet then kneels down in front of him and clasps each of his hands in hers. I watch their interaction in fascination and honestly, in the hopes of learning something.

"Don't be in a rush to grow up sweetie, you will be big and strong like your daddy in no time, but you will also be brave and fearless like your mommy. But for right now, let's just enjoy you being a fearless, strong willed and loving little monster." She ends it with tickling his sides and he squeals in delight; I smile and get lost in watching my mom and son play. My attention is snagged when I hear squeals and hoots coming from below, I peer over the railing and spot a...pool! Fucking hell, how did I not know there was a pool? Another peel of laughter has me snapping my gaze to the two guys in the pool with girls on each of their shoulders, I laugh but the laughter dies in my throat when I zero in closer to who they are. One of the guys is Cairo with Callie on his shoulders and the other is Zeke with...Fuck! I spin around and race down the stairs leaving Harlem behind with my mom, anger is radiating off me. People hustle out of the way, one thing about being a shifter is you can sense and smell the rage of another, so everyone in this vicinity knows now is not the time to fuck with me. As I round the corner I slam to a stop, Cole is now in the water with Sky on his shoulders. I turn to Jess and see that the bikini she has on barely covers her tits, I growl and storm over to the edge of the pool. None of them notice me for a minute and continue to laugh and try push each other off their perch on the guy's shoulders. Cole and Sky are the first to spot me and both the smiles on their faces die when they see the look on my face.

"Come on Callie, that all you got?"

"You're going down Hastings." Jess laughs and reaches out with her arms to push Callie off but then spins her head to the side and the smile on her face drops when she sees me. Due to her being distracted by me she doesn't have time to dodge my sisters attack as she is shoved from Zeke's Shoulders. Zeke spins around and grips her hips to help her up, Jess being the smart cookie that she is, as soon as she breaks through the water again, she tries to step out of Zeke's hold, but he won't let her. Her gaze snaps to me and he follows her, a frown mars his face.

"Unless you want to lose those fucking hands you will take them off her now!" The carefree look Jess had is gone and I see some of the happiness in her eyes dim.

"Dude, there is a pool table over there, go and play a game

with Kyle. If you can't find a cue just pull the one out of your ass and use that." I glare at Cole and open my mouth to reply but Jess beats me to it.

"It's okay, I should go anyway--"

"Nah, fuck that. Get lost Reeves, my sister was having fun and you ruined it." I recoil internally, fuck! I keep fucking things up and I don't want to treat her like a possession, so I think on my feet and do something I would never normally do, I grip the bottom of my shirt and pull it off, I don't miss the way Jess's eyes double in size. I kick off my shoes and dive in jeans and all, I make sure to surface right between Jess and Zeke. I focus all my attention on her as I push my hair back out of my face.

"Dick." I ignore Zeke and smile at Jess as I grip her hips and pull her flush against me, she reaches up and wraps her arms around my neck. I move my hands to cup her ass but frown when I feel skin instead of the material of her bottoms. I peer over her shoulder and... fuck me sideways. She is wearing a G-string!

"Princess." I growl out, she at least has the courtesy to look semi sheepish.

"They are called bikinis, don't freak out...please." I squeeze the globes of her ass and relish in the gasp it elicits from her.

"You can wear those tonight--."

"Those are *our* sisters swimmers dick face." I release Jess and jump backward like she burnt me; everyone laughs including Jess.

"On second thought, burn them and anything else she has given you." My head snaps forward and I turn to glare at the little shit I share blood with.

"I will have you know, Sky looooves everything I wear--." I strike out and cover her mouth with my hand, when I hear Sky laugh, I pin her with a dirty look.

"I do not, I repeat do not need to know what you and your mate do in the privacy of your own room. Something's are better left private, kay?" I release her and step backward, Jess comes to stand in front of me and I wrap my arms around her middle and savor this moment.

"Fuck off with that bullshit, if Callie has to do that, then so do you, now get away from my sister. You're like a fucking blow fly that will never die." Even I bust out laughing at Ro, riling him up is becoming my favorite thing to do. Once we get our laughter under control Jess faces off against her brother.

"Did you just call my mate, slash baby daddy a *blow fly*?" Ro looks to me and smirks as he answers.

"It was either blow fly or pedo?" I recoil and glare at the fucker, Jess gasps and places her hands on her hips. I can feel Sheba close to the surface and I preen like a proud peacock at the way my mate is ready to throw down for me.

"The fuck would you call me a *pedo* for you fucking asshole?" A sly look crosses his face.

"You literally pretended to be a high school senior so you could bone my sister you fucker." I can't help it, laughter bubbles out of me and within a second Jess begins to laugh as well. Everyone eyes us like we have lost of minds.

"You two are weird as fuck." I ignore my brother and clear my throat before asking.

"You guys wanna have a re-match? Bet ya Jess and I can

take you all on." A devilish glint enters both Ro and Sky's eyes.

"Deal, Sky's with me--."

"Hey! She's, my girlfriend!" Sky turns toward Callie and wraps her arms around her mate.

"Baby, I love you, but you are terrible at sports." I cough to try and hide my laughter when my sisters mouth drops open in shock. "You go with Cole, and I promise I'll make it up to you later." Callie opens and closes her mouth like a fish out of water.

"Fuck no!" We all turn to Cole. "I'm down for Jess and Sky rubbing their ass cheeks all over me but like fuck is my twin doing that, I bow out, Z can take my place." We all laugh again; I can't blame my brother though. Because I am trying to change my ways, I reach out and grip his arm as he is about to hop out of the pool and speak.

"After Jess and I beat the shit out of these guys you can take Jess and beat their asses again." Cole looks at me in shock and I can feel everyone else's gaze on me as well.

"Uh, yeah sure bro, okay thanks."

As shore comes into view it's bittersweet, these past couple of days have been the best of my life. The anger and rivalry between me and my brother is gone, since leaving that island both Cole and I have agreed that the anger within us... vanished. Neither of us know what was the cause, and both of us refuse to believe Davina, that it was over power and wanting to rule the vampires. Callie and I reconnected, and it was interesting to get to know this new version of my sister, she isn't a little girl anymore she is a woman. Callie let a big secret slip and I have to say it hasn't stopped playing on my mind ever since she told me the first night on the boat. Jess and I even seem to be more at ease and getting along so well, Cairo and I have gotten back to how we used to be which I am thankful for. Sky is...Sky, so nothing much has changed there but Zeke-- I know he loves to push my buttons about Jess but after spending some time with him I must say, he is a good guy.

I wouldn't trade the time I've spent with my friends and family these past couple of days for the world. My siblings and I have even noticed that mom has relaxed a lot and isn't so worried that we are going to run off and jump on team Davina, Cole and Callie still can't stand the sight of her. Me on the other hand, it's not that I like her or anything, but I feel like there is more to her than meets the eye, whether or not I find out is yet to be determined.

"We'll ride together, it will be tight but at least the monster and my sister won't be unprotected."

"Agreed Ro, but I just have to check and make sure my mom is sweet to get back." Cairo nods and I head off to find mom, she stands to the side of the boat gazing out at the ocean. She doesn't turn toward me as she speaks.

"As soon as we leave this boat the happiness, we have built over the past couple of days will be gone." I share in her misery, if it was up to me, we would keep sailing around the world and never leave the damn boat.

"Mom, the carefree part may leave us but the memories of what happened here will remain. It won't always be like this--"

"Don't make promises you can't keep son, when your father comes back everything will change–"

I growl and pull on her arm until she turns to face me, I ignore the look of sadness in her eyes as I meet her gaze. She needs to see the truth in my eyes as I speak these next words because I will not say them again.

"He will change nothing; you are our mother what more do we have to do to show you that? You want to adopt us? Fine, I can have the paperwork drawn up, but a piece of paper doesn't change how we view you. We may not share DNA mom but we sure as fuck share love and loyalty and that is all you need in a family." Tears stream down her face, I wrap my arms around her and hold her against me as she sobs. Her tears soak my shirt, and it hurts me to know that she has been carrying these doubts around with her since she learned that Davina is alive. Anger simmers inside me, not at my mom but at myself for not making sure that she was reassured and made to feel like she isn't someone or something that can be replaced. I rest my chin on top of her head and just hold her. "I love you mom; nothing will ever change that."

"I love you to son, more than you will ever know." She pulls back and wipes her face, I look away to give her some semblance of privacy. Once she has herself composed, I fill her in on what is about to happen, she tells me that she is going with Connie and George so that eases my worries slightly, I know George would die protecting his mate and my mom.

We have been in the car for two hours and already I want to throttle my siblings, Cole, Sky and Callie sit in the back while Jess, Harlem and I sit in the middle. Z sits shotgun while Ro drives, I can tell from how stiff they are that they are about as ready as I am to smash the twins' heads together.

"Your leg is touching mine!"

"Close your fucking legs then, it's not like you have balls and need the space, Callie."

"I have bigger nuts than you, just ask Sky." Sky groans but doesn't comment, they have been arguing over stupid shit like this the whole way.

"Mommy, Daddy?"

"Yeah monster?" We both answer in unison.

"I don't want a brother anymore." This clever four-year-old has no idea that thanks to him cracking that joke he saved his aunt and uncle. The car erupts into fits of laughter, the only ones who are not laughing are the salty ass twins in the back.

"I'm so glad Sky doesn't have a penis." I snap my head back and glare at my sister.

"Watch your mouth California." I grit out, she pokes her tongue out and rolls her eyes.

"Oh please, if Sky was a dude and knocked me up, the world would implode, mother earth isn't ready for two California Reeves. Plus, I would hate for it to come out like the monster and say stupid shit." I glower at my sister; she really needs to get a filter. No brother ever wants to hear about his sister's sex life,

I shudder at the thought of my baby sister doing the horizontal tango.

"We still have a really long drive; I know everyone is antsy and on edge, but can we please not fight. Also, while we are all here, everyone needs to stop having sly digs at my son, he is four and says it how he sees it, so don't act like a dick, and he won't call you out!" we all stare at Jess, she doesn't waiver under the pressure of our gazes just merely shrugs and turns to look out her window again. The twins manage to remain quiet which is a miracle in itself! Cairo and I refused to let any of our guys lead the convoy of cars, as the alpha's it is our job to lead, but with that being said when we are about halfway we pull over into a gas station to swap Harlem into my mom's car. Jess of course refused to ride with them, I don't trust the council or Jacob not to have set a trap for us, and if there is an ambush, I want my son as far away from it as possible. After transferring his seat and strapping him in, Jess and I both cuddle and give him a kiss, I feel a lump rise in my throat as I look at my son. A renewed sense of determination flows through me, I never want to be separated from him or my mate again and if that means killing every member of the council and Jacob-- I'll do it.

As we near Rosewood the tension in the car amps up, we instructed the cars travelling with young and the older members not to enter the town and stay hidden on one of the dirt roads until we sent for them. I want to make sure everything is secured, and no one is waiting for us, I don't know this Belle woman and I sure as fuck don't trust her. For all I know someone could have forged that note and we're travelling into a trap. I reach over and clasp Jess's hand in mine giving it a gentle squeeze, I can tell the smile she gives me is forced but I don't have time to dwell on it as we are finally crossing into Rosewood. I stare out my window stunned speechless.

What the fuck?

I can't scent anyone.

No shit Corbin, it looks deserted.

"What the hell happened here?" Zeke took the words right out of my mouth. The whole main street is void of people; I wouldn't be surprised to see some tumble weeds rolling through the township. As we head toward my pack lands, I begin to scent humans but there isn't many, where did everyone go?

"We need to figure out what the hell happened here. I get that the pack left but why have the humans up and left as well?"

"That is exactly what I want to know Cole." I reply, the rest of the car ride to the pack lands is quiet as we all stare out the windows and get lost in our own thoughts. As we get closer to my pack lands, I begin to get anxious about what awaits us, this could be a trap for all we know. "Stop the car." Cairo does as I say and pulls over. Before they speak, I hop out of the car and run to the vehicle behind us, Asher, and Tommy both jump out to meet me and I can feel Cairo and Zeke coming up behind me.

"What's going on Creed?" I can tell Asher is worried and already on high alert, good. I need all my men to stay sharp until I am sure there is no threat.

"I want some of you to drive up to the pack house and the rest to shift and take a wide birth around and see if you can scent anything or find anything. Something isn't right and I want to know what that is before my mate and son get caught in a crossfire." Both Asher and Tommy nod then turn to go fill the rest of the pack in, Cairo motions for Zeke to go do the same with their pack.

"We gonna wait for them or go at the same time?"

"No, the wolves will go first and when I'm satisfied it is safe, I'll mind link Jess and let her know." Cairo lets out a low whistle and raises his brows.

"Yeah, that isn't going to go down well with my sister at all." I sigh, I know he's right, but I am the alpha, and it is my job to lead my pack. I am no coward, and I will not stay back and send my men into the unknown where I am not willing to go myself.

"I'll go tell her."

"Yeah bro, better you than me."

What a drop nuts!

CHAPTER FORTY FOUR

Jessica

I have been a ball of nerves ever since I relented to Creed and agreed that I would stay behind while he and the others scout the pack lands. I hate the thought of him out there and potentially in danger, I know Creed isn't the type of alpha to stand down from a battle, but the selfish part of me, wishes he would.

"He'll be fine." I release the breath I didn't know I was holding.

"You don't know that Ro." My brother scoffs and Cole chuckles which earns him a glare from me.

"My brother is to stubborn to die, Jacob is sly and cunning, but he is no match for Creed." My brow furrows, I feel like I am missing something here. "Look, Creed is strong and resilient. He was raised for this shit and thrives off the danger, don't insult him by assuming that he can't hold his own. I have seen my brother go into battle when other alphas would try to claim our land, Creed always won." A thought hit me then.

"If Creed won those fights, then doesn't that mean he would have to take over the other packs?" Cole smiles but it doesn't reach his eyes.

"Creed will never deliver the killing shot; he would always let the other alpha leave with his pack if they swore never to return." I reel back at a loss for words. "Creed never wanted to be like our father so he... changed things."

"I-I had no idea."

"Don't beat yourself up over it sweetheart, Creed doesn't know that Callie and I know. We overheard him and dad fighting about it one night, dad told him that it made him look weak not killing. In truth, if Creed had of done it, we might not be in the position we are in now."

"Don't put that on him Cole, he couldn't have known anything like this would happen. He was just trying to do better than dad--"I cut Callie off.

"Wait, so if Creed let the other alpha's go then that means they would feel indebted to him then, right?" The five of them have funny looks on their faces but it's Z that catches on to what I am asking first.

"You might be right, if we can use that to our advantage, we might have a shot. How many alphas would you say Creed has fought?" Zeke asks Cole.

"Including Jacob?" My mouth drops open in shock.

"He fought Jacob?" My voice is high pitched as I ask.

"Uh, yeah?" Cole looks at me like I'm slow.

"Why didn't he kill him?" I grit out, if the others are shocked by my bloodthirst, they don't show it.

"Okay first, including Jacob, Z I think he fought around nine. Now, to answer your question love, if he could spare the person he hated most in the name of peace, then other alphas might do the same. Turns out he was wrong and should have just ripped the old fuckers throat out when he had the chance." I slump back in my chair and remain silent, as the others try to revise a plan, I'm so lost in my own thoughts that I don't hear him the first time.

Princess? The worry in his voice has me sitting straight.

I'm here, are you okay?

Yeah, I'm fine. What took you so long to answer?

Uh... I was just distracted. I lie not wanting to worry him, I'll speak with him about what I have learnt later.

Tell your brother it's clear and to come up to the house.

Okay.

We pull up to the house and I can't help but stare, it's like someone entered my mind and used everything I wanted and made it come true. When I was younger, I used to sketch out what my dream house would look like, I drew this exact house pretty much. I see wolves start to come around the front of the house, I scan my eyes over them until I land on Creed's wolf. He is a giant of a man, and you would think dropping down to four legs would diminish his stature, but it doesn't. Creed is a regal looking beast and even when he tries not to look daunting, he can't help it the aura that surrounds him is power and dominance. I don't see how I am supposed to be this big bad alpha when I want nothing more than to submit to my mate. Sheba scoffs inside my head.

I will not roll over and allow him to lead us.

I don't want to lead Sheba.

You must!

We'll talk about this later.

I follow the others out of the car and don't stop until I'm standing in front of Corbin, Sheba pushes forward and takes partial control. She refuses to drop her gaze from Corbin's, and I begin to panic that he will view this as a challenge and the last thing I need right now is to be at odds with Corbin. Except...

nothing happens. Corbin and I stand there staring but even with Sheba at the forefront I don't feel the need I used to, the urge to control and dominate isn't present. Before I can dwell on it too much he turns and heads around the back of the house, I follow Cole and the others inside, we expected to find the house trashed but... nothing is out of the ordinary. Callie takes Sky's hand, and they check out the back half of the house, Zeke and Cairo search the kitchen, so Cole and I decide to check out the rooms. We all meet back in the living room and the others found the same as we did, everything is fine and not out of order.

"Why the hell didn't they torch the place?"

"Morbid much sister?" Callie glares at Cole but I ignore them and ask.

"Where is Creed?" Callie and Cole's faces scrunch until they see the look I shoot them, their eyes drop, and their posture stiffens. "What's wrong?" "He'll probably be at his house..." I choke on air as I stare at the pair of them.

"What does that mean?" Callie meets my gaze, and it annoys me to see sympathy shining in her eyes.

"Creed should fill you in, if you follow the path out the back of this house it will lead you to his. We'll bring your bags out to you." I nod and follow her instructions and head out the back to follow the beaten path toward the woods. I don't know why I am shocked, I guess being with Creed means I'll learn new things every day. As I break through the dense brush of trees a simple log cabin comes into view, it looks like something out of a story book that I read to Harlem. Two windows in the front with a simple porch and two rocking chairs, the front door is slightly ajar. I take a few deep breaths and roll my shoulders back as I head inside, I push the door open and decide to let myself in. I close the door quietly behind me and spot a small cozy looking kitchen to the left, a lounge room in front of me, my ears perk up at the sound of running water. I follow the sound to the right of the lounge room and down the hallway, I pass by two closed doors and enter the room at the end with the door open. I can tell immediately that this is the master bedroom, Creed's scent clings to everything in here. I scan the room and see an open wardrobe, my nose gets the better of me, so I take a to peek inside and I'm stunned. I stand here staring with my mouth hanging open, I'm so lost in what I'm looking at I don't hear him come out of the adjoining bathroom.

"I didn't want them sitting in boxes." I spin around and stare at him with tears in my eyes, he stands there with a towel wrapped around his waist and water droplets dripping from his hair, I follow the droplets as they run down his chest--." You gonna keep checking me out or?" I shake my head and quickly spin around; I feel the heat in my cheeks I don't know why I am embarrassed after all the things we have done together. I gasp when he warps his arms around my waist and rests his chin on my shoulder.

"Why?"

"Because..." He clears his throat and tries again. "I had always hoped you would come back, or I would find you, so I figured it was a good idea. Are...Are you mad about it?" I turn around and look at him, he seems so unsure, and it warms my heart. I wrap my arms around his neck as he places his hands on my hips. I reach up on tip toes and plant a soft kiss to his lips and pull back. He stares at me like I'm some strange being which causes a smile to stretch across my face.

"I'm not mad, I'm just so surprised that you would hang my clothes and keep my stuff that I left behind." He cups my face between his hands.

"It was all I had left of you so of course I would keep it. They may be just material things but when they are all you have left, they mean so much more." I swoon a little inside, the way he ducks his head to hide his eyes I realize he's shy about discussing his feelings. It's endearing to finally find something that he isn't comfortable with, I feel in power now that the shoe is on the other foot. Deciding to take pity on him I ask instead.

"Why didn't Sheba fight for control when you were in wolf form?" A sexy smirk graces his lips.

"Because our wolves have finally seen each other as equals." I gasp and open the link to Sheba.

Is that true?

Yes, our mate is strong and fearless.

So, you won't fight him anymore? Sheba scoffs and I fight the laugh that wants to bubble out of me.

Never! I can't hold back, I laugh, and Creed narrows his eyes playfully at me.

"What did Sheba have to say?"

"Ummmmm, I think she really is my soul mate."

"Why?"

"She agrees you're a good mate, but she refuses to never fight you on anything." He chuckles and shakes his head as he plants a featherlight kiss to my forehead.

"I would expect no less from her... or you."

Chapter Forty Five
Jessica

We've been back in Rosewood for two weeks now and everything is...quiet. We aren't fooling ourselves though, we know this is the calm before the storm. We have learnt from some of the towns folk that remained that Jacob and his pack chased most of them out, it was a relief to know that they did that in human form and didn't expose our secret. The pack has been busy trying to help cleanup the town and with the re-opening of the stores. We have tried to reach out to as many of the humans that fled, some of them refused to return and sold their homes to us or their businesses. The ones that did return were happy and willing to help with re-opening stores. Creed and I agreed that it would be a bonus for the kids in our pack and Ro's to attend school and return to some form of normality. The kids will start back next week, Callie has even agreed to teach in the local Kindergarten, and Meg has signed on as principle for the high school. Zeke and Cole offered to take over teaching the sporting programs and honestly, I couldn't have picked two better people for the job. Asher and Tommy are both going to run the local hardware store, everyone seems to be pitching in, and honestly Creed and I couldn't be more grateful.

"I don't want to go with Aunt Callie." I shake my head to clear my thoughts and sigh. Creed shoots me a pleading look to take over this talk with our son. He has not been open to the idea of going to school with Callie next week. We have to prepare him so Creed and I can plan and prep for an attack, I know it will be good for him to be around other kids his own age. I reach out and run my fingers through his hair, I'm still taken back that he will let Creed cut it considering he refused for years!

"Monster, you need to go so you can learn and make friends." He slumps back in his chair and crosses his arms over his chest.

"I don't want friends, daddy says they oberated." I glare at Creed as he tries to hide his smile.

"Friends are *not* overrated; friends are great, and they help you. If you don't make friends, who will you invite to your birthday party in a couple of months?" That seems to pique his interest.

"Your mother is right, if you make friends then we can have a big party and invite them all here."

"Promise?" I shoot Creed a look urging not to make a promise he can't keep; he ignores the look and smiles wide.

"I promise buddy. I missed four birthdays already, and I will not let another one go by where I don't get to throw my favorite guy in the whole world a party fit for a king." A lump forms in my throat as I watch Creed and Harlem embrace each other, I really hope Creed is able to fulfil his promise to our son.

That evening Creed and I decided to hold a small meeting at Meg's house, I know Creed still feels a bit awkward coming here because it holds dark memories for him, I squeeze his hand as we enter the house, he smiles but it doesn't reach his eyes. I sigh and let him lead me to the dining room, I smile when I see my son on a small stool in the kitchen cooking with Meg.

Harlem has been a great distraction for her, I know she misses Kane even though he hurt her, she has been pushing Creed to search for him. Creed being the stubborn ass that he is, refuses, he thinks I don't know that he has been sending out search parties every couple of days, I haven't said anything about it to him. Creed releases my hand and makes his way toward our son and his mom; he places a kiss on her cheek and ruffles Harlem's hair which earns him a dark scowl from the moody four-year-old.

We all take our seats around the table, Ro, Z, Callie, Sky and Cole join us for dinner. Everyone makes small talk and it's nice to see everyone relaxed and not so on edge like we have been for the past few weeks. This false sense of eutopia that we have allowed ourselves to fall into is just a mask.

"We have to hunt and flush them out, I won't keep looking over my shoulder." All conversation around the table stops and all eyes swing to me. Creed sighs then turns to our son and says.

"Why don't you go into the living room and play with your trains, and I'll bring you desert soon?" Harlem nods his head eagerly and jumps from his chair.

"Jess is right, this shit has to end."

"How do you propose we do that when we can't find them?" Ro and Z exchange a loaded look before answering Creed.

"We may have a lead." I stare at my brother with my mouth hanging open.

"How?" Callie asks. Cairo doesn't give anything away; he remains stoic and his face an emotionless mask, but Z very quickly darts his gaze to Sky and back to us, that's all I need to know. They have a lead, and it is something to do with Skylar Cage, Sky is like a vault, you won't be able to crack her unless she wants you to know. Callie must have seen Zeke's subtle glance at her mate because now she is scowling at Sky. "Care to fill the rest of the class in on what we are missing, *darling*?" The way she says darling has Sky cringing and both my brother and Z leaning back into their chairs.

"Oh shit, hurricane California is brewing." Creed and Cole may act tough and like alpha males but at the first sign of their sister about to pop off they both scoot their chairs toward the end of the table where their mother sits shaking her head.

"Fuck up Colton!" Callie doesn't take her eyes off Sky as she snaps at her brother.

"Mom, can Cole and I be excused?" I gape at Creed; he has to be joking. He shrugs his shoulders and then mouths *she's crazy.*

"You fucking pussy, stay the hell where you are!" Creed snaps his mouth closed and averts his gaze to the ceiling, I have never seen him, and Cole behave like this before, mind you I have never actually seen Callie lose her shit properly either. "I'm waiting, darling!"

"Babe--"

Callie scoffs. "Don't fucking *babe* me. You promised not to keep me in the dark with any of this, you always shut me out where *he* is concerned!" She shouts while pointing at my brother, Cairo at least has the decency to avert his gaze and keep his mouth shut. Sky doesn't waiver as she meets Callie's gaze, these two fiery women are a match made in heaven.

"You knew where I stood with *him* before we became an

item, he is my alpha, and I can't betray him."

"Can't or won't?" I hear the watery tone in Callie's voice and know she is close to tears; I hate that this shit is coming between them. I know Sky is loyal as fuck to my brother and I still have no idea why, but from the look on her face I can tell she is trying to find a way to let her mate down gently.

"California... Please don't--"

"No! I have told you before I don't want to be treated like my bro--"Callie quickly clamps her mouth closed and then faces me with wide eyes, I smile sadly and reach out to place my hand on hers.

"Like your brother treated me?" She nods and I can feel Creed's gaze boring into the back of my head but ignore it. "You and Sky are nothing like Creed and me, maybe just let her keep you in the dark?"

Callie shakes her head. "I don't want to be in the dark, Jess. I have been in the dark most of my life and I don't want my own mate to treat me like that." I wrap my arms around her and hold her close, I'm surprised when I feel both Cole and Creed press up behind me and each of them land a hand on their sisters back offering their silent support.

"I respect the fuck out of you Sky, always have and probably always will, but I will not let you hurt my sister because you have some misguided loyalty to your alpha. My sister loves you and she is right, she deserves way fucking better than how I treated Jess, don't make the same mistakes I did because believe me, it isn't worth it in the end." I'm so proud of Creed for speaking his truth, he becomes my soul focus and it's hard to tear my gaze from him when Sky speaks.

"You know nothing Alpha--"

Ro cuts Sky off. "Enough, she is your mate, and she has a right to know." For the first time since I met Sky, I get a clear read on her emotions, her mask has slipped, and her emotions are on display for all to see. The silence in the room stretches for so long, I begin to think no one is going to talk, Callie pulls out of my hold and turns to face her mate who is solely focused on my brother.

"Take it from someone whose been in love with a compulsive liar for more than half my life. Whatever is keeping you from telling my daughter the truth or whoever you are protecting, is that thing or person worth risking losing the love of your life over? Forgive me, I don't mean to overstep, but as California's mother, my daughter deserves more from her mate and sure as hell does not deserve to be lied to." Meg runs her gaze over each of us and it pains me to see the unshed tears in her eyes, she still loves Kane. "Now, I will leave you kids to sort this out while I take my grandson some desert. If it's okay with you and Jess son, I would like to take Harlem with me to the pack bon fire tonight, I will have him back before bedtime?"

Is that okay with you? It doesn't shock me as much now that I'm used to hearing him in my head.

Yeah, I think he will like spending time with your mom.

"Go for it mom, I think the monster will love to spend some time with you." Meg smiles and scurries from the room grabbing a couple of chocolate muffins on her way out. Cole and Creed move back to their seats, but Creed pulls his close enough to me that his leg brushes against mine. Sheba stirs inside me and purrs at the contact from our mate. My wolf has some serious issues, right now is not the time to be thinking about our mate and how he can make our body soar when he is inside me--.

"Jessica!" I snap my gaze to my brother, and I feel the heat coating my cheeks and hope to God no one around the table can scent my arousal.

"Sorry, I was... distracted." He narrows his eyes at me but lets it go.

"I was just saying now that Callie and Sky have agreed to sort their matters out privately, we should go over the plan."

"Yeah Ro, why don't you fill us in on how you and Zeke know something we don't." Z rolls his eyes and scoffs.

"Yeah, that isn't going to happen but what we can say is that we have it on good authority that Jacob and his pack has taken to hiding in the mountains." What the hell.

"Why?" Cole grits out.

"Apparently some shit went down between him, and the council and they have closed him out." Ro raises his hand to stop Creed from interrupting Zeke. "We honestly don't know what happened between him and the council all we do know is that he and what is left of his pack are in the mountains somewhere."

"Wait, what do you mean what is left of his pack?" Z and Ro share a look before Ro takes over the conversation.

"According to our source, when the split between Jacob and the council happened some of his pack fled with the council and the others just left... on their own I guess."

"How many remain with him?" Cole asks.

"I don't know, that is where the biggest problem is." My shoulders slump slightly, we can't just charge in there blind without knowing how many he has with him it's a death warrant for all of us. I meet my brothers gaze and ask the one questions that has been burning in my mind.

"If we take Jacob out then the council will know we are coming for them." His face gives nothing away as to what he is thinking.

"Ask me what you really want to ask." I take a deep breath and square my shoulders as I hold his gaze.

"I don't want just Jacob; I want the council to pay as well. How do we get Shelley and the others back without them knowing we are coming?"

"I'm not sure, we don't have the numbers to be able to launch an attack simultaneously. We need to scout out where Jacob is and get a read on his numbers and try to find the whereabouts of the council's location. I am not going to make any promises Jess, I don't know if we can pull something like this off, if we can't, we will need to go with the easier of the two which is Jacob." Sheba smashes against my ribs and a gasp spills from my lips, I feel everyone's gaze on me, but I don't acknowledge them. I'm fighting to stay in control here and trying to push Sheba back down inside me or I risk her taking over and going after my brother.

I want his blood to coat my tongue!

Sheba...stop...we--

We go after him and then the council!

Why?

He tried to break us and caged us like a rabid animal. I will not allow him to continue to breath, he needs to be put down!

I wish I could say Sheba is wrong but she isn't, being taken by Jacob has changed me in ways I can't even begin to describe. Just hearing his name spikes my fears that I thought I had gotten over. Jacob nearly succeeded in breaking me, if it wasn't for... I cut myself off and ask.

"Do any of you know where Kayla is?" I see Creed stiffen out of the corner of my eye but ignore him as I run my gaze over each of them.

"Why?" I face Creed and speak.

"Because she is the one who saved my life, I think *you* and I both owe it to her to at least care enough to ask where she is." Creed pales and nods his head stiffly, Kayla and I may have started out on the wrong foot, but I'm the type of person who believes that everyone deserves a second chance. I know she and Creed share a past but that is exactly what it is, the past.

"I haven't seen her, we scoured Jacob's land to try and flush out any wolves that remained, but she wasn't among them." I nod my thanks to Z. The day after we arrived here Ro and a dozen others went to Jacob's land and searched the houses and outskirts and found over twenty wolves hiding. They were malnourished and frightened, it angered me to see them so skinny and gaunt.

"Look, now seems like a good time as any to tell you all I have set up a meeting with thirteen alphas tonight." Everyone snaps their gazes to Cole; he sits there and shrugs his shoulders like he didn't just drop a bomb on everyone. "What?"

"The fuck do you mean *what?*"

"Calm down Credence--"

"Don't tell me to calm down, you are not the alpha of this pack and had no goddamn right to go behind my back and call this meeting!" Cole slams his fist down on the table growling at his brother, Creed begins to vibrate and growl. I reach across and quickly place my hand on his shoulder to garner his attention, he shakes me off. Callie gives me a shove and I turn to her.

"Stop him, please." The worry in her voice snaps me into motion just as Creed is about to stand, I quickly push in front of him and drop into his lap. The shock of me doing something so bold like this in front of everyone has him snapping out of his anger and just staring at me.

"Jessica!"

"Cairo, now is not the time, you can thank me later for stopping the fight between these two goons." My brother groans but remains silent, I focus on Creed and cup his face between my hands. I need to tell him the truth and I'm honestly not sure how he is going to take it after that display.

"Don't blame Cole--"

"Why not?" I can his eyes flicker between hazel and blue, Corbin is close to the surface, I let Sheba come forward but remain in control, so she is able to calm Creed's beast.

"Because I asked Cole to call the alphas." Creed reels back taken off guard, by what I just said. I ignore the other chatter around us and focus on my mate, his eyes search mine but I'm not sure what he is looking for.

"Why princess?" I know the hurt that laces his tone is because I hid this from him, but I knew if I didn't, he would never have consented to it. Creed has tried to find a way around me meeting with the alphas because he is scared, they will challenge me or try to take me from him. But that will never happen because I have a plan and I just hope he trusts me enough to go along with it.

"Because, if we plan to go against Jacob and the council, we need their numbers. I know you love me and want to protect me, but I will not put the others in harm's way. You and I both know we don't have the numbers to take the council, given the situation with Jacob now and him being so close isn't it better that we have more wolves on our side?"

"And what if they don't want to help and just want to challenge you for the pack?" I hear growls sound out behind me.

"I'll fucking kill them for even thinking it!"

"I agree with your brother princess." I shake my head and hop off Creed's lap and move to the end of the table, so I have them all in my line of sight.

"They are coming tonight, so either get on board or piss off, because this is happening! I am not putting any shifter at risk because my mate was scared some big bad alpha wanted to fight me." Creed scoffs but I push on and shoot him a glare. "They will arrive tonight at 8pm so be ready and do not... I repeat, do not instigate any disagreements with any of these alphas, as I said before, I have a plan and you will ruin it if you start something!"

Chapter Forty Six
Credence

I stand here in the middle of the field next to Jess and Cole, grinding my teeth, my idiot brother needs to be taught a lesson and my mate... she needs to be punished. I plan to punish her over and over again tonight when these assholes leave. The bon fire was canceled tonight so I asked mom if she can keep Harlem with her. Cairo, Zeke, Sky, and myself, shit even Callie for once is on my side, agree that this idea of Jess's if fucking crazy.

They have invited thirteen fucking alphas to our pack lands when we are at our lowest, we don't have half the numbers each of their packs have. If they wanted to, they could annihilate us all tonight, on my own fucking land! Corbin has been pacing inside me, restless and edgy just waiting for one of them to attack. I have fought about half of these alphas and let them live, they are all strong and deadly, but of the ones I have fought Eric was the toughest. He isn't like the others and fights with brute strength he analyzes and studies his opponents for a weak spot before attacking, I hate the way he cocks his head to the side trying to get a read on Jess. I grit my teeth and take a few deep breaths to reign my temper in, if I attack him now in the open, I will start an all-out war that we can't afford right now.

"Colton, why are we here?" I turn toward Andrew, the alpha of the mid-west pack. He is a big fucker; he stands at around six-foot-six and is built like a brick shit house. I have never fought against Andy and honestly, he and I have never had a reason to cross paths except at the yearly summits. I snap out of my thoughts when Jess steps forward, she draws the attention of the alphas, and it angers me to see all their eyes on my mate!

"Cole asked you here on behalf of me." Even though I'm

angry at her for going behind my back I'm also proud as fuck at how strong she sounds, and the fact that she isn't cowering under the intensity of their gazes is also a testament to how brave she really is.

"Why did you need us here urgently?" Comes from Kyle, alpha to the Desert pack.

"Because we need your help." They all begin to murmur but stop when Jess growls, they each pin her with a curious look but say nothing. "Jacob Michelson and the council have declared war against us, they have taken over our land--"

"Why would we risk the wrath of the council to help you miss...?" Jess turns her head and focuses on William; he has only been alpha for a short time since his father passed. His dad was a respectable man and a great guy, but he did something that pissed the council off and a few days later wound-up dead. William being the alphas son means he was automatically named alpha of the Woodland pack the next day by the council.

"Because from what my brother tells me Will, you hate the council as much as us." Jess runs her gaze over each of the alphas as she speaks. "We will not force you or make demands, but what I will *ask, is* for your help. I specifically asked each of you here because I know you all have personally had an encounter with the council or Jacob. I won't lie, my brother and Creed wanted to visit each of your packs and ask for help and if you refused, they would have taken turns battling for the right to be named alpha of your packs." Each of them snaps their angry gazes to me, I stand tall and don't flinch under the weight of their accusing glares. "Don't blame him, he was backed into a corner and was only trying to protect me and our son." Tomlin steps forward and I growl out a warning, if any of these fuckers even so much as think to take on my mate, fuck the consequences, I will start a war right here and now! Tomlin eyes me for a second before focusing on Jess, she doesn't cower or step back, she stands tall and meets his gaze head on.

"Why would the council scum and Jacob be targeting you and your son?" I see Jess stiffen, bad move princess. With all eyes on her, it is impossible for them not to notice her tension, Tomlin cocks a brow at her as he says. "You want our help, then we deserve the truth, if we are to risk our packs safety to help a virtual stranger. We may know Credence, but we do not know you."

"Fine... My name is Jessica Has--Cruz, I am the daughter of two alphas and rightful alpha to both the Reeves and Michelson packs. Jacob has been after me ever since I came back to Rosewood, he killed my mother and then claimed I was his mate so I... killed his... son." That manages to shock all the alphas, I know that was hard for her to say out loud, but I cannot comfort her right now and undermine her in front of these guys or they will view her as weak, and my mate is so fucking far from weak. "I fled for five years and gave birth to mine and Creeds twins, the council and Jacob have hunted me since then."

"Twins?" Andy asks, Jess takes a shuddering breath and clenches her fists. I refuse to let her do this on her own, so I step up beside her and wrap my arm around her shoulders and draw her into my side as I answer.

"Jess and I *had* twins, our daughter, Katy, didn't make it.

The council has taken my father and two others hostage to draw us out, they know about Harlem and are coming for our son--"

"They want him because he is pure alpha blood." The horror in Tomlins's voice is so thick I can taste it on my tongue.

"Yes, Jess has asked you all here to help us save our son and our packs." Eric eyes me warily as he asks.

"Packs?" Before I can answer Cairo comes out of nowhere with Zeke and Sky on either side of him, all thirteen alphas may have never seen Ro before, but they sure as shit can sense the power radiating off him.

"My name is Cairo Cruz, and I'm Jess's brother, my pack is here to fight alongside of Creed and my sisters." Eric stumbles back as he stares at Ro.

"You are Austin and Shelley's son; you're supposed to be dead." Jess gasps beside me.

"You know our mother?"

"You said Jacob killed your mother!" Tomlin grits out, fuck this is going to take a long time. Cairo fills the alphas in on how Jess was raised by their aunt and how he fled, we tell them about Shelley and Dela being the other captives of the council.

"Right, now that you are all up to speed, decide whether it's a yay or nay, because if it's a nay, Creed and I will battle you for your packs?" Growls sound out and each of the alphas shift to fighting stances, I let go of Jess and push her behind me, then crouch ready to strike like Ro and the others. Jess rushes out from behind me and stands in the middle of us dividing the alphas.

"Please, these were not my intentions to fight amongst

ourselves. There is a greater threat out there and this is the last thing we want. If you don't want to help us take them down and get revenge for the things they have done to you and your pack personally then leave now!" I stare at her in shock, if they all leave, we're fucked. "But, if you choose to stay, then please stop this, too many lives have been lost already and the last thing I want is for anyone else to get hurt because I asked you all here. You don't owe us a thing, but I am asking for your help anyway?"

Twelve out of the thirteen alphas agreed to help us, Zion refused because a lot of his pack members are too old to fight. He did offer to aide us with planning but that is it, I respect his decision to protect his pack, he is a great alpha. We offered to bring their packs here and told them they could all stay on Jacob's land, they each agreed and said they will return with their packs. They were all shocked to learn about the vampires, we made sure to keep Davina and her lot hidden during the meeting, so we didn't spook them. We told the alphas we'd hold a meeting the next day to go over a plan and work out the logistics of it all. Plus, that will give them time to get their packs here and set up.

"We should get up." I roll over and bury my face in the crook of her neck near her mate mark and tighten my hold around her waist. She chuckles but doesn't push me away, it's not like we have to rush and get Harlem from mom. Plus, the meeting with the alphas isn't till this afternoon.

"Let's just stay here." She sighs and leans back into me. We lay here silently for a long time, each of us lost in our own thoughts.

"We'll make it out of this right?" I furrow my brow and pull back so I can stare down at her.

"I can't make that promise princess, but what I can do, is promise to try my hardest to keep us all safe." She smiles sadly and cups my cheek.

"I feel like all of this was for nothing, Jacob started this shit with the council because he wanted me due to the fact that I am of alpha blood and now look."

"What do you mean?"

"I don't want to lead Creed, the alphas all agreed to help because they were asked, not because they were forced. My brother doesn't want to lead either, so when all of this is over, I don't want to be alpha." I frown at her.

"What are you trying to say princess." She lets out a nervous breath and says.

"I want you to be alpha of the Reeves and Michelson pack, I'll help you however I can, but I don't want the title or the responsibility and let's be real, you thrive off of the power and stress." She chuckles and I playfully glare down at her. "You're a control freak and there is no way in hell you will ever take an order from me." I scoff.

"Would so."

"Yeah, right. When?"

"In the bedroom, you can boss me around whenever you like." She tries to turn and hide her face, I grip her chin and turn her to face me, the blush that coats her cheeks forces a smile from me. I capture her lips in a searing kiss that steals the breath from my lungs, I pull back and grip her face between my hands. "Thank you, princess."

"For what?"

"For giving me another chance and for just... being you. I never thought I would ever be lucky enough to find a mate who could rival me, and challenge me, but here you are, as perfect as ever. I love you Jessica Cruz-Hastings and I want you to share the same last name as me and our son, so would you marry me and become Mrs. Jessica Reeves?" Tears trail down her cheeks and her bottom lip begins to quiver; my bravado begins to dwindle.

Did I just make a horrible mistake?

No, she is overjoyed, I can scent her happiness.

I wish Corbin's words could reassure me, but they don't, her silence is deafening, and I don't think I can take it much longer!

"Princess?" She begins to smile but still doesn't speak. "Can you answer me?" She reaches up and wraps her arms around my neck and pulls me down so she can kiss me, I get lost in the kiss for a moment until I realize she still hasn't answered. I pull back and glare down at her. "Jessica––"She cuts me off.

"You became the center of my universe the moment you walked into that classroom all those years ago, you have been my sole focus from that moment. Well, until I gave birth to our children, but you were still there in my mind and heart. There isn't anyone else out there for me Creed, you and I were made for each other." I furrow my brows.

"That still doesn't answer my question." I growl out.

"Let me spell it out for you then Y.E.S." I smash my lips to hers and we both laugh, I pepper kisses all over her face, I never thought I would be *that* guy who falls in love and wants to get married, but Jess changed everything the moment I saw her. As soon as our eyes met, I knew it in my heart that she would be it for me, I guess it just took my mind a while longer to get the memo.

Chapter Forty Seven
Credence

The meeting with the alphas went better than I had expected, Tomlin and five other alphas volunteered to hunt for the council and hopefully locate them. Everyone was in high spirits knowing that six alphas and at least two hundred wolves will be out scouring the country, until Davina and Vince busted into our meeting with grim looks on their faces. I trailed my gaze over them and stop when I spot the letter clutched in Davina's hand, before she speaks, I already know who that letter is from. I cut my gaze to the twins to see they've taken a glimpse at the letter as well, I turn to Ro and Jess and watch as he wraps his arm around his sister. The alphas have no idea what is going on, they are more focused on Davina and Vince, this being the first time they have seen a vampire. Zeke, scurries over to Ro while Sky moves toward my sister, I stay where I am and meet Davina's gaze. She averts her eyes and turns to my mom who is bouncing my son on her knee, her eyes soften for a moment before her mask is back in place and she meets my cold stare.

"Is there anyone that's able to take Harlem from Meg?" My stomach drops, the tone of Davina's voice and the look in her eyes tells me everything. I nod and turn to Z; he meets my gaze with a shocked look.

"Zeke, can you take Harlem for a walk?" He doesn't hesitate, he moves toward my mom and reaches out to my son who goes willingly and laughs as Z puts him on his shoulders and disappears out of the room. Mom stands and comes over to me, I wrap my arm around her shoulders and pull her into my side, she is going to need my support shortly.

"Would you like to do this in private?"

"No Davina, they agreed to join us, so they have a right to

know. Just say what it is you came to say and get it over with." For the first time since learning that she is alive Davina drops her mask completely and lets us all see the pity and hurt on her face, but the hurt isn't for herself it's for...us. She looks between me and the twins and takes a deep breath before reading the letter.

"Before I start, I just want you all to know that this letter came with a package." I open my mouth, but she raises her hand to stop me. "Please Credence, just listen to the letter. None of you need to see or know what is in that box, let me carry that burden for all of you." When none of us answer she begins to read the letter.

"I told you I will never let you go Jess, you took something from me that I can never replace, and now it's my turn to return the favor. Your so-called mate is nothing but a parasite and when I take him and his useless pack out, I will take you as my own personal mate, you will give me a new heir. I hope you enjoy the time you have left with him because his days are numbered, I hope you like the gifts I have sent; it was such a pleasure to watch them break, and then destroy what remained of them. See you son, J.M."

The silence is deafening, my mom begins to tremble in my hold.

"I-I." Mom stops and clears her throat before she continues. "I would like to see the package please." I can hear it in her voice that she is close to tears, and it devastates me that I can't save her from this heartache. I'm going to fucking kill that slimy piece of shit. Davina moves toward and reaches out to grab one of my mom's hands, the only reason I don't bite her head off is because I'm stunned by the look of understanding in her eyes.

"Meg, I urge you not to look in that box, it will do nothing but cause you heartache and pain." A sob tears out of my mom but before I can wrap her in a hug Davina yanks her forward and wraps her arms around my mom's sobbing form. I just stand there and stare at the two of them, I never thought Davina had an ounce of compassion in her body, but I guess I was... wrong. "He was a good man Meg, he loved you so much and you both raised three amazing children together. Keep the memory you have of him and don't tarnish it by viewing the contents of the box." My mom begins to scream and thrash in Davina's hold, but she tightens her arms around my mom. Tears fill my eyes as the reality of what she is saying finally sinks in. I hear my sister begin to cry and face her only to find my brother and Sky holding her between them, Cole's gaze meets mine and I see the unshed tears in his eyes, and it guts me. I was so angry at my dad and banished him, but I never wanted him dead, I feel her approaching me from behind, but I know as soon as she gets near me, she will force me to face my feelings and I can't afford for that to happen. I move past my mom and Davina and head to Vince; he meets my gaze and whatever he sees in my eyes has him nodding and motioning for me to follow him out of the house. We head out back toward the woods, as we clear the first line of trees the scent of blood assaults me, it's my dad's blood, but I can also scent someone else's blood mixed with his.

"Who else Vincent?" He doesn't pretend to not understand

what I'm asking, he doesn't stop to answer, he keeps trudging forward and says.

"Shelley and Dela, the three of them are gone." My heart sinks for Jess, I know her, and Cairo are pissed she lied, but at the end of the day that was still the woman that gave them life. I snort, what a hypocrite, here I am condemning Davina, and yet I pity my mate and her brother for losing a woman who done the exact same thing my bio mom did. We come to a halt in a clearing and there in the middle sits a large cardboard box on top of a tarp, I can see the blood has seeped through the sides, and the scent of the rotting flesh is worse than smelling the vamps. "We moved it out here so no one else would be able to scent the blood, we didn't want to cause a frenzy amongst the pack and my kind." I nod my head; no words will come out of my mouth no matter how hard I try. I just stand there and stare at the box, as the minutes tick by the blood-soaked edges start to trail off the tarp, but I still can't bring myself to open the lid.

Do I want to see?

Will it be real if I don't see it with my own eyes?

Questions keep running through my mind and before long the sky begins to turn dark, Vince still doesn't move or say anything, which I appreciate. We hear a branch break and we both spin around; I scent the air and my shoulders slump.

"You both shouldn't be here." I say as Cairo and Cole come into view.

"I want to see it with my own eyes." I reach out and place my hand against my brother's chest as he attempts to walk past me, he growls but I brush it off. I know he is hurt and angry, he is lashing out and if need be, I'll take everything he has to throw at me.

"Colton, if you see it, then you can never unsee it, is that what you really want?" Before he can answer Cairo speaks.

"He isn't alone in that box, is he?" I meet his gaze and nod. "Have you seen it?"

"No, I've been sitting here staring at it trying to work up the courage to finally open it." I drop my hand from my brother's chest and turn to face him, it breaks me to see the defeated look on his face. "Go home brother, let me take care of this." I can see he wants to argue and it fucking hurts me to do this, I bring Corbin forward and let him take the lead and give an alpha order so I can spare my brother the pain of seeing what's in that box. "Go home, stay with mom and Callie and don't leave them until I get there." His eyes widen, I expect to see anger in his eyes, but instead all I see is appreciation. He wraps his arms around me and pulls me in for a hug.

"Thank you, brother." I pat his back and release him; I watch until he disappears inside the dense trees and turn toward Cairo.

"How did you know it wasn't just my dad in the box?"

"Because I know Jacob would want to hurt my sister, and the best way to do that is to kill Shelley."

"Does she know?" He shakes his head.

"She suspects it, so I told her to stay with the others."

"Thank you, I don't want her to see this, she has been through enough."

"Agreed!"

"I don't mean to break this up, but the blood is turning...

ripe and the scent will travel to the vamps. We need to get rid of it now, before they come searching." I release a long exhale and nod; Vince is right I can scent the change in the air. Ro and I move in unison toward the box and pause in front of it.

"On the count of three we both take the lid off?"

"Deal." I answer, we both begin to count.

"3...2...1." We both flip the lid off, and I fight the gag that wants to break free as I stumble away from the box, I see Ro retching out of the corner of my eye. I try to take in deep breaths through my mouth to try stop myself from gagging and throwing up. I'm so disoriented and lightheaded that I don't even see her pass me until the sound of her growl snaps me out of it, I spin around to see her standing there gazing into the box. Cairo is quicker to react than I am he hauls her away by her arm and tells Vince to get rid of the box, I follow after them as Cairo begins to drag Jess back toward the house.

Chapter
Forty Eight
Jessica

I sit here and stare out the window of Meg's lounge room, but not really seeing anything. Zeke, Ro, Sky, and I have all gathered here with the Reeves family, even Davina and Vince, but they like me are standing alone and away from the grieving family. My brother has asked me more times than I can count how I am going or how I am feeling and honestly-- I don't know. I have no idea how I feel about what I saw, of course my heart hurts for Creed and his family for the loss of their father but that's... it. Seeing Kane like that is horrific, but to see the woman who gave birth to me like that is unimaginable.

Shelley, Kane and Dela had no eyes, their teeth were pulled and made into a necklace that was wrapped around the tops of each of their heads, but the most disturbing part was seeing their eyes in their mouths. Their faces were battered and bruised. My anger begins to spike just thinking about it again.

We will avenge their deaths.

And then what Sheba? We keep fighting and killing people because they hurt us?

No, we get revenge and then we stop.

We may be able to take Jacob out but let's be real, we don't have the numbers to take the council.

We have the alphas.

Even with their help I don't know if it will be enough to take them out, we have hundreds of wolves they have thousands.

Why are doing this?

Because I have been so blinded by rage that I was willing to let everyone fight when the reality of it is I would have got them all killed!

They know the risks--

No, they don't!

"Jess?" I shove Sheba back in her cage and turn to Vince.

"Yeah?" I didn't mean for that to sound as harsh as it did.

"I just wanted to check and see how you were holding up." The air rushes out of me, I'm being a bitch and taking my frustration out on Vince.

"I honestly don't know; I feel for Creed and the others but that's about it. Shelley was our mom, but we never knew her, I know she sacrificed a lot for my brother and I but..."

"I understand."

"I don't think you do."

"You feel like you have to be sad because of who she was to you, but then you don't want to be sad because you think if you are that it will make you seem like an asshole, because Creed, Cole and Callie actually knew their father whereas you never knew your mother?" I reel back in shock and just stare at him, how the hell does he know that? "Your feelings no matter how big or small are warranted and valid, don't ever let someone tell you otherwise." Too stunned to utter a word, I just nod my head and watch as he goes back to standing by Davina. Just as I begin to turn back to the window, a thought hits me. I turn toward my brother and Z and make my way over to them, Ro smiles when he sees me coming once I'm close enough, Zeke wraps an arm around my shoulders and pulls me into his side giving me a side hug. I smile up at him and am just about to thank him when I'm suddenly ripped out of his hold by a growling Creed.

"Don't fucking touch her!" I pull out of Creed's hold and glare at him, I know he is hurting but that doesn't give him the right to be an ass to Zeke.

"Dude, I was just giving her a hug to comfort her." Creed sighs and shakes his head; his shoulders droop and a defeated look crosses his features which guts me to see. I grip his hand in mine and smile apologetically at Zeke as I lead Creed from the room and down the hallway to his old room. Once inside I kick the door shut and release his hand then head over to the bed and sit down, he paces back and forth stopping every once and a while to look at me then continue pacing. He tugs on the strands of his hair in frustration I don't know how to get through to him, so I decide to try switch things up, I stand and begin to undress which catches his attention. He stops and stares at me open mouthed as I stand before him butt naked, he takes a step toward me but stops when I begin to shift. Within seconds I'm on all fours and shaking out my coat, letting Sheba take control.

"You're beautiful little alpha." Sheba chuffs at being called *little* which elects a small laugh from Creed, He comes toward us and drops to his knees, he reaches out and buries his hands in our fur. Sheba rubs up against his face then he hauls us forward and buries his face in the side of our neck and... weeps.

Holy fucking shit.

Is he?

Sheba, Creed is literally crying!

Sheba stands there stiff as a board while our mate clings to us and breaks down, I have never seen him cry before and it is breaking my heart. I'm at a loss as to what I should do until it hits me, I open the link between Creed and me.

Shift, let Corbin take over and numb the pain for a while.

I can feel him nod against our neck, a few moments pass and then he jumps to his feet and opens the door, Sheba stares at him in confusion for a moment until he says.

"So, we can get out when I shift." *Ahhhh*, that's really smart, I hadn't thought about that. Creed begins to undress and much to my utter dismay Sheba turns away and I growl at her.

Humans.

What the hell does that mean?

Why do you all get weird over skin, seeing their butthole is much better.

I cringe and balk at the idea of judging Creed on the fact that he has nice... asshole. Oh god, I couldn't think of anything worse than that. Creed has shifted and this is the first time we are both in our wolf form together, Sheba and Corbin circle each other until Sheba stops and stands tall, Corbin follows her lead but a moment later he closes the space between us and nuzzles our neck, Sheba to my shock does the same and she makes a weird noise which reminds me of a cat purring.

Do you want to go for a run?

Now?

Yes princess, Corbin needs to let off some steam and I think Sheba does as well.

I-I I've never--

Sheba won't run princess; she has Corbin with her now.

The thought of finally running freely as a wolf fills me excitement and I can feel Sheba itching to get out and explore, and not be limited to how far I will let her go now that I know she won't take off.

Okay.

Sheba is beautiful princess. If I wasn't in wolf form, I know I would be blushing.

Let's go!

We take off out of the room and bound into the lounge, shocked eyes land on us, and for a moment I think we may have made a mistake coming in here, until I see Cole begin to strip, with Callie and the others following suit. The only one that doesn't, is Sky. I cock my head at Sky trying to ask her with my eyes why she isn't coming with us when she says.

"I'll stay back with the monster." Oh my god, I can't believe I forgot about my son sleeping in Meg's room! Before guilt can consume me, Sheba shuts down my emotions and tells me that he is okay and safe. Once Cole, Callie, Zeke and Meg are shifted I turn toward my brother.

"Are you gonna be okay if I shift?"

Sheba will you be, okay?

Yes, I have my place with my mate.

So, you won't fight my brother for alpha?

No, even though you told Creed you don't want the role we are still alpha because we are his mate, so I am content.

Excitement fills me as Sheba nods her head to my brother, he begins to strip, and I quickly avert our gaze.

"I'll get the door." Creed growls his thanks to Vince and we follow him toward the back sliding door, as soon as we're outside, I take in a huge whiff of air and finally after years of feeling caged and restrained it is all lifted, standing here and seeing my friends and family all around me in wolf form and being able to join them for the first time is... everything. Creed tips his head back and lets out a long and loud howl, Sheba follows his lead and throws her back and howls up at the night sky pretty soon other howls begin to join in and it's like a symphony. The sound of the howls together and knowing that mine is mingling with everyone's is euphoric. With the news that we got today I think this is exactly what we all needed, to get out and let our beasts run free. Within minutes both of the remaining packs join us. The other alphas have returned to Jacob's land, which is great because it gives us all time with just our pack. The howls die off and Sheba moves to stand beside Corbin, Ro and Z follow me and then we face the others. It's so surreal to stand here and see all these wolves.

This is what we have been missing?

Yes, we will never have to miss out again now that we are with our mate.

If I was on two legs, I know I would be crying right now, this moment will forever be ingrained in my mind for the rest of my days. I feel the link between Creed, and I open and turn to face him, he nips at me playfully to make sure he has my attention.

Are you ready princess?

For what?

A pack run, tonight we will run with our pack and Cairo's. I'm nervous and excited at the same time.

I'm so ready for this and so is Sheba, she is chomping at the bit to run with our pack.

I can feel Creed's pride through the link with me referring to the pack as *ours.* He lets out a yip and then turns and starts to run, I watch as he and other wolves run past me, Ro knocking into my side snaps me out of it, and I follow my brother.

Running has never been my strong suit, but running in wolf form is freeing and exhilarating at the same time, I see wolves playing as we run past them. I've never played before in wolf form. It's almost as if the thought of it brought it to reality, one minute I'm chasing my brother and then the next thing I know I'm smacked into and rolling around on the ground with Callie's wolf nipping at me and jumping all over me, Sheba seems to know what she is doing.

We run and play for hours, by the time we make it back to the house I'm tired but still wide awake. The excitement of the night has me amped up and wanting to do it again every night, I follow Creed through the open back door of Meg's house and into his old bedroom. He pushes the door shut with his nose, once in the room and then he shifts back, Sheba doesn't fight me as I gain control and shift back. Creed has mud coating his body and bits of leaves in his hair, I look down and see mud is caked all over me and when I reach up and feel my hair I cringe, I can feel how tangled it is and manage ton feel debris in hair, Creed chuckles at the look on my face I narrow my eyes at him.

"Come on little alpha, join me in the shower." I ogle his ass as he passes me to head to the bathroom, the chuckle that escapes him lets me know that I just got caught checking him out and I'm not even shy about it. I follow after him and head into the bathroom, steam billows out of the shower stall and I'm momentarily stunned as I watch Creed in the shower with the water cascading down his body, my eyes trace the droplets of water that roll down his chest and past the V to his hardening-

-." You gonna keep looking at my dick or hop on it?" I snap my eyes to his and see the devilish smirk on his face, I won't lie and say that his words don't have liquid pooling between my legs.

"Uh, I-yeah I'm just...yeah." I shut my mouth to stop my rambling and hop in, within seconds he has maneuvered so my back is against the tiled wall. He doesn't mess about as he bends down and captures my lips in a heated kiss that steals my breath away. I reach up and wrap my arms around his neck and moan into his mouth, he grips the backs of my thighs and lifts me. I wrap my legs around him and can feel his cock pushing against my opening, I try and wiggle so I can impale myself on him, but he holds firm which pulls a frustrated growl from me. He pulls back and smiles up at me, I scowl at him. "I think I liked it better when you were angry at me all the time, at least then you wouldn't tease me." He throws his head back and laughs, seeing him let go and laugh is the most magnificent site in the world. His laughter dies off and focuses back on me, he holds my gaze as he lowers me onto his cock, we both moan at the feeling of having him sheathed inside me. He begins to move at a slow steady pace and still maintaining eye contact.

This feels different, to all the other times we have had sex, this feels more... intimate. It's like for the first time we are both finally seeing each other and not hate fucking or just trying to fuck our point across to the other. This time feels different because we are no longer bound by past or harbor any anger toward each other, we both are letting our guards down and showing how we really feel. I see nothing but love in his eyes and I show him with my own how much I love him. A moan slips past my lips and I begin to feel my orgasm build but it's still out of reach, Creed leans his head down and captures one of my nipples in his mouth and sucks. I pull on the strands of his hair and moan--loud. He switches sides and does the same thing to my other nipple but this time as he releases it, he scarps his teeth along it and it sends a shudder through me.

"Do that again but fuck me harder, I need to come." His eyes darken and a growl of approval rumbles out of his chest. His pace picks up and I tighten my hold on him as he lowers head to do as I ask. "Oh god, that feels so good!" He slams into me at a relentless pace, and I love every second of it. He bites my nipple, and it sends shockwaves through me causing me to cry out. He switches sides but this time he slaps my ass at the same time and my orgasm slams into me without warning, I scream out in pleasure. He quickly covers my mouth with his to mute the screams coming from me as I clench around his cock and ride out the aftershocks of the most intense orgasm ever. His pace remains the same and within seconds he groans into my mouth as he cums deep inside my tight wet hole.

CHAPTER FORTY NINE
Credence

We stayed in my old room last night, I didn't want to leave the twins or mom alone last night. We're all sitting around the breakfast table, but the vibe in the room is dull and tense, the only one who seems to be happy and cheerful is Harlem. His laughter and smiles seem to be the only thing that is keeping everyone from breaking down or losing their shit. I sit here and watch my mom, the twins, Sky and Jess avoid looking at each other and I'm annoyed at myself because I don't know how to fix this situation. A knock at the front door pulls me from my thoughts, I jump to my feet to answer it. I scent the air and relax when I pick up on Zeke and Cairo, I open the door glad for the distraction and reprieve from the gloom in the dining room, but when I see their faces my stomach drops.

"You both have faces like a slapped ass, so this clearly isn't a happy visit." Ro glowers but steps back and motions for me to come outside. I sigh and close the door behind us and move over to the old wooden chairs on the porch. Ro and Z both take a seat, and we look out over the pack lands, we sit in silence for a moment and I'm grateful for the peace, they look pissed off, so I know whatever they are about to tell me is going to make a shit day even worse!

"Tomlin sent word; the council isn't in the states they fled to Russia." I spin so fast toward Ro I feel my neck crack.

"Come again?"

"They fled brother; I don't know what else we can do." The defeated tone in Ro's voice is annoying me. I need solutions not problems, and that seems to be all he is bringing to me these days.

"Now that we know they are not in US that means we deal with Jacob first, and then we travel to them." Cairo and Zeke both have the same look, they stare at me like I have lost my mind.

"You're joking right?"

"No. Jess won't be able to relax and move on if they are still out there, I won't have her looking over her shoulder. She deserves better than that and so do we. They killed my fucking father Cairo and sent his head back to me, they will die for that--every last one of those sleezy fucks!"

"Okay, we deal with Jacob first but after that is done, we send the other packs home. I will not bring them into this."

"We need the numbers Ro--"

"No, if they have fled the country then that means they left with minimal numbers, they would only take a few with them so they don't raise suspicion." I sit back and think on that for a moment, he has a point. If they fled the country, they wouldn't take hundreds of wolves, but that doesn't mean they haven't roped the Russian packs in and forced them to protect them. If we are going to take this fight abroad then we will need to enlist the help of other packs around the globe and that is going to be difficult, we may have some sway here over other alphas, but we don't have shit overseas. I hang my head in frustration, how the hell are we going to work this?

"I have an idea." I lift my gaze slowly to meet Zeke's stare. "We all work together to take Jacob out, but when it comes time for the council, our pack will take care of them." Has he lost his ever-fucking loving mind?

"What part of we don't have the numbers did you not

understand?” Zeke narrows his eyes as he glares at me, Cairo leans back in his chair and remains silent, clearly, he and Zeke have already discussed this before coming to me.

“We all go to Russia, they will know we’re coming, but if a small group of us land there they won’t be alerted, take out Jacob for your mate, and after that well take over.”

“No Zeke, I won’t--.” A growl that tears out of Cairo has me pausing.

“Your fight is over after this, you will not help, follow or have anything to do with taking down the council. Let us do this for you, so you, my sister and nephew can live in peace, she deserves that Creed.” The alpha part of me wants to tell them to go fuck themselves, but the rational side of me is entertaining the idea of not fighting anymore and being able to live in peace. After everything the pack has been through, they also deserve a peaceful life.

“I will only agree to this if I know when and how you are going to do it.” They both nod, but I raise my hand to stop them from celebrating too early. “Also, you have to tell Jess and the others.” They both nod reluctantly; I don’t envy them, I know for a fact they are going to have an even harder time convincing Jess than they did me.

“You are out of your fucking mind Credence!” I growl at the ballsy son of a bitch and allow Corbin to come forward so he can feel the raw alpha power surging inside me. Andrew may be an alpha, but he is also one of the ones that I beat and let live.

"We are on my fucking lands; you will show me the fucking respect that I deserve you prick." I yell, I clench my fists at my sides trying to tamper the burning rage inside. We have been trying to work out a plan of attack for nearly two hours and I'm about ready to smash their skulls in. Whoever thought it might be a good idea to group so many alphas together was going to be easy is sorely mistaken. We can't seem to agree on anything and whenever I think we are getting close to finalizing the plan one or two of them will pipe up and shut it down. I turn to Jess and glower at her, she shrugs her shoulders and stands from the log she was sitting on. We thought it would be a good idea to host this meeting out back incase tempers flared, and someone shifted. At least that way there'll be no damages to the house.

Jess claps me on the shoulder and moves in front of me. "Gentlemen I asked you all here to help us not fight but more than that I want to give you all the opportunity to be free. Do you like living under the council's rule? Being at their beck and call?" She looks over each of them, taking her time to make eye contact with each of them, no one answers, but their body language is enough. "We could have gone about this a different way, but we didn't. None of us wanted to come your lands and pick a fight just so we could take over your packs and use you and your people for our gain. That is not who we are or how we want things to be done moving forward--"Ashton the alpha to the Nomad pack stands, he isn't the type to speak often or ever be away from his pack lands. Dad told me he is an honorable man... just thinking about my father has a pit forming in my stomach. I push my feelings back down and promise myself I will deal with them when this is all over.

"Without a council to lay down the laws and rules we will become savages, what do you propose then?" That... is a good question.

"You may all think I am bias and swayed, but I can assure you I am not. I think we need to elect someone as our... king, I guess we will call it, and I think that person should be Creed." My mouth drops open in shock, but before I can ponder what she has said chaos erupts and everyone begins to shout and curse, men begin to volunteer themselves as our *king*. They carry on shouting for a few minutes before Jess screams at the top of her lungs, it's so loud everyone including myself covers our ears. We all shoot her a glare which she shrugs off and smiles sweetly.

"Please take your seats so we can discuss this like grown adults. I get you all want to measure dicks and prove who has the biggest. I know for a fact that half of you have challenged my mate for his role as alpha and failed." Half of the assholes drop their gazes or look around not wanting to acknowledge that what jess is saying is true. "I know he is one of the youngest alphas and new to this, compared to a lot of you, but let's be clear, can any of you that fought him, say that you would have done what he did? Would any of you have shown each other mercy or compassion?" She doesn't give them a chance to answer. "No, I didn't think so. You would have happily killed him and taken what is his so you could brag about how big and mighty your dick is. I personally would trust him with my life, he is rash and blunt, but he is also smart and cunning. The plan he has come up with to take Jacob out is the best one I have heard, and you all know it--"

"Why the hell should we listen to a woman? You are no alpha; you have no standing or title here amongst us." I growl out a warning, my nails turn to claws as I fight back the shift, Corbin doesn't like our mate being underestimated before I can even open the link between me and Corbin, Sky shocks the hell out of me when she jumps to her feet and comes to Jess's aide.

"Because Albert, she is the daughter of two alpha bloodlines and the rightful heir to both these packs, which makes her superior to you, *you* gutless fucking drunk. Now sit the hell down before I break your fucking nose you slimy pig, we are in the 21st fucking century and woman lead now, so get used to it or we will take your pack from you!" Each of the men here may be alphas and rulers where they come from, but each and every one of them have heard about Skylar Cage, I guarantee it. Sky's reputation proceeds her and if these fools are smart, they won't push her or antagonize her in any way.

We finally managed to come to an agreement on how to take Jacob out, it was like pulling teeth, but I refused to leave that clearing without a day and plan on when Jacob would meet his maker. Ending his life will be my greatest honor, just the thought of ripping his throat out has Corbin growling his approval inside me. I've been lying here for hours unable to sleep, rather than tossing and turning and waking Jess I decide to get up and check on Harlem.

I make my way across the hall and poke my head in to see him sleeping soundly, Jess and I agreed that after Jacob is… dealt with, we will give his room a makeover. I want him to have the room of his dreams and know that this house is his home, the prospect of watching my son grow in the house that I built with my bare hands fills me with warmth.

We have our mate and pup; the pack is behind us as well.

Yes, we need to make sure that everything pans out Corbin, I won't risk anyone's life.

They all know the risk; they have chosen to follow us, and the others have chosen to follow their alpha. Their choices are not ours to make.

Yeah, you're right, I just want this to be over.

It will be, then Cairo and Zeke can take the council down, and then we will finally be free.

Hearing that from Corbin filled me with a sense of longing, I never really knew what I wanted out of life or what I wanted to do aside from being alpha. Having Jess and Harlem with me shows me that there is more to life than just ruling a pack. I want my son to grow and be proud of where he comes from, I can't promise that there won't be other battles, but I can promise they won't be as bad as the ones we are facing now.

I quietly pull his door closed behind me and head out the front, I drop into one of the wooden chairs on the porch and look out at the night sky. The stars shine bright, the wildlife make sounds in the woods and the breeze carries the scents of my pack around me. The loss of my dad hit me harder than I thought it would, I was so angry at him for what he did to mom and how he used me, he lied to us our whole lives! No matter how hard I try to latch onto the anger to mask the pain it keeps slipping away from me, I feel a lone stray tear slide down my cheek and quickly swipe it away. I'm shocked that I am actually crying, I don't cry!

"Why are you out here alone?" I spin toward her voice and glare, what the hell is she doing out here at this time of night?

"Why are you even here?" A sly smirk cuts across her face.

"I asked you first." I growl, she chuckles and shrugs her shoulders. "I was hunting, believe it or not hunting prey at night is easier than in the day."

"Wicked." I deadpan. She sighs and moves toward the porch, I should stop her or tell her to fuck off, but I don't, not even when she drops into the seat beside me. We both sit here silently, I'm tense wondering what the hell she is up to, but she seems relaxed with not a care in the world. As I stare at her I notice she looks different, her hair isn't pinned up in its normal style, its flowing around her shoulders, she's even dressed differently in a plain shirt and dark wash jeans. Davina seems so... at ease here.

"I never thought I would ever be back here, don't get me wrong I always wished I would be able to come back, thanks to your mate she made my wish come true." I huff in exasperation.

"What are you getting at Davina? If you're here to try mend shit then don't, I don't have the energy to deal with your drama right now."

"I don't want to fight Creed; I know I can't turn back time and rewrite my wrongs. All I am asking of you and the twins is just give me a chance to try and be your... friend. I would never disrespect Meg in any way, she is a great woman and honestly not a lot of women would have done what she did, she raised the three of you as if you were her own. I fucked up and made horrible choices, but if I didn't make those mistakes, then you and the twins wouldn't be who you are today. I just want a chance to get to know you all--."

"You gave up on us and ran! You didn't give a shit about us back then so why care now?" Her shoulders slump forward.

"You're right, I did run, but I never gave up on you three. Your father promised me that when I got the thirst under control that he would bring you three to spend time with me. I found out later on when he cut contact with me that he had told everyone I died, I tried to come back but I was stopped by Alexander's guards. They told me that if the council caught me, they would torture me for information on the original family, I didn't care about being hurt, I wanted my children. But Alexander didn't mean they would torture me, he meant they would hurt you and the twins to get me to talk and I couldn't take that risk. It is wrong of me to speak ill of the dead but... I hated your father for keeping the three of you from me, he made me a promise to never cut me out and he fucking lied. I didn't choose to leave you Credence, your father made me leave under the ruse that it would be safer for you kids." I can't tear my gaze from her as I slump back in my seat. Her eyes, the same color as my own are filled with unshed tears. I hear the truth and heartbreak in her voice, and I honestly believe every word she just told me. My father kept her from us but... why?

"Why would he do that? What did he have to gain out of keeping you away from us?" Davina shakes her head as she answers me.

"I don't know. Kane was a great man, but he also had many secrets, he had his fingers in a lot of pies so to speak. I don't know if it was for fear of the council or the fact, he just wanted to make a family with Meg, why he kept the truth from you all."

"I guess we will never know his reasons now." Davina turns to face me and hesitantly reaches over to place her hand on top of mine, I don't pull away like I should, instead I sit here and stare at her hand.

"Sometimes it's better to not have all the answers. I know you were angry at him in the end for what he did to your mother, channel that anger and use it."

"Use it for what?" I'm slightly horrified when she smiles at me, Davina smiling is as rare as a solar eclipse.

"Use your dislike for what he did as fuel to make sure you never become like him. Your father wasn't a bad man, he just had terrible luck in who he married first." I can hear the regret in her tone.

"Why did you marry him if you knew he wasn't your mate?" She removes her hand from mine and stands, she leans over the railing and gazes out at the woodlands.

"Because it's what my father told me to do. Plus, your father had said and done all the right things to get me to believe him. It's a long story and one I'm sure you don't want to hear, so I won't bore you with the details."

"Do you regret it?" She turns her head and smiles at me sadly.

"No, if I didn't marry your father, you and the twins wouldn't be here. You may think of me as nothing but a bitch, but the truth is you kids are the reason why I rescued so many wolves and gave them a sanctuary on my island. I knew the council was getting worse and every time a new shifter arrived a part of me hoped it might be you three, but then another part was relieved it wasn't. I'm sorry I was such a fuck up as a mother Credence, I never meant to hurt you three." Hearing her say that is like getting struck by lightning, it's everything I ever wanted her to say, but now that she has said it, I wish she hadn't. I'm so confused and conflicted about the way I feel toward her, I know the twins hate her and haven't softened a smidge toward Davina.

"Be that as it may, Meg raised us, she is our mother in every sense of the word. I will not push her aside or shit on her because you say you're sorry. Too much shit has happened for you to get a clean slate--."

"I'm not asking for one, I know I can't undo what I have done, all I can do is try to make up for it and show you all that I am sorry. I will never ask you to view or treat Meg differently, she is your mother in every way. I was just the vessel that brought you into the world. Meg has done a fantastic job raising the three of you, I owe her a lot."

"You owe me nothing." I jump to my feet and Davina straightens as we both turn toward my mom. I didn't even hear her approaching; she makes her way toward us, and I gulp. She doesn't look mad to see Davina and I standing here alone, she smiles at the both of us as she makes her way up the porch and motions for me to sit, she claims the chair Davina vacated. I'm as tense as can be and just watch her as she crosses one leg over the other and smiles kindly at Davina.

"How much of that did you hear?" Mom laughs and waves her hand at Davina.

"Enough to agree with you that I did a great job raising them." Davina nods her head as I keep darting my gaze between them. "I don't want any animosity between us, I have spoken to the twins, and they are... hardheaded shall we say. I wanted them to clear the air between you and them before you all go after Jacob, I can't speak for you Davina, but I know *my* children, don't give them any time or space like they ask, break down their walls and barge into their lives and don't give them a chance to push you away. Also, if anything happens to my twins when you take Jacob down, I will hold you responsible." I scoff.

"What about me?" Mom turns and rolls her eyes as she pats me on the cheek.

"Sweetheart I gave up telling you what to do when you were sixteen, you are a pigheaded alpha who will do whatever he wants. Plus, I know Jess will keep you in line so there is that." Mom and I chuckle.

"I'll keep them safe Meg, you have my word." I hear the truth in each of Davina's words, it's good to know I will have someone else watching the twins back.

CHAPTER FIFTY

Jessica

The three days pass by in a blur of chaos, everyone has been on edge, half of the pack has spent more time in their wolf form because of their nerves. The ones that didn't shift have been helping us move the young pups and the older shifters to safety. Creed told me his grandfather had a cellar built out in the middle of the woods in case they were ever attacked. To be on the safe side we all decided it was best if we hid the pack members that couldn't fight there. The other alphas have managed to work together, and I think having them here and showing them the respect of us not trying to take over their packs has formed an alliance of sorts. Eric is still quiet and reserved with me and I don't know why, Creed told me it's because Sheba is an anomaly, and he doesn't like not being able to control things. I have kept to shifting in the woods with Creed and the others because when I shifted in front of the other alphas, they went nuts claiming that my wolf was challenging theirs, I wish I could say they were being dramatic but they weren't. Sheba has been pushing me to challenge them and take their packs. So, I was left with no choice but to shift in the woods or risk blowing our plan out of the water before we could even get a chance to take Jacob down.

"You talking to me yet?" I turn away from the sink in our cabin and face my brother. I haven't spoken to him or Zeke since they told me about their plan to hunt the council without us, I know my brother, and there is more to this than he is saying. As I'm about to answer him I snap my mouth closed when Davina walks in behind him, I growl at the sight of her. Davina being the asshole that she is, just smirks and moves over to the dining table and pulls out a seat then drops into it. I tear my gaze from her and glower at Cairo.

"If you wanted to suck up to me, bringing her isn't the way to go about it!" He smiles sheepishly and motions for me to take a seat, I narrow my eyes at him.

"Smalls, I brought her here because come tomorrow we must have everyone onside, and not have to worry about a fight breaking out on our own team. I know you are pissed at me, but we have to table that shit until we finish what we started; can you do that?" I want to tell him to eat a fat eggplant but deep down I know he is right.

"I can table *our* problems." He opens his mouth, but I raise my hand to stop him. "Now, if you want me to fix shit with her, then you need to leave and take Harlem with you, please." My brother pales slightly as he looks between Davina and me, I cock a brow at him when he doesn't move immediately. He sighs and raises from his seat and pats Davina on the shoulder and speaks.

"It was nice knowing you." I growl and he chuckles, then calls out to Harlem. Once they leave the cabin I move and take the seat opposite Davina, the both of us lock eyes and it becomes a battle of wills, Sheba is bursting to break free and teach her a lesson, but I manage to push her back---barely.

"Say what it is you have to say, to move on from this, if it is an apology you want, then you won't get it." I scoff at the audacity of this woman.

"How dare you--"

"No how dare you, Jessica! You allowed yourself to fall into a dark hole that you couldn't pull yourself from, Creed tried to reach you, but you pushed him away. He was so desperate to save you that he came to me!" I'm floored at the sheer manner of this woman and how she thinks she is right, her words hit the mark though. I did everything she said and that is what pisses me off more.

"You have no idea what I went through Davina--"

"I know exactly what you went through!" The watery tone of her voice has me slouching back in my seat. "You think I was changed into a vampire and welcomed with open arms?" She doesn't give me a chance to answer. "You are a fool if that is what you think, I faced horrors that make your worst nightmares seem like a pleasant dream. If there is anyone who understands, it is me!"

I can hear the truth in her words, I can feel her pain as well. I close the link between Sheba and me, I don't want her to distract me right now.

"You and I may have experienced similar situations but that does not mean you understand what I went through." She laughs a humorless laugh and I clench my hands into fists.

"You mean how you felt so useless and like you didn't deserve to live because you were about to give up? Or, do you mean how you felt like if you just lasted one more day someone would come, but no one ever did so you lost all hope? Should I go on?" She takes my silence as her que to continue. "You went through hell Jess, I will not demean that but you made it out, you fought hard and came home to your family." I feel tears building and try to blink them away, I try to bite my tongue to stop the words from spilling out, but I can't stop them once they start.

"I just wanted the pain to stop, I thought I could beat him if I showed him, I wasn't weak and he couldn't break me but, in the end, I just wanted him to end it. I didn't care that Harlem wouldn't have his mother, I knew Creed would raise him." I begin to sob uncontrollably, Davina doesn't move to comfort me or say a word, she just lets me cry out my pain and finally let all my anger go. I don't know how long I sit there with my face buried in my hands and just cry, I only stop when Davina hands me a box of tissues and then reclaims her seat. I wipe away my tears and clear my nose when I face her, the harden look in her eyes is gone and all I see is understanding and respect.

"You are not a victim Jessica; you are a survivor. Do not let the past define who you are, the past is called the past for a reason and the present is called the present because it is a *gift*. Don't dimmish the gift you are given every day by living in the past. I lived as you are now and it will not do you well to dwell on matters you can't change, get your vengeance and then let it die with Jacob."

Davina and I sit here and talk about things in her past and mine, she even gives me tips on how she dealt with her anger and tools she used to cope. When Creed, Harlem, the twins, Sky, Cairo, and Meg enter the house they all freeze when they see Davina and I in the kitchen cooking together and laughing.

"The fuck did I miss?" We turn to face our stunned guests and smile. "Blink twice if your under-duress sweetheart." I roll my eyes at Cole and tell them all to find a seat because we are ready to serve up. The others move to the living room while Creed makes his way over to me, he places his hands on my hips and plants a kiss on my lips. I blush knowing that Davina is standing right there, but Creed doesn't seem to care.

"Everything okay?" I smile up at him and nod, spending the

day with Davina has been very therapeutic, it was great to talk to someone who actually understood what I went through.

"Perfect, now go sit and D and I will serve you shortly." Creed reels back and darts his gaze between us.

"D? since when did you two become friends?" Davina saves me from answering.

"That is between your mate and I. I do believe she told you to sit, so I suggest you do as she says, or she may just put something in your food." D and I both laugh at Creed's horrified look; I shoo him out of the kitchen after placing a quick kiss to his lips.

Sitting here with our loved ones and sharing stories and laughs is something I thought would never happen. The tension between the twins and Davina has eased enough for it not to be awkward and uncomfortable, I lean back into Creed's side and rest my head on his chest smiling at my brother as he plays with Harlem. This may not have been what I had planned for my life, but I wouldn't change it. Laughter and conversations are flowing easily Sky is even laughing at something Cole said, this night couldn't get any better.

Something's wrong! I stiffen in Creed's hold, being the perceptive person that he is he immediately cuts his conversation off with his mother and asks.

"What's wrong?" I shake my head and focus back on Sheba. *What is it?*

We're under attack!

I jump to my feet and the conversation stops as I turn and face everyone. "Sheba said we're under attack--"Before I can finish speaking the front door bursts open, Vince and Z barrel inside with stricken looks on their faces. Within seconds everyone is on their feet, Cairo scoops Harlem up and passes him to me as he brushes past to speak to the two guys.

"What is it?"

"Jacob and his pack, we need to move now, I have Tomlin and Andy's beta's moving the children and elders to the bunker." Vince barely finishes speaking before chaos ensues and everyone is barking out orders. I block them out and turn to Meg, her eyes are filled with tears of worry, but I can't let that affect me know.

"I need you to take Harlem to the bunker and stay with him until Creed or I return." I don't give her a chance to respond, I pass my son to her and cradle his beautiful face between my hands, I stroke his cheeks with my thumbs and fight back the tears that want to spill. As a mother it kills me to part with him when there is a chance that this may be the last time I see my son, but the other alpha part of me knows this is the only way to keep him safe and give him a future.

"I love you Monster; mommy will be back soon."

"No, stay mommy!" The fear in his voice threatens to break me.

"You go with grandma and then mommy and daddy will come get you later. Always remember you are the son of two alphas who love you more than anything in this world, okay?"

Hearing Creed's words causes a pang in my chest, I shut that feeling down and lean forward and place a kiss to my son's forehead. "Mom, go with Zeke I promise I'll keep the twins safe."

"Just promise me the three of you will all return?" Creed sucks in a large breath before answering.

"I promise." Even I can tell he was lying just to appease his mother. Meg nods and follows Zeke out of the cabin.

"You should go with them." Vince says to Davina, she glares at Vince and if looks could kill he would be burnt alive.

"I will not hide, now let's end this!" Everyone rushes out of the cabin, but Creed pulls me back, Cairo stops and turns and looks to both of us and speaks.

"Keep her safe no matter what, if shit goes sideways you take her and Harlem and run. Do you understand?"

"Ro no--"I'm cut off by Creed.

"Yes, I swear I'll protect them." Ro nods and turns to me with a smile on his face that doesn't reach his eyes.

"You were always meant for greater things smalls, I love you." A sob tears out of me when he disappears through the door. Creed pulls me into his hold as I weep against his chest.

"Princess, you can sit this out and go with our son." I pull back and quickly swipe away the remnants of my tears before I answer.

"No, we do this together for our son." He nods and then grips my hand in his then leads us out of the cabin and into the chaos.

Chapter
Fifty One
Credence

The smell of smoke is the first thing to assault my senses when we exit the cabin, then comes the sounds of screams and growls. I lead Jess out of the woods heading toward my mom's house but stop when I see that her house is engulfed in flames. I stand here and watch as my childhood home goes up in flames, I hear Jess gasp beside me and that is enough to snap me out of my stupor. I turn to her and see anger and fear simmering in her eyes, I want nothing more than to ease her fears but right now I can't. I cup her face between my hands and lean down and capture her lips in a kiss that I hope conveys how much I love her without words. Before I can overthink everything, I pull back and meet her gaze as I say.

"I love you, now shift!" Her eyes immediately change to the color of her wolf as she recognizes the alpha command in my voice. I step back and begin to strip; Jess does the same and within minutes we are both shifted and standing on all fours. Corbin takes over and bounds around the side of the burning house with Jess hot on our heels, it's sensory overload once we get to the front, wolves in both their human and fur form fight, vampires are in the midst battling alongside us. I pause to scan the area and take in the sheer number of people; Jacob has more numbers than we could have planned for its like he has the councils' numbers and every pack at his call. I hear a yelp to my left and spin around and find that it's my brother pinned beneath a huge wolf with another one about to go for the kill shot.

Corbin! I scream as my wolf takes off toward my brother, before one of the wolves can latch onto his throat, I throw myself at the wolf pinning Cole to the ground, we roll a couple times before skidding to a stop. We jump to our feet and that's when

I notice it isn't one of Jacob's wolves it's Sean, one of the alpha's who was supposed to be helping us. Anger courses through my veins as Corbin releases a growl and launches at Sean, just before I manage to pin him on his back, he sinks his teeth into my shoulder and I howl out in pain. Corbin shakes him off and latches onto his throat, then tears his flesh, the gurgling sound and flow of blood that rushes from his exposed wound fills Corbin with a sense of...power. I don't dwell on the fact that I just killed an alpha and inherited his pack instead I look for my brother and find that he is okay and moving toward me. I turn to the spot I was with Jess and panic when I can't see her!

Colton, Jess is gone.

She ran into the fight when she saw Sky taking on three wolves.

Shit, where is Callie?

I-I don't know! I can hear the panic in his voice and try to mask my own worry.

You find California and I'll get Jess. There is too many of them Cole and some of the alpha's have switched sides.

No, we end this tonight, Creed, we don't have a choice!

Before Cole and I can finish speaking a group of wolves' head in our direction, we split up, so we don't get cornered. As I make my way through the battle to Jess, I dodge bodies of fallen wolves, renewed determination flows through me, I will not let my pack fail. My worry for Jess is clouding my job as alpha, so I do the only thing I can and pray that she can hold her own. I push away my worries for her and focus on trying to find Jacob, if I take him out then his pack will fall under my rule and I can stop this killing.

By the time I spot Jacob on the ridge I'm limping and bloodied, Corbin is tired after fighting off so many wolves. I wanted to give them a chance to stop fighting and leave but Corbin wouldn't allow it, in his mind it is *killed or be killed.*

Creed! I spin around to see Callie and Davina sprinting toward me, Davina has claw marks over her arms and chest, her clothes are torn but she hides her pain behind her mask. Callie has blood dripping from her jaws, and I notice she isn't putting too much weight on her left hind leg.

I need to go to Jacob now--

Jess and Cole are already up there! I tried to stop them, but I got attacked and couldn't chase after them.

My stomach sinks, I turn back toward the ridge and strain my wolf eyes to see clearly and that's when I see it. My brother's wolf lay limp on the ground while Jess and Jacob circle each other, with my heart in my throat I take off. The pain and exhaustion I felt seconds ago has vanished as I focus on saving my mate and my little brother, I just hope I make it to them in time. My legs won't move fast enough, I hear Callie and Davina trailing behind, thanks to Davina's vampire speed she is able to keep up with us. Corbin pushes us to newfound limits in order to get us to our mate before Jacob can harm her, but still it isn't fast enough, the seconds feel like minutes and the minutes feel like hours as we navigate our way through the woods and up to the top of the mountain ridge.

CHAPTER FIFTY TWO

Jessica

After helping Sky take down the three wolves, I scan the carnage around myself to hopefully catch a glimpse of my brother, a relieved sigh slips from my snout when I spot him and Zeke ploughing through our enemies like they are but a bug beneath their paws. When I hear a howl that sends shivers down my spine, I turn toward the mountain ridge and that's when I spot him, standing there in his human form. Rational thought flees me as Sheba takes off toward Jacob, I hear paws pounding the earth behind me and chance a look over my shoulder, when I see it's Cole I don't bother to stop or slow, if he wants to follow us then he needs to keep to our pace. I dodge fallen branches and debris as I move through the woods and up the incline to the top of the ridge, I feel Cole right behind me trying to nip at my flanks, but I push Sheba harder. Cole is trying to stop me from facing Jacob and I cannot allow that, this is my fight not his or Creed's, I need to do this in order to face my demons and come out stronger.

As soon as I break through the last of the brush and emerge at the top of the ridge I see him, he stands there in a Henley, jeans and shit kicker boots, his brown eyes hold so much malice as he looks at me. I dart my gaze to the others with him and growl when I see Kayla is bound and gagged kneeling in front of that council fucker Phillip, he still wears an ill fitted suit and his yellow crooked teeth grind together as he stares down at me and Cole, I don't know who the other man is that stands next to Phillip but he seems to have an edge of sorts to him that I can't quite explain. I push thoughts of why Phillip is here and not with other members in Russia from my mind.

"I knew you would find me, I'm a bit chuffed that you

thought it wise to come here without your mate though. I mean, who will save you from the big bad wolf now?" Phillip and Jacob chuckle at his stupid joke, having had enough of their shit I growl and snap my jaws toward them. Cole releases a long and loud growl from beside me, Jacob glares at me before turning to Phillip. "Shift and deal with the Reeves mutt while I subdue my mate." The way he says *mate* sends a shiver through Sheba.

We take him down or die trying.

We won't get caught again Jess; I promise.

If we don't make it out of this Sheba, just know I'm so thankful you chose me as your human.

She doesn't respond, instead she breaks away from Cole and moves toward Jacob who is standing near the edge with a smug smile on his face.

"I'm going to make the rest of your life a living hell for what you took from me, you will give me a new heir!" If I was on two legs I would have thrown-up, the thought of his hands on me makes me feel ill. First rule of training Vince taught us was to never take your eyes off of your enemy, but as Jacob grips the waistband of his boxers, I force Sheba to look away, his appendage is not something I want to see. It was a mistake to let my human side take over for even a split second, he uses that to his advantage and attacks before Sheba can even face him. He slams into our side, and we skid along the hard compact dirt, Sheba jumps to her feet in time to dodge his jaws, she backs up to give us some space to assess our opponent. I haven't seen him in wolf form before, he may be a slimy human, but he is a formidable wolf. His long black coat ruffles in the breeze and his eyes look almost onyx, Jacob's wolf is a nasty looking beast. Sheba doesn't seem to feel the way I do, if anything she is giddy at the idea of facing off against a wolf of this size and proving that she is stronger. I hear snarls from beside us but I don't dare take my eyes off him again and risk him getting the upper hand just so I can check on Cole. I have put off being initiated into pack because of everything that has been going on and now I'm regretting my decision, without that ceremony I am unable to link with any of the pack including Cole.

Jacob launches toward us, and Sheba fakes right only to bounce to the left and sink her jaws into the side of Jacob, the taste of his coppery blood fills our senses but before we can celebrate the small victory a searing pain shoots through our side and we release him with a howl of pain, and he jumps back. Our shoulder burns where he sank his teeth, she growls out in anger as she faces Jacob, our blood drips from his snout and it sends a surge of hate through my wolf.

We need to make this quick Sheba; we'll tire before he does.

Your confidence in me is awe inspiring.

Sheba shuts the mind link down between us and pushes me back to the furthest part of our mind, I thrash against the cage she has locked my conscious in, but it is futile, the last time she did this I was helpless, maybe it's better this way at least then she can focus and hopefully take Jacob down once and for all.

Sheba bounds toward Jacob and leaps into the air but he's quicker, he moves out of the way and manages to use our forward momentum against us and knocks us to the ground then jumps on top of us, Sheba tries to wiggle free and get off her back, but she can't move him. She manages to dodge his bites twice but isn't lucky the third time, he sinks his teeth into the side of our neck and Sheba let's out a horrible yelp of pain. The pain is excruciating, he clamps his jaws down harder and Sheba stops moving or she risks him tearing our throat out. Thoughts of Harlem and Creed plague my mind, if this is the end, then their faces are who I want to see in my mind before I leave this world.

Sheba manages to twist slightly, and I feel the tear of our flesh, I scream inside her mind at the pain, but she doesn't stop as she bites into his leg so hard, I feel the crunch of his bone. He releases his hold on us with a growl, he yanks his leg free which inflicts more damage tearing the skin from his bone. Sheba rolls and is on her feet, the pain is agonizing but she blocks it out and focuses on Jacob, he limps around us, and Sheba does the same circling him, I can scent our blood and from the sluggish movements Sheba is doing I know we don't have long before we either bleed out or pass out. Jacob is favoring his leg and it fills me with satisfaction to know that we are the ones that caused that pain for him. He stops in front of Kayla and the other man, Sheba crouches and is about to launch at him but stops when he clamps his jaws down on Kayla's shoulder, before I can make a move Cole's wolf sails through the air toward Jacob, before I can even process what the hell is happening, Jacob has half shifted, his torso is human while his lower body is still wolf. He grips the hilt of a knife from the man's jeans and then swivels enough to plunge the blade into Cole. My restraint snaps as Cole yelps and falls to the ground with the knife sticking out of his chest. I rush to Jacob and as Sheba launches through the air, he has fully shifted back to his wolf, but he was too slow, Sheba clamps her jaws on his neck and shakes him like a rag doll, his cries and howls of pain fill her with glee. Sheba is like a wild animal; his pain is like a balm to her almost as if his pain is making up for what he put us through.

Jacob tries to shake us off and he even manages to get a hold of our leg but still Sheba won't let go, as he clamps his jaws on our front paw, I feel the snap and know he has broken it but Sheba is too rabid to feel it, she yanks backward and then the satisfying feeling of his flesh tearing and his blood soaking the fur around our jaws lets us know we won, Sheba jumps backward careful not to land on our front paw and spits the flesh from our mouth, we stand and watch as Jacob gasps and staggers until he falls to his side in front of Kayla. His soulless eyes meet mine and Sheba finally lets me take control back, I shift and stagger slightly, the pain in my arm and loss of blood is catching up to me, but I refuse to pass out. I stumble over to his dying wolf and spit at his snout.

"That's for my mother you piece of shit, I hope you rot in fucking hell!" I grit out, I watch as the life leaves his eyes, and he slowly starts to shift back into human form. I tear my gaze from his and look to Kayla who is bleeding from her shoulder and shaking with silent tears, I look to the man next to her who raises his hands and nods his head respectfully.

"I am not your enemy; I only came to make sure you were the victor." His gaze darts to the woods behind me. "Our paths will cross again Ms. Hastings, your father was right, you truly are a prize." I furrow my brow in confusion as the handsome stranger turns and disappears into the woodlands behind him. I make quick work of untying Kayla and then quickly rush over to Cole. He's shifted back into human form and clutching his side where the knife sticks out, I drop to the ground by his head and help him lift his head with my good arm to rest on my naked thigh.

"You're going to be okay, just stay awake Colton." I plead, he smiles up at me and winks.

"He didn't hit anything vital sweetheart, I won't die." The air rushes out of me and the adrenalin begins to wear off. The sound of footfalls snags our attention as we focus on the woods, I scent the air and relax. Creed clears the brush first, then Callie and Davina. His gaze lands on Jacobs lifeless body before he scans the area, when he spots me and Cole he shifts back to human form and rushes over, he drops down beside me and cups my face, I flinch when his hand drops to my neck, he growls when he sees my wound. Before he can overreact, I reach out with my good hand and cup his cheek, I try to smile reassuringly.

"I'm okay, I swear--"He cuts me off by smashing his lips against mine, the kiss ends to quickly when Cole begins to whine.

"Dude! I'm good with her being naked by head but not you, and if you get a fucking boner right now, I'll beat your ass." I can't stop the chuckle that comes out, but immediately regret it when the pain in the side of my neck intensifies, I hiss and Creed narrows his eyes.

"Davina, you and Callie help Cole down the ridge. I'll help Jess down so she can call an end to the fight." Creed scoops me up and before he can rush us out of here, I stop him with my words.

"Kayla." His brow furrows.

"What?"

"She was by Jacob." Creed turns us toward Jacob's lifeless body, but Kayla is nowhere to be seen.

"Princess, it's only you and Cole up here." I don't get a chance to answer, Creed races us down the side of the ridge and a few times I thought he might stumble and fall but he doesn't, I bite my lip to stop me from crying out in pain when he jostles me, I hold my arm against my chest to try minimize its movements. I know that being a shifter means it will heal quicker but that doesn't mean it still doesn't hurt like a bitch!

CHAPTER FIFTY THREE
Credence

I don't stop until we get to the center of pack lands, wolves and vampires still fight around us, I place Jess gently on her feet and turn her toward me. She looks so confused and unsure; I know she is in pain, but she has to do this, or the fight will never stop. I can see that her wounds are affecting her and it kills me to make her do this, but I can't let more lives be lost.

"You have to shift and call your pack off."

"Huh?" I reach out and cup her face, I know she never wanted this, and I wanted to protect her from being an alpha, but I can't change that now.

"Jacob was an alpha Princess, you killed him which means that his pack is now yours. Shift and call them back before more lives are lost, please!" I don't know if it was the tone of my voice or the look in my eyes, but she nods, steps back and then shifts. I sink my hand into the fur along her back and relish in her warmth. "Close your eyes and feel for your pack, once you can feel that connection you need to pull on it, and then issue an alpha command." Sheba huffs, I know she knows what to do but I say the words for Jess's benefit not hers. As minutes tick by I begin to worry, if she doesn't hurry, we will have no choice but to join the fight soon. My pack has managed to hold the other wolves back while Jess concentrates, but they won't be able to hold them back for long. Just as I'm about to shift and help Asher and Tommy hold back six wolves Sheba throws her head back and lets out a loud, long howl. A few seconds tick by as I scan the area and see that wolves, vamps and wolves in their skin stop fighting as they face Jess. When all the fighting stops Jess shifts back and wobbles slightly, I wrap my arm around her waist to steady her.

"Jacob is dead!" A mixture of gasps and then cheers ring out around us. "No wolf is to attack another, there will be no more fighting here tonight. Enough blood and lives have been lost because of the greed of one man." I stare down at my mate in awe, the way she handled herself tonight and just spoke to these shifters is a moment I will never forget. "We are all the same, we may be from different packs but that doesn't mean that fighting is the answer to everything."

It's nearly noon by the time we manage to clear most of the debris and deal with the fallen shifters, we can't salvage my mom's house. She didn't give a shit about the house, all she cared about was that Cole, Callie and I were all safe. Cole's wound has pretty much healed, Davina's doctor took a look at Jess's wounds and cleaned them, Al had to apply butterfly stiches to the wound on her neck. He said they will heal fine, as long as she didn't shift for a couple days, she agreed and was happy to have the pain meds he gave her. Exhaustion is creeping in, and I know everyone must be feeling it as well, but I refuse to let them rest until we care for those that lost their lives helping us, Jess was devastated to find that her friend Carmi had lost her life, Callie, Asher, Tommy, Ashely and Jess all chose to dig and bury their friend together. I spy Davina standing near one of the cabins talking to Vince, I decide that I have to thank her for her help, without her and her vamps we would have been fucked. They stop talking when they see me, I reach up and rub the back of my neck as I speak.

"Thank you, without your support we would have been fucked plain and simple." Vince grunts and then excuses himself to help the other vamps deal with their dead. The tension between Davina and I isn't as bad as it normally is, I have a newfound respect for the woman who gave birth to me, that is something I never thought I would say. I can see in her eyes the toll this battle has taken on her and a part of me does feel bad but another part, the part of me that is still bitter toward her doesn't give a shit.

"I appreciate it, but you don't need to thank me, well not after what I have to tell you." The ominous tone of her voice sets me on edge, the tiredness I felt moments ago is gone.

"What is it?" She lets out a whoosh of air and darts her gaze around to make sure no one is listening to us.

"Vince went to recover Jacob's body--."

"Why?"

"Because Cairo wants to return the favor an send his head to Russia." *Jesus!* "Well, when he was there, he caught a familiar scent."

"Whose scent?" Her shoulders stiffen as she tears her gaze from mine.

"Alexander's."

"The guy that gave Jess's dad the vampire blood that turned you?"

"Yes." She grits out through clenched teeth.

"Why?"

"I have no idea; Vince and I will look into it, but him being back isn't a good thing. We will leave in a couple of days and

track Belle down, if he's come back, it's because he's after her."
I have no idea who this Belle is but from what I can gather from
Vince and Davina she is someone very important to their race.

"After what you all did for us, we will help you locate her
and protect her." Davina smiles sadly.

"No, if Alex is here and coming for her then he will lay waste
to anyone who tries to stop him." She reaches out and places her
hand on my arm. "Your fight is over, go be with your mate and
son and enjoy your freedom. You have both earnt it, Cairo has
offered to help us, and I accepted."

"Why the hell would Ro offer?" The sound of footsteps
approaching draws my attention to see, Ro, Z, Sky and Callie
coming to us.

"Because my wolf won't allow me to live with two alphas." I
deflate a little on the inside, Cairo leaving is going to gut Jess.

"We'll figure something out--." He shakes his head and
cuts me off.

"Nah man, you and smalls don't want me hanging around,
I'll come back though. But for right now, I have to do this."

"Jess is going to try and stop you." He smiles sheepishly.

"That is why we're going to sneak out while she is distracted
sorting out her new pack."

"Fuck no! If she finds out I knew and didn't tell her she is
going to castrate me!" Everyone chuckles well I glare. "I'm very
fond of my dick thank you very much." Cairo's laughter cuts off
immediately as meets my stare.

"Creed, for the first time ever, my wolf won't let me rest and
it's because of something to do with this Belle. I need to find her

and figure out what hold she has over my wolf, or I will go mad." The truth is clear in his words and if anyone can understand what he is saying it's me. I reach out and pull him in for a bro hug.

"Don't fucking die or your sister will kill me." He chuckles and pats me on the back as he steps back.

"That's not such a bad thing." I shake my head at him, when my sister steps forward, the smile vanishes from my face and my shoulders slump.

"Does mom know?" She bites her lip and shakes her head; I release a sigh and focus my gaze over her head to Sky. "If anything happens to her, I'm coming for you Skylar, guard her with your life." Sky has an evil smirk on her face, but she nods. Callie wraps her arms around my waist and rests her head against my chest, I hold her close to me and breath her in.

"I love you big brother." I'm man enough to admit that I have to force the lump down in my throat so I can talk.

"I love you to California, you have to call me every second day or I'm coming after you!"

"I'll make the calls." I lift my gaze to see my brother standing next to Sky with his hands stuffed in his pockets, my eyes widen when I realize what he means.

"Not you to!" I whine, he smiles sadly and nods.

"Look, after what happened on the island with us it showed me that I have to do my own thing, or risk fucking up our family. I'm not leaving because of you; I'm going with them because I have to do something different." I release Callie and move toward my brother, I never realized until now how much he has changed in these past few months. He isn't that carefree quarterback anymore, he looks like he has the weight of the world on his shoulders and if this is what will help him, then who am I to stop it. I grab him and hug him.

"I love you brother."

"Love you to Creed." I take a deep breath and step back; I look to my siblings and smile sadly as I say.

"I, Credence Reeves of the Reeves pack release you both from my command as your alpha." The twins' eyes widen, a sob comes from my sister. "You both deserve a fresh start, the least I can do is give you both the freedom to do that. It goes without saying, this pack is yours and if either of you choose to return, then I'll welcome you both back." They each thank me and give me a hug; I stand beside Davina and watch as Cairo instructs those of his pack that want to come with him to follow. A lot of the elders and younger wolves choose to stay behind, Cairo cuts his gaze to me, and I nod, they will remain here with us as part of our pack should they choose it.

"What you did for the twins... that was--." I cut her off.

"I did what mom would have wanted me to do, after everything they have been through, they deserve this." Davina nods and then steps in front of me, she meets my gaze, and I can see the unshed tears in her eyes which stuns me.

"You would think I would be used to saying goodbye by now, huh?" She chuckles but there is no humor to it. I admit standing here in front of her is hard. "Look after that beautiful boy and love him right." I nod, we stand there staring at each other for a moment before she sighs and turns to leave, when she is two feet away, I call out to her. "Yeah?"

"The same offer applies to you as well; my pack is always open to you." I see a stray tear fall from her eye, but she quickly swipes it away. "I'll...send you pictures of Harlem, at least well your away you can see your...grandson grow." Her hand covers her mouth, another tear leaks out as she nods and walks away.

Mom and Jess lost their shit when I told them, mom tried to call the twins numerous times and Jess tried calling Cairo but none of them got through. They have both been giving me the cold shoulder for two days, but Jess has no choice but to speak to me today. We have sent all the other alphas home and thanked them for helping us, each of them lost wolves and it is a debt I will never be able to repay. This battle has opened a link between all of us that wasn't there before and it's all thanks to Jess. Cairo's pack members have decided to stay with us but not join which is fine, they have been given homes and the elderly offered to help out at the school and other places of work which we appreciate. Jacob's old pack was sent back to their land on the other side of town until Jess decided what she wanted to do, thanks to her giving me the silent treatment I have no idea what she has planned. She called a meeting for her pack and the Reeves pack today to discuss what happens from here. We stand out in the middle of the field under the glaring sun, there is at least four hundred shifters here including what small amount I have from my pack. Pack members that chose to join Jacobs pack stand among those numbers with their heads bowed in shame.

Jess and I stand before both our packs with our son in the middle of us, Jess looks fucking sexy and badass in her ripped black denim jeans, Converse and plain white shirt, her hair blows subtly in the light breeze. She runs her gaze over each of the wolves standing in front of us, some of them shuffle from foot to foot nervous.

"I know you all think you were asked here so I could punish you for going against us." Mumbles break out but Jess continues. "That will *not* happen, I know some of you were taken from your original packs or forced to join Jacob's so, I want to give those of you who wish to leave or return to your packs a chance to do so now." My mouth drops open in shock, this woman never ceases to amaze me.

"You'll just let us go?" Someone calls out.

"Yes, I am not Jacob. I will not force you to stay here, I'll be honest, I never wanted to be an alpha, and this is all new to me as well. I'm going to make mistakes, but I promise I will learn and do my best, if you choose to stay then you have to know that our pack will be joined to the Reeves pack." Holy shit, this is news to me! Jess turns to face me, and I can see the uncertainty in her eyes as she asks. "Is that okay?" I smile and reach over gripping the back of her neck to pull her to me so I can smash my lips to hers in a quick kiss.

"Of course, it is princess." She smiles widely at me before turning back to face the others.

"I want us all to live happily and peacefully. None of you will be forced to fight or do anything of that sort, we are trying to raise our son to do better than us. I want him to grow and see how a pack should be lead and how to treat people right, no one is better than anyone here, we are equals."

CHAPTER FIFTY FOUR
Jessica

Six Months Later

Things have finally settled around the Reeves-Cruz pack, everyone is happy and thriving. Since the day in the field over eighty members left to return to their own packs which they were so grateful for, the rest stayed and helped us rebuild and reshape how we *now* do things. Both packs are joined together, and I am finally able to mind link everyone! That took a long time to get used to.

Harlem had his very first birthday party with friends and family, Cairo and the others came back to celebrate with us, which just made mine and Harlem's day to see them again. I hated having to say goodbye to my brother, but I know him, and he won't rest until he fulfils his promise about taking down the council and finding Belle. Davina and Vince returned with them, and I don't think any of us were shocked to find out that they finally made their relationship official. The twins and D seem to get along better than when they left, Creed may not admit it, but I know he was happy to see her as well.

The day before Ro and the others left, Creed said he had something to show me, so here we are driving to who-knows-where with our son in the backseat. Creed refused to tell me where we are going, we head toward a part of Rosewood I have never been before. He pulls the car over and I quirk a brow at him in question when I see my brother and Davina's cars parked here as well. We hop out of the car and Creed gets Harlem from the back, when I look around the car I gasp and cover my mouth with my hand. Tears well in my eyes, I see the others standing toward the middle, I don't wait for Creed to lead, I take off toward them with him and Harlem following me. The closer I get the more my nerves begin to frazzle inside me, as I near Cole,

Callie, Z and Davina step aside.   When I see her name, I drop to my knees and sob, I didn't think Shelley would keep her word, but she did! Cairo kneels down beside me and rests a hand on my shoulder.

"Creed thought this might help give you some closure, plus it gives you a chance to see our father as well." I search the other stones and gasp when I see his name, *Austin Cruz.* I turn back to my mom and reach out to run my fingers down her headstone and read the words inscribed on it.

Katharine Hastings

Beloved aunt, friend and sister.

Mother of Jessica Hastings.

Seeing the last line has more tears leaking from my eyes, I know she wasn't my real mother biologically but her giving birth to me wouldn't change anything. She was everything a mother should be, without her love and guidance I wouldn't be able to raise Harlem the way that I do.

"We'll give you some time with Aunt Kat and dad. Just in case you wanted to know, Shelley has a plot beside dad, we...uh...buried what we had of her here with him." I nod and thank my brother, each of them lays a hand on my shoulder and speak words of love as they head back to the cars.

"Ro, take Harlem with you please, I'll be there in a second." Creed asks, he and Davina remain behind as the others leave.

"I just wanted you to know that your father was a great man and he loved you and Cairo more than anything. I am truly sorry for the part I played in his death Jess, I loved him with every fiber of my being. Please don't hate him for his transgressions with me." I don't bother to respond to Davina, once she walks away Creed kneels down beside me, I can feel his gaze on the side of my face, but I can't manage to look away from my mom's stone.

"I'm here for you always princess."

"Why did you bring me here?" I whisper.

"Because you needed to say goodbye to your mom." It hits me then; I turn to the side and meet his stare.

"Shelley didn't bury my mom, did she?" He shakes his head. "Why did you do it?"

"It was the least I could do after everything I put you through. Your mom deserved better than she got, and I wanted to make sure everything was done right and she was laid to rest with dignity and respect." Tears roll down my cheeks faster now.

"Thank you." He smiles sadly and stands heading back toward the others to give me some time with my *parents.* After a few moments I stand and stare at the graves in front of me, my dad is buried between my mom and Shelley. I turn toward my father and Shelley and speak to them first. I wrack my brain for something to say, what does one say to the dead? I decide to speak from the heart in the end.

"Thank you for giving me life, I didn't get a chance to know either of you really. A part of me wishes that I did have the chance but... another part of me is glad. If things didn't work out the way they did then I wouldn't have had my mom, I hope you are both proud of the woman she raised me to be." I turn my gaze back to my mom; I fight past the lump in throat as I speak. "I miss you. I wish you had the chance to have met Harlem and

Katy, I hope she is up there with you. Thank you, mom, for everything, I wouldn't be who I am or where I am today without you and your guidance. I love you." I turn and head back toward the others feeling lighter than I have in years.

Creed, Asher, Tommy and the other pack members have been working tirelessly on re-building Meg's house as well as other houses on both the pack lands for all the new shifters we have with us. Creed offered to build us a bigger house, but I refused, I love our little cabin and it's just perfect for the three of us. I have begun teaching at the school, I love being able to help mold the minds of our future generation. I handed over the day to day running of the pack to Creed, he understands and supports my wishes not to lead. He has been nothing but encouraging and supportive toward my choices and what I want for the future. He is the best dad and helps Harlem every night with his homework while I cook and grade papers.

We have all fallen into a routine and it feels so normal, we fought hard to get to where we are today. Somedays the guilt of the lives lost and the lives I have taken still eat at me, but Creed is always there to reassure me and help me through my guilt. We have even talked about seeing a doctor to help us get pregnant, after having the twins and all the complications I had we need professional help to get pregnant again. I didn't think Creed would be open to this option but when he came to me and told me he found a specialist a few hours away and I agreed.

"Princess, why are you out here?" I shake my head to clear my thoughts and smile at my mate slash soon to be husband, I trail my gaze over him in appreciation. He's wearing a flannel shirt, dark wash jeans with saw dust clinging to them and steel toed boots, the whole construction look is working wonders for him. When my gaze finally travels back to his face, he has a sexy smirk firmly in place and a lustful look in his eyes. "Keep looking at me like that and we won't make it to dinner with mom." I stand from my seat on the porch and saunter over to him, I stop when there is a sliver of space between us and trail my pointer finger down his chest and stop at the waistband of his jeans, a growl of approval sounds from his chest.

"Harlem is with your mom." Is all I manage to get out before he lifts me and flings me over his shoulder, I squeal in surprise but begin to laugh when he stomps inside our cabin. He slams the door behind us then heads toward our ensuite, he sits me on the bathroom counter and undresses faster than I can blink.

"Your turn princess." I smile and slide off the counter, I slip out of my sweater and push the straps of my dress down and let the material pool at my feet, Creed sucks in a sharp breath at the sight of me in just my bra and panties. He still manages to set my body ablaze with his touch. "You're killing me princess." I trail my gaze down his chest and take a minute to appreciate that V before letting my eyes drift to his hard veiny cock that juts out, I dart my tongue out to moisten my lips. Clearly, I don't move fast enough for him as he yanks me forward and unclasps my bra and chucks it to the side, he drops his head to capture one of my nipples in his mouth and I cry out in pleasure, he nips it with his teeth electing another moan from me. He releases it with a pop and then kneels down in front of me, he reaches up and pulls my G-string down. I stand before him bare and ready for him to ravish me. "I can smell how wet you are already."

"Hmmm, what are you going to do about it?" His gaze snaps to mine as I stare down at him, his eyes are full of hunger. He has never looked as powerful as he does now kneeling before me.

"I'm gonna make you scream my fucking name!" Before I can sass him back, he buries his head between my thighs and devours my wet pussy like he hasn't eaten in days. I lift my leg and hook it over his shoulder and then brace my hands behind me on the counter. His tongue circles my clit and I cry out in pleasure, if there was an award for the best pussy eater, I'm sure Creed would win! He inserts two fingers inside me and pumps them in and out as he laps at my clit, I feel my orgasm begin to build.

"Oh, yes...fuck...Creed, don't stop!" My orgasm is right there and about to rip through me when he stops and pulls back, I watch in shock as he climbs to his feet, licks his lips then winks and hops in the shower. My mouth hangs open in shock.

"Close that dirty mouth of yours or I'll fill it with my cock, princess."

"What the hell was that?" I snap angrily at him, the bastard smiles and motions for me to join him in the shower. I'm way to freaking horny to think clearly so I stumble into the shower with him before I can say something he grips my hips and hauls me against him then smashes his lips against mine. When his tongue invades my mouth and I taste myself on him and moan, he pulls back and stares down at me, water drips down his face from his hair and my pussy clenches at the sight of him. Credence Reeves is a wet dream come true.

"Turn around and put your hands on the wall baby and spread your legs." Excited and beyond turned on I do as he says and brace my hands on the wall then spread my legs, I watch him over my shoulder and feel more wetness building when he stares at my exposed pussy and begins to pump his cock in his hand. He continues to stroke his cock with one hand and reaches out with his other to squeeze my ass, in one swift move he drops his cock and lands a swift smack to my ass which has me jolting forward. He rubs the spot he hit and then does the same to the other side. He does this three more times and by then I'm a withering mess and can feel my wetness dripping down my inner thigh. He drops to his knees behind me and then uses his hands to part my cheeks, him fucking my ass has become my new favorite way of having sex. I know most woman think it's taboo and hurts but for me that isn't the case, when Creed sinks his cock deep into my ass it takes me mere minutes before I'm coming and screaming his name. "You want me to fuck this hole baby?" I open my mouth to answer but a moan slips free when he begins to lick up and down my ass.

"Yes." He pulls back and then runs a finger from my asshole to my wet cunt, he sinks his finger inside me and I automatically clench his finger trying to keep him inside me.

"I'm gonna fuck this pussy and finger your ass at the same time, you want that princess?" I moan in answer, he chuckles then withdraws his finger. He sits down and then turns so his face is to my front and slides backward until his mouth latches onto my clit. I keep my hands on the wall and look down at him and watch as he eats my pussy but keeps his gaze locked on mine as he does it. "Ride my face and make yourself come." I do as he says, I grip his hair and hold him in place as I begin to ride his face, his moans spur me own.

"Oh yessss, hold your tongue out like that, I'm gonna come!" He does as I say and holds his tongue out so I can rub my clit on it, and I come undone within seconds doing exactly as he said, I scream his name.

He doesn't let me come down from my climax, he slides out from between my legs and then stands, he lines his cock up with my pussy and I hold my breath as I wait for him to slam inside me. There is no better feeling than his cock sliding inside me.

"Fuck princess..." He cries out when he slams into me, I moan at the feeling of having him inside me. He spreads my ass cheeks as he pounds in out of me, I feel liquid drip down my ass, and I know he has used his spit as lube. He rubs his spit around my hole with his thumb and when he finally pushes his digit inside me, I cry out. "Fuck, I love it when your pussy clenches my cock when I finger your ass." I can't formulate an answer, the pleasure he is dolling out on my body is too intoxicating to focus. He continues to fuck me and finger my ass at a ruthless pace.

"I-I'm gonna come!" I wheeze out.

"Come all over my cock baby." It's as if my orgasm is his to command, as soon as he utters the words my orgasm rips through me and I'm screaming his name until my throat is hoarse, Creed shouts out his release a second later. We stay there panting and trying to get our breathing under control, Creed pulls out of me and spins me around to face him. He cups my face between his hands and then kisses me, I can feel everything he is trying to convey in this kiss. He pulls back and then rest his forehead against mine.

"I love you too, *eggplant.*" I jest.

"You will never love me as much as I love you princess."

The End.... Or is it?

Turn the page to find out....

EPILOGUE
Cairo

Six Months!

That's how long it has taken to even get an accurate lead on where Gabrielle Wilder really is, apparently the family that took her in skipped out on where Davina had them stashed and ran. With the council off the grid and the local packs in Russia unable to find them we decided to focus on Belle first before going after them. We don't know if Phillip is still in the states, Cole told me he took off the night Jacob died. Fucking pussy, he was always a spineless prick.

"You sure you good with this plan?" I turn to face Sky; her eyes still have that haunted look in them and I want nothing more than to wipe that look from her eyes.

"If it means saving your life, then I'm good." She grinds her teeth. "Skylar, I would burn the fucking world down for you, if she is the key to helping save you then I'll do it."

"What about your wolf?" The closer we get to Belle's location the more out of control my wolf is getting, he's antsy and on edge and I have no idea why. He forced a shift yesterday and nearly attacked Z.

"He'll be fine once we get to, Belle."

"You gonna tell Davina?" We decided it was best if we split up, Davina, Vince and the vamps went to search on the west side of the country while we took the east. My pack and I have been through hell and fought numerous packs along the way, seems alphas don't take kindly to me not being able to be controlled.

"No, we get the girl and find out what is wrong with my wolf. Then we see if she can help you, then maybe we call Davina. We don't owe her shit; she may be Creed and the twin's mother but she isn't mine." Sky glowers at me, Callie can be pissed all she wants but she chose to follow me and what I say goes.

"Cole and Z say we're at least a day out from her pack."

"Good, I'm ready to go hunting and show little Belle what a real beast is."

443

Cairo and Belle's story will be coming soon!

Thank you!

Dear Lord have mercy!

Holy shit on toast, this bad bitch was a monster to write. Jess and Creed sent me on a wild as fuck goose chase! Every time I thought I was getting somewhere with the story they changed their minds and made me start over.

This book is something I never thought I would write, I never thought anyone would love Book 1 – Savage Lies, I wrote it for me, ya know? But it blew my mind when it took off and people demanded book 2. Jess is a bad ass in her own right, Creed is a alpha-fucker who needed a woman to stand up to him. They are the perfect pair and I am sad that their story has ended but also glad that they got HEA.

Don't fret though, you will see them again in Book 3 *Savage Beast*. Cairo's book will be out in August this year.

Thank you so much for taking a chance and reading this series, it means way more than you will ever know.

Xxx

If you would like to stay up to date with all my releases follow me on the links below. If you loved Savage Lies, please leave a review on, Amazon, Bookbub, or Goodreads, your feedback would be much appreciated.

Stalk me on the links below!

Instagram - @author.samantha.barrett

Facebook – author.samantha.barrett

Tiktok - @samanthabarrettauthor

Twitter - @author_sbarrett

Feel free to join my readers group on Facebook – Sam's Dreamers.

Acknowledgments

Firstly. Shout out to my mum man, she is a boss and bad ass woman. She edited Savage Lies and Brutal Truth, these books wouldn't be what they are without her, so thank you mummy you the real MVP girl!

Amber…My PA, my go to when I'm having a moment lol. Thank you babe, for everything you do for me behind the scenes and all these beautiful covers. You are the best and I appreciate you so much!

Huge thank you to Kylie Kent and Mel Bennett for all your guys help on helping me launch this book and Savage Lies. You ladies are freaking incredible and I cannot wait to get lit at the clubhouse in 2023!

To my man, thank you Marcus for standing by me and loving me. I never thought happily ever after's existed until I met you, I slayed a lot of dragons to get to you my king!

My ARC team! Thank you all so much for reading and reviewing my books it means a lot to me and I apricate each and everyone of you!

To my amazing readers, thank you!

your support and recognition to these characters is the reason that drives me to follow my dreams.

If you loved *Brutal Truth* please leave a review.

Sam. Xxx

About the Author

Samantha is a book lover and writer. She is originally from the land of the long white cloud, New Zealand.

Sam loves anything Twilight and is a TWIHARD proudly.
#TeamEdward

She loves fantasy-romance novels with strong Alpha males.

Samantha loves to write complicated love stories with a twist. A strong and badass heroine is a must!

She lives in Brisbane, Australia with her husband, two children, and four dogs.

If her books leave you wanting more or you feel as if you connected with the characters in some way, she takes that as a win!!
Sam loves writing anything that is out of the box!

If you would like to read Nico and Ryan's journey turn the page to read their blurb.

If you would like to know more about Dom and Soph, turn the page for their book – Redemption.

You can find her on –

Amazon - amzn.to/3vsmuxy

Bookbub – bit.ly/2NvIJl4

Goodreads - bit.ly/2NsCSx2

Also, by Samantha Barrett

<u>The Dream Trilogy (Complete)</u>

<u>A Beautiful Dream</u>
<u>A Twisted Fate</u>
<u>A Beautiful Nightmare</u>

<u>The Dream Trilogy Spin offs (Can be read as Standalones)</u>

<u>Redemption – Brothers best friend</u>
<u>Anarchy – Best friends' daughter</u>

<u>Brutal Savages Series</u>

<u>Savage Lies</u>

<u>Brutal Truth</u>

<u>Savage Beast</u> – Coming August 2022